KISSING SHADOWS

Also by Sally Stewart
and available from Headline:

Playing With Stars

KISSING
SHADOWS

Sally Stewart

HEADLINE

First published in 1999
by HEADLINE BOOK PUBLISHING

A HEADLINE hardback

10 9 8 7 6 5 4 3 2 1

British Library Cataloguing in Publication Data

Stewart, Sally
Kissing shadows
I. Title
823.9'14 [F]

ISBN 0-7472-2176-6

Typeset by
CBS, Martlesham Heath, Ipswich, Suffolk

Printed and bound in Great Britain by
Mackays of Chatham PLC, Chatham, Kent

HEADLINE BOOK PUBLISHING
A division of Hodder Headline PLC
338 Euston Road
London NW1 3BH

Some there be that shadows kiss;
Such have but a shadow's bliss.

Shakespeare, *The Merchant of Venice*

Chapter 1

Christmas was approaching in London, with its customary lack of peace, goodwill, or even whiteness. Instead of snow, a spiteful sort of rain was falling on Knightsbridge, and umbrellas held like battering rams suggested that no quarter was being asked or given among the crowds of quietly frenzied shoppers. Trapped in a traffic jam that looked unravellable, Jessica Smythson suggested to her taxi-driver that she might make better progress on foot. His jaundiced view was that Christmas brought out the worst in people, and it was hard to disagree, but she over-tipped him in the hope of cheering him up and then plunged into the pedestrian battle herself. She was going to arrive not only late but bedraggled and breathless as well, to complete the displeasure of a woman who was never any of those things.

Under the awning of the hotel she finally hurried into, a news-vendor's placard caught her eye. Somewhere on earth there was certain to be a drought, or a forest fire raging, but in Venice it was flood time again, apparently. With so little moderation all around, she reckoned that God's human creatures couldn't be blamed for imitating Nature and often going wildly to extremes. But whatever the hubbub outside, within the hotel order was around her now, and the receptionist's well-bred stare would stop the most determined hell-raiser in his tracks. A lifted eyebrow suggested to Jessica that *she* might have wandered in by mistake, but her mention of Elizabeth Harrington's name worked its usual magic. She wasn't even left to find her own way to a sitting room on the first floor. A snap of the fingers produced, as swiftly as a rabbit appearing from a conjuror's hat, an escort for the journey upstairs.

Her grandmother managed not to glance at the clock on the marble mantelpiece as she went in, although Jess's damp shoes and splashed tights, and the sodden raincoat that dripped water on to the pale carpet were registered instead with a hint of pain. It was right to have come back to London, Elizabeth was deciding; the girl needed taking in hand before it was too late. They exchanged smiles, but no more than that this time. Their cheeks had briefly touched a week earlier at the funeral that had brought Elizabeth to London; another show of affection could await her next visit.

'I thought you were going straight home after Paris,' Jess observed,

1

since for once her grandmother didn't seem inclined to launch the conversation.

'I was, but I realised I'd left something undone here.'

Her English accent sounded unchanged after nearly forty years of New York life. At seventy-eight she looked very little different as well – still elegant, still perfectly presented to the world. Age hadn't been allowed to wither her, and her glance remained as sharp as a surgeon's knife. But there was this one small alteration: no errors of omission had been admitted to before. Unlikely as it seemed, Jess wondered if her grandmother was finally aware that 'Time's wingèd chariot' might even be at *her* heels as well.

'I had dinner with Gerald last night,' Elizabeth said next. 'You were out at the opera, I gathered, with some elderly admirer.'

The admirer in question was almost young enough to be her son, but Jess ignored the temptation to make so hurtful a correction. 'Only a concert performance of *The Mastersingers*, but better than nothing while Covent Garden is closed for renovations.'

Elizabeth supported the Metropolitan at home, but only as a self-sacrificing public duty. That kith and kin of hers should actually enjoy Wagnerian outpourings was strange; that her granddaughter's reticent face should light up at the recollection of them seemed out of character enough to suggest that in other ways she might not be exactly what she seemed.

'You're wearing grey again,' Mrs Harrington pointed out next. 'It's a dismal, mourning colour, but I suppose you'll say that you *are* still mourning your mother.'

'I'm more inclined to say that I wear grey because I like it,' Jess insisted gently. 'I was gaudier when young and wanting to be noticed.'

'Rubbish, Jessica – you're thirty-eight. At more than twice your age I can tell you that I *still* want to be noticed, and make sure that I am.' Elizabeth took a sip from the glass of Evian water beside her while she decided how to go on. 'I'm glad the subject has cropped up, though, because I'm concerned about you. Of course you looked sad and exhausted at the funeral – you'd had to watch your mother die a slow and painful death. But life must go on now. Gerald isn't left alone – he's got his sister living with him in that huge house. It's time for *you* to make a fresh start, and you ought to do it in New York, where I can help you. It's the most exciting city in the world for anyone with talent, and although you're stuck in a rut at the moment, there isn't any doubt about what you're capable of.'

She liked to deal in these crisp certainties, Jess reflected. It was one of the reasons for her success – opportunities hadn't been lost while she considered anyone else's point of view. Her first husband, William Carstairs, had been killed during the slow Allied advance up Italy, and after the war she'd made her own fresh beginning alone in New

York. She'd landed a job as a journalist for the owner of a powerful newspaper empire, and finally succeeded to the extent of marrying him. Walter Harrington was also dead now, but she was still the company's major shareholder, and with as many friends as enemies in high places, her offer of help amounted to something.

Jess tried to sound grateful. 'It's kind of you . . . very kind . . . but I think the answer's no. London is exciting enough for me, and I doubt if New York and I would suit each other so well. In any case, this isn't the time to leave Gerald. The last few months *were* dreadful – and now I think we have to help each other back to normality.'

Her gratitude had sounded real but so was the tenacity that Elizabeth knew was typical of her. She was a living reminder of the large, quiet man who'd walked away one day to go to war. William had bequeathed to this granddaughter he'd never known not only his height and Northumbrian colouring but an unbudging obstinacy as well.

'You're still young, but you can't afford to waste time,' Elizabeth said sharply. 'The race is to the swift now. Gerald is happy to potter on at his own unadventurous pace, but *you* mustn't be.'

As usual she made the mistake of sounding irritated by the mention of Gerald Smythson, even knowing that it was unfair, as well as stupid. Gerald – her brother's son and therefore her nephew before he became her son-in-law as well – had married a distraught, pregnant girl and then gladly accepted the role of father to her child. Jessica had always regarded him as such, loved and revered *him* as much as she despised the unknown man who'd actually begotten her. With Gillian Smythson now dead, the story should have been ancient history, but for once Elizabeth seemed perversely inclined to dwell on the past, as if her own part in it needed an apology of some kind.

'I know I left my daughter behind when I moved to America, but it was her choice – she was convinced about becoming the next Margot Fonteyn, and I went believing that she'd be safe at the Dutch House with my brother and sister-in-law. Afterwards, of course, she blamed me for what happened. I'd have invited you to New York long ago but whenever I came back here Gillian always showed me how things were: I'd made *my* choice; you and she were the indispensably close daughter and mother that she and I had never been. Gerald was included in her little circle – though I think she almost even resented that – but there was to be no room for me.'

'You had Walter instead,' Jess suggested gently.

'I did, and I'm very proud of the fact. But now that he's dead, and so is Gillian, I can't help regretting that you and I haven't been friends. That's really what I came back to London to say. It's why I'd like to take you away from the Smythsons.'

After a little pause Jess found her voice. 'Thank you, but I don't need rescuing. I could leave the Dutch House if I wanted to, but why bother when I have a comfortable home there? I could leave the firm and work for myself or someone else but it would seem ungrateful as well as stupid – Gerald has been the kindest of teachers as well as the very best and most loving of fathers.'

Elizabeth lifted her shoulders in a shrug that mixed acceptance with disappointment. 'All right, but if you change your mind you'll have to let me know – I shan't ask again.'

It seemed to conclude the interview. Her offer had been made, and rejected because the barrier erected by a woman who was dead still held. But for once Jess felt saddened at being given permission to go; the woman in front of her might seem indomitable still, but she wasn't immortal, and soon it might be too late to discover that they could have liked each other. The strange idea suddenly prompted her to stoop and kiss Elizabeth Harrington's cheek.

'Safe journey home, Gran dear. Don't regret the choice you made in going to New York – you've been a tremendous feather in our caps!'

She had William's trick of smiling with a straight mouth. The woman left alone was momentarily hurt by its remembered gleam before Jessica was gone and the door closed behind her.

Outside, early-winter darkness had fallen but the rain had stopped. Jess decided to walk down Sloane Street to the Smythsons' design studio, where she and Gerald planned beautiful houses for the rich and mighty. Gerald would probably still be there and she could share his taxi home as usual. Everything *was* just as usual – the familiar neighbourhood, their windows, when she reached them, aglow with the rich cascade of fabrics she'd arranged there. Her mind insisted on the normality of what she could see, denying the echoes of the past that her grandmother's conversation had set loose – wisps of recollection that the child she'd been then might not even have registered correctly.

It was late enough for the others to have left – Pinky Todd, who ran the studio with a Cockney's cheerful, sharply intelligent drive, and young Jane Harrison, their new trainee designer. These two, with Jess herself and the flock of curtain-makers, upholsterers, and furniture-restorers they used, made up what Gerald referred to as his monstrous regiment of women. But he liked working with the opposite sex, treated them as he treated the duchesses on his list of clients, and received their devotion in return.

He looked up as Jess went in and she tried to judge dispassionately the man her grandmother seemed to despise – an interesting but unhandsome face had given rise to a self-sketch long ago that he'd entitled *Picture of a Well-bred Camel*. She'd had to acknowledge the resemblance at the time, but his gentle, welcoming smile was a truer reflection of the past than the other memories the afternoon had stirred up. His kindness had never failed her or her beautiful, neurotic mother. Gillian Carstairs had made him a troublesome and eventually a tragic wife, but Jess had never seen him lose patience with her or regret his choice of partner.

'A swig of clients' sherry before we leave, I think,' he suggested now. 'I can see you've had the usual bruising interview with your grandmother.'

She accepted the drink he poured for her but shook her head at what he'd said. 'It *wasn't* quite as usual, although poor "elderly" James Hatherley came in for a merry swipe, and she pointed out – rightly, because I saw myself in a mirror as I went downstairs – that I looked a depressing mess! But this time at least I had the feeling that her malice was well intentioned. The past few months entitled me to depression, apparently, but now I must pull myself together, and she even offered me the chance to do it in New York.'

Jess sipped the bone-dry sherry Gerald favoured and smiled ruefully at him. 'I'm afraid I turned the offer down not very graciously, but when she began to talk about the past I suddenly realised that she *wanted* to help. I still have no ambition to set New York alight, but I wish she hadn't looked so . . . so spurned. I've always thought of her as being invincible.'

'She still is,' Gerald insisted calmly. 'You saw her at a vulnerable moment, that's all. She's just lost her only child – it *must* have an effect, even on a woman as immune to emotion as my dear aunt and mother-in-law.'

There was an edge to his voice that only Elizabeth Harrington seemed capable of putting there; they were connected by blood and by long association, but not by sympathy. Jess had always supposed them merely incompatible, but it occurred to her now for the first time that the hostility had a deeper cause: Elizabeth resented having to feel grateful, and Gerald judged her to have been that worst thing in women, an unnatural mother who'd abandoned her child.

Jess emerged from the uncomfortable train of thought to find that she was being stared at.

'I don't normally have an opinion in common with your grandmother,' Gerald said quietly, 'but I had to agree with what she pointed out to me last night. Gillian's final illness was something we *had* to bear together, but there were years before that when her sufferings were much more imaginary than real. I should have been firmer then – made her let go of you – turned you out of the house, even, to live your own life.'

He smiled but his eyes looked so haunted by the past that to reassure him Jess would have denied the last grain of truth in what Elizabeth had said. '*You* bore the brunt of Mother's ups and downs, not me. I

5

had all the friends I wanted, all the freedom I had a taste for. If a string of ardent young men didn't pant to get me away and into bed with them it was because I wasn't sufficiently seductive!'

She spoke cheerfully, refusing to remember the pain of scenes buried in her memory. Urged to bring home fellow-students from the college of art, she'd watched Gillian either destroy them with a pitying smile or dazzle them out of their wits with her still-astonishing beauty. Ailments and unthinking neglect had been bravely borne in front of *them*; she'd charmed any prospect who seemed to offer a threat. Secure in the knowledge that, beside her, Jess wouldn't even be noticed, she'd extolled the virtues of a plain but much-needed daughter, for whom she was nevertheless doing her best.

With lessons learned, Jess had kept later friends away, but confidence had been lost, and she'd made a humiliating failure of the only love affairs that had seemed promising. She wasn't sure whether she'd loved or hated Gillian by the time illness of the most dreadful kind had finally become a reality; but death had ended the uncertainty and now it didn't seem to matter which it had been.

'Time we went home,' she suggested after a long pause. 'I promised Imogen we'd both eat with *her* this evening.'

'Oh God – half-cooked vegetables again, and one of my sister's many variations on the indigestible theme of pasta!'

'Well, maybe, but you're a snob when it comes to food and wine, and in any case we go because it gives Aunt Immy pleasure to minister to us!'

Gerald's unenthusiastic nod agreed, but he poured more sherry as if still in no hurry to leave.

'Jess dear, something still to say to you,' he confessed in a sudden plunge. 'I hadn't quite decided earlier; now I have.'

'You're going to turn me out after all,' she suggested, with a faint smile because he hesitated and looked so grave.

'Well, yes . . . in a way I am!' he agreed astonishingly. But her change of expression made his own face relax and he went on more easily. 'I was invited to lunch today with a friend of your grandmother's – Elvira Acheson, the wife of Nathan Acheson, no less.'

'I'm impressed! Even I have heard the name. Does she want you to do some work for her?'

'Yes, but not here. Her husband has acquired a Venetian *palazzo* – nearly derelict for years, but now being rescued by an architect and an army of workmen. The American restoration committee that Nathan's money largely funds is celebrating an anniversary there this summer, and the *palazzo* is required to be got ready for some large-scale entertaining. When your grandmother met Elvira Acheson in Paris she suggested Smythson's for the design work.'

'Sensible of her – you'll do it beautifully,' Jess agreed.

'I'd like to tell Mrs Acheson that *you* would do it even better,' Gerald insisted quietly. He saw her about to protest and shook his head. 'It's true, my dear. I'm a very good designer, but you're getting ahead of me now, and I'm *glad* to be able to say that, not regretful. How do we ever make progress if a teacher isn't overtaken by his pupil?'

Her answering smile was full of gratitude and affection. 'Even if it were true, I doubt that many teachers would have the grace to agree with you! Anyway, whatever *you're* kind enough to think of me, Elvira Acheson will certainly have asked for you, not me.'

'I told her I'm too busy, which also happens to be true.'

He stared at Jess's white, tired face and almost abandoned his suggestion. She needed a change badly, the fresh start that her grandmother had so categorically recommended; but was a demanding assignment in a strange and alien city likely to be the challenge she needed, or only an ordeal that would simply lay her low? He could scarcely risk that – she was the most precious part of his life, his joy and daily consolation.

'You're free to turn it down. It's two months' gruelling work, and although Venice is incomparably lovely you'd have to be there in the middle of winter. Shall I tell the lady she must look for someone else?'

Jess opened her mouth – to say yes, she thought; at the moment she felt too tired, and altogether too unadventurous. But a picture of her grandmother's disappointed face suddenly floated into her mind, and with it, the memory of something else as well.

'Oddly enough, Venice has already cropped up once today – I saw a placard about it being flooded again. If I wait much longer it might not be there at all, so I think I'd better accept the job, don't you? I could hand some work over to Jane and be ready to leave soon after Christmas.'

'Good. I'll telephone our illustrious new client at Claridges tomorrow and tell her so; but now, I suppose, we must defer the pleasure of Imogen's spaghetti à la something or other no longer! Let's go home, my love.'

Christmas came and went almost unnoticed by Jess, so intent was she on brushing up a scanty store of Italian previously acquired for holidays in Florence and Rome. Her days at the studio grew longer too, as she struggled to complete work in hand, but at last she was ready – a long discussion with Elvira Acheson concluded, goodbyes said, and only her packing left to do. She was immersed in clothes and tissue paper when a knock sounded on the front door of her own rooms at the top of the Dutch House. She went to open it, imagining that Gerald on the floor below had suddenly remembered some last-minute message. But it was her aunt, Imogen Smythson, who stood there, breathless from the climb up from her own quarters on the ground floor.

'Jess dear . . . can I come in? I expect you're frantic, but I need to . . . to talk to you.' The need was obvious – her eyes looked feverishly bright behind the large round spectacles she always wore.

Her niece stifled a little sigh. In between illustrating children's books quite beautifully, Imogen made a habit of blundering into other people's lives with the tenacity of a well-meaning tank, giving offence and unwanted advice in roughly equal quantities.

'Come in and tell me what's wrong, Immy,' Jess suggested, imagining some new storm in a teacup. 'Or shall I make coffee first?'

Imogen shook her head. 'Just let me confess what I've come to say . . . I've agonised over it until a moment ago; then I suddenly *knew* what I had to do.' She stopped, hand held to brow for maximum dramatic effect, while Jess waited patiently for the final dénouement. But when it came, it took her breath away, catapulting her back into the sad, embittered years of her mother's life – because it was into the deep end of Gillian's story that Imogen suddenly plunged, boots and all.

'It isn't only your client's *palazzo* that's in Venice . . . your father, your *real* father is there too. His name is David Llewellyn Matthias.' She hesitated for a moment, frightened by the sudden shocked whiteness of her niece's face, then stumbled on. 'I'm sure it's *meant*, Jess – your going there. With Gillian dead it's time to . . . to look differently at things . . . see more than just her point of view. I didn't tell you while she was still alive . . . there was never any point, but . . .'

'There isn't any now,' Jess interrupted her sharply, when she could speak above the sudden thumping of her heart. 'How do I begin to look differently at a phoney Welsh artist who seduced a girl of scarcely eighteen, and left her desperate and pregnant, with a promising career in ruins? How am I supposed to view someone who destroyed her health and happiness and let another man spend *his* life taking care of her?'

Imogen winced at the truth she was being made to face, but with the worst of her confession behind her she managed to take hold of self-control and even a kind of unexpected dignity.

'You despise *him*, of course, as Gillian taught you to, and you rightly love my brother. She blamed me, too, because it was I who brought David Matthias here . . . mainly to give him a square meal; he was always short of money, and more often than not short of food as well. I should have guessed what would happen – my cousin was beautiful as the dawn, and my Welsh friend could charm birds from a tree; but their rapture didn't last. He wanted to paint more than anything else in life, and a jealous girl who expected him never to leave her side was a handicap he couldn't afford.'

'So he abandoned her,' Jess pointed out coolly.

'Yes, but without knowing that she was pregnant. Gillian didn't even know herself; she was hurt and mortified, but not distraught until she fainted one morning at rehearsals and the doctor told her the reason why.'

It was a fact that Gillian's subsequent plaintive retellings of the story had overlooked, but Jess clung to another aspect of her mother's story that couldn't be denied.

'He must certainly have known how young and vulnerable she was . . . how completely she loved and trusted him.'

Imogen had to agree sadly that this was so, and then silence fell for a moment, disturbed only by the faint sound of the evening traffic outside.

'How do you know about my . . . my father?' Jess finally asked, stumbling over a word that it seemed a disloyalty to Gerald Smythson even to use.

Her aunt hesitated for a moment, not sure whether what she must say would make things worse or better. 'David borrowed money from me . . . all I could afford at the time. I believed in him, you see – thought his talent couldn't be wasted. For years after that I didn't hear from him; then one day a letter arrived with a banker's draft for half the amount of the loan. He was living in Venice by then, married to an Italian girl whose parents owned something called the Pensione Alberoni. His wandering days were done, he said, and respectability had finally caught up with him. The remainder of the money also came in time. When I wrote and thanked him for it I said that Gillian had given up her ballet career, married Gerald, and had a child, but I didn't think I had the right to mention whose the child was.' Imogen took off her spectacles, and peered at Jess with earnest, short-sighted eyes. 'My dear, isn't it time to mention it now? You'll be so lonely and sad by yourself in a strange city – and Venice is *very* strange, I'm told. Gillian isn't here to be hurt, and Gerald wouldn't mind. He'd be grateful to anyone who helped you . . . probably agree with me that you *ought* to know your father.'

The temptation to shout at her was very strong, but Jess made a tired grab at self-control. 'Immy dear, you've made your suggestion, but now forget it, please. I've no wish to meet my father, and I doubt if an unknown daughter arriving on his doorstep would greatly appeal to him, or his Italian wife. In any case, I don't need help, and I forbid you to put into Gerald's head the idea that I can't manage on my own. Now you must go away and let me finish packing. I shall be back in two months' time, speaking Italian like a native and eating spaghetti to the manner born!'

Imogen found herself shepherded firmly to the door, bewildered as always by the fact that her well-meant advice never seemed to get the response it deserved. This time she'd been so certain, too. But the idea that had taken root in her mind couldn't be dislodged . . . Jessica had tried to sound cheerful but looked desperately tired. In her sad, exhausted state how could any young woman see clearly?

Imogen waved her off to the airport the following morning, smiled absent-mindedly at Gerald, and then retired to her own rooms. Having slept on it, she was *certain* of being right, and her very first task of the day must be to compose the letter that her niece had fortunately *not* forbidden her to write.

Chapter 2

The Pensione Alberoni closed its doors at the end of every October. From then until the great festival of Easter came round, its *padrona*, Signora Maria Matthias, could be a private Venetian citizen again. Apart from flurries of Japanese, who seemed to be year-round travellers, most visitors sensibly accepted that the winter climate was vile and stayed away. Without them there was no need to fight for standing room on the *vaporetti*, and no need to hurry through the days. Maria had time to haggle properly in the fish market, and to look for friends sipping coffee at Florian's in the Piazza.

Winter brought the joy of Christmas as well. She still believed in the miraculous power of the Nativity, and confided daily in the Madonna, certain of being listened to. She'd wept as usual at the midnight moment when all the bells of Venice rang their chime of celebration, discordantly out of tune but triumphant all the same. This year, though, joy had quickly fled away, and she knew why. Born and bred in the Lagoon, she was also aware of heavenly influences that were *not* divine. The astral times were out of joint and playing havoc with her family's tranquillity. They were quarrelling again now at the breakfast table and, of course, it was Claudia's fault. Llewellyn indulged her too much, insisting that his younger daughter's quick mind and readiness to argue sprang from his Welsh blood. Maria could see that it might be true. Lorenza and Marco caused her anxieties, but never wilfully; only Claudia seemed determined to spare them the risk of being bored by living peacefully together.

'We're the worst of Europeans,' she was claiming now, with her unfailing sense of drama. 'Look at us – venal and self-interested. We deserve our fate, which is to be swallowed whole by the hungry, hard-working millions on the Pacific Rim!'

'You know nothing about it,' said Marco with the blunt authority that came of being twenty-four to her mere twenty. 'They've got problems enough of their own now over there. But in any case, we're Venetians first, then Italians, and Europeans only when it suits us. That's what Zio Pietro says, and I think he's right.'

Claudia dismissed her brother with an airy wave of one hand. 'Venice for the Venetians! Throw out everyone else – including the tourists and the rich incomers whose money keeps this crumbling city afloat. It's called biting the hand that feeds us!'

'It's called proper pride,' snapped Lorenza, the eldest of the children, joining battle on her brother's side. 'We should rely on ourselves, not on other people.'

To this extent, at least, she could be certain of agreeing with him; it was harder to follow him all the way along his unswerving march towards pure socialism, because in her heart of hearts she didn't want the old order swept away in the bright, egalitarian dawn he dreamed of.

Maria looked at the flushed faces of her children – alike in their dark hair and lustrous eyes and warmly tinted skin, but otherwise such very different people. She knew what would come next – they would all begin to talk at once. But Llewellyn suddenly banged his fist down on the table, making the cups and saucers rattle.

'*Basta!* Can't we have one meal in peace? If you must argue, do it somewhere else. I'm tired of listening to you.'

The outburst briefly united them. Llewellyn had always been a born arguer himself, opinionated and excitable. They couldn't be expected to anticipate the moment when age and a longing for peace would suddenly catch up with him. About to say so, Claudia registered her mother's pleading glance and smiled seraphically instead. Marco stood up, shoulders still hunched in disapproval, announced to Lorenza that if she wanted a lift he'd be leaving in five minutes' time, and marched out of the room. She gave her mother a resigned wave and followed him, leaving Claudia in no hurry to dawdle towards a college lecture that threatened to be tedious. There was time for another cup of coffee and a little gossip with her mother about events along the rio.

They had barely started on it when Llewellyn opened the first of several letters lying beside his plate, and let out a shout across the table. Ugly, mobile face screwed up in a mixture of astonishment and pleasure, he sat staring at the sheet of paper in his hand. Maria looked at the discarded pink envelope inscribed with purple ink – a woman writer for a certainty. A *French* woman, she knew with a twinge of apprehension – she was familiar enough with the stamps that came from France. She asked Llewellyn to remember they were there, and finally he stared across at her.

'A ghost from the past, *amore*,' he began to explain in his still-beautiful Welsh voice. 'Someone I knew in Paris a long time ago. She was called Fanny Lessage then – now she's Madame Duclos, a widow with a grown-up son.'

Maria identified correctly the cause of his sudden frown – Fanny had been young and beautiful, but there sounded something sadly middle-aged about a widowed mother. Even so, the mention of Paris was disturbing. Long years might have passed, but Maria knew how

12

vividly her husband still remembered the time he'd spent there.

'How . . . how did Madame Duclos know where to write?' It seemed a reasonable question to ask, and aware that her daughter was listening, Maria managed it calmly.

'She became a successful actress – it was her one ambition in life when I knew her. In fact our ambitions clashed rather painfully . . .' Llewellyn's inward gaze lingered on the memory of that youthful, intoxicating time. Claudia waited interestedly for more disclosures, but Maria dragged him back to the present again.

'The *letter*, Llewellyn.'

'Some of Fanny's theatre friends happen to have stayed here,' he was obliged to continue. 'They said the *pensione* was comfortable, and the *padrona – you*, beloved – very kind; but when they mentioned her husband as well by name, Fanny naturally recognised me.'

Naturally, Maria admitted to herself. Having once known David Llewellyn Matthias, where was the woman who could fail to recognise or remember him? She waited to be told next that the successful actress now suggested visiting the *pensione* herself, but Llewellyn went on differently.

'Fanny has a favour to ask – she wants to send us her son, Jacques, as a paying guest for three months.'

There was a little silence before Maria answered. 'The *pensione* is closed now. There are hotels open if he must come immediately.'

'But *why* now?' Claudia enquired. 'Doesn't the poor creature know about Venice in winter . . . thigh-boots needed to wade across the Piazza, and a freezing wind blowing straight down from the Dolomiti?'

'*Now*,' her father answered, consulting his letter again, 'because he's recovering from an ambush that nearly killed him in some war-torn African swamp. His companions *were* killed; Jacques was badly damaged, and he has to learn to walk again. Where better to do that than here? God knows, walking's a necessity in Venice.'

Ashamed of her first instinctive reaction, Maria agreed with her daughter. 'Claudia is right – the *poverino* needs a kinder place than this in winter.'

But Llewellyn added further information. 'He also needs something to do, and a publisher friend has asked him to make a picture portrait of Venice and the Lagoon. That's what Jacques *is* – a rather well-known news cameraman, who is about to become a photographer.'

Already late for college, Claudia could see no alternative to getting ready to leave. But she kissed her parents reluctantly, doubting that without her advice they could decide sensibly on anything important. 'Let him come, Mamma,' she recommended from the doorway. 'I'll show him what to photograph, though he may be too French to be told what to do . . . they *will* think they're twice as clever as anybody else, poor things.'

'My darling daughter should know about *that*,' Llewellyn reflected as the door closed behind her. 'You've let her grow up too pleased with herself, I'm afraid, *amore*.'

'You're very pleased with her yourself,' Maria pointed out, not labouring what they both knew. He loved all three children, but the youngest was his favourite. There was silence in the room for a moment while Llewellyn saw again in his mind's eye the young woman who had once enchanted him in Paris, and Maria struggled to accept gracefully the prospect of a visit from the woman's son.

At last she made the little gesture with her hands that accepted what Fate had in store. 'You must telephone Madame Duclos . . . say that Jacques may come when he likes. We shall have to pray that he's French enough for Claudia not to neglect her studies.'

Llewelyn blew his wife a grateful kiss, not unaware that it had cost her something to accept a guest she would rather have turned away.

'Thank you, *amore*. Now, it's time I settled down to work.' He smiled brilliantly at her, crammed into his pocket another forgotten letter lying on the table, and walked out of the room with a more jaunty air than usual.

She was left alone to begin the tasks of the day . . . the pleasant ritual of service to her family that ruled her life and made it valuable. But for once her mind rebelled, dragging her back to a time that Fanny Duclos' letter had brought alive again. Llewellyn's arrival in Venice all those years ago was still a vivid memory. Heartsick and out of money, he'd been in desperate need of what Maria Alberoni could offer him – a home, a resting-place, somewhere to belong. He'd married her out of necessity, not love. That had since come slowly, but never with a young man's passionate joy in his beloved, and never with the completeness that Maria had offered love to *him*. She no longer expected it now . . . could make do, and be content, with what she had; but a reminder of his life in Paris was hard to accept with grace.

Llewellyn's studio was at the top of the house. He climbed there, set up paper on his easel, and then stood staring at it, not seeing the blank sheet in front of him. The past refused to be packed back into its box again just yet; it was seeping into the corners of his mind like the incoming tide in the Lagoon that nudged its way into every rio in the city. At last he gave up the pretence of working, pulled on the cape and wide-brimmed hat that his children liked to laugh at, and let himself out of the house.

Force of habit led him to a favourite spot – the wide quayside of the Zattere. Here in front of him was an island-dotted expanse of watered silk, pearl-grey and unruffled this morning because for once the day was calm. Behind him lay the city that a wandering life had finally brought him to – the old marketplace between 'the morning and the evening lands'. He wouldn't wander any more; it was home now, this huddle of russet, rose and faded brown, laced with the green ribands of its canals. For the moment its colours were hidden under the winter veil of mist and rain, but soon, for a month or two of the year, Venice would be heaven on earth, especially if the spring came early and the tourist hordes arrived late.

In front of where he sat, across the wide gap of the Giudecca canal, the pale bell-towers of Palladio's Redeemer church fretted a metal-coloured sky. It was highly paintable, that great, severe temple resting so lightly on the water. But his clients only wanted to take home with them the familiar 'views' they recognised. He could reproduce in his sleep now what they'd ask for – the Rialto Bridge, of course, or a flock of gondolas tethered along the Riva, and – most inevitably of all – the Piazza itself, complete with San Marco and that bloody Campanile that he hoped might one day fall down again, as it had once before. Then at least he could stop painting it.

Those endless, picturesque, sunlit views – *they* were the rub that had prevented him from working this morning, mocking him with their futility. Suddenly aware of the rawness of the morning, he thrust cold hands into the pockets of his jacket beneath the cape. One of them found the unopened letter he'd crammed there – with an English stamp, he noticed idly; probably left over from Christmas because it had a Nativity picture on it.

A photograph fell out when he opened it – a girl he didn't know. He turned the untidily written sheet and saw the letter's signature – another unexpected jab from the past; the morning was too full of them. Then he began to read what Imogen Smythson had written. The girl in the photograph was Gillian Carstairs' daughter – and, dear God in Heaven, *his* daughter too. Gillian was dead, and Imogen had decided that it was time he knew the truth. It didn't occur to him to doubt her – she'd been his only friend, always constant, always kind.

Across the span of years he was made to remember a time before his hectic liaison with Fanny. Then, in a different city, an exquisitely beautiful young dancer had listened to him boasting that he'd make her immortal. He'd believed it; even believed afterwards that he had the right to abandon her for Paris, because a true artist couldn't be caged by domesticity. But instead the Welsh genius had settled for turning out copy after copy of the famous Canaletto views . . . 'It's all a question of sea light, dear lady, and the changing water reflections – that's what I try to capture – that's where the magic lies!' . . . how many times had he spouted nonsense like that to some credulous American matron from the Mid-West? It sounded plausible, of course, and he always told himself at the same time that she was getting a painting to hang over her fireplace at home no worse than a hundred others she might have been talked into buying. But great art it was not . . . nothing to have justified his treatment of the vulnerable girl in London who'd begun his education into the more gentle ways of people who lived outside the mining valleys of Wales; nothing to have abandoned a child for.

At last, stiff and cold, he set off slowly towards home, but he ignored the entrance to the *pensione* and walked on instead to a palace that lay almost at the sea entrance to the Grand Canal. The water-gate at the front was boarded up for the winter and he went in through the courtyard at the rear. While he waited for the housekeeper to answer his ring, the door was opened by someone else, hurrying out of the *palazzo*.

'*Buon giorno, signore*. The greeting was polite, but cool. Giancarlo Rasini wasn't a man to offer him two words if one would do, nor to pretend that he liked his grandmother's visitor.

'Well met, my dear boy. You're in a rush, I see. Another *acqua alta* imminent, no doubt, and more duck boards to be laid across the Piazza!'

'Perhaps, although I don't actually lay them myself.' No glimmer of a smile softened the steely politeness. Rasini's expression seemed to say that keeping the city from being entirely waterlogged, or even upright at all, was no matter for flippant badinage, especially on the lips of a foreigner.

Llewellyn waved him extravagantly on his way, unable even on this most unsettling of mornings not to overact the part of amiable, theatrical buffoon. It was the effect that Emilia's stern grandson always had on him – amusing if it hadn't also been sad. Like his own children, Giancarlo wasn't impressed by the artist's get-up, but while they laughed at him with an affection that removed the sting, Llewellyn felt this man's disapproval as a personal diminishment; he was always aware of needing admiration as other people needed air.

The housekeeper was waiting for him at the top of the first flight of stairs – smilingly arms akimbo in the classic pose of the old and valued servant. No fear of overdoing things here at least – Battistina adored him. Most women did – it was a comfort he could still rely on.

'Signora la Contessa will be glad to see you, Signor Davide. She is *un po' triste* today. Well, it stands to reason . . . *è tempo brutto, non è vero?*'

It was certainly ugly weather, but he grinned at Battistina's typical mixture of phrases. In many ways Venetians were only ever themselves, and therefore unlike other Italians. But in this matter of '*il tempo*' they were all the same. Let the sky turn grey for a moment and their gaiety went out like a spent match. The Veneto's months of winter rain brought his neighbours to the very edge of despair – only God knew what would become of them if the sun forgot to reappear.

Still grumbling about the weather, Battistina led him to the *piano nobile*, where the Contessa received her guests. In some palaces it was on a still higher floor than this, but the Rasinis had never been rich merchants, conducting business on the *mezzanino*, and storing there out of reach of floods the source of their wealth – the exotic silks and spices they traded with the East. The family Emilia had married into had been aristocrats from the Republic's earliest years, founder members of the Golden Book, even providers of a *doge* or two. But there was no proud Republic now, and the Serenissima's empire had gone the way of all such. *She* was reduced to being a mere provincial city, and Count Rasini's heir had to earn his living in one of the departments of the Municipality.

Emilia Rasini was waiting for him at the far end of the long, shadowy room that stretched from the canal frontage to the back of the house. Hat in hand, he bowed over her outstretched fingers and then kissed her on both cheeks with a grace that had been carefully learned. He and Emilia were friends, even business colleagues now, but he treated her with the respect and gentleness that a medieval troubadour might have offered his lady. In her youth he would have fallen in love with her for sure, but the uncouth Welsh boyo that he'd been then could have found no favour with this aristocratic lady. Fate had been kind and given him time to grow civilised.

Upright and slender, in the way of high-born Venetian women, and groomed to the last detail as they always were, she smiled warmly at him. She wasn't a Rasini by birth; he had to remember that whenever he thought of the man he'd met on the way in, or of the gentle, ineffectual scholar who was her husband. Wit and vitality still sparkled in her dark eyes, and a vivid interest in the oddities of human nature accounted partly for her enjoyment of the game they played together. But he knew that the revenue it brought in was also badly needed – ancient Venetian palaces soaked up money as desert sand soaked up water.

'*Caro*, how glad I am to see you,' she said in the English they mostly used together. It was good practice, she insisted, since even the American visitors he brought her liked to imagine that it was the language they were speaking. 'My dear Paolo is distressed today – he made the mistake of glancing at the *Gazzettino* and read about some new scandal in Rome! And Giancarlo is burdened with anxieties as usual. At any moment the next spring tide may bring disaster, yet *still* the politicians argue among themselves. The rest of the world could be forgiven for washing its hands of us.'

'The rest of the world won't,' Llewellyn said firmly. 'It has to have a lost cause with *some* hope of saving, and Venice perfectly fits the bill. Giancarlo would rather save it single-handed, of course, or at least tell well-intentioned foreigners to stop interfering; but if they provide some of the money I'm afraid they expect some of the fun as well!'

'It's interference we should be grateful for – without it our government might never have been persuaded to release a single lira.'

Emilia waved a long, thin hand at a side table set with decanters, and he obediently busied himself with pouring the Madeira that she favoured as a mid-morning aperitif. But she noticed that he sat down afterwards more heavily than usual, and then stared out of the window at the traffic on the canal. There was nothing unusual to attract his attention – only the normal coming and going of barges and motor boats required to keep a water-borne city supplied with food and fuel and services. The aimless, colourful hordes who provided the gondoliers with work and choked the water-buses wouldn't be back for several months yet.

'You're thoughtful today, my friend,' the Countess said gently. 'There is nothing wrong with Maria or the children, I hope?'

Llewellyn thrust a hand through the thatch of thick silvery hair that by contrast made his brown face look younger than it was.

'Nothing especially wrong, although Maria always finds herself able to worry about the children through sheer force of habit. But I . . . I had some unexpected reminders of the past this morning, and I've reached the age when such memories inspire melancholy!'

He waved the subject aside and pointed instead down at the canal, where barges jostled against the mooring-posts of the building next door.

'I thought the Ghisalbertis' *palazzo* was left empty, Emilia, but something seems to be going on there.'

'Something indeed! They seem to have sold it to an American couple who are now, with their usual vigour and disregard for money, making it habitable again.'

Llewellyn stared at her with astonishment in his face. 'Americans? But Mario Ghisalberti was granted money for repairs on the understanding that the *palazzo* stayed in Venetian hands. At least, that's what my well-informed son believes. Marco and his cronies even had some scheme for renting it and turning it into a charitable youth centre – like an old-time *sculoa*.'

Emilia smiled at him wryly over her glass. 'Then I'm afraid it sounds *just* like Mario Ghisalberti! Battistina gives me the information, of course – she talks to the workmen all the time. The American lady has sent someone from London to help her decide how the *palazzo* should look. It didn't occur to her, perhaps, to consult a Venetian about this!'

For once she was disappointed in her friend, who hadn't even seemed to hear her small joke; instead, white-faced, he was staring out of the window again, seeing not the busy scene below but the phrases penned in Imogen's flamboyant hand . . . 'Jessica is on her way to Venice, to do some interior design work for an American – she's rather brilliant at it . . .'

He struggled to remind himself that there were probably a dozen houses along the Grand Canal owned at any one time by foreigners, and more still scattered over the squares and alleyways of the city. Americans, especially, were prone to these ill-considered romantic purchases until the drawbacks of Venetian life proved too much for them and they found themselves a less atmospheric but more convenient home. He shook himself out of the moment's shock and tried to retrieve normality. His observant friend was staring at him, but not even to her could he talk about an unknown daughter who had chosen to have nothing to do with him.

'They never stay long, do they, the rich visitors?' he asked, almost wildly. 'The damp, the heat, the smells, the mosquitoes, and the Venetian genius for making money out of them always spoil the fairy-tale in the end. Then they hurry away, pretending that they hadn't intended to stay.'

She heard a note in his deep voice that puzzled her until she remembered that he might still be under the spell of the melancholy past. He was a Welshman, as much inclined to gloom as to sudden irrational moments of gaiety.

'We make a little money out of the visitors,' she reminded him, and saw his taut face relax into a smile.

'Of course! Don't you remember that the eighteenth-century pickpockets used to take their haul to the city guards in order to be allowed to keep a percentage of the value? The authorities justified this system by saying that it encouraged "an ingenious, intelligent, and sagacious activity among the people"! Why should you and I not be sagacious? It has a fine, respectable ring!'

Her deep, rich laugh answered him and he could take his leave of her while they were both still smiling. But when she was alone again she remembered the strange moment when she was sure of having seen anguish in his face.

Chapter 3

Three days later a stranger limped into the Pensione Alberoni and announced in excellent Italian that he was expected by Signora Matthias. Summoned by the housekeeper to deal with a visitor who looked alarmingly on the point of collapse, Claudia found herself for the first time in her life afraid of saying or doing the wrong thing. She had never seen a man whose gaunt face and body proclaimed so shockingly that tragedy had been experienced at first hand. 'Let him come,' she had recommended blithely to her mother. Well, he was there, but what could safely be offered to someone whose hold on life seemed so precarious?

'My parents are out . . . we expected you later, I think . . . Shall I help you to your room . . . bring you coffee?' she stammered.

'With a lot of luggage needed, I decided to take the night train from Paris.' He stared at the flushed, vivid face in front of him. 'Which are you – Lorenza . . . or Claudia?' His worn face managed the vestige of a grin, and weary and unamused though it was, she felt slightly reassured. A man who was about to die at her feet surely couldn't go to the trouble of smiling?

'I'm Claudia . . . the terror of the family, Llewellyn calls me, but in fun, you understand. I never do any harm – I just like to . . . to be busy, I suppose.'

He couldn't guess her age – twenty, but perhaps younger; Italian girls came early to full physical maturity, and she was a perfect specimen of rounded, youthful beauty. Her mixed parentage probably accounted for something about her that wasn't entirely Italian, but at the moment he felt too exhausted to work out what it was. Flames of agony were beginning to shoot up his unhealed leg, and his only other conscious thought was that he'd been a fool to be talked into coming here at all. Henri Clément could have found himself another photographer, and his mother's erstwhile lover would almost certainly prove an embarrassing host.

'If you could be busy to the extent of showing me my room and bringing me some coffee, that's all I require,' he said curtly. 'I also make a point of carrying my cameras myself,' he added as she moved towards the aluminium case at his feet. 'Perhaps someone else could deal with the rest of my luggage, which is still outside on the path, getting rather wet.'

'Of course,' she said with dignity. 'Giovanni will bring it in; you need only follow me, *monsieur*.'

He made no comment on the excellent French she'd hoped to impress him with, nor on the charming room her mother had prepared for him on the ground floor. One must be sorry, of course, for so damaged a man, but Claudia reckoned that unless Gallic charm was another of the myths that life was constantly exploding, some vestige of it might have been expected to survive even his present condition. She'd been prepared to forgive him Napoleon's brutal treatment of the Serenissima, but it was going to be hard to help him; still harder to see in him any of the charm that his mother must have possessed in order to subjugate Llewellyn.

The gondola journey from San Samuele to the Ca'Rezzonico was brief enough for Jessica to decide that it was safe to ignore the boatman's surly instruction. Native-born passengers managed to keep their balance standing up, and if *they* could, so would she. She reached the far side of the canal in safety and the victory, though trivial, offered the comfort she needed. However many thousands of eager visitors poured across the causeway in summer, the Venetian lagoon in January was a desolate place. She could put up with the knife-edged wind that flicked across the water, and rain was something she was used to at home, even though there it didn't stream down from every cornice and leaking gutter quite as extravagantly as it did here. But while she waited for Elvira Acheson to arrive from a shopping spree in Paris, her sense of lonely isolation from the world around her seemed almost more than she could bear. Imogen would probably say it served her right for disowning the father she might have claimed, but Jess felt no more inclined here than she had been in London to imagine that a stranger called David Matthias would want to have anything to do with her. Loneliness would have to be endured.

With the canal crossing made, the gondolier now turned his craft towards the landing-stage and showed her what a standing passenger had concealed before. Someone else *had* chosen to sit down, and she could see why when he climbed out awkwardly with the help of a stick. She pitied the man for a moment – Venice seemed no place for the infirm – then forgot him in the surprise of the morning's second victory. The Ca'Rezzonico *was* open; she'd had time to learn that the city's museums and galleries preferred to function in bloody-minded defiance of all advertised times of business. There was something to be said for January after all – she seemed to have the huge house entirely to herself. But its eighteenth-century grandness was lost without people to provide the necessary sense of scale; one vast, painted ceiling, and one room full of Chinese lacquered furniture were enough to ram home the message of past wealth and glory; more only turned out to be less, as usual. Smiling at the idea, she turned to descend the staircase but found that she wasn't quite alone after all.

'I shall make a guess at English,' the other visitor said. 'That would explain why you were looking at all those fleshy goddesses above our heads so disapprovingly a moment ago!'

It was the passenger from the gondola – recognisable because still leaning on his stick; but not elderly, as she'd imagined, now that she could see his face. Not an Italian either – French perhaps. He spoke American-English well, but still with his native habit of stressing the final syllables. Jessica glanced at the ceiling again before she answered him.

'They do rampage a bit too much for my taste,' she agreed coolly, 'but I dare say men might see them differently.'

Nettled by a gleam of amusement in his face that she feared she might have caused, she gave him a small farewell nod; being solitary was preferable to offering entertainment to this sardonic-looking Frenchman. She went quickly down the stairs and left the building, only to discover that the drizzle had settled into a persistent downpour again. It was absurd to think that Venetian rain was worse or wetter than rain anywhere else, but she was assailed by the feeling that it was true. The whole heaven-soaked, water-sodden decrepitude of a place that had survived against the odds too long seemed suddenly more than she could manage after all. With low tide in the Lagoon, the level of the canal she walked beside had shrunk to reveal the peeling, scabrous brickwork of the houses on the other side. A scum of refuse eddied on the water and, final horror, a rat scavenged among the rotting timbers of a landing-stage.

The need to escape such insistent awfulness drove her into the first lighted doorway she came to. Warmth greeted her like a friend, and the cheerful sound of the espresso machine hissing on the counter offered a reassurance that life, not death, was possible here after all. Steamy windows veiled the cheerlessness outside, and even the *padrone* smiled more kindly than usual at an early customer he hadn't been expecting.

'*Buon giorno, signorina . . . inglese?*' He offered a menu written in English and she noticed that for the second time that morning she'd been easily identified.

'Minestrone, *per favore.*' Her command of Italian could manage that, at least, and if she stared at her guide book hard enough it might discourage a conversation that as yet she was unable to continue. The arrival of another customer seemed providential, but only until she saw who it was.

'Third time lucky – isn't that an English saying?' The limping

Frenchman had followed her own route from the museum and been similarly driven indoors. Rain still trickled down his lined face from a head of cropped, tightly curling hair. 'I saw you not only at the Ca' but standing up for the gondola crossing as well, I think. An intrepid race, *les anglais*; the rest of us have to admit that!'

The edged smile that she found disconcerting twitched the corners of his mouth again. He wasn't obliged to admire or like the English, but since he clearly didn't do either she wished he'd move to a distant table and leave her alone.

'If not intrepid, we *are* well known for being bloody-minded,' she explained briefly. 'I objected to the boatman's order to sit down.' That made clear, she went back to her book again, but sensed him still lingering in front of her.

'Are we to sit at opposite ends of an empty restaurant while the unfortunate *padrone* walks up and down between us? Or shall we share our impressions of the Ca'Rezzonico? A chilly place, I thought – I'm not surprised your poor Robert Browning caught cold and died there.'

Surprise trapped her into staring at him and she discovered that he wasn't looking sardonic at all, only pleasantly amused.

'You're more acquainted with our poets than most Englishmen I know,' she commented. 'Are they part of the normal French curriculum?'

His smile suddenly broadened. 'Perhaps only for those of us who read English at university! You have a good ear – most people take me for an American, because I spent several years there.'

'Not long enough if you hoped to disguise your nationality – though the French usually don't, in my experience of them,' Jessica said calmly.

'Chauvinistic to a man,' he agreed. 'And that's something that has already been pointed out to me here.' He abandoned the conversation to talk to the hovering *padrone*, but then seemed to assume that he'd been given tacit permission to sit down. 'Our friend recommends a red from the Friuli,' he explained when the man had bustled away, 'but perhaps you followed the conversation anyway.'

Jessica answered honestly. 'Faint but pursuing, I'm afraid – I should do better if Venetians spoke something resembling the little Italian I know. There's no need for you to offer me wine, though; I could have managed to order that for myself.'

'There is always a need to share wine,' he answered firmly. 'Now, did you enjoy the museum, or not?'

'I wasn't there to enjoy it . . . only to see what an eighteenth-century *palazzo* looked like from the inside. I'm in Venice to advise a client on the decoration of her house. She hasn't arrived yet, and I'm slightly unnerved to be given *carte blanche* to start work without her because it's a race against time.' It was a lot to have explained about herself, but she suspected the Frenchman of being fully prepared to ask for whatever he wanted to know.

'Your client's husband is an industrialist from Milan, I expect, or an American tycoon,' he suggested. 'Who else could possibly be rich enough?' He paused while their wine was being poured, took a slow sip, and then nodded to the *padrone*.

'Not French . . . but not bad!' he decided before returning to his companion. She'd removed the waterproof hat that had been crammed down over her hair and he could study her now – not conventionally beautiful and not very young, though younger than his first glimpse of her had suggested. But her reddish-gold hair was unusual, and her grey eyes were lovely. They also observed the world around her, he suspected, with intelligence and an amused detachment rare in women; his own experience of the opposite sex was that an objective judgement was usually beyond them.

'I wouldn't have guessed interior decoration as your job,' he admitted next. 'No, something more . . . more cerebral – a lawyer, perhaps, or a lecturer in higher mathematics. That seems to be the sort of male territory women now feel obliged to conquer.'

'And the sort of career that men feel obliged to resent.' Her eyes seemed to be coolly examining *him* for traces of resentment, increasing his suspicion that in her directness and lack of artifice she wasn't like any other woman he'd ever known.

'You've chosen a strange time for a visit if *you* came purely for enjoyment,' she suggested, suddenly deciding to turn questioner.

His unamused grin reappeared. 'The time chose me – I've been commissioned to produce a portrait of Venice in winter. But at least it gives me the chance to take some photographs that are original. High summer here has been done to death; I prefer to see the city, and the Lagoon as well, as they are now – wintry and desolate, but still strangely beautiful.'

She stared at him while he considered the red glow of the wine in his glass. He seemed scarcely fit enough for any task, much less the arduous one he'd chosen. The bones of his face were sharply visible, surplus flesh pared away by some inner distress as exhausting, she guessed, as the physical weakness that he also struggled with. It seemed a strange thought to have about a chance-met stranger, but when he looked up and caught her watching him she didn't feel embarrassed – and there was strangeness in that as well.

'Is being original what you enjoy?' she heard herself ask. 'Or are you just determined to frighten people with the ugly reality of something they come here expecting to find romantic and beautiful? Most of them will never see Venice in January – why not let them keep their illusions intact?'

He shook his head, almost roughly. 'You miss the point, I'm afraid.

25

Their sunlit summer vision *isn't* all illusion, and nor are the sores and shabbiness that my images will show. Reality is the *whole* truth, not the bit of it that each of us accepts because it happens to fit our point of view.'

The idea he'd just offered her was reasonable enough to be agreed to without question, but it reminded her sharply of Imogen's plea that she should try to see more than her mother's view of David Matthias. No doubt this rational Frenchman would insist that the 'whole' truth was something even her father had a right to.

'If I wanted to be contrary,' her companion was saying now, 'I'd insist that the real beauty of this place is in its mid-winter desolation, not when it's gaudy with sunlight and bloated with foreign crowds like maggots feeding on a dead carcass!' It was a grossly brutal analogy and he expected to see revulsion in her face. Instead there was a kind of pity that he wanted to reject. 'I dare say *that* would put your rich client off her splendid *palazzo*!'

Jess still stared at his drawn face, wondering what tragedy had come so close to destroying him. 'I'm put off myself by rat-infested canals, and churches that smell of damp and decay,' she answered. 'In any case, you aren't acquainted with my client, so why make rash assumptions about her?'

'I'm acquainted with others of her kind – cocooned by wealth, using places simply for enjoyment until their novelty wears off.'

Ruffled by his certainty, Jess shifted to firmer ground. 'Far from merely making use of Venice, Mrs Acheson's husband provides a handsome contribution towards keeping it above water.'

With the score now in her favour, she began counting out lire notes to end the conversation, but his thin hand reached across the table to pick up her bill.

'The minestrone is on me, please, but I'm afraid you haven't eaten enough to make the *padrone* happy.' He heaved himself to his feet as she stood up, thinking that her defence of the people she worked for had been pleasant. He was even, he realised, sorry to see her leave. 'The Correr Museum's full of decorative things that might be useful,' he suggested, half tempted to suggest going with her.

'I know . . . that's where I'm off to now.' From beneath the drooping brim of her hat, now back in place, she surveyed him with the same openness that he was applying to her. She didn't offer her hand to say goodbye, but the omission didn't surprise him; the English shied away from such physical contact, fearing to give away information about themselves. Something troubled her, though, enough to keep her standing there.

'You look very tired,' she said suddenly. 'There were too many stairs at the Ca'Rezzonico, for me as well as you.'

A smile that was genuinely amused showed her the young,

carefree man he might once have been.

'Since I arrived here a week ago I've had a determined minder to watch over me, but she was otherwise engaged this morning. I shall sit here a bit longer and then limp back home to my friends at the Pensione Alberoni.'

He thought he felt for a moment a sharp and inexplicable withdrawal in the woman in front of him, as if she'd winced away from an unexpected blow. Then she nodded and walked out, and he told himself that he'd imagined that strange reaction.

Outside himself on the path that bordered the canal, Jacques Duclos stood hesitating. Even without rain the raw afternoon wasn't much improved, and its sullen grey light neither softened dilapidation nor encouraged photography. So much for all his fine talk earlier. The truth was that at the moment there was nothing beautiful, mysterious, or even bearable about this dank waterway beside him, and in honesty he ought to find that odd woman again and tell her so. It would provide an excuse to go to the Correr Museum – she was sure to be still there, painstakingly busy with her research and looking as lonely as she'd seemed at the Ca'Rezzonico. But he could imagine her taking fright if he turned up again; she wouldn't know, because he'd be unable to tell her, that an anonymous conversation with a stranger was the best he could manage at the moment. All war photographers probably ended their career in one of two ways – either sick to the heart of witnessed horrors, or too bludgeoned by them to notice even one more tragedy. This mournful, rotting place suited him now; anything more hopeful would have seemed a lie he couldn't tolerate.

But the afternoon still waited to be filled. He must either mortify the flesh by walking again until his unhealed leg screamed a protest, or admit that he was the cripple he actually was and make for the nearest *vaporetto* station. He hadn't made up his mind when a motorboat passed him, and then slowed as its engine was suddenly throttled down. He caught up with it and glanced down to see Maria's aloof son looking at him.

'A lift needed, or not?' Marco called out.

'If I can manage to climb in, yes please.'

Even with the boat skilfully held almost motionless, embarkation was an agonising, leg-jarring business. When he'd finally managed it and they were moving again he turned to his rescuer, now steering with one-handed, careless competence, Italian-style.

'I'm still not quite accustomed to being given lifts on roads filled with water,' he commented as he wiped away the beads of perspiration on his face.

The youth beside him didn't smile, but Jacques knew why: Marco didn't want him there. Fanny Duclos was part of Llewellyn's past – they were all aware of the fact now – but in the past they thought she

27

should most certainly have remained. This glowering young man might have mixed feelings about his father, but there was no doubt at all about his devotion to Maria, whom he loved with the fervour that an Italian male reserves only for his mother, and occasionally also for the Blessed Virgin Mary. Marco's view, shared with his elder sister, was clear – Jacques Duclos wasn't welcome at the *pensione*.

'I've still a trip to make over to San Giorgio,' Marco announced now. 'I'll drop you off at the Accademia *vaporetto* stop if you can manage the walk from there.'

Jacques glanced at the neatly stacked crates of fruit and vegetables that waited in the well of the boat to be delivered – Marco's stock-in-trade; or, more accurately, his uncle's. Among other enterprises Pietro Alberoni owned some of the large market-gardens on the island of Sant' Erasmo that kept Venice supplied with food. It was Marco's job to run them for him. He was still only twenty-four, Jacques had already discovered, but looked older than that – a stocky, powerful young man whose only un-Italian characteristic inherited from his mixed parentage seemed to be a rare inclination to listen rather than talk.

'I can certainly manage the walk,' Jacques answered at last, 'but why don't I come with you? For the moment I've nothing else to do.'

Marco reached into a locker and pulled out a heavy waterproof jacket. 'Better put this on then. It will be cold out in the Bacino, and choppy too – the tide's coming in hard.'

With all that could be expected of him attended to in the way of comfort for an unwanted guest, he hunched himself over the wheel and edged them out into the traffic on the Grand Canal. His passenger abandoned the effort of talking above the noise of the engine and thought instead about the extraordinary work of salvage on the island they were going to. Like most of the Lagoon settlements, San Giorgio Maggiore had fallen into almost complete dereliction by the time Count Cini decided to turn it into a memorial to his dead son. Now Palladio's superb church – essential focal point of the lagoonscape that Llewellyn painted so often and so profitably – was pristine again. The rest of the island's beautifully restored monastery buildings housed Vittorio Cini's foundation for the study of arts and crafts. It was an inspiring story, a counterblast to the pessimism that Venice usually inspired.

Jacques wondered what his companion thought of it, because here was one young Venetian at least who hadn't joined the general exodus to the mainland. Marco's usual expression was a frown that said the world was a troubling place, but for once he seemed perfectly content – happy to be steering his boat through the treacherous, shallow channels as confidently as any local fisherman. They came alongside the island's little quay, where a child waited for the mooring rope that Marco threw him. The crates were unshipped, loaded on to a waiting trolley, and quickly wheeled away, with the lack of fuss that came from a thousand-year-old tradition of living surrounded by water. A few minutes later Marco came back stuffing a wad of lire notes inside his jacket – following another local tradition, Jacques reflected. No doubt Uncle Pietro believed in the good Venetian rule, time-honoured since the Crusades, of cash payment in return for services rendered, no matter how illustrious the customer; it was the principle that had made the Serenissima rich enough to acquire an empire. Jacques smiled at the thought, then braced himself for the cold, wet trip home. But instead of starting the engine, Marco delved under a seat again and pulled out a canvas bag.

'I was too busy to eat lunch today, but my mother's sure to ask when we get home . . . she always does!' He offered his passenger a roll lavishly stuffed with salami, but Jacques shook his head.

'No food, thanks, but if you were to offer me some hot coffee from your flask I wouldn't say no. I've seen some desolate places in my life but none to beat the Lagoon on a January afternoon like this one . . . but perhaps that isn't how it strikes you?'

He expected an answer that would be no more than a shake of the head, but for once Marco went to the trouble of finding words.

'I like it however it is . . . winter or summer, it's always beautiful . . . always interesting.'

Encouraged by the admission, his companion tried again. 'Is that why you stay, instead of moving to the mainland?'

'If you mean Mestre or Marghera, I'd rather *starve* here.' The tremble in Marco's voice gave away his youth and the strength of his feelings on the subject. 'We ought all to be able to live and work where we belong, but who cares what the ordinary people want?'

'Venice for the Venetians,' Jacques suggested, 'and to hell with the tourists and the interfering doers of good who only care about scraping dirt off painted saints and propping up churches that you'd rather see fall down!'

'In a perfect world I wouldn't mind looking after the saints and their churches as well,' Marco allowed, 'but we're far from that, I reckon. Venice can only stay alive if *Venetians* go on living here. What's the use to us of rich Milanesi or foreigners from abroad who can bribe officials to bend the rules for them, and then stay for two months of the year? We need more than a good mayor *here* – we must have honest politicians who'll speak for us in Rome, and a system that isn't rotten through and through.'

Watching his young, earnest face it seemed to Jacques that here, perhaps, was one honest politician at least in the making – who could talk, after all, when he wanted to.

'I'm afraid I heard this morning about more of the foreigners you dislike,' his passenger remarked. 'Americans who've acquired a *palazzo*

29

on the Grand Canal. I happened to meet the Englishwoman who is decorating it for them, but at least she was taking the trouble to discover how it ought to look!'

He smiled at Marco's wry shrug – the gesture that said things were as they were, not as one hoped they'd be; he'd already seen it time and time again during his painful trudges about the city. It prompted him to a confession that took them both by surprise.

'I came here selfishly, I'm afraid – not having given any thought to the embarrassment or pain I might cause your mother. Now I am aware that I should have found a lodging elsewhere. It's a bit late, but I can still move if you'd like me to.'

It seemed a long time before Marco answered him, with a shy and unexpected smile. 'Bad for trade, Mamma would say . . . it might give the *pensione* a bad name if you left too suddenly!'

Jacques' answering grin acknowledged the true Venetian response but he soon grew serious again.

'Claudia is being enormously helpful, but if your mother is anxious about *her*, I can always insist on managing on my own.'

Marco's glance now was rather pitying. 'Try insisting if you like, but it won't do any good. Claudia isn't even sure that God Almighty can manage without her up above, much less the rest of us.'

Then, abandoning the remainder of his lunch to the Lagoon, Marco restarted the engine. The cold dampness of late afternoon was turning to fog, and it made haloes of light round the *bricole* marking the navigation channels. Across the water Venice now floated in a faint wash of gold, insubstantial as a dream. The old sea-witch city looked entirely beautiful at last, and Jacques found himself hoping that the odd Englishwoman of his morning encounter was seeing it like that, too.

Chapter 4

Count Rasini preferred to emerge into the hurly-burly of the modern world only when obliged to – that was to say on the second Thursday of every month, to meet with fellow-scholars. Otherwise there was little enjoyment to be found outside; quietness had been destroyed by the diesel-engined boats that churned the waters of the canal, and privacy invaded by the foreign hordes that clogged the arteries of the city. Ancient courtesy had been lost, too, in a feverish determination to profit from so many bemused strangers. But, worst of all, he suspected his dear wife of being more involved in this last shameful exercise than she admitted to. He never asked about it, fearing to see her smile and explain that she was behaving like a true Venetian.

It was safer to remain in his library, even in the comparative quietness of winter, but this morning, despite the raw dampness of the day, he was obliged to venture out; courtesy demanded it. He dressed carefully for the visit he was about to make, regretting that the temperature made his ancient tweed overcoat a necessity – it had belonged to his father and was consequently no longer quite à la mode. The old Count's hunting bowler, with a hole in the back where the cord had hung, might also be thought to have seen better days, but one had to have something to raise when calling on a lady.

The water entrance next door being, like their own, boarded up, he approached the building from the courtyard at the rear. It was heaped with discarded timbers, and shards of plaster and glass – the usual detritus from an ancient house that was in the course of renovation. A workman ambled past, with a casual greeting, and Paulo Rasini feared that he'd been precipitate . . . perhaps come too soon to be welcome. On the verge of turning back, he saw that he was already observed. A lady stood at the top of the stone staircase leading up from the courtyard, waiting for the visitor she'd noticed.

The tall, thin figure reached her level and lifted an antiquated hat. Courtly grace was in the gesture, and she smiled at Cervantes' quixotic knight come to life. He peered back, aware that he wasn't quite what he'd expected. In his limited experience of rich American ladies they tended to the loud, but there was none of that quality about the youngish chatelaine in front of him. Perhaps stridency diminished as wealth increased – he knew there was no doubt about her husband's gigantic fortune.

'Signora Acheson, *buon giorno*. I have come to offer the assistance of a neighbour,' he explained in slow, precise English. She looked blank, and he remembered Emilia's teaching that Americans dealt in titles and full names. 'I am from the *palazzo* next door – Count Paolo Rasini is my name.'

On closer inspection she was still surprising – younger than he'd supposed, dressed simply in thick, high-necked sweater, plaid skirt, and low-heeled, buckled shoes. For once a modern woman's face didn't frighten him – no white or plum-coloured mouth, no black-rimmed eyes, and her smile was gentle.

'I'm afraid there's a misunderstanding, Count. Signora Acheson hasn't arrived yet. She's employing me to get the *palazzo* ready for her.'

'And you are not even American, I think,' he ventured, listening to her voice.

'No – Mrs Acheson merely hired me in London. My name is Smythson – Jessica Smythson.'

A shy smile lit his face. 'Shylock's daughter, I believe – how very appropriate, *signorina*, even if you haven't come to spend his ducats on the Rialto!'

She nodded, scarcely surprised now by the well-read company she seemed to be keeping. Everyone she bumped into appeared to be rather more familiar with the giants of English literature than the people she met at home.

Disappointed of the lady he'd come to find, the Count still hovered there. 'I'm afraid the bulletin I received from the Amici di Venezia was at fault. It informed me that the Signori Acheson – to whom we are greatly indebted – were already here,' he explained earnestly. 'Hence my visit, you see . . . to welcome them.'

'The *signora* arrives soon, to stay at the Danieli until the *palazzo* is ready. Her husband travels a good deal – he isn't expected until nearer the summer, I believe.'

The Count's conversational style was catching! But now she thought her aristocratic caller would bow again and take his leave. When he continued to linger she realised why he stayed – there were precise rules governing the duration of the visit, and these had to be obeyed.

'It's marginally warmer inside,' she suggested diffidently, 'and I could even offer you coffee if you don't mind drinking it in the kitchen.'

'Coffee anywhere would be delightful,' he announced with another bow that seemed to ennoble her modest invitation.

She led him along a corridor void of anything but ladders and stacked tins of paint, but from the adjoining rooms came the various noises of a small army of craftsmen at work. In the room they entered,

32

an electric fire, kitchen table, and chairs offered at least a little comfort, and the early flame-coloured tulips Jess had bought at a stall on the Zattere glowed cheerfully in a jam jar on the table. Her visitor gave them an approving nod, laid down his venerable bowler, and smiled at her.

'How cosy this is . . . if I have the charming English word correctly!'

It seemed to draw a sad picture of the cosiness available in his own stately home but she hoped that he was simply being tactful about the hospitality now on offer. He was perfectly mannered altogether and she was suddenly glad to have him there, smiling shyly at her. Apart from a brief, occasional visit by the morose architect Nathan Acheson had employed, she had only the painters to talk to, and their English combined with her Italian confined them to only the most basic conversation.

'I used to know this house very well, of course,' her caller explained. 'But it's several years since the Ghisalbertis lived here; they prefer the mainland, I believe.'

A faint note of disapproval sounded in his voice which she decided not to ignore. 'Perhaps you think that Venetians should stay *here*, Count Paolo, and not dispose of what they own to foreigners?'

'Whenever it is possible, yes,' he felt obliged to confess. 'But although my dear wife accuses me of living in the sixteenth century, even I am aware that many Venetians must nowadays abandon what they cannot make habitable themselves. Not everyone is grateful to people like the Achesons, *signorina*, but they preserve what the original owners could not.' He frowned as the memory of something Emilia had said came back to him.

'We have schemes at home to help people – grants from the state,' Jessica pointed out. 'Doesn't that happen here?'

'I believe it does,' he admitted unhappily. 'In fact my wife seems to think it happened in this case, the quid pro quo being that the property would be kept in *Venetian* hands. Individually we are very ready to help each other, you must understand, but I fear that the principle of acting unselfishly for the general good makes very little appeal to my countrymen.'

If what he said about the *palazzo* was true, she realised that it might account for something that had puzzled and irritated her. The architect employed by Nathan Acheson had seemed to take no pleasure in his work; in fact his manner had been hostile. Extended to his clients, it would mean trouble ahead. Elvira Acheson was certain to take popularity for granted, believing that no one could fail to love a rich man's wife, especially one who came as a benefactor.

Jessica would have liked to pursue the subject but the Count already looked depressed enough by the thought of his absent neighbours, and she cast around for something else to talk about. 'Why would

33

you choose to live in the sixteenth century particularly?' she asked instead, remembering his wife's complaint about him.

His sadness disappeared in a sudden twinkle of pleasure. 'My dear young lady, think of the richness of the first fifty years of that century – alive then, I could have rubbed shoulders with Erasmus, here to see his *Adages* through the Aldine Press. I should have gone every day to watch Titian painting the *Assumption* behind the great altar of the Frari, and Sansovino overseeing the building of his library in the Piazzetta.'

'And Venice itself would still have been rich and mighty,' she said, joining in the game, 'with the arsenal building ships to keep it safe from the "envy of less happier lands" . . . rather like my own country in its Victorian heyday, as a matter of fact!'

He smiled again, delighted to find so kindred a spirit in his new friend. 'There are other similarities between us, don't you think? Our trading empires have gone, and we have both had to accept a less dominating position in the world. Nevertheless, one has a *little* inherited influence left, and mine shall be entirely at the service of Signora Acheson.'

Jessica decided that there was no need to worry about her employer after all. A charming nobleman living next door couldn't be counted on for certain even in Venice, but Mrs Acheson's luck seemed to be in. Nathan's wealth and generosity could open most doors for her, and this gentle old man's connections would see to the rest.

She sipped coffee and remembered something else he'd said. 'If you knew this house long ago I hope you won't be horrified by what I'm doing with it now. I can't re-create the sixteenth century, and even if I could, my client wouldn't want to live in it. She's a very present-day American.'

'As we must expect,' he agreed courteously. 'But I hope I may be allowed to see what you *are* doing.'

'The drawing room is fit to be inspected,' she admitted, with a sudden feeling of nervousness. 'It isn't furnished yet but the men have just finished working in there.'

Should she implore him not to say if he thought she'd made a disastrous mistake? There was probably no need . . . he would try to be polite but his face was too guileless not to give him away.

They walked along the corridor together, but when she'd ushered him into the huge, airy room she left him and turned away to the long windows overlooking the Grand Canal. Even today the water outside threw changing reflections on the ceiling, but she had tried to visualise it on a summer morning – with casements thrown open and wonderful Venetian light pouring down. Between panels picked out in gold, she'd chosen to have the walls painted a delicate celadon green. The panels themselves were hung with Chinese silk – birds of paradise and flowering trees rioting against an ivory background.

'There'll be pale curtains and armchairs,' Jess said almost defiantly, 'but the cushions will echo the same rich colouring as the birds, in case you think it's all going to look too subdued.'

She didn't know what to expect – certainly not that he would offer her another courtly bow.

'I think only that it is perfect, *signorina*,' he said simply, 'and I now see why a wise American lady leaves you to handle these decisions alone. Western comfort combined with Eastern beauty – what else should the *Signora* want for a Venetian *portego* like this one?'

'Nothing, I hope; but if Mrs Acheson doesn't like it, at least I shall now be able to insist that *you* think she ought to!'

'I shall tell her that she is fortunate,' said the Count, in no doubt that it would settle the matter. 'Now I must leave you to your work, but may I beg you to visit the Palazzo Rasini and meet my wife? You must use the side entrance, on the Rio della Fornace, and I will tell Battistina, our housekeeper, to expect you. Shall we say tomorrow, at five o'clock?'

She found herself agreeing to an arrangement that, though diffidently suggested, was not to be refused, and a moment later he carefully descended the staircase to the untidy courtyard. There he turned back to give her another little salute with his raised hat before setting off to find Emilia, who would scarcely believe that he'd invited a chance-met young lady to call. He smiled all the way home with the pleasure of for once being able to surprise her.

Jessica returned to her shade cards and swatches of material on the kitchen table, but her mind lingered on what the Count's conversation had given away. The architect would have to be asked if the Ghisalbertis *had* been guilty of double-dealing, and her client would have to be told if he said yes; but it probably wouldn't spoil her pleasure in the *palazzo* – she must have lived long enough by now in the world of rich men to know the tricks and dodges that they found acceptable. Jess put down her pen and walked back to the drawing room. No mistake had been made, and it still looked beautiful, but the Count's disclosure had taken the bloom off her pleasure, even though it had nothing to do with her if his neighbour had cheated. Rectitude could easily get lost here, it seemed, but that should have come as no surprise. Hadn't there always been something lax and self-indulgent in the Serenissima's air? Every book she'd read about it had certainly said so, and even a famous Venetian theologian and Servite friar, Paolo Sarpi, had once admitted that though he told no lies, he didn't tell the truth to everyone. Il Conte Ghisalberti had Venetian history on his side, it seemed.

The persistent rain was no help to a photographer but in other respects

Jacques was beginning to find that his Venetian assignment was proving unexpectedly enjoyable. Learning to walk again about this traffic-free city was almost a rediscovered pleasure, with something to catch his camera's eye in every *campo* and alleyway; but for the first time in his life he was also enjoying a totally new experience – he'd never been part of a family before. There had been, to begin with, a certain awkwardness in the air, not lessened by Llewellyn's rather forced and overpowering joviality; but Maria was incapable of not taking to her heart anyone who looked in need of kindness, Marco was relaxing into wary friendliness, and Claudia had recovered from the bad start they'd made to become guide, counsellor, and friend. Only Lorenza still remained aloof, but only from habit it seemed to Jacques; something kept her withdrawn from the exuberance that her father and sister couldn't fail to generate around them.

One morning, forced to stop work by yet another shower of rain, he found himself in the Frezzeria outside the elegant flower shop that Lorenza helped to run. On impulse he went in and invited her to lunch. She was about to refuse, but when he insisted that he hated eating alone, the invitation was accepted unsmilingly. In the nearby *trattoria* that she led him to, her choice of salad and mineral water seemed to dampen enjoyment so deliberately that he suddenly lost patience with her.

'Marco resented my being here, but he's getting over that now – why aren't you?' he asked bluntly. 'Am I supposed to remind Llewellyn of the past too much, and upset your mother?'

The directness of it brought colour into Lorenza's pale face, making her beautiful. She was more perfectly featured than Claudia, but normally lacking her sister's vividness and brightness of spirit. Now, for once, she seemed suddenly determined to assert herself. 'Mamma doesn't seem to mind now, but I think she *was* upset. It's too late to expect Llewellyn to be more like other fathers – quiet and respectable; but he's so extra-temperamental at the moment that Mamma is worried about him.'

'Claudia seems to adore him as he is,' Jacques pointed out, trying not to smile. 'She overshadows you at home. Why do you let her? Out of an elder sister's kindness?'

Lorenza repeated her familiar little shrug. 'There's noise enough already – Mamma doesn't need the two of *us* squabbling as well!' Then, as if what she'd just said sounded disloyal or unkind, she made a more difficult confession. 'I expect you've noticed that Claudia's different from me – braver and much more like Llewellyn. She'll go looking for adventures. Even as a tiny child she always wanted to know what lay beyond the rim of the Lagoon.'

'I know . . . that's why she takes trouble with a wreck like me – she thinks I've *had* adventures!'

36

Lorenza shook her head, smiling a little sadly. 'There's no bother involved for her – instead of disapproving, she's decided to fall in love with you. She never does anything by halves, I'm afraid, so we shall all suffer when you go away!'

Jacques thought – hoped – that he was being faintly teased; then he saw Lorenza's face stiffen into its more usual expression of aloofness. She was offering a brief nod to a man who'd half risen from a table across the restaurant to acknowledge her.

'A friend of yours?' Jacques asked, ignoring the evidence to the contrary.

'An acquaintance who happens to live near us, that's all. I don't know what he's doing *here* – he's supposed to be out in the Lagoon, holding back the high water for us with his bare hands.'

For a mere acquaintance he seemed to merit a surprising amount of venom, and Jacques was about to say so when Lorenza glanced at her watch and then stood up to go. But the man she'd nodded to was also leaving, and courtesy obliged him to stop as he passed their table. He bowed to the stranger this time and Lorenza was equally obliged to introduce them.

'I keep forgetting how small and friendly Venice is, compared with Paris,' Jacques said bravely, in the face of the waves of cold disapproval that seemed to be flowing from Lorenza's rigid body to the man she'd named as Giancarlo Rasini. 'I'm invited to call on a Countess Rasini later this afternoon . . . we have a mutual friend in Lorenza's father.'

Giancarlo's pleasant smile faded immediately. 'The Countess is my grandmother, *monsieur*. I regret I shall not be there. I hope you like looking at paintings of Venice, because I'm afraid they will certainly be on show.' He bowed yet again, in a gesture that minimally included Lorenza, and walked away.

She took a deep breath and tried to smile. 'There you have one of our bluest-blooded aristocrats – part of the shabby ruling clique that sold Venice out to Napoleon and the Austrians.'

'It was a long time ago,' Jacques reminded her gently. 'In any case, I thought you said something about a job . . . did I misunderstand, or does the Countess's lordly grandson have to work for a living like the rest of us?'

Lorenza looked down her lovely straight nose. 'He works now and then, I believe, but his main concern in life is to despise the rest of us who don't happen to live in a Gothic ruin that ought to have fallen into the Grand Canal years ago. It doesn't bother *me* – I'm a socialist, like Marco.'

'I'm not sure what I am, except that I'm prepared to listen to opposing points of view,' Jacques admitted gravely. 'Will two diehards like you and Marco forgive me if I seem to hobnob with the enemy?'

'Why not?' Lorenza asked bitterly. 'We have to forgive Llewellyn.

37

It's he who keeps the Rasini *palazzo* upright, and Giancarlo dares to despise *him* as well.' Angry tears made her eyes suddenly look very bright, but Jacques thought he understood at last who it was that made this quietly intense girl so unhappy.

'He didn't look stupid,' he suggested calmly, 'and to despise *any* of you would be very stupid indeed.' There was no reply except a careless shrug, and Jacques deemed it time to leave the subject of the Countess's grandson alone.

'I was in the Frari church yesterday and couldn't help noticing the wedding flowers Maria said you'd arranged – no wonder Llewellyn boasts about his artistic daughter!'

The compliment was genuine and well deserved, but Lorenza quickly disclaimed it. 'Llewellyn's *florist* daughter, engaged in trade – not nearly artistic enough for our grand neighbour along the canal!' Then, as if disinclined to end the meal on a sour note, she smiled warmly. 'If it weren't for Claudia getting hurt, I'd be glad you'd come to Venice.'

He frowned for a moment, half inclined to believe this time that he was meant to take her seriously, but he brushed the idea aside. 'I'm a trial run for the real love affair she'll throw herself into one day; meanwhile, working with me on the book is very good for her journalistic career, or so she tells me!'

'It sounds like Claudia,' Lorenza agreed, getting ready to go back to the flower shop. She refused Jacques' offer to escort her there, and he was free to return to work himself until it was time to keep his appointment at the *Palazzo* Rasini.

Chapter 5

Remembering the Count's own visit, Jessica thought there were certain to be formalities governing a social call. She consulted her friend at the flower stall and was assured in terms she hoped she understood that it would be impossible to go wrong with a gift of snowdrops because, apart from being suitably *piccoli*, they were undoubtedly *molto carini* as well – small and very sweet certainly summed them up. That wasn't the end of the transaction – the posy had then to be charmingly encircled for her by a ring of glossy ivy leaves. Watching it being made, she knew that she observed one of the grace-notes of life in Italy. Here, presentation itself had been made into an art, and even the fishmongers along the *fondamenta* by the Rialto bridge took pride in turning their merchandise into glistening, colourful heaps of beauty. If this talent for improvement meant that the Italians also touched up harsh truths occasionally, she'd had time to learn that it was only out of the same pleasing desire to show everything to maximum advantage.

The *Palazzo* Rasini's landward entrance proved harder to find than the Count had airily suggested. Baffled by the local system of naming and numbering, Jess finally had to consult a passer-by. She expected a flood of Venetian dialect to be unleashed, since the usual '*sempre diritto, signorina*' in this case would clearly lead her straight into the canal, but she was taken by the arm instead and delivered to the very door she needed.

She parted from her guide and found herself in one of the many gardens that the city managed to keep secret. In the summer a cascade of greenery and blossom over stone walls might give it away, but for the moment every stem of climbing rose and honeysuckle and jasmine was bare. Alone impervious to the season, an ancient stone well-head took pride of place in the middle of the garden. It had been carved, Jess supposed, at the beginning of the Count's favourite century.

There was only time for a glance as she went by because she *was* being watched for, as he'd promised. The woman who waited for her at the door wore the afternoon dress of an upper servant, but there was nothing subservient about the bright dark eyes that examined the visitor, her clothes, and the flowers in her hand before she was offered an accepting nod. It wasn't hard to imagine that, having been summed up differently, she might have been told that a mistake had been made in the address or the day.

'*Signora la Contessa Lei aspetta, signorina*,' Battistina announced instead, with the satisfied air of the messenger who'd brought the good news from Aix to Ghent.

Awaited as she was, inside the house they climbed a flight of stairs of uncarpeted stone and the same coldness as charity; then the servant led her into a small chamber that seemed to serve as hall and cloakroom combined, and detached Jess from her coat and flowers.

'*Io faccio tutto qui*,' she declared firmly, and it seemed impossible not to believe her – everything that needed doing here, she *would* do. Then she threw open a tall, carved door and ushered the *palazzo*'s guest inside. '*La signorina inglese*,' she shouted to the couple waiting in a small oasis of lamplight at the far end of the room, and Jess began the perilous business of groping her way towards them. There was some distance to go and the path was strewn with hazards – small tables laden with ornaments hid themselves in the gloom, and the worn rugs beneath her feet slid dangerously on the polished marble floor. She could spare scarcely a glance for the huge, shadowy room itself, with its occasional gleams of gold where lamplight picked out an antique frame or gilding still clung to old wooden panelling. It seemed to be beautiful and sombre, rich and slightly threadbare, all at the same time.

Armchairs were grouped around the further of two immense fireplaces, where Count Paolo stepped forward to lead her to the slender, finely spun woman who waited there. Jess's first impression of Emilia Rasini was never to need adjusting. Here was someone who perfectly matched her setting. She belonged in this noble, time-worn room, among its faded velvet hangings and shabby rugs and small, priceless works of art; the treasures and the poverty were both the badge of honour of a family that had done the Venetian Republic much service in its time, but now – like the Serenissima itself – had seen glory vanish.

'*Signorina*, here is my wife,' the Count said proudly. 'Emilia, may I present Miss Smythson.'

'She of the lovely Shakespearean name, I think!' the Countess answered in English more fluent than his own.

'But *yours*, Countess, comes from a happier play,' Jess suggested with a smile.

The Count looked momentarily baffled, like a terrier surprised by some unexpected scent, but even as he began to edge away from them Emilia firmly called him back. 'Not now, *caro*; you must consult your library afterwards, please. Here is Battistina to say that our other guest has arrived.'

But the housekeeper was advancing down the room only to bring

Jess's snowdrops, arranged in a delicate glass bowl.

'From the *signorina*,' she announced approvingly. There were callers at the *palazzo* nowadays who wouldn't have been received in earlier times, and with a servant's fierce snobbery she regretted the fact more than her employer did.

The Countess took the flowers from her, and put them on a low table beside a framed photograph of a young couple in wedding dress.

'Thank you, my dear,' she said to Jess after a moment. 'Yours is a prettier word for them than ours, I think.' She turned to smile at Battistina, still lost in admiration of her own floral arrangement. 'There is another visitor yet to come, *cara*.'

'*Si, si, lo so, signora . . . vado subito*,' the housekeeper agreed, and finally ambled away.

The Countess held up long, thin hands in a gesture of defeat. 'Battistina has spent her entire life in this house – we belong to her, you understand, not she to us.'

They were all three smiling at the thought when she reappeared again, this time followed by the missing guest.

The advantage was with him, looking from dimness towards comparative light. He made out his elderly hosts easily enough, and, standing with them, a tall, slender woman whom he might have guessed to be American if he hadn't already known that she was English. He limped towards them, even more concerned than Jess had been not to trip over something, and finally was near enough to bow over the Countess's hand.

'We have been practising our English, *monsieur*,' Emilia explained with a charming smile, 'but we can struggle on in French now, if you prefer!'

He glanced fleetingly in Jessica's direction before answering. 'English by all means, Contessa.'

'Then . . . let me introduce Miss Smythson to you. Jessica, this is Jacques Duclos, the guest in Venice of a dear friend of ours.'

Jess hesitated, wondered fractionally why she did, and then held out her hand, but spoke to the Countess.

'Venice is small, and wonderfully empty in winter – Monsieur Duclos and I happened to share a wet morning at the Ca'Rezzonico when everyone else had sensibly stayed at home!' Then she said to Jacques, 'The Correr Museum was as useful as you reckoned it would be.'

Freed from the task of pouring wine, the Count was able to join in the conversation. 'I can't believe that Miss Smythson needs any help; I've seen what she is doing for her fortunate American friends next door, and it is extremely beautiful.'

The smile with which he was thanked for this commendation interested Jacques for several reasons. It seemed to indicate that Jessica

Smythson already stood on the friendliest of terms with her aristocratic hosts, and it intriguingly transformed her quiet face; it also set up in his mind the strange idea that he was reminded of someone else. But while he struggled to pin down this elusive resemblance, the far door opened and there walked into the room the tall, austere-looking man he'd already met that day, at the *trattoria* with Lorenza.

The Countess made the introductions again – unnecessarily in a way, Jess thought, because in thirty years from now, Giancarlo Rasini would be an exact replica of his patrician grandfather.

The conversation under Emilia's tactful management centred on Paris and London until the subject of museums led them to the next Venetian Biennale, and from that to modern art in general. It seemed to be all the spur the Count needed; he was mounted on his favourite hobby-horse and galloping away.

'Dear friends,' he cried, looking round the circle, 'name me *one* modern painter that we can put beside Veronese or Carpaccio, much less speak of in the same breath as Titian, or the great Tintoretto himself. And I mention only Venetian painters, you notice; there were many more spread throughout Italy and Europe at the same time. By comparison we live in a barren, barbaric age, I fear.'

Jacques smiled at his agitated host. 'At least, Count, admit that we live in an age that tries to preserve, even if it can't create. How many different organisations are there now funding restoration work here?'

'Dozens, I'm thankful to say; and inspired by them even the central government is doing its share,' Paolo Rasini had to concede. 'But my despair remains. What monuments will the present century leave behind – for architecture, the Pirelli Building in Milan? For art, today's obscene graffiti scrawled wherever there is a blank wall?'

'Perhaps the obscenities and mistakes of previous centuries also existed but didn't survive,' Jess pointed out quietly. 'I doubt if ours will, either.' Then she pointed to the painting that hung above the fireplace. 'If I'm right in saying *that's* modern, Count Paolo, you needn't despair. It's beautiful . . . no disgrace to any age of painting, surely?'

They were all bound to stare at it, but it was the Countess who identified for her guests its small, scrawled signature – 'Llewellyn', the single name, she said, that David Matthias always used.

'You are right, my dear. It *is* beautiful, and my husband thinks so too, of course.' She turned to smile sadly at Jess. 'I feel guilty, you know. If it weren't for the little enterprise we run together, my dear friend might have time to paint more pictures like this one. But it isn't what most visitors to Venice want.'

Jessica scarcely heard the last sentence, remembering instead the name Imogen had mentioned – David Llewellyn Matthias. She stared at the painting, mutely thanking God that, a moment before, she'd set down the fragile goblet of Murano glass in which the Count had brought her wine. But the picture suddenly wavered before her eyes, and she ducked her head, overcome by the knowledge beating in her brain that these kind, cultured people were even more her father's friends than Jacques Duclos, a guest at the Pensione Alberoni, seemed to be. The moment of dizziness passed, and perhaps hadn't been observed, because when she lifted her head she saw that the Frenchman had moved across in front of her, apparently the better to study Llewellyn's delicate impression. It was worth studying – San Giorgio Maggiore's campanile rising like an arrow pointing straight at Heaven out of a mysteriously mist-hung lagoon. Then, with another glance down at her, Jacques walked away, and she was composed enough again to hear the Countess talking to him about their mutual friend.

There was still wine to be drunk, and another half-hour to get through, before the appropriate time for leaving seemed to have arrived. When it did, Giancarlo offered to escort her, but Jacques firmly announced that it was unnecessary since her hotel lay on his own route.

Outside in the cold, fresh dark she would have preferred to be alone. She'd been brought much nearer to her father than she'd been prepared for, but the unexpectedly haunting beauty of his painting at least confirmed what Imogen had always maintained – the man *was* an artist. Artists, according to Imogen, had to be excused the restraints imposed on ordinary people, because the impulses that drove them were *not* ordinary, but Jess still refused to believe it was anything other than a theory dreamed up by selfish men to enjoy whatever licence they pleased. Married life in Venice might have sobered David Llewellyn Matthias, but surely neither talent nor change of heart could wipe away past wickedness.

With that clear in her mind, she heard the man beside her ask where she would like to be given dinner. As in the matter of an escort home, apparently she wasn't to be asked whether she even wanted his company at all. Irritated by what seemed like arrogance, she sounded very firm. 'I shall be dining in the hotel, where a friendly waitress allows me to practise my Italian on her.'

'Polenta and dried cod, or liver *alla Veneziana*,' Jacques predicted gloomily. 'Well, we'll just have to hope the wine is drinkable.'

'It will be,' she said, smiling in spite of herself. 'The *padrone*'s brother has a vineyard up in the Trentino.'

Annoyance with him couldn't survive, it seemed, and the truth she couldn't admit to was that dinner shared with him looked an infinitely more attractive prospect than her usual lonely tussle with Italian irregular verbs. Even the hotel dining room when they went into it together seemed suddenly a much less gloomy place than she'd found it to be so far, and she saw the approval in the waitress's smile – the Inglese had found herself an attractive friend; well, that was how it should be.

When they were left alone, Jacques broke open a chunk of bread and handed her a piece in a gesture that seemed casual and yet disturbingly intimate at the same time. It was a needed reminder that her safe, middle-aged acquaintances in London might not have equipped her for dealing with this more complicated man. She couldn't even be sure that he would tactfully ignore her moment of disorientation in the Countess's drawing room, as one of her own countrymen would surely do. He was examining her now too intently for comfort, and she was hard put to it not to seem to care.

'You don't look a typical Englishwoman, if that rather stupid phrase can be said to mean anything at all,' he announced abruptly. 'Where did your strange colouring come from?'

'It isn't strange in Northumberland, where my grandfather's family hailed from. I take after *him*, unfortunately, not after my mother, who was divinely beautiful and golden-haired.' She doubted that a glib and insincere compliment would be forthcoming in any case, but quickly turned the conversation away from herself to make sure.

'You speak Italian so well that I'm sure you also read it easily. Did you look at the *Gazzettino* this morning, by any chance, and come across an article that seemed to touch too closely on what I'm doing here?'

'You mean the piece about unscrupulous property-owners making deals with foreigners that are frowned on? Yes, I saw it . . . heard some argument about it at the *pensione* as well. The Matthiases' son, Marco, is part of the protest group involved. They aren't concerned only to preserve Venice; they don't want it used as a holiday playground by the rich. "Venezia Viva" is their cry – a living city, in other words; not a museum to the long-dead past.'

'I can understand that,' Jess agreed slowly, 'but if my foreign clients didn't know about any possible illegality it seems unfair that they should be pilloried. Mrs Acheson will be arriving here soon, expecting gratitude for her husband's generosity to the city – not blatant hostility in the local press.'

'Advise her to consult the lawyer who handled the sale,' Jacques suggested. 'It was his job to discover whether there was any illegality or not.'

'Of course!' Jess's frown of worry faded. 'That's exactly what she must do.' Amusement glimmered as she looked at him. 'Imagination was beginning to run riot to such an extent that I could seeing Elvira being barricaded out of her own home! I should have remembered that this is a non-violent city, where diplomacy was invented and guile is part of the usual stock-in-trade!'

Jacques' shout of laughter made the other diners stare. He acknowledged their attention by giving them a little bow, and then considered Jess's amused face again, as if there he might find the answer to something that was puzzling him.

'I came to Venice feeling suicidally bored and very sorry for myself. My only intention was to scramble through a tedious job while I discovered whether I could get fit enough to return to work I no longer wanted to do.'

'But you aren't bored any longer?' she prompted him gently, and saw amusement light his face.

'Boredom can't survive at the Pensione Alberoni. I arrived in my surliest frame of mind, but found myself pitched headlong into the Matthias family – nominal head Llewellyn, the artist whose painting you admired at the *Palazzo* Rasini; he's twice as alive as most men but not quite as respectable as his children would wish! He knew my mother rather intimately in Paris when he was a young man. The matriarch in charge of the family is his lovely, kind wife Maria. I've mentioned their son, Marco, already, but there are two daughters as well – Lorenza, who can't decide whether to help her brother grind the aristocracy into the dust or adore it in the forbidding shape of the Countess's grandson; and Claudia – an investigative journalist in the making. Her self-imposed task in life at the moment is to steer me around the city. She isn't as beautiful as her sister, but she has other charms that more than make up for it.'

The note of affection in his voice identified for Jess the 'determined minder' he'd spoken of once before. Claudia Matthias had made an impression on a man who'd had time to pick and choose among attractive women. It was a suddenly depressing thought, but she was firm about pushing it aside, concentrating instead on what he'd said about her father.

'The Countess referred to a "little enterprise" with Llewellyn,' she commented. 'Do you know what she meant by that?'

'Of course I know – I'm part of the Matthias family now. A friend of Llewellyn's organises city tours for the rich tourists who stay at the Danieli, and the Gritti Palace. The tour ends with tea at the *Palazzo* Rasini, where the punters get to meet its real live Countess. While being shown round, they also happen to see her artist friend crouched over his easel, and naturally clamour to buy whatever happens to be there. Most of the proceeds go towards the upkeep of the *palazzo*, which Giancarlo seems to resent as much as Marco does, but for different reasons.'

Jess thought of the austere face of the Countess's grandson and wasn't surprised by what Jacques had just said. 'Too much proper pride . . . too much sensitivity? They're inconvenient virtues nowadays, though not all aristocrats seem to suffer from them if Count

45

Ghisalberti is anything to go by.' She looked across at her companion, almost tempted for a moment to confess her connection with the Matthias family. But it wasn't possible, and she must find something else to say instead.

'I knew that my job here would be a challenge, but it's becoming complicated in ways I didn't expect. I'm not even sure whose side I'm on – ancient or modern! I'm not usually so confused at home.'

Jacques' lined face creased into another smile. 'Don't sound indignant about it – just accept the fact that visitors from the north must expect to be lost the moment they set foot here! The certainties and comfortable moralities of a lifetime suddenly disappear in this strange, water-borne city of illusions and magical tricks, where nothing is quite what it seems.'

Jess met his bright, speculative glance across the table but wished she hadn't, even though she had sufficient northern common sense left to know that provocation was all this odd man had in view; for some reason it amused him to unsettle her.

'I admitted to being confused, but not entirely lost; I can still tell a hawk from a handsaw, and I shall return to London with all my puritan habits perfectly intact!'

She saw his eyes gleam but at least he resisted the temptation to cap her quotation with another about the heroine who protested too much. Instead, he spoke almost gravely.

'Before you leave Venice resolutely unbewitched, promise me that you'll take the boat over to Torcello. There's something in the cathedral there that you mustn't miss.'

He didn't say what it was – she was expected to recognise it, and felt strangely certain that she would. But she was also aware of needing to escape from the intimacy he seemed to insist on so carelessly. She stood up to bring the conversation to an end and felt both relieved and disappointed when he didn't argue, said a brief good night, and limped away.

Chapter 6

The following morning, expecting to see Maria smiling a welcome from behind the coffee-pot on the breakfast table, Jacques found only Claudia instead. 'You're late,' she pointed out cheerfully. 'Marco and Lorenza have gone already and Llewellyn's in his studio. Mamma isn't here either because I had the brilliant idea of taking breakfast to her upstairs. I told her she was to be an eighteenth-century lady recovering from a night of dissipation at the Ridotto!'

Jacques hoped very much that Maria knew her daughter well enough to be sure whose scheme this was. Seduction at the breakfast table wasn't on his mind, though given Claudia's clinging silk négligé it might well be on hers. He'd begun their acquaintance by thinking of her as a charming, impulsive adolescent, but she wasn't that at all; she was Llewellyn's image in her relish for life, and disregard of the risks that frightened other people. With her gaiety and warmth, she was exactly what he'd needed when he arrived at the *pensione*, and her smile for him now said that she had no doubt of it herself. He tried all the same to sound friendly but avuncular.

'Shouldn't *you* be at college?'

'It's Saturday . . . I don't have to go today. I can look after you instead,' she assured him, giving his hand a tender pat.

Jacques withdrew it and reached for a roll. 'All I need at the moment is a cup of your mother's excellent coffee. If yours isn't as good I shall go upstairs and implore her to leave the eighteenth century.'

Claudia considered him with lambent eyes over the coffee-pot. 'You're looking jaded this morning, darling Jacques. I'm afraid it's the result of going roistering last night. You didn't come home to supper so I suppose you dined with someone you met at the Rasinis'.'

'We were discussing modern art,' he pointed out with some degree of truth. 'The conversation was too interesting not to continue, but the food on offer at the lady's hotel was dreadful, and in case you're wondering whether or not to ask, life's other pleasures were neither offered nor required.'

'I should hope not,' Claudia said virtuously. 'In any case, I doubt if you're quite up to them yet! But you soon will be. Venice brings people back to life – it's a well-known fact.'

She was the handful that Llewellyn, with a certain amount of pride, liked to claim, but she had her mother's sweetness as well, and Jacques found it impossible not to smile at her.

'I needed something nice like this to happen,' she said next, 'because Lorenza and I shouted at each other earlier on. We never do that as a rule, but we quarrelled about you visiting the Rasinis. Lorenza pretends to hate them on the grounds of being a socialist, like Marco, but if Giancarlo would only look her way and smile, she'd help him rebuild his crumbling *palazzo* brick by brick.'

Jacques remembered the encounter in the *trattoria* Lorenza had taken him to. 'Is it very likely – that Giancarlo *will* smile at her?' he asked slowly.

'I don't suppose so, because he despises us. We come from a long line of merchants and boarding-house keepers, which is bad enough in itself, but poor Llewellyn makes matters worse by always overacting the part of mad bohemian artist.'

She sounded wistful but resigned; though sadly unfortunate, this was how their life was arranged.

'My dear girl . . . it can't have mattered for at least a hundred years what your antecedents did for a living, or how your father behaves,' Jacques nevertheless felt obliged to protest.

'It still matters here,' she said with certainty; 'such things don't change among Venetian families who had their name in the Libro d'Oro, and the Rasinis *did*, of course. Lorenza knows that, which is why she snubs nice young men who'd like to take her out, and pretends that lovely old buildings should be torn down and replaced with workers' apartment blocks. Giancarlo thinks she's a revolutionary like Marco, and he blames Llewellyn for the rich, vulgar tourists who get taken to the *palazzo*.'

'I heard about that last night. Giancarlo might at least be grateful for what keeps the *palazzo* roof over their heads.'

'He isn't grateful at all. His idea is that if Venice and the Venetians can't survive by their own, preferably more dignified, efforts, better to let the whole place sink beneath the waves. As a matter of fact, I rather agree with him about that,' Claudia added unexpectedly. She saw surprise in her companion's face and smiled ravishingly at him. 'Nothing's simple here – haven't you discovered that yet?'

'I'm beginning to.' He might have admitted to embarking on a voyage of discovery all round, but the door opened and Maria appeared, looking unrested by her stay in bed. For once she spoke firmly to her daughter. '*Tesoro*, I need you to come shopping with me, but more clothes than you're wearing at the moment are going to be required.'

Claudia blew her a loving kiss and agreed to go upstairs, while Jacques offered Maria a smile that for once had no bitter edge to it, only real affection. 'It all goes quiet when she disappears, but I dare say there are times when the rest of you are thankful for that!' He saw the shadow of worry still lingering in Maria's eyes and decided not to ignore it. 'If you're feeling anxious because of me, you needn't be. Claudia has decided to forgive me for being disagreeably French, and thinks I need guidance in a strange city. I promise you I shan't hurt her, but if our friendship makes you unhappy, I'll manage without her.'

Maria shook her head, smiling at him gratefully. 'No, *caro* . . . she is happy helping you, and it's important to be happy at her age – sadness comes soon enough.'

'You worry about them all, I think,' he said after a moment's pause. 'Perhaps worry most about their future here.'

Maria smoothed into a neat heap the crumbs scattered on the table – the automatic gesture of a woman who thought more clearly when her hands were busy. 'Claudia's future won't be here; she will insist on seeing the rest of the world, and putting it to rights if she can.'

'Perhaps, but at least Marco loves the Lagoon and the city – he told me so.'

'The poor boy is very torn. My brother thinks he should be content with what he does – it's useful, necessary work, helping to make sure people are fed. But Marco has different ambitions – he wants to fight against what we call here *"clientelismo"* . . . corruption, perhaps, is your more truthful word for it. It seems to mean going into politics, but how can he achieve that sort of influence and remain honest himself?'

Jacques thought it might sum up most people's attitude towards politicians, but given the Italians' post-war experience of government it could scarcely be avoided here. He took refuge in an evasion that didn't properly answer her question. 'Anything is possible, Maria, in this country. The rest of us regularly write Italy off as being beyond hope or redemption, but before we've finished wringing our hands over the corpse, she's made fools of us by springing to glorious life again!'

Maria examined the idea, then nodded. 'It's true that we're survivors . . . we've had to be,' she agreed, but followed it with a wistful sigh. It would have been a relief to explain what was worrying her most of all at the moment; but content though she now was to have Jacques included in their family circle, she couldn't bring herself to confess that for the first time in their married life she didn't know what ailed her husband. Something kept him for long hours at a time shut away in his studio upstairs, but when he went out and she crept up to look, there were no new paintings to be seen.

Jacques saw the anxiety in her face and surprised himself by kissing her as he got up to leave the table. 'They'll be all right with you praying for them,' he said gently. 'My dear, they're certain to be.'

Jess was awake early as usual, listening for the sounds she'd come to expect. There was bound to be rain again – pattering on the little balcony outside her window, and spouting noisily into the canal like a miniature waterfall because the pipe suddenly ended halfway down the wall. This was Venice in late January, and the only doubt was whether the day would bring merely drizzle or the deluge she was becoming accustomed to.

But this morning the sounds she anticipated were missing – so far not a gurgle to be heard; and instead of a grey veil hanging outside the window there was a kind of brightness slanting through the gap between the hotel and its neighbour across the narrow slice of water. An hour later, convinced that the dawn's fine promise would hold, she revised the programme she'd planned. A visit to the Basilica, followed by another dutiful onslaught on the paintings in the Accademia, would have to wait. This was her first sunlit Sunday, and she'd follow Jacques Duclos' advice and make the lagoon journey to Torcello.

It wasn't difficult – she could find her way now 'through the linings' of the city, as the local expression had it, to the Fondamenta Nuova where the No. 12 *vaporetto* stopped. The bright day was sharply cold and, waiting there for the boat, she could see why – the snow-capped line of the Dolomites showed clearly on the horizon to the north-west, and from that direction blew the morning's icy wind. But nearer at hand winter sunlight had made the colours of Venice spring to life. All about her was a gorgeous huddle of umber, chrome yellow, and faded rose, and the silver lagoon unrolled to meet a sky as delicately tinted as a blackbird's egg. Her French acquaintance had been right after all; everyone's vision of this extraordinary place *was* part of its reality. Beauty was wherever it could be seen, however briefly it pierced the watcher's heart with gladness. Gerald had been right to send her here; Venice wasn't something to have missed.

But it was of Jacques Duclos that she found herself thinking again on the boat. Even in the shelter of the glassed-in cabin it was bitingly cold, and the young couple opposite her sat entwined, probably as much for warmth as for affection. They smiled at each other often, but occasionally spared a glance for her as well. The boy considered her legs, which she was glad to think could stand his scrutiny, but the girl's expression was touched with pity – a woman on her own, poor thing. Jess had met a similar though not so blatant reaction at home without it troubling her, but here she was perilously close to agreeing that to be alone in Venice was a mistake. Her mind shied away from the memory of a voice insisting that northern heads were turned by this intoxicating city, but she could at least agree that there would have been more pleasure in having someone to share it with. She was probably getting tired of conversations only half understood . . . heartsick for something familiar.

But a small, unknown island awaited her instead, and she must step ashore on to it because that was what she'd come for. There was only one route to take – a concrete pathway that lay between a stagnant canal and some neglected market-gardens that waited drearily for the spring. It led merely to a grassy square, an ancient church, and an even older, austere cathedral – all that time had left of the first and greatest of the Lagoon settlements.

A handful of people wandered about – not enough to make Torcello seem inhabited by anything but ghosts – and she wondered for an unhappy moment whether it had amused Jacques Duclos to send her on a wild-goose chase to this depressing remnant of the past. Then, as she walked into the cathedral, all regret at coming disappeared. The story of the Last Judgement told in mosaics covered the entire west wall and it was stunning enough, but she was drawn on to something else. From the curved ceiling of the apse, black-robed against a background of pure byzantine gold, the figure of the Madonna seemed to lean over the entire church. The memory came back to her of having once read a child's perfect description of it – 'a tall, thin lady holding God'. But the sadness of the world was in this Lady's tear-stained face, and she already knew how the life of the child in her arms was going to end.

Jess sat transfixed by it for a long time, scarcely aware that in the end she was seeing something else as well – her own life, running in reverse like a film fed into its projector the wrong way round. Each sequence had been the inevitable result of something earlier, leading back to the very moment when Imogen had taken a fiery young Welshman to the Dutch House and introduced him to her impressionable cousin, Gillian. None of it was cancellable now, but all of it was in the past and it was time to start again. Her grandmother had been right about that, as she so often was.

Jess considered for a moment what Elizabeth Harrington would have thought of her decision to avoid the family at the Pensione Alberoni – *her* family in a way, hard though it was to assimilate the fact sufficiently to make it seem real. But Elizabeth's clear, sharp mind would surely have agreed with hers for once – starting again required leaving the past behind, not getting more entangled with it.

Sure at last of the path she'd chosen, and suddenly aware of having grown rigid with cold in the wintertime frigidity of the Basilica, Jess knew that she must move or freeze to death. She had almost reached the door when someone else's footsteps sounded on the stone floor behind her, and a man's voice spoke in English – his mother-tongue it seemed to be, with no trace of Italian accent or inflection.

'You left without noticing that your Ruskin had slipped to the floor.'

She was glad not to have lost it, but disinclined for the company of a compatriot who, perhaps because he'd read the English title of the book, now hopefully lingered there, glad to have found someone to talk to.

'Thank you . . . yes, it's mine,' Jess agreed – absurdly, she realised, when there was no one else in the church.

It should have been the moment for him to nod politely and walk away but he was staring at her instead. Looking at *him*, she saw a man dressed with lavish eccentricity – a heavy, dark cape hung about him in extravagant folds, and the velour hat in his hand was wide-brimmed and definitely arty. His face beneath a mop of silver curls had the same theatrical quality – eyes, prominent nose, and full-lipped mouth all insisting that they merited attention. She felt her heartbeats begin to race, knowing that it wasn't absurd to think she recognised him, because, in some way that seemed inexplicable, he was identifying *her* with equal certainty.

Chapter 7

'I couldn't be sure,' he said hoarsely. 'The photograph Imogen sent wasn't clear . . . but when you moved to the door you had a different way of walking from Italian women.'

'You're David Matthias,' Jess managed to force her stiff mouth to say.

'And you're my daughter – Jessica.'

She felt for the first time in her life incapable of knowing what to do next; anywhere but in this lovely place she might have raged at her aunt's intolerable interference. She could just as easily have exploded with hysterical laughter – hadn't she decided only a moment ago on the rightness of ignoring her father? But still under the spell of the Madonna's presence in this great, quiet space, she could only stare at the man who watched her, and offer him the one simple denial that came to mind.

'My name is Smythson, not Matthias.'

He lifted brown hands, as if to ward off a blow, but whatever he might have said next was altered by the sudden tremor that shook her body.

'It's too cold in here; you're shivering . . . need some hot coffee. The little *ristorante* across the square is closed in winter, but the owner is a friend of mine.'

He saw in her pale face the decision to refuse, and stretched out his hands again, this time in a gesture of pleading. 'Don't say no, girl – we have things to say to each other.'

Jess hesitated a moment longer and then nodded her head. In silence they stepped into the different coldness of the air outside, and walked across the shrivelled grass. The friend he'd spoken of, a small, ample lady who seemed not to mind being disturbed, kissed him on both cheeks, smiled at the stranger, and promised that hot coffee would be instantly forthcoming for the *povera signorina inglese*. Left alone again with her father, Jessica decided that she would be the one to begin the conversation; the first shock was over, she'd stopped trembling in the warmth of the house, and she could manage this interview after all if she stayed resolutely calm and clung to that new acceptance of the past just worked out in the Basilica.

'I should have guessed that Aunt Imogen would ignore what I said, and write to you – she can never resist believing that she knows what is best for the rest of us.'

Llewellyn had removed his cape; now, sweater and shabby corduroy trousers made him seem less exotic, but his fierce stare was still formidable. 'She believed I should know about you, and she was right. I *didn't* know, when I left Gillian in London, but I can't promise that it would have made any difference if I had – I was young, you see; barely able to keep myself, but certain that my day as an artist must come.' He broke off to welcome the arrival of the coffee, then grew sombre again. 'At least that sort of arrogant ambition doesn't survive – we have to learn to accept that what we can do is trivial after all.'

Jess registered a fact that she knew she must be careful to remember: he was actor as well as artist. The deep, beautiful voice and tragic expression were used with the same theatrical effect as his showy cape and hat. He was trying to manipulate her into feeling sorry for him, but God knew she'd been manipulated too much already in the past. From childhood up she'd been expected to share her mother's wasted, regretted span of years; she couldn't – wouldn't – be worked on any more.

'You've made your life here,' she said quietly. 'Mine is in London, with the man who took devoted care of my mother, and of me. All that links me with you is an accident of begetting; otherwise we're strangers. That's why I rejected Imogen's suggestion . . . it's why I still do.'

Llewellyn's hand suddenly seized hers. 'No . . . don't say that, please. Gillian's dead and there's nothing I can do for her. But you're alone here – I can *help* you. We should know each other . . . you should know your brother and sisters.'

'And what should I tell them?' Jess asked in a voice that broke with sudden anger because the past couldn't be quite done with yet. 'That my mother gave up hope because of you? That instead of the brilliant career she ought to have had, she became an invalid eating her heart out with bitter regret? She was only fifty-eight when she abandoned the pretence of living altogether and welcomed an illness that she wasn't prepared to fight.'

'I abandoned her,' Llewellyn muttered after a small pause, 'but I should have made her very unhappy if I'd stayed, and I knew the Smythsons would take care of her.'

He poured more coffee for them both, then sat with broad brown hands laced about his cup, but he stared at Jessica's face as if committing it to memory. There was a subtlety of colouring and feature in his eldest daughter that hadn't come from his own rumbustious Welshness; and it was a quality that would make her an elusive subject to paint. But she had to be in *some* way a Matthias – his heart insisted upon it.

'I made up my mind I wouldn't track you down,' he went on slowly, 'although I guessed where you were working from what Emilia Rasini said. The choice had to be yours, but I had a battle with myself over that.'

'I've met Jacques Duclos as well as the Rasinis,' Jess pointed out. 'It was he who told me to come to Torcello.' She was tempted to suspect more interference; but that was silly, of course, and unfair. Jacques couldn't have known whose daughter she was.

'I come here regularly to visit an old friend,' Llewellyn explained as if he'd followed her train of thought, 'but I always call in at the cathedral first – it's a special place, I think.' Then he remembered something else. 'Paolo Rasini is a difficult man to please – because he's immensely knowledgeable, especially about Venice; but when he praised what you're doing at the *palazzo* next door it was all I could do not to boast and say that you had your skill from me!'

Jess abandoned the dregs in her cup to stare at him instead. 'I think I had my skill, whatever it amounts to, from Gerald Smythson. As well as being a brilliant designer, he's been generous enough to share what he knows. Since I was a small child he's been my truest friend.'

She was at pains to make it clear, Llewellyn thought; he was to understand that her real father, missing all her life, had been to her nothing at all. It was simply the truth – not something that she'd hoped might hurt him. He doubted if she was in the habit of hurting people.

'Will you change your mind?' he asked suddenly. 'Come back with me now and meet Maria and the children.'

She shook her head, knowing that she would have refused in any case, but remembering clearly what Jacques Duclos had said: the Matthias family preferred not to be confronted by his vagabond past, and already his wife had had to accept the reminder that Jacques represented of his time in Paris.

'Your family life sounds complicated enough – it can do without including me,' she said finally. 'There's no point in even mentioning me at all – I shall soon be back in London.' But Llewellyn's tragic face compelled her to say something else. 'I saw your San Giorgio Maggiore painting in the Countess's drawing room and it's anything but trivial – on the strength of that I don't think you have to apologise for what you can do.' A smile touched her mouth at the sudden change in his expression but she got up to leave. 'Thank the *signora*, please, for the coffee. Now I feel strong enough to brave the cold inside Santa Fosca – I haven't seen that yet.'

Llewellyn watched her for as long as she was in sight, but when she disappeared inside the beautiful Byzantine church opposite, there was nothing left to do but say goodbye to his friend and walk slowly back to the landing-stage. Daniele, Marco's boatman friend, sat waiting for him, but for once they made the journey home in silence while Llewellyn framed over and over again in his mind the news that he must take back to Maria and the children. They had to be told about Jessica; he couldn't, wouldn't, shrink from that.

They were waiting for him when he let himself into the *pensione* – Maria and the girls still dressed with the formality that meant they'd been to Mass. Lucia announced that lunch was ready, and they sat down to food Llewellyn couldn't afterwards remember eating. Then, while Maria poured coffee, he knew the moment had come to begin.

'I went to Torcello this morning.'

It wasn't a surprise; he quite regularly did. No one but Jacques stared at him, remembering the woman he'd directed to Torcello himself. There were tiny beads of perspiration on Llewellyn's forehead now, and suddenly Jacques recollected something else – the scene in the Countess's drawing room when her white-faced guest had been mesmerised by the painting over the fireplace. There was more to come, he realised, and slowly Llewellyn went on with his story.

'I bumped into the Englishwoman who is working at the *Palazzo* Ghisalberti – her name is Jessica Smythson.'

'Mousy-haired, and talking her own language in a loud, clear voice?' Claudia hazarded. 'They usually do.'

Llewellyn ignored his coffee and poured more wine instead with a hand that shook. He should have told Maria the story first, he thought; as usual, he'd realised the most important thing too late, but now he must finish what he'd begun.

'Jessica isn't mousy-haired or loud, I'm glad to say . . . seeing that she's my daughter.'

There was moment of rare silence round the table, as if his listeners had stopped breathing. It couldn't be a joke – his face convinced them of that; but how could it possibly be true?

'I was told about her for the first time a little while ago,' he explained painfully, with an imploring glance at his wife. 'I was a young man in London – Marco's age – and I fell briefly in love. It was a mistake and I abandoned the girl to move to Paris – I didn't know I'd left her pregnant. She married her cousin, Jessica was born, and given his name, Smythson.'

'Why . . . why were you told about her now?' Maria falteringly asked. '*Who* told you . . . Llewellyn, perhaps it isn't true.'

'I recognise her,' he said simply. 'I *know* it's true. Her mother died recently. That's why I was told, and because she was coming to Venice.'

Marco glanced at his mother's stricken face and got up to stand behind her chair, so that he could put his arms around her. 'Your

56

English daughter chooses bad people to work for,' he said fiercely. 'We don't want them here.'

Jacques stared at Llewellyn's Italian children, thinking that they were behaving very typically. Lorenza looked shocked – her dear but unreliable father was even less respectable than she had always feared; Marco was angry for his mother's distress; only Claudia was intrigued, and rather excited. None of them, he noticed, gave a thought to Jessica herself, but what had that reticent and wary English creature made of her extraordinary father? He would have liked to ask, but he was an onlooker at this family scene, and probably shouldn't have been present at all.

'What happens next, Papa?' It was inevitably Claudia who asked. 'When are we going to meet Jessica?'

Llewellyn stared at her with tragic eyes. 'You aren't going to meet her at all. She made it quite clear – she wants nothing to do with any of us. We're to forget that she exists.' He stood up, made a gesture with his hands that said he could bear no more discussion, and walked slowly from the room.

His family left behind would have all begun to talk at once, but Maria chose that moment to exert herself.

'You heard what your father said . . . we're to forget Jessica Smythson. Now, if you're going to Sant' Erasmo, you'd better go, or your aunt and uncle will think you aren't coming.'

She watched Marco herd his sisters out of the room, but stayed where she was herself.

'Are you worrying about Llewellyn's other daughter?' Jacques asked gently.

Maria shook her head, unable to say that she was thinking of the girl her husband had loved in London all those years ago. Abandoned, and now dead, poor thing, her story wasn't over. The daughter Llewellyn had given her was here in Venice, and he would no more be able to forget that she existed than he could stop breathing. None of them would be able to forget – she had to be included in their thoughts from now on.

Alone as usual that evening, Jess decided what she should take downstairs to read over dinner. She'd seen Torcello for herself – now was the time to wallow in Ruskin's marvellous description of it. But the book wasn't to be found in her shoulder-bag, nor anywhere else in her bedroom, and she suddenly realised why. Llewellyn's cape and hat had been flung over it when they were drinking coffee, and she'd left the room too hastily to remember to pick it up. He would return it to the *Palazzo* Ghisalberti, she felt sure – an artist couldn't help knowing how indispensable it was; but it would mean another meeting with him and that she had wanted to avoid.

Hard at work the next morning, she was interrupted by one of the workmen bringing her a small packet which she felt sure contained her missing book.

'Is for you, *signorina*,' the man who carried it in kept insisting in case she failed to understand. 'The young man said is for the *signorina inglese*.'

'Is he still here . . . is the young man still here?' She couldn't frame the Italian words, and unpardonably shouted the question in English.

'*Credo che no . . . ah, si, guarda fuori – il poverino non puo andare via.*'

She looked out as she was told and saw why the bringer of the packet hadn't been able to leave. A funeral cortège of black-draped gondolas was travelling along at the slow pace deemed suitable for the journey to San Michele, and for as long as it took to go past no traffic could emerge from the side canal. Jess fled down the stairs and across the courtyard, and flung open the gate to find a boat still waiting beside the pathway with its engine idling. She looked down at the youth who was frowning at the funeral procession still going past, and knew the answer to her next question even before she asked it.

'Are you Marco . . . David Matthias's son?'

'*Sono io.*' He made the cool admission in Italian deliberately, she thought, to underline his preference not to be there at all. Her father was mistaken if he imagined that *this* member of his family was ready to sound welcoming, but she assumed that the resentment in his face was because he disapproved of her work at the *palazzo*.

'If you speak English, and can spare a moment or two, I should like to talk to you.'

He hesitated and she expected him to refuse, but when she shivered in the bitter wind that raked the gap between the buildings his hand moved suddenly to switch off the engine.

'I prefer Italian, but I speak English, of course. You should go inside; it's very cold out here.'

She assumed it meant that he'd agreed to follow her, and gave his mother credit for the small concession. Jacques Duclos had seemed to think highly of her influence on Llewellyn's children. Having tied his boat to a mooring-pole, Marco *was* walking behind her, but as she led the way indoors to the kitchen – still the only warm place to sit in – she regretted the impulse that had sent her out to capture this reluctant caller; it would have been far better to let him escape as he'd intended.

'I'm sorry I gave you the trouble of returning my book,' she said quietly. 'I stupidly left it behind yesterday on Torcello.'

An inimical glance almost warned her of what was coming next. 'My father told us about that . . . he told us about *you* as well. I think it would have been better for us not to know.'

'Because your mother is upset? I'm sorry if that's so. I didn't intend to meet any of you. I came here to do a job of work, but as soon as it's finished I shall go back to London. You can forget that I was ever in Venice at all.'

His expression made it clear what he thought of so silly a remark, and she was obliged to agree with him; a sibling, however much unwanted and embarrassing, was a fact, and mere wishing didn't make facts go away. She had to make a guess at his age, but thought he was probably younger than he seemed. Perhaps gravity had had to be assumed to counteract his father's Welsh theatricality; or perhaps it was the burden of being involved in local politics that made him look so careworn and intense.

'What happened in London happened a long time ago . . . nearly forty years ago,' she said, suddenly wanting to ease the unhappiness in his face. 'My mother was a young ballet dancer – young and very beautiful – but before I was born she married someone else; her . . . her connection with Llewellyn was too brief for you to worry about.'

Marco's shoulders lifted in a shrug that disclaimed all interest in the woman she was talking about; instead, he fastened on a principle – they talked a great deal about principles at meetings of the *gruppo*, and he felt more comfortable with them than people.

'Ballet, opera . . . these are luxuries that only the rich can afford and pretend to enjoy.'

He saw Jess frown and waited for her to point out that his experience of the rich sounded too limited to be taken seriously. His argument was as stupid as hers had been a moment ago, but the truth was that he was feeling very confused – he'd imagined someone different from this quietly spoken, soft-haired woman. He insisted to himself that she was alien nevertheless . . . another complication in their already chaotic family life that his father should have known he must ignore; but instead of looking hostile, she was smiling at him now, as if they could share amusement together.

'All Italians have to be devoted to *opera*, at least – it's an article of faith with the rest of us!'

He was aware of being at a disadvantage – she was much older, and sophisticated enough to be able to make him feel gauche. His pride was hurt, and in a sudden gesture that reminded her of Llewellyn he waved his arms at her own sketches an the table.

'You work for rich people – of course you stick up for them; but we don't want them here. Especially we hate rich foreigners.'

It wasn't one of the extravagant phrases his father might have used. She could see how passionately he believed what he said. His young, set face suggested that he was prepared to hate her as well because she was on the side of the enemy.

'What *do* you want instead?' she asked. 'To see lovely old buildings like this one crumble until they fall to dust?'

59

'They belong to the past. Venetians need a future. There isn't room for both here – the city is too small.'

'Everyone needs a past,' Jess insisted. 'We need it more than ever now. If we can't create beauty for ourselves we must cling with all our might to what earlier generations have created for us.'

'Fancy architecture and paintings are one kind of beauty,' he almost shouted. 'Decent houses for poor people, and hospitals, and schools, and jobs are what I'd rather cling to. Have you any idea how many Venetians leave here every year because they can only find those things on the mainland?'

She had enough of an idea to accept the truth of his argument, but he was bigoted as well as right, and too accustomed to talking only to people who shared his views.

'I know a little about the problems here; not as much as you do,' she admitted. 'Even so, you might remember that it isn't only the undeserving rich who come to enjoy Venice. Thousands of ordinary people – the ones you think you represent – flock here because it's unique. If you let treasures that can't be replaced rot from damp and pollution and neglect, the rest of the world will stay away.'

'Then we'll manage on our own – it's what we should be doing anyway,' he insisted furiously. 'We don't need any of them – the millionaires who'd turn Venice into a museum, or the day-trippers who just want to say they've fed the pigeons in St Mark's Square.'

He believed it, she realised, with a young man's heroic conviction that would defy reason or common sense if it had to; fanatics and martyrs were made of the same stuff as Llewellyn's son. But she'd been in Venice long enough to know that *everyone* who had a point of view clung to it with a passion that made compromise impossible and concerted action unlikely. Paolo Rasini revered the past just as single-mindedly as Marco dreamed of the future. The city seemed to send people almost madly to theoretical extremes, and she pitied anyone whose job was to struggle with the reality of its present-day survival.

'I just have work to do,' she said at last. 'I can't properly claim the right to a point of view. But although you may not want my rich Americans here, at least admit that they provide employment for Venetian craftsmen, even if it's only going into keeping this lovely building standing.'

'There are things here that you don't know enough about,' he said with a quiet fierceness now that was more compelling than a shout. 'The *Palazzo* Ghisalberti's reconstruction was paid for just so that it shouldn't be bought up by foreigners. We had plans . . . to rent it afterwards from the Municipality and use it as a meeting-place for young people. But the noble owner sold it off anyway. He thinks he can bribe the people who are in a position to make difficulties for

60

him, but it's less easy now than it was to cheat and swindle, and we aren't at the end of the battle.'

Jess held up her hands in a little gesture of appeal. 'I can't argue with you about that – only beg you to remember that the people I work for probably don't know about the Count's dishonesty, and so don't deserve to be vilified.' She watched Marco's unrelenting expression for a moment longer, and then admitted defeat.

'We aren't going to agree, but I'm glad you came, because at least I've got one thing quite clear now. I was right all along to guess that you wouldn't fancy having a rather elderly half-sister wished on you! The fact that I like opera and old buildings, and don't even draw the line at working for rich Americans, only makes things worse. But you needn't fear that I have any intention of being a nuisance to you at the *pensione.*'

He stared at her, uncomfortably aware that his mother would think he'd behaved badly. He'd come meaning to hate this woman, which was wrong; but he'd completely failed and in a way that now seemed even worse.

'I'm sorry if I shouted at you,' he said stiffly, marched as far as the door, and then halted there to turn and stare at her. 'The wind is changing quarter, which means that you may see something rare in Venice – a sudden fall of snow. It will look very beautiful, but the paths and bridges will become treacherous. You must take care.'

Before she could thank him for the warning, he'd bolted out into the corridor and a moment later she heard the roar of his boat engine down below. She felt unexpectedly saddened by the knowledge that her brief acquaintance with him was over. She'd been right to want to avoid her father and his Italian family, but Imogen had been right as well – they *would* have been worth knowing, and perhaps she'd even admit that to her aunt one day when she was back in London.

Chapter 8

Once Llewellyn shut himself away upstairs, Maria normally left him undisturbed, to reappear sooner or later, buoyant or depressed according to how the morning's work had gone. Today she found an excuse to interrupt; the attic studio he preferred not to heat would be very cold – some hot chocolate might be welcome.

He wasn't working when she went in, and a painting on the easel, barely sketched in, seemed to suggest that most of the morning had been spent in staring out of the window, as he was now. Persistent sadness was rare and worrying in a man she was accustomed to see swing easily between high and low; she knew the cause of it now, but felt powerless to help him. Since breaking the news of the unknown daughter who had suddenly come to work in Venice, he'd sunk into a mood that isolated him from the rest of them.

Maria glanced at the easel again now and risked a snub. 'Why *that, amore*? I'm sure I've heard you say that artists only heap fruit on a dish when they can't find something more interesting to paint.'

'You've heard me spout far too much rubbish over the years,' he said with bitter frankness. 'The truth is that I never could bring a still life off – still can't, by the look of it; but I'm sick to death of painting bloody "views" of Venice.'

She put the mug of chocolate in his mittened hands. 'Drink this – it's too cold in here for you to paint anything at all.' The habit of making excuses for him was fixed now after nearly thirty years of marriage; in summer she would be just as ready to suggest that he couldn't work because the studio was unbearably hot.

'Was Jessica unkind yesterday?' she ventured bravely, determined that the subject of his daughter was better discussed than buried.

He thought it a question only his wife would ask. Kindness, her own special grace, was the one yardstick she felt ready to measure people by.

'She was truthful,' he answered after a while.

'Beautiful . . . like her mother?' Maria suggested again.

'No, not beautiful – interesting, though.' He stared at his wife and she could see the sudden shine of tears in his eyes. 'I asked her to come back with me, Maria, but she wouldn't; apparently it was more important to visit Santa Fosca instead. Her life is in London, she said

– nothing to do with us here. That's why I left it to Marco to call at the *Palazzo* Ghisalberti this morning with a book she left behind yesterday. He didn't want to go at all, and he won't have stayed to talk to her, but that's wrong, too – they're kin.'

His grief would have seemed excessive in another man, but it wasn't in this one; she'd seen him weep over an old woman who'd collapsed on the *fondamenta* outside, and rage against what he called the dying of the light when a neighbourhood infant drowned in the canal.

'You invited her, *tesoro* . . . what more could you do?' she murmured. There was another question to ask that Maria found more painful. 'Why don't you want to paint Venice any more . . . is it because seeing Jessica made you homesick for London?'

He banged down the mug he'd been holding and came to wrap her in a fierce hug. '*No* . . . you dear, stupid woman! I hated London, and Paris wasn't much better. *This* is home . . . has been since the day I walked in and you took pity on me . . . although I remember you were also very severe!'

She smiled because he was wanting her to. 'I thought a tramp had arrived, but you cleaned up very well; even Mamma thought so after a while!'

Signora Alberoni had come reluctantly, nevertheless, to accepting a rootless painter as a son-in-law; he knew she'd understood that for him it had been a marriage of necessity then, not love – he'd been a vagabond for longer than he could bear. Looking at Maria's gentle face now, he wondered how many times since then he'd hurt her, sometimes meaning to, but mostly not. The shock of his announcement yesterday had stunned her into silence for a while, but she'd dealt firmly with the children afterwards when they wanted to pester him with questions. His whole life seemed suddenly to be strewn with the wounds he'd inflicted carelessly on other people, and mostly on his long-suffering wife. He lifted his hand to touch her cheek in mute apology.

'I talk too much as a rule . . . brag too much to show everyone what a devil of a fellow I've been; but I doubt if I've told *you* nearly often enough that you're the only woman I wouldn't have been able to do without. I shouldn't even have asked you to let Jacques come – I realise that now; but, as usual with me, repentance comes too late.'

She shook her head, anxious to be truthful, as he was being. 'I *was* afraid he'd remind you of Fanny, but he seems to belong with us now. It's only Claudia that I fear for. She's out with him again now, studies forgotten while she shows him Venice and falls more and more in love at the same time. I try to make her remember that he'll go away as suddenly as he came, but she just smiles and I doubt if she even hears what I say.' Maria made a little helpless gesture. 'It's your fierce Welsh blood, my dear – they're all-or-nothing creatures . . . look at Marco, thinking of no one but his socialist friends instead of enjoying himself when he's finished working for the day. My brother says that isn't natural.'

Llewellyn swallowed the comment that in all matters except business Pietro Alberoni was a fool. 'Fighting injustices and righting wrongs,' he said instead. 'That's proper work for a young man.'

'But dangerous work as well,' she pointed out sadly. 'His meetings get *very* rowdy at times, I'm told, and what good can they do? Things are as they are – one brave heart is never going to change them.'

She spoke with a conviction that he knew most Italians shared. In the long history of their country, right had seldom triumphed over might, and people in power had never yet failed to '*sistemare*' things to their own advantage.

'All right, but you can't stop a brave young man from trying,' he said gently. He gave her cheek a little kiss and then released her. 'Now it's back to those bloody grapes and lemons . . . I shall get the better of them, sweetheart; see if I don't!'

She agreed that he would, and went away hopeful that his worst dejection had passed. The children always smiled when he boasted a little, not understanding that it was only to give himself the Dutch courage he needed. But his new-found eldest daughter already lived richly in his imagination; she'd refused to understand him at all, and it was Maria's sad belief that he might never quite recover from that failure.

Jess was surveying the food she'd set out on the kitchen table when her next caller arrived. In working clothes he looked younger and more approachable that when she'd seen him in his grandmother's drawing room. She was more aware, too, of a rare, masculine kind of beauty; no wonder it had snared Llewellyn's elder daughter.

'Miss Smythson, forgive me . . . I see that I come at a bad time, but my grandfather, who is not well enough to come himself, was very insistent that I should call. He wishes his English *signorina* to know that she must take special care in the snow that is being forecast!'

Jess smiled but looked concerned. 'Your grandfather isn't *very* poorly, I hope.'

'I don't think so. Donna Emilia only confines him to his room today because the wind is very sharp.'

'Thank Count Paolo for his kindness,' Jess said, 'and I also thank his messenger as well!'

He gave a little bow and gestured to the laid table. 'You expect a guest, I think . . . I mustn't delay you any longer.'

'I was expecting Signor Moro, the architect,' Jess explained, 'but he telephoned just before you arrived, cancelling our appointment.'

She considered her visitor's face for a moment, decided that shyness rather than arrogance might lie behind his aloofness, and surprised them both with her next suggestion. 'If you have no luncheon engagement of your own, perhaps you would stay and eat Signor Moro's share of this food?'

She expected him to refuse the stopgap invitation – almost certainly his life was arranged more formally – but after a small hesitation he offered his elegant bow again instead. 'If I may ring Battistina, who is expecting me home, I should like to stay,' he insisted gravely.

She pointed to a telephone out in the corridor, and when he returned a few moments later, found him smiling pleasantly.

'Donna Emilia is absent today, visiting cousins on the mainland, but I'm assured that "*tutto va bene*" next door – which means that my grandfather is doing as he's told, and Battistina is delighted to be in sole charge!'

He poured the wine Jess had provided in the expectation of a guest, and she had the impression that, perhaps to his own surprise, he might even relax enough to enjoy himself. Jacques Duclos had described him as forbidding, but she was more inclined to think that his stiffness of manner came from an upbringing governed by ancient family rules of behaviour. He'd chosen not to abandon them for today's headlong, slapdash intimacy; it made him unusual but not hostile.

'It's a daunting task you have here in a foreign place,' he said seriously. 'Perhaps more than it was fair to ask of you.'

'I *was* nervous until your grandfather confirmed that I was working on the right lines!' Jess admitted with a smile. 'Fortunately Mr Acheson employed a good architect in Signor Moro, and surly though *he* is, the workmen he has found for me couldn't be bettered.' Jess put down a piece of cheese she'd cut and stared at Giancarlo Rasini with Marco's outburst still in her mind. 'It's impossible for an outsider like me to know whether Venice can survive or not. It seems too small and vulnerable a battlefield for all the opposing forces who are determined *not* to meet each other peaceably halfway.'

'It can survive physically, I think,' Giancarlo answered with care, 'although fresh problems are always cropping up. It might have been harder to sound optimistic twenty years ago, but a huge amount of work has been done now to ensure its future. The problem of what it survives *as*, however, still remains to be solved. Young men like the son of our near neighbours, the Matthiases, staunchly support "Venezia Viva", at any cost to what we now call the "historic centre". The most extreme of them would see the canals filled in and an underground station in St Mark's Square! Ranged against these modernists are the people, including my grandfather, who would accept a great deal of foreign ownership as the price for keeping Venice looking as it's looked for a thousand years.'

Jess thought of the treasure-filled huddle of palaces and churches all around them, crammed precariously out of reach of Adriatic tides, threatened not only by them but by other hazards as well. Its astonishing accumulation of beauty *was* too precious to lose, but she could visualise just as clearly the stagnant canals that the tides no longer reached, and ancient, scarcely habitable slums in which people still had to live if they didn't give up the struggle and move to the mainland.

'It can't accommodate everybody's point of view,' she said sadly.

'No,' he admitted, 'but essential improvements are slowly being made, and perhaps it survives simply *because* we rather muddle along in the way we do – at least nothing decisively wrong gets done if not very much is done at all!'

It was, she thought, a sublimely Venetian piece of reasoning, and his smile seemed to agree that he thought so too.

'You've been so careful not to say whose side *you're* on here that I can't even make a guess!' she pointed out next.

He looked amused again at her persistence but didn't answer immediately. She thought it would be his usual approach; expect no hasty, emotional reaction from Giancarlo Rasini – life was too weighty a business to be conducted without due thought.

'I don't even know myself which my side is,' he admitted ruefully. 'I'm that useless creature, a man who takes no action because he can see both the opposing arguments! But it doesn't affect the job I do for the Magistrato alle Acque; our duty is very clear – to keep the Lagoon healthy, because that is the very life-blood of Venice, and to prevent the city itself from being washed or worn away.' She heard the ring of commitment in his deep voice and amended her careless summing-up of a moment ago – emotion was there after all in his devotion to a hypnotically beautiful but problem-ridden city.

'It's enough of a task,' she agreed. 'Let others argue about the rest. But at least Count Paolo is prepared to welcome the Achesons as neighbours, even if others are not.'

Giancarlo's rare smile shone again. 'My grandfather would welcome the Devil himself if he came bearing gifts that would help to keep the Serenissima intact!'

'I envy you *both* your grandparents,' Jess told him. 'I hope you realise your good fortune!'

'Emilia and Paolo brought me up,' he confessed after a moment's hesitation. 'My parents were drowned in the Florence floods of 1966, when I was a child of five. My home has been here ever since.'

And a small, orphaned boy had become a water engineer because of it, she thought painfully – determined that, if he could prevent it, no one else should die in some catastrophic disaster that might have been averted. It explained, too, why Donna Emilia had placed a gift of snowdrops beside the wedding photograph of her only son, and perhaps why Count Paolo had mostly chosen to retreat into the sixteenth century.

'I'm so . . . so very sorry about your parents,' she murmured, aware of how hopelessly inadequate it sounded. But when she looked at him across the table she found only a kind of quiet astonishment in his face.

'It is *I* who should apologise, not you. I don't usually embarrass people by talking about a tragedy that happened a long time ago. But, according to my grandfather, I *may* blame you – he assured me that I would find Signorina Jessica very easy to talk to!'

For the lonely child who'd become a shyly reticent man, he was doing very well, Jess reflected; the Count's charm of manner was in him too, when he exerted himself to use it. Her idea of the duties required of a Venetian water engineer were vague in the extreme, but she thought they couldn't help being arduous and often uncomfortable or dangerous. He *looked* an indoor sort of man, studious and aesthetically inclined, but Jacques Duclos had warned her against believing that anything Venetian was what it seemed. She dragged her mind away from another sudden vision in her mind – of a lame, camera-encumbered man slipping on icy, snow-covered steps – and instead held out her hand to the man actually beside her who was getting up to leave.

'Thank the Count for his message, please, and tell him that I shall walk like Agag if the snow does arrive!'

Giancarlo bowed again, offered her a shy, sweet smile, and went away. It wasn't hard to see what had appealed to his grandfather in this Englishwoman if he'd felt drawn to her enough himself to talk about his lost parents.

The last interruption of Jess's day occurred while she was deep in consultation with the foreman painter, Luigi Arredo. Venetian reserve in this skilled and careful craftsman had slowly melted in the certainty that, between them, he and the Englishwoman were bringing back to life something that had once been beautiful. She was young enough to be his daughter, and a foreigner as well; but her instructions were given to the men courteously, and there'd been time enough already for them to see how well she knew her job.

It was Luigi who, looking over her shoulder, saw the visitor first, and tactfully walked away. She turned to find Jacques Duclos there, leaning on his stick, and the little spring of pleasure that she felt at the sight of him flustered her into tactlessness.

'I'm told it may snow soon, and the surface will be treacherous under foot. Perhaps you should be at the *pensione* out of harm's way.'

'I hope I can still take a little snow in my admittedly halting stride.'

68

The edge to his voice was a warning that the reminder of lameness had been resented; he might refer to it himself, but others must assume that he was still capable of anything he had a mind for. She wasn't sure what to say next – it would have been natural to talk of the visit to Torcello that he'd recommended, but she couldn't be sure whether he knew what had happened there or not.

As if he understood her difficulty, he plunged into the subject himself. 'Your agitation at the sight of Llewellyn's painting has been explained to us now. It's an eventful time you're having here . . . fact proving stranger than fiction, as it so often does.'

'I saw no need for this particular fact to be known at all,' she pointed out sharply.

'I realise that.' Jacques inspected her face and decided on more interference than he usually felt prepared for. 'Llewellyn is not himself – he hoped to be allowed to lavish affection on you; everyone whom he's inclined to love is required to love *him*, instantly.'

'He must make do with the loving family he already has, I'm afraid. The man I regard as my father lives in London.'

'Stubborn,' Jacques murmured as if talking to himself, 'but understandably so, and rather splendidly loyal as well!' His smile was without the bitter edge for once, as if he'd meant what he said. 'I sent you to see the cathedral; did finding your father there spoil it for you?'

'No . . . I was on my way out, after staying far too long. When I got there I found I had a lot of thinking to do – was *that* why you sent me?'

The directness of the question not only marked her out from any other woman he'd known, but also restored the missing ease of communication between them that he'd been aware of even that first rainy morning at the Ca'Rezzonico; if he'd been a Buddhist he thought he might have insisted that this present incarnation wasn't the first time they'd known each other. Their minds fitted comfortably, but there was more than that. Physical closeness might provide even more pleasure.

'I didn't know what your need was, but I doubted if you'd come out empty-handed,' he said after a pause.

His eyes were as sad as a monkey's or maliciously bright, but always intelligent as well. There was something simian about him altogether – the shape of the skull very apparent under a pelt of thick, close-cropped hair, the lined skin stretched too tightly over the bones of his face, making him look older than his years. He had none of Giancarlo's austere, masculine beauty, but he had the trick of walking into the mind of anyone he was with. Given his smile, and his highly individual ways, he could probably invade women's hearts quite easily as well, she thought.

'Marco was sent here this morning with a book I forgot yesterday,' she said abruptly. 'He came unwillingly, and I should have done better to let him go without an argument. But at least it convinced me that I should stay away from the *pensione*. He was kind enough to relent at the end and warn me about the snow, though. I suspect him of being a very kind young man altogether.'

'He is,' Jacques agreed. 'Kind and idealistic. No wonder Maria fears a future for him amid the political sharks in Rome.'

'Giancarlo also came to warn me about the snow,' she went on. 'It will be a nuisance, I suppose, but at least it should give you some interesting photographs.'

'I only take interesting photographs,' he pointed out. 'I told you that once before.'

'So you did . . . my apologies, *monsieur*!' He was smiling now and, for no reason that her mind would supply, it was suddenly easy to smile back until he made his next suggestion.

'Shall we brave the weather forecast and dine *out* this evening? Not even for the pleasure of your company will I face a second helping of polenta and cod. Dinner with a woman is supposed to be enjoyable, not a penance that kills any hope of further pleasure!'

It was happening again – his practised leap on to another branch of intimacy, careless of whether or not it would bear his weight. Perhaps she'd made her loneliness too clear, seemed too readily available for anything he suggested; the very longing to accept was a warning in itself. They were in this strange, phantasmagoric lagoon city; full of marble, alabaster, and *verdantico*, cloth of gold and silver tissue, and the haunting scents of saffron, musk, and cinnabar – even now everything about it conspired to mislead or tease the senses; Venice was a deeply unsettling place. But as long as she remembered that, the vapours of desire that still drifted like smoke along its secret alleyways could be resisted.

'I must dine *in* by myself this evening,' she said with all the firmness she could muster, 'with lists and sketches and invoices for company! My client is finally due to arrive here tomorrow and having been several times interrupted today, I'm very far from ready for her.'

'You allowed your neighbour to stay too long, perhaps, discussing the weather,' Jacques suggested coolly, more aware of disappointment than he liked.

'Giancarlo came only at lunchtime with a message from Count Paolo.'

'Then I concede defeat. A dashing rival would be worth my powder and shot . . . but *your* dreary puritan work ethic I refuse to fight over! *Un' altra volta, signorina*'

He lifted his hand in a little salute, and then limped away, leaving her with the sad suspicion that he'd had no need to persist because another dinner companion would be readily available. Resolution was left intact, and so was virtue, but they'd won an empty victory.

Chapter 9

Elvira Acheson and the predicted snowstorm arrived in Venice almost simultaneously. For so valued a guest, brave enough to come in early February, the Danieli went out of its way to make her feel at home – with the glow of imitation logs in the fireplace of her sitting room, and the exotic perfume of hothouse white lilac to scent the air.

Across the Grand Canal, Jess anticipated and soon received a summons to the hotel – her employer being frank about forgoing the pleasure of a gondola ride when the opposite bank was veiled in snow. She was stretched out on a chaise-longue when her visitor arrived, but got up to offer a muted welcome and a complaint.

'*Snow* in Venice! Nathan won't believe it when I tell him.'

'It's temporary,' Jess assured her, 'but very rare. You may never see the Rialto bridge fringed with icicles again.'

'I can live without them!' Elvira answered with a snap. 'Icicles aren't unknown in New York; I don't need them here.' She abandoned the chaise-longue and chose an armchair near the fireplace instead – a small, neat woman encased in some of the spoils from her Paris raid. A skirt and jerkin of pale-blue suede testified to her excellent taste in clothes, but Jess was suddenly aware that a single meeting in London hadn't told them enough about each other to make collaboration easy. She really only knew what Pinky Todd in the studio had discovered about this second Mrs Acheson. Rather as Elizabeth Carstairs had done with Walter Harrington, she'd proved herself a loyal, intelligent aide, whom Nathan had eventually wedded after extricating himself from a disastrous first marriage. In London Elvira had seemed friendly, brisk, and sensibly inclined not to interfere once her interior designer had been hired, but there were aspects of this commission, Jess feared, that she might have to become involved in.

'There's a lot for you to inspect,' she reported first. 'The men that Signor Moro found for you are doing beautiful work, and it's been a joy to take my pick of the wonderful Venetian fabrics and craftsmanship that are still available here. But there are things we shall need to go to Padua to find.' She waited for a laden tea-trolley to be wheeled into the room, but when they were alone again Elvira Acheson still sat with her gaze fixed on the windows that overlooked the Lagoon. If she'd even listened to the suggestion of a trip to the mainland, she seemed scarcely enthusiastic enough to comment on it.

Jess hesitantly embarked on a more immediate hurdle instead. 'One small problem needs tackling, I'm afraid – provided you know the name of the lawyer who handled the purchase of the *palazzo* for your husband.'

'Of course I know. Nathan expects intelligence in his wife, not fluttering eyelashes and helpless femininity.'

She listened with renewed attention and no noticeable alarm to the story of the newspaper article and the reason for needing to see the lawyer; only the implication that her husband could be suspected of being outsmarted by a Venetian seemed to ruffle her at all.

'It's something they're good at here,' Jess felt bound to insist on with a faint smile. 'Venetians are often very kind to strangers, but they've been keeping an eye on the main chance for centuries, and milking the unwary is an activity that still comes naturally to them!' She realised, belatedly, that the same could probably be said of Nathan Acheson – Greek must have met Greek when he sat down to negotiate with Mario Ghisalberti.

'I'll get the lawyer here tomorrow,' Elvira said, sweeping aside a problem she didn't propose to worry about; Nathan had given her a *palazzo* – how could it not be hers?

She sipped the tea she always drank at four o'clock – not, Jess suspected, because she'd ever acquired the taste for it, but simply because it was what she was expected to do. Much of her life was probably run on the same principle – charitable lunches, duty visits to art exhibition previews, opera evenings at Covent Garden or the Met; such were the tasks that filled the lives of women whose husbands were enormously rich and often absent as well. Those born to the charade probably saw nothing wrong with it, but Elvira Acheson hadn't been, and Jess would have liked to feel justified in asking what she made of it. Even in the lavish comfort of the Danieli she looked lonely, and it was a pleasure to be able to tell her of someone who was anxious to offer her friendship and concern.

'By the way, your neighbour at the *palazzo* next door, Count Rasini, has been waiting for you to arrive so that he can make you feel welcome.'

Elvira looked unsurprised. 'Let me guess . . . he's as poor as a church mouse, and the crumbling ruin he lives in just happens to need a new roof!'

'You guess wrong,' she was told with sudden crispness. 'Paolo Rasini reckons that your husband is already a good enough friend to Venice. He is not only grateful, but anxious to be helpful – in his old-fashioned philosophy, that's how a gentleman behaves to an incoming neighbour.'

Elvira blinked at an unexpected frontal attack but yielded no ground. 'I think I'll make up my own mind all the same.' Then her blue eyes fixed themselves on Jess's face. 'If I detect a chink in *your* maidenly armour, my advice is never to trust an aristocrat. Nathan would agree with me – they're the ones you have to watch, if only because you *expect* them to behave honourably.'

'Count Rasini is old and frail, and married to a Venetian lady called Emilia. It's true that their grandson lives with them next door, but we needn't beware of *him* because he scarcely has a moment to spare from keeping Venice out of reach of the Adriatic tides.'

'Then don't let us distract him,' said Elvira. She was staring out at the desolate seascape beyond the windows again, and when she suddenly shivered despite the warmth of the room, Jess came to the strange conclusion that what had disturbed her perfectly made-up face was a flicker of something approaching fear. It seemed necessary, if slightly absurd, to offer comfort.

'Venice in winter takes a little getting used to,' Jess suggested matter-of-factly, 'but in a month or two you'll see how beautiful it is.'

'I shall still see water wherever I look . . . hear it slapping against the walls, trying to get in!' Elvira's taut mouth made an effort to smile. 'You come from a very small island – it probably doesn't bother you. I prefer what I'm used to – a good, solid continent beneath my feet!'

It seemed useless to pretend that she might grow not to notice what surrounded the new home she'd been given. Instead, Jess tried to fix Elvira's mind on the building itself. 'The *palazzo* is secure enough in the Dorsoduro; it's the part of the city with the hardest, highest foundations. Your home is also beginning to look beautiful, so I hope when you see it you'll decide that you *can* live happily there.'

Mrs Acheson's expression went blank for a moment. '*Live* there? What makes you imagine we shall do that? I don't exactly know what Nathan's got in mind, except to use the *palazzo* for some entertaining this summer while his Save Venice Committee is celebrating its twenty-fifth anniversary. After that we shall come for a month or two each year, I suppose – late spring maybe, or after the crowds have gone. Nathan hates crowds, although I rather enjoy them myself.'

She sounded momentarily forlorn again, but Jess was hearing Marco's fierce voice instead, railing against just such people as the Achesons . . . people he hated, and now she could see why. He'd give them no credit for saving what he reckoned Venice was better off without. And the truth was that she was rapidly reaching Giancarlo's position herself, of not knowing whose side she was on. She was as convinced now as Paolo Rasini of the irreplaceable beauty of the place, but there was much more to save than a museum to the past. It was enough of a problem to struggle with, but she couldn't help considering as well whether a globe-trotting, all-powerful entrepreneur had the faintest idea of his wife's strong aversion to the place he'd marked out for her.

Aware at last of the silence in the room, and of Elvira Acheson's last remark hanging unanswerably on the lilac-scented air, Jess smiled at her and stood up.

'I told the workmen I'd be back to lock up. Shall we see you tomorrow if the weather improves?'

'You may, but first I'll need you here to help me with the lawyer. I'll ask his office to let you know when to come.'

It wasn't unreasonable, of course, and Jess nodded agreement, but she felt reluctant nevertheless. Supposing that Llewellyn's son was involved in the protest campaign, her own position was likely to become extremely embarrassing. There was no need for Elvira Acheson to know of her connection with the Matthias family – in fact it was much better that she shouldn't; but Jess could see her Venetian adventure becoming complicated in ways that she had never bargained for. She'd written to Gerald and to Imogen, briefly explaining how her meeting with Llewellyn had come about; she hadn't, as yet, in her evening telephone calls to report progress, mentioned that their clients' ownership of the *palazzo* was being hotly disputed by her own half-brother.

Jess pushed the problem aside, said goodbye to her employer, and left the warm, overscented room with a feeling of relief. It was a claustrophobic world the rich lived in and she felt happier to be breathing the freezing air outside. In the space of an hour or two the scene around her had completely changed, its colours now reduced to the basic simplicities of black, white, and silver-grey. The gondolas huddled together at their moorings along the Riva made fretful little noises as the tide jostled them against each other. They were densely black, archaic shapes riding the icy water, and she could imagine the images of them that Jacques Duclos would capture on film.

He was much more often in her mind than she liked and she couldn't help feeling anxious about him – the going underfoot *was* treacherous, especially for someone who was lame. But there was, of course, his determined minder to remember . . . a girl Jess conjured up in her imagination as having inherited some of her father's extravagant qualities. Claudia Matthias had youth on her side and probably, as well, the proud confidence that all Italian girls of her age seemed to have, whether they were beautiful or not. This hallucinating place was where Claudia Matthias belonged; there would be no difficulty for *her* in believing in the actuality of things she couldn't clearly see.

The cold was too intense for standing still. Forced to start moving again, Jess dragged her mind back to what ought to be concerning it. Tomorrow's meeting with the lawyer would probably confirm Elvira's right to own the gift that Nathan thought he'd given her; if not, the objections Marco had hinted at would have to be investigated. Her feet carefully negotiated the snow-covered steps of the Accademia bridge while her mind admitted that it was unable to decide which of the two things she now believed should happen.

But on the other side of the Canale Grande, she altered direction for long enough to climb the staircase of the Palazzo Rasini and leave a message with Battistina. Whatever happened tomorrow, one thing was certain: it was time Count Paolo was told that his long-awaited American benefactress was safely here, wrapped in the comfort of the Hotel Danieli.

After Maria's visit to the studio, Llewellyn hadn't referred again to the subject of his English daughter. The silence was unusual – a warning to the family at the *pensione* that if he was anywhere within earshot, discussion of Jessica was forbidden. Not even to his wife had he been able to confess that the memory of the woman met at Torcella refused to dislodge itself from his mind. He'd even tried, in the privacy of his studio, to exorcise the image of his daughter's face by committing it to paper, but every sketch under his hand failed; not one of them brought to life what he remembered so vividly – the flash of anger in her clear eyes, or the humour that might have lurked about her mouth if only they'd been friends. He tormented himself by imagining what *she* had seen when looking at him – an old fool got up in some sort of artist's fancy dress? She'd probably judged Marco as well – again on the strength of one brief meeting. Would she have seen *anything* of the man who was himself, or understood the fervour with which his son believed that a corrupted world needed changing? He thought not; but with more self-discipline than usual he locked grief away, and astonished his children at the *pensione* by forgetting to shout at them.

For once, though, he overlooked the fact that life along the Rio della Fornace didn't allow for privacy; the network of relationships was too complicated. Giovanni, the husband of Lucia at the *pensione*, was a cousin of Battistina's at the Palazzo Rasini, but even without this family connection the two ladies would have thought it necessary to meet in the course of almost daily shopping in the Campo San Vio, to compare neighbourhood news, and assess the local *situazione*.

Lucia's latest titbit of information, carried hotfoot back to the *pensione*, was startling enough to be shared not only with Giovanni but with Signorina Claudia, who liked to keep her finger on the pulse of things. The Countess's grandson had gone to call on the *Inglese* working in the *palazzo* next door. That was *miracolo* enough in a man they'd given up for lost when it came to the indulgence of normal pleasures, but he'd stayed there hour after hour in Battistina's rendition of the story, even refusing to come home to the lunch that she had waiting for him!

Given this information, Claudia brooded long over it before deciding at last to share it with her brother.

'I think I've found her,' she said mysteriously. 'Our unknown sister, I mean. Didn't Llewellyn say she'd come to decorate some rich Americans' *palazzo* for them? Well, there can't be two *inglesi* doing that in the middle of winter – so it *must* be Jessica at the Palazzo Ghisalberti!'

Marco tried to sound authoritative and calm. 'There may be a dozen Englishwomen working here for all we know, but in any case it doesn't matter. The subject of Jessica Smythson is closed – Llewellyn said so.'

She only smiled at him, pityingly he feared. 'Don't be silly . . . how can it be when she's still here? But you haven't heard the rest of the story yet – *Giancarlo* of all people has been enjoying a sort of picnic with Jessica, and goodness knows what else besides, in the kitchen of an empty *palazzo*! I'd scarcely believe it except that Battistina got a telephone call while he was actually *there*. I've made up my mind not to tell Lorenza. He might only have been showing kindness to a stranger – after all, she's nearly middle-aged – but it would still be hurtful in a man who's not supposed to notice the women beneath his feet.'

Not yet certain what she proposed to do instead, Claudia absently regarded her reflection in the mirror opposite. Their mother might say – in fact she often did – that a beautiful nature was the only gift from God that counted, but in this one important matter Mamma had to be mistaken. Claudia knew that lovely dispositions were the consolation prize given to those plain women who didn't allow their handicap to embitter them. She patted her neat bottom, pleased to think that even in such a danger zone as this she had nothing to fear. Jacques was very critical of the female Venetian behinds encountered on their walks, and it was sadly true that Italian women *were* all too prone to spread as they got older.

'Of course you're not to prattle to Lorenza,' said Marco sternly, dragging her back to the problem in hand. 'In fact, don't do anything at all. Just for once remember what you were told – it's Llewellyn's affair, not ours.'

'Then *he* should do something more than just look tragic because a guilty conscience about her is paining him. We have a duty to be kind and welcoming,' Claudia insisted virtuously, and then gave her ravishing smile. 'Besides, I'm curious as well; our English relative must be a poor, sad thing if even Giancarlo feels she needs taking on!'

'You're *stupido*,' Marco roared suddenly. 'You think you've got everyone taped, but you don't know what I know. Jessica Smythson isn't anywhere near middle-age, and if you picture her as a sexless, dowdy spinster, think again, little sister!'

For once he'd managed it . . . reduced her to stunned silence. The triumph was worth a great deal, because it was so rare; but he was aware that more than the pleasure of finally putting Claudia in her place had led him to blurt out what he'd just said. The image in his mind of a woman with pleasant ways and humour in her eyes had somehow insisted on it.

'You've *seen* her,' Claudia shouted as soon as she'd recovered enough to frame words to hurl at him. 'You wicked, deceiving *pig*, Marco . . .' There would have been much more, but the door opened, and her face changed as Jacques walked into the room.

'*Tesoro*, listen to this, please – Marco has *seen* our English sister, without telling us. Llewellyn pretended *he'd* met her accidentally, but I suppose that wasn't true either.' The thought of her father's deception was even more painful than Marco's, and there was the glisten of a tear in the huge eyes she fastened on Jacques. 'Men aren't to be trusted . . . all except you.'

She expected to see sympathy in his face, and it was there, along with another fleeting expression he wasn't quick enough to conceal.

'*Dio mio, you* knew as well about Marco meeting her,' she said almost disbelievingly. 'I suppose he made you promise not to say.' Even Jacques, it seemed, wasn't entirely without flaw after all. 'It was wrong of you,' she said with rather touching dignity. 'You should have told me.'

He thought that she was probably right, but thanks to Jessica's stubbornness and Llewellyn's wounded pride, the whole damned business had now got thoroughly out of hand.

'You're mistaken, *ma petite*,' he said with all the firmness he could muster. 'Marco didn't tell me.'

She inspected his face and decided that she must believe him. 'Then I'm sorry I said what I did . . . forgive me, please.' Her tremulous smile faded almost at once into a frown again. 'Marco says Jessica *isn't* the sad, lonely creature I imagined, and that seems to be true, because according to Battistina, she's throwing herself at Giancarlo Rasini in the boldest way. I'm inclined to *hate* her now, for Lorenza's sake, and I hope she goes back to London very soon.'

The temptation to take the coward's way out and let the conversation end there was very strong. Expediency was something Jacques had made use of before in his relations with women, but he couldn't fall back on it now; Claudia deserved better than that, and so did Llewellyn's English daughter.

'Don't ill-wish Jessica . . . she isn't someone to hate,' he said deliberately.

Claudia stared at him for a long time, made aware for once of the gap in age and experience between them. She was determined to catch up with him . . . *must* do so because, although he didn't know it yet, she could see their future clearly planned. She knew that her family watched, but didn't understand; she could see them waiting for the moment when infatuation for a man nearly twice her age could be thrown off like some new dress she'd suddenly got tired of. It didn't matter what they thought, although she wouldn't hurt them yet by saying so; only her dear, damaged Frenchman mattered. She wasn't even dismayed by the knowledge that Jacques himself might need convincing – she would win in the end. It was something Llewellyn had taught her: failure only came when the prize to be fought for wasn't wanted badly enough. But with heart and body and soul she would offer herself to Jacques when the time came.

'I suppose *you've* met Jessica too.' She said it with heroic restraint, in a voice that barely trembled.

'We met by accident at the Ca'Rezzonico one morning,' Jacques felt obliged to explain. 'I knew nothing about her, not even her name; when I went to meet the Rasinis she was there as well, but I still didn't know who she was until Llewellyn came back from Torcello and told us.'

'And *she* was the woman you liked enough to have dinner with that evening. Marco is right. Jessica Smythson doesn't need any help from us – she can manage *very* well.'

There was spitefulness in her voice for once, but also pain, and for both things Jacques felt responsible. The girl who expected to love everybody was suddenly discovering that it wasn't possible after all. It had been easy to be generous until now; friends not endowed with her beauty and intelligence and verve had always been treated kindly, because she felt sorry for the comparisons they were bound to make. But suppose all her own advantages now were not quite armament enough against a woman with age and sophistication to help her? The fact that the woman shared her blood only seemed to make a contest between them more dreadful.

'She seemed lonely here . . . as *you* would be if you were on your own in London,' Jacques said firmly. He didn't explain that Jessica had met her father in Torcello Cathedral because he'd sent her there; it was something he found he couldn't talk about. But when he spoke again it was in the gentle voice he seemed to reserve for Claudia. 'She'll be gone quite soon, you know, and none of this will matter.' It was the moment – he knew it – to go on and say that he himself would leave as well, one day or another, and that would be something else that needn't matter. But her tragic expression made it impossible now. She wouldn't believe him, and he must wait for the day when the image she had of him began to dwindle into something resembling reality.

80

Claudia pushed tendrils of dark hair away from her face as if she were brushing aside doubts that had troubled her but must be overcome. 'You're wrong . . . because everything matters, I find . . . but I shall have to learn to deal with it, that's all.' She sent a glance in Marco's direction that said she wasn't ready to forgive *his* deception yet, and then walked out of the room.

It was he who broke the awkward silence left behind. 'She is right, I'm afraid. It would be nice to pretend that in a week or two, a month or two, life will go back to normal . . . but I don't somehow think it will. We tease Mamma for believing that everything that happens is preordained; Claudia, especially, is normally convinced that *she's* in charge. But your coming here, and Jessica's, has changed things . . . we *can't* go back to where we were before.'

It was a long speech for Marco to have made, born – Jacques realised – of an anxiety that had needed putting into words. He recognised it because the same anxiety was in himself – life *had* changed, almost from the moment he'd arrived from Paris.

'I'm afraid I agree with you, my friend,' he said bleakly, before he gave a little shrug and then followed Claudia out of the room.

Chapter 10

Countess Rasini entertained friends formally as a rule. Her invitation to Signora Acheson should have been no different matter, but for once she had to submit to being hurried. Paolo was insistent that a lady staying at the Danieli on her own must certainly be lonely, and it was well known that Americans saw nothing wrong with informality.

'A small, pleasant dinner party,' he recommended earnestly, 'to which we must, of course, invite the *signorina* who works for her – and perhaps the Matthiases as well. No one is likely to be a more kind and helpful neighbour to the Achesons than Maria.'

'Very true, but she has a guest of her own to consider.' Paolo looked blank and his wife was provoked into being almost sharp with him. 'My dear, he *came* here, don't you remember? The Frenchman, Jacques Duclos.'

'Then he may come again,' he said with faint surprise. 'Didn't you find him a pleasant, interesting man?'

He smiled at her very sweetly and trotted away, convinced that he'd been not only helpful but unselfish. He would have preferred an evening's quiet reading in his library, but to be remiss in courtesy to the wife of a benefactor and close neighbour was simply unthinkable.

Left alone, Emilia reluctantly made her first telephone call. With an American's unfailing ability to remember names, Elvira 'placed' the Countess and pronounced herself free to dine that evening. She was even ready to brave the weather, and would expect the boatman who'd be sent to collect her at eight o'clock. Emilia was pondering her next call when Giancarlo, dressed for an arctic inspection of sea defences out in the Lagoon, looked in to enquire about his grandfather.

'He is sufficiently restored by the news of Signora Acheson's arrival to insist on entertaining her this evening,' Emilia said tartly. 'I am also instructed to invite Jessica Smythson, together with Llewellyn and Maria and their French guest! I should prefer to make the *signora*'s acquaintance more slowly, but your grandfather is suddenly determined to behave with the vigour he imagines all Americans are blessed with!'

Giancarlo grinned at this dryness but kept his parting shot for when he was at the door. 'It sounds too good to miss! If I'm to be allowed to come, will you tell Miss Smythson that I'll call for her at her hotel?' Then he smiled at his grandmother's astonished face, and went away, leaving her with this unexpected development to ponder. It wasn't his usual habit to share in whatever entertaining was done on the floor below his own, and it was a long time since she'd fought her last rearguard action to prevent him from becoming a reclusive bachelor upstairs. She knew, with continuing regret, that she'd also failed to get him to value her friend Llewellyn as he should; and the knowledge that the Matthiases would be present made his behaviour now all the more remarkable.

She put the puzzle aside, sent Battistina next door with an invitation for Jessica, and telephoned the *pensione*. Ten minutes later, after a conversation that had to be interrupted because Maria found it necessary to consult Llewellyn, the Countess absent-mindedly replaced the receiver and thought about what she'd just heard. Then she went in search of her husband. It was time to explain to him the complexities of the evening he'd insisted on providing for them.

Avvocato Bossi was asking for his client at the Danieli just as Jess arrived, but she thought she would have identified him anyway. He was as elegantly turned out, and had the same gravely watchful air, as the white-tabbed men she'd seen along the Rialto, making for the law courts in the Palazzo Grimani. He listened to Elvira's explanation of the problem already aired in the pages of the *Gazzettino*, and then pulled out of his briefcase a copy of that morning's newspaper.

'I've had a rough English translation of this made to save time,' he said, laying a typed sheet of paper in front of them. 'I'm afraid it carries the original protest a stage further.'

He allowed them time to skim through it, watched a flush of colour disturb his client's delicately tinted face, but neatly forestalled the tirade she was about to launch.

'You see that the implications are twofold now – property-owners, obviously identified by the writers although they are not named here, have betrayed the spirit and perhaps even the letter of what was offered them; but their foreign buyers are reckoned to have benefited as well, by being spared the cost of huge structural repairs that they would otherwise have had to face. The only losers have been the local people who hoped to see the restored buildings put to a different, communal use.'

'I understand the implications,' Elvira said in a voice that trembled with rage. 'You must find out who wrote this . . . because Nathan never lets libel go. He's *poured* money into saving this . . . ungrateful, decrepit place, and all the thanks he gets are cowardly, anonymous attacks.' Silenced for a moment by the sobs of anger in her throat, she sat banging the table with hands made into small clenched fists.

Jess filled the gap with the only question that seemed worth asking.

'*Was* the sale illegal, Signor Bossi? It all seems to hinge on that.'

He delayed answering for a moment – like an actor, she thought, unable to resist screwing the tension a little tighter. 'The transaction wasn't illegal,' he said at last, 'because technically it wasn't a sale at all.' He heard Elvira give a little gasp, but went calmly on. 'Count Ghisalberti is still the nominal owner of the *palazzo*, but for as long as your husband continues their agreement, the Count waives all right to live in it, or to dispose of it to anyone else.'

'In other words, it's a legal dodge,' Jess suggested bluntly.

The lawyer answered with Venetian tact. 'Let us say that it permits a considerable benefactor to remain here as long as he wants to.'

'Thank you,' said Elvira, with a steely smile for her designer. 'I don't care for the word "dodge".' Then she tapped the article with scarlet fingernails. 'I just want to know what we do about *this*.'

'All that we can do has already been done, *signora*,' Avvocato Bossi replied. 'The *Gazzettino* has been informed that since there has been no infringement of the law, any further article will be considered libellous. The people responsible have had the satisfaction of venting local anger, but that must suffice. I think you will find that the protest ceases now.'

It was clear from Elvira's expression that she was anything but satisfied – a retraction followed by a ringing tribute to the generosity of foreigners like her husband was the least the *Gazzettino* could offer. She wasn't insensitive, though, and unmistakable in the lawyer's manner was a hint that she mustn't expect more than local feeling could deliver. He bowed over her hand very gracefully, permitted himself the faint smile for her companion that her different status required, and then left the room.

There was a silence that Jess felt obliged to break, although how to do it tactfully was beyond her. It didn't seem worth trying to suggest that Nathan Acheson had perhaps been outmanoeuvred after all, or had misunderstood the terms of the transaction. Elvira was perfectly aware that his life was spent reading the small print of anything he put his name to. But instead of looking angry, deceived, or at the least deeply disappointed, to Jess's astonishment she was now beginning to smile. Perhaps *she* hadn't fully understood – Signor Bossi's English, though fluent, was strongly accented.

'It seems that your husband is, in fact, only renting something that Count Ghisalberti knows he couldn't justifiably sell,' Jess ventured at last.

'I realise that, thank you,' Elvira said cheerfully.

'You . . . you don't seem to mind . . . I was afraid you might have done.'

The idea was waved aside, with Elvira's face getting brighter by the second as she examined the new situation. 'I misunderstood what

Nathan said, that's all. I should have *known* he wouldn't saddle us with something we might decide we don't want after a year or two. This way, we just end the agreement whenever we feel inclined. To tell you the truth, I wasn't very happy before, but now I can put up with being here.' She glanced at her watch, and then stood up with a forgiving smile. 'I'm due at the hairdresser downstairs. I've to dine this evening with those people you think so well of – the Rasinis!'

'I also,' said Jess, ashamed of the hope that it would make Elvira's smile fade. But even that didn't happen, and she went away before she was tempted to fracture the harmony of a business friendship that Smythsons were supposed to prize. Still, a feeling of sick disgust needed to be walked off before she could return calmly to work. A beautiful house would stay empty and unused for most of every year; Venice would have acquired another largely absentee resident, while Mario Ghisalberti and Nathan Acheson no doubt congratulated themselves on the astuteness of their deal. The very rich operated by standards that seemed acceptable to them, which Jess had to suppose was reasonable enough; but they always seemed hurt when other people resented the fact, and that didn't seem reasonable at all.

That evening she dressed with care; a black velvet suit would, she hoped, defeat the chill factor of the *palazzo*'s vast rooms but also meet Battistina's critical opinion of what the occasion merited. She was ready much too early, having not clearly registered when her promised escort was due to arrive, but Giancarlo was announced almost immediately by the receptionist in the hall.

'You weren't intended to hurry down,' he said apologetically. 'I just hoped there would be time to enjoy a peaceful drink together before we need leave.' He signalled to the waiter-cum-barman, who put in front of her something she didn't recognise. 'It's a Venetian speciality . . . a mixture of Prosecco and peach juice invented at Harry's Bar, which everyone else here has now adopted. If you dislike it I'll order something else.'

'It's delicious,' Jess decided after a sip. 'No change needed, thank you.'

She felt no awkwardness in his company, only a definite sense of surprise; he seemed far removed from the sort of men she was acquainted with at home who sought bar conversations with women they scarcely knew. In fact her impression of him was that he preferred to seek no company at all. Then his next remark left her with the stomach-churning feeling that she'd stepped on a stair that wasn't there.

'My grandmother's other guests this evening come from the Pensione Alberoni – Jacques Duclos, Maria, and . . . your father. Maria told Emilia about your connection with Llewellyn.'

Suddenly white-faced, Jess tried to smile. 'Now I understand why you came early – to give me a kind warning of the . . . the little ordeal in store! I arrived in Venice believing like a fool that if it didn't matter to me that my father was here, it needn't matter to anyone else. I've been proved wrong about that.'

'*Is* it an ordeal – to share a dinner party with him?' Giancarlo asked gravely, then at once retracted the question. 'Forgive me, please. I had no right to pry into your life.'

Jess shook her head, smiling to reduce his embarrassment, which now seemed greater than her own. 'It felt more like concern than prying. In any case I shouldn't have used the word "ordeal" – it's no such thing to meet Llewellyn again, or to be introduced to his wife.' She watched Giancarlo's face, wishing that it wasn't schooled to such unrevealing self-control. 'All the same, I feel a little anxious. Your grandparents belong to a more disciplined, more sternly moral generation than ours; I shouldn't like the fact of my existence to affect their friendship with Llewellyn.'

'You're much more generous than he deserves, I think.'

Cool disapproval was visible in her companion's face at least, and it made matters clear – he, certainly, was not her father's friend. The memory of David Matthias as she'd seen him at Torcello was vivid in her mind – a flamboyant, theatrical man hovering on the edge of the absurd. What saved him was the sheer conviction of the performance, but she could see that nothing might save him for so reticent a human being as Giancarlo Rasini. It would have been tactful now, probably, to change the conversation, but she chose not to.

'I can understand you not approving of my young half-brother's socialist politics,' she suggested, 'but I get the impression that you equally disapprove of David Matthias. Am I right about that?'

Her candid eyes – set, he noticed, under brows darker than the strange colour of her hair – asked for the truth, and he reluctantly produced it. '*You* seem to share some of Marco's egalitarian views, but your father doesn't. He colludes with my dear grandmother to sell his paintings to the tourists who get brought to the *palazzo* during the summer. Most of the proceeds go on repairs to the *palazzo* which we would otherwise be unable to afford.'

'And you disapprove of that?'

'Yes, because the means in this case don't justify the ends. Credulous people are parted from their money by a combination I find distasteful – my grandmother's title, and your father's gifts as a salesman!'

Feeling the heat of unexpected anger in her face, Jess supposed that it was something else to blame on Venice. Anywhere else, she might easily have agreed with what he'd just said; here, with the old illusionist city still playing its tricks, she had to contradict him.

'Salesman my father may be – I hope he *is* for Donna Emilia's sake; but judging by the painting I've seen, the people who buy what he offers aren't as credulous as all that.'

She'd spoken too vehemently, she realised, for a man who probably still expected females to be docile and grateful for being told what to think. While he'd devoted himself to nursing his ailing Lagoon, the present age had passed him by, and he hadn't even noticed that today's new woman was supposed to be opinionated, bold, and self-assertive.

At last he found something to say. 'Maria told my grandmother very little, of course, but I think I expected you to hate your father, not defend him.'

Jess shook her head. 'You gave me credit for being generous a moment ago, but the truth is that I've spent my entire life so far thinking very ill of him . . . that's why it now seems important to at least be fair.' Her thin hand trembled a little on the table, and suddenly his own covered it in a small, shy gesture of apology.

'I may dislike the tourist scheme, but I had no right to seem to belittle your father. Forgive me, please.'

Her quick nod wiped the offence away, and he was at liberty to withdraw his hand. That he should have touched her at all was something he found astonishing. It was years since he'd offered a woman anything except a formal gesture. But her hand had been warm and companionable, and the truth was that his own felt empty now.

Jess thought she saw sadness in his face, and supposed that it had to do with regret for his own lost father. They had something in common, he and she – a childhood that had been unusual enough to distance them from normal family life, and make relationships difficult. But whatever memory troubled him he now put aside and a sudden gleam of amusement made his face more youthful.

'I was eight or nine when our neighbours along the *rio* were electrified by the news that Maria Alberoni was going to marry a wild English painter. It was generally agreed that no good would come of it – foreign artists being even more unreliable than those who sprang from the locality. But according to my grandmother, who knows them both well, it has been a successful marriage.'

'I'm glad,' Jess said truthfully. 'Whatever else I've yet to learn here, I've already come round to understanding the futility of being haunted by the past.'

Giancarlo seemed intent on staring at the golden wine in his glass, then put it down to look at her with eyes full of regret, 'I still am – haunted by it.'

She supposed that he still thought of his lost parents, and knew that her grandmother would say he'd mourned them for too long, but she wasn't Elizabeth Harrington, and felt less ready to offer such advice.

'Your job reminds you all the time of what happened, and you live with people who share the same grief,' she said instead.

Another faint, rueful smile twitched his mouth. 'My grandfather lives mostly in a different world, but Emilia did her best to keep us up to date. When I came back from school and university she struggled to entertain a generation she found mystifying – the girls spoke a language she didn't understand, and wore clothes she could only try to ignore. It was a relief when she finally admitted defeat. Perhaps she realised by then how little I had to offer – a title, that when the time came would probably be meaningless, and a beautiful but decrepit house I should have to give away.'

He sounded sad but resigned – much too resigned, Jess wanted to insist – ridiculously so given the considerable man he was. But his diffidence was at least real, not the pretence of self-deprecation that some people offered in order to have it denied. She found him very likeable altogether, but refused to sound as if she felt sorry for him.

'Donna Emilia found you the wrong girls. My own rather forceful grandmother would say you should have found one for yourself.'

'I did,' he announced with a mixture of pride and sadness. 'She was French . . . an expert in the restoration of old stone work. We used to laugh and say she'd never be out of a job in Venice – it had more crumbling buildings than anywhere else on earth!'

He was looking back into the past now, and Jess had to prompt him gently. 'Even so, she didn't stay?'

'She went home to tell her parents that she'd agreed to marry me. I didn't see her alive again – she was hit by a car in Paris.'

There was nothing to say, and Jess simply repeated the gesture he had made earlier, by stretching out a hand to touch his where it rested on the table.

'It isn't recent history – Jeanne was killed five years ago,' he said after a little while. 'But I decided to stop looking for happiness after that. All the people I loved seemed to get taken away from me in some horrible way or other.'

It explained the man he'd become, and the conviction in his voice made contradiction difficult, but Jess did her best. 'Perhaps you should have reckoned instead that, more than most of us, you were about due for some lasting happiness.'

He heard the compassion in her voice but didn't mind it any more than he regretted the extraordinary confession he'd just made. He'd never talked to another woman about Jeanne . . . always imagined that he wouldn't ever do so. A smile and the wave of one long brown hand put the past aside.

'It's time to go but, this being Venice, I'm unable to summon a taxi for you at the door – we must walk instead!'

Jess accepted the deliberate change of tone. 'This being Venice,

I'm already prepared – overcoat, scarf, and boots are waiting in the lobby!'

'*Allora, signorina . . . andiamo!*' he said, almost with gaiety.

When they stepped outside there had been a fresh fall of snow, although Giancarlo predicted that it would be the last because a thaw was on its way. But for the moment the whitened paths and dark ribbon of the canal echoed for Jess the stark contrasts of the traditional Carnival disguise – white mask, black domino and tricorne hat. Already the shops were full of these, and fancy-dress costumes, some alluringly beautiful, some grotesque – the twin elements of a madcap, make-believe season that had traditionally to be relished before the austerities of Lent set in. It was peculiarly suited to a city where nothing was what it seemed. She knew now that its 'marble' was often merely stuccoed brick; San Marco's glorious bronze horses were an amalgam of metals, not bronze at all; and even the Salute's imposing stone scrolls supported nothing but a great grey dome of wood. By the same token the emotional dramas in which she seemed to have been caught up – her own and other peoples' – were probably just as illusory, and when she was back in London even the memory of this snowy, silent walk would become as dreamlike as the rest of the whole extraordinary visit.

Chapter 11

They were the last to arrive, and six pairs of eyes registering the fact added considerably to Jess's feeling of embarrassment. But Llewellyn dealt with it in his own way, tempering his usual panache with a little, unexpected air of dignity. As if he'd been on the watch, she was intercepted almost at the door and led to where their hosts were standing.

'Emilia, dear lady, and Paolo . . . you've met Jessica already, but not knowingly as my eldest daughter.'

Jess heard a sharp intake of breath from Elvira, stationed next to the Count, but the others were able to take calmly what they already knew. She held out her hand, trying to smile. 'Our family skeleton is out of the cupboard at last, Countess . . . no more rattling of bones!'

'Much more peaceful,' Donna Emilia agreed calmly. She gave her guest's hand a little pat as if to say that no awkwardness need be felt, because a Venetian aristocrat was certain to be perfectly accustomed to the illegitimate daughters of old friends turning up. Then she made the next introduction herself.

'Monsieur Duclos you already know, of course, but not my dear Maria.'

Jess offered her hand again to the woman the Countess had spoken of with such affection. At first glance Llewellyn's wife wasn't what she expected. With her comfortable roundness, sober black gown, and smoothly coiled hair, Maria Matthias looked the archetypal Italian matriarch, not the sort of woman to have captivated a man with a highly developed eye for beauty.

'Your father has been anxious about you,' Maria was saying gravely. 'It isn't good to be alone in a strange place.'

She was torn, Jess thought, between Llewellyn's disappointment and an understandable reluctance to add to what already sounded like a complicated household. The result was that between innate kindness and her natural preference for her own children, she couldn't decide quite how to behave.

'Venice no longer feels strange, although it did at first,' Jess admitted. 'But I didn't stay away from the *pensione* to cause hurt – it just seemed the . . . the best thing to do.'

Maria's serious expression relaxed into the smile she'd passed on to her son. 'Best to us perhaps, but if not intended by the Fates they always have the last word.'

'Jessica won't grant you that, *cara*,' said Jacques' voice suddenly beside them. 'The English are pragmatic people – not inclined to allow for unprovable influences on their lives!'

The Countess chose that moment to lead Maria away to talk to her chief guest, and Jess and Jacques were left confronting one another. It was the word that came into her mind because there'd been an edge to his voice that reminded her of their first encounter. She'd refused a casually given dinner invitation; it didn't seem enough to have made him sound hostile again.

'You're looking very Parisien,' she suggested, refusing to be intimidated.

'Raffish, I expect you mean,' he corrected her, adjusting the roll neck of the white silk sweater he wore instead of a shirt. 'My motto is comfort at all times, and in any case, I abominate bow ties.'

He inspected her in his turn, aware that part of his present irritation was due to the extent of his original error about her. The woman he'd met at the Ca'Rezzonico had certainly been lonely, but only his own bitter introspection could have fabricated the memory of plain, repressed spinsterdom. The real Jessica Smythson was this elegant woman in front of him now – dammit, not only elegant but seductive as well. Her skin looked creamy-pale against the red-gold glow of copper that the lamplight gave her hair, and her eyes were beautiful.

'You missed a treat earlier on, but it serves you right for letting Rasini make you late,' he said disagreeably. 'Your employer's entrance into the portego would have done credit to the Queen of Sheba.'

Jess registered the full effect of Elvira's tunic and trousers of dazzling gold brocade, before answering truthfully. 'She looks very splendid to me.'

'The Count suspected her of having come in fancy dress, but he rallied gamely . . . even thanked her for a charming compliment to the Serenissima's past Eastern glories!'

Lips twitching, Jess managed not to sound amused. 'Perhaps that's what it was.'

Jacques' answering grin was still edged with malice. 'I doubt it – she looked very surprised! She's irked with you, by the way . . . thinks you've been *very* secretive.'

Jess shook her head sadly. 'Either dinner parties don't agree with you or trudging about in the snow has tried your temper.'

'It's my usual company style!' But her grave grey glance compelled him to apologise. 'It's nothing of the sort. I'm just feeling irritable. By the way, congratulations on a conquest – Rasini's air was very proprietorial when he ushered you in this evening, and he's not known for being a ladies' man.'

She took the small apology for an excuse – a self-contained man's refusal to say what really ailed him. He was improving physically, even to the extent of being without his stick tonight, but she still sensed in him a distress of spirit that hadn't yet healed. It might never do so – perhaps he'd witnessed too much human madness across the globe. She wanted, to her own astonishment, to put out her hand and reassure him . . . wanted to insist that homo, though not yet so very sapiens, *would* survive, despite all the evidence he'd seen to the contrary, simply because God willed it so. But she could imagine the derision in his face if she offered him that comfort; little as she knew him, she was sure that he would reject it. No nonsense for *him* about Divinity shaping their ends – men did that themselves, he'd say.

She dragged her mind back to what he'd said about her employer. 'Elvira may be irked with *me*, but at least Llewellyn is making her forget that she doesn't like Venice in winter without her husband.'

Jacques watched the performance critically, and grinned this time with sudden, pure enjoyment. 'Llewellyn's death-or-glory impersonation of a man swept off his feet by yet another beautiful woman – Maria says it never fails!'

Jess watched too, with a judicial air. 'She sees the kindness that's intended, I expect – I think it reflects great credit on both of them.' She thought about what she'd just said and then added to it. 'But I doubt if it would have occurred to me to say *that* before I came here. You were perfectly right to warn me about the deplorable effect Venice has on newcomers.'

There was no malice in his smile now, only teasing, warm and wholehearted amusement. 'I hope I said liberating, not deplorable!'

He had some of Llewellyn's chameleon quality, she realised; it made him an exciting but dangerous companion, especially for the inexperienced girl she supposed Claudia Matthias to be. The anxiety in Maria's face wasn't to be wondered at – she was looking in their direction now, as if obliged to judge Jacques' interest in another woman. He seemed suddenly aware as well of her glance upon them, and Jess saw the affection in his answering smile. These two knew and trusted each other, and *she* felt excluded. It was a relief to hear Battistina summon them into dinner, and find herself seated between Llewellyn and her host.

It was time to forget about the *pensione*'s involved household, and store away in her memory a picture of the people gathered in the beautiful, shabby room. She wanted not to forget any of it – the Countess's profile, as delicately and precisely carved as a head on an old coin, Giancarlo's brown hands cupped gently round a fragile wine glass, even Battistina, smiling and indispensable as usual – each was a tiny piece of the mosaic to be embedded in her mind. Jess registered it all intently, knowing what it was that she watched – the final tableau in a play that couldn't last much longer. Paolo Rasini and his wife were old and frail, and with their ending would come the ending of the *palazzo*'s story. That vision of the future left Giancarlo unaccounted for, but she found herself reluctant to think about a man who'd abandoned all hope of happiness; it might almost begin to seem a duty to make him change his mind. She looked instead at Jacques Duclos, now deep in conversation with a smiling Elvira. It was his special gift, she remembered rather painfully, to concentrate with such flattering intensity on whichever woman was to hand.

The guests left not as they'd assembled, because the Countess felt obliged now that it was late to send her chief guest back to the Danieli in Giancarlo's care. Before she could nominate another escort for Jess, Llewellyn intervened, asking Jacques to see Maria home while he delivered his daughter to the Hotel agli Alboretti. Given only a brief farewell bow, Jess was glad to see Jacques walk away, but it took her a moment or two to find something to say to the shadowy figure beside her.

'I should have written to thank you for sending Marco with my book,' she said at last as they walked along. 'The reason I didn't is stupid – I couldn't decide what to call you.'

A grin suddenly spilled light over his sombre face. 'Llewellyn, of course, as the others do. It's not as respectful as I'd like, but probably as respectful as I deserve.'

Jess hesitated about what to embark on next, but her father filled the gap himself.

'Claudia couldn't see why Emilia didn't invite them all tonight – she likes to be where the action is, but most of all to be where Jacques is, and I'm afraid Maria worries about that. Lorenza is beautiful and good, but her sister's a different kettle of fish . . . argumentative, but clever and brave.'

He said it with pride, and Jess could see her as a girl after his own heart; the passively beautiful, however much loved, would make less appeal. With very little encouragement he'd have gone on talking about Claudia but Jess turned the conversation in a different direction.

'When Marco came to the *palazzo* I made him talk to me, so I know a little bit about his views. He probably has nothing to do with the articles that have been appearing in the *Gazzettino*, but I'm sure he approves of them; they're saying exactly what he said to me.'

Llewellyn lifted a hand in one of his expansive gestures. 'He has a young man's idealism, Jess . . . belongs to a group of hotheads who believe they can fight a system they reckon is crooked, which I'm bound to say it usually is.'

'Not entirely so in the case of the Palazzo Ghisalberti. Marco hinted that the opposition would continue, but will you tell him, please, that no illegality took place? Mr Acheson's lawyer confirmed that when

Elvira and I saw him this morning. The *Gazzettino* has been reminded of the laws of libel, and they'll be invoked if necessary by a man who punishes impertinence. If Marco *is* involved, it won't make him feel any happier, but at least he'll have been warned.'

'It will simply convince him that he's right, I'm afraid – the rules *are* different for the rich. The law protects *them* instead of people who deserve protecting.'

She turned to look at her father by the light of the wall-lamp they were passing. Under the brim of the old velour hat his eyes were amused and sad at the same time, reminding her of the complicated creature he was, constantly changing mood and expression.

'Is it something you get used to here?' she asked suddenly. 'Heaven knows things aren't perfect at home, but the loopholes don't seem quite so blatantly designed as they are here for the benefit of the wrong people. Count Ghisalberti is allowed to make a fool of the law while a poor man probably gets hammered for some petty crime indulged in to make his slum habitable.'

The grave enquiry brought him to a halt. 'If you stay in Italy you have to accept it as it is, Jess – largely disorganised, often devious, and plain daft most of the time; the system that governs it certainly is. But for all that it's still a place where you can live in the middle of kindness and astonishing beauty. I was born in a depressed mining valley, remember – that makes a man thankful on his knees for what he finds here.'

His grim past was part of her too, she suddenly realised; she valued beauty because he did, probably loved music and the rest of life's variety because he did. Giancarlo had wanted to pity her for lacking a father, but she could see at last that she'd been luckier than most. This man's relish and talent for living had in some unexpected way been handed on to her, and in place of the disaster that his marriage to her mother would have produced, she'd been given Gerald Smythson's steadfast generosity and love.

'Forget the dishonest politicians, and the ridiculous laws, and the sheer bureaucratic muddle of it all,' Llewellyn pleaded, afraid that she still wasn't convinced. 'Every small town here owns some priceless treasure, and much of the landscape is achingly lovely, but it's the ordinary little *people* who really make Italy worth living in.'

She nodded, not doubting that he knew. He'd lived the sort of life that taught a man true from false, lasting from fly-by-night. Whatever he'd been as a young man, he'd grown generous in spirit and she was glad to know him.

'I think I was right to stay away from the *pensione* . . . I can't conveniently forget my mother's unhappiness, even now. But I shall thank Imogen when I get home for writing to you. It's much more than I bargained for!'

His transfiguring smile appeared, making her thankful to have offered him even that small gift. It seemed in fact to be what the whole unforgettable evening had left her with – the conviction that no chance of giving or receiving happiness should ever be wasted, because life was short and joy spectacularly uncertain.

'Maria would tell you that I've been like a bear with a sore head lately,' he confessed. 'I knew *why*, of course – I was afraid I might never get another opportunity to say what I *should* have said at Torcello; that I'm truly sorry for the damage I did. But I can't help feeling proud as well – that you've managed so brilliantly without me.'

They walked on again after that, content to be silent until Llewellyn asked a final question as the hotel entrance came in sight.

'How much longer will you be here?'

'I'm not exactly sure . . . another month at the most, but less if I can manage it. Gerald sounds very tired when I talk to him on the telephone . . . without me there he's having to work too hard.'

Llewellyn tried to call to mind the youth met once or twice when Imogen had taken him to the Smythson house at Holland Park. A dandified, bloodless creature he'd thought Gillian's cousin then, but it wasn't possible to despise Gerald Smythson now.

'You and he have *something* in common,' Jess insisted as if she read what was in her father's mind. 'You both go in search of beauty, and create it when you can.'

'Then you can tell a fellow-searcher that I'm aware of what I owe him,' Llewellyn said. 'My thanks to Immy too, please, Jess; she's been a very constant friend.'

She nodded, smiled to see him sweep off his hat in a final theatrical gesture, and then walked into the hotel, while he still stood there, watching her.

Chapter 12

Claudia was usually an entertaining companion, talkative and alert to anything worth noticing. But the morning after the Countess's dinner party she had so little to say that Jacques suspected her of having grown tired of their association. Apart from the hours she spent helping him, there was still her college work to attend to, however carelessly she did it. If she'd grown bored with her self-imposed task of being a photographer's assistant, it was only what he should have expected. Much *more* unexpected, he now realised, was his own reluctance to part with her as a companion, but it must be done.

She smiled when she caught him watching her, but it wasn't only in his imagination that some effort was needed now that hadn't been there before. They'd been at the Erberia since early morning, photographing the wonderful vegetable displays; now rain was setting in, and they'd taken refuge in a nearby café to drink coffee. The stalls were being dismantled in any case, but the scent of fruit and herbs still lingered on the damp air.

Suddenly, taking her by surprise, he said what was in his mind.

'It's time we ended this very nice arrangement, I think. You've been a most wonderful help, but I'm not a stranger here any longer – I can manage on my own; *you* must return to your own friends, *tesoro*, before they give you up for lost.'

Claudia's dark head was turned away from him; he could have thought her more concerned to watch the passing traffic on the canal. Only the trembling of her fingers when she put down her coffee cup spoke of the agitation she wanted to hide.

'Mamma's been talking to you – I knew she would.' Claudia's voice was slow and quiet for once, almost grave. 'She doesn't understand . . . thinks I'm still a silly teenager, dazzled by a much older, sophisticated man. They're all waiting at home for the infatuation to wear off.'

'It's what happens to infatuations,' Jacques said gently. 'As the man in question, I can promise you that.'

He smiled as he spoke, affection and wry amusement combining in his face to transform him from the ill-humoured stranger who'd limped into the *pensione* one morning. She hadn't liked him then; now she understood how completely she loved him. But it wasn't the

97

moment to say so – she knew that too. She understood everything about herself and him, and the time would come when she could tell him so; but not quite yet.

'Mamma's afraid I'm wasting time . . . neglecting my studies,' she went on in the same reasonable tone, as if he hadn't spoken. 'She doesn't realise, poor love, that it's my college work that's futile, whereas working with you is the best training I could have.' Composure wavered for a moment and she looked at him with huge, imploring eyes. 'My captions *are* good, aren't they . . . you haven't just been saying that?'

It was a moment that he knew to be crucial – he could slay her now with unkindness, but it would mean a lie she didn't deserve. 'Your work is excellent – concise, accurate, and to the point,' he agreed after a small pause. 'Henri Clément in Paris is rather impressed with what I've been sending him.'

She smiled at last with something of her old radiance. 'Well, that's settled then; the nice arrangement stands. Dear Jacques, what *were* you thinking of!'

'Your future, I expect, and your parents' peace of mind, and the poor friends who don't get a look-in because you devote yourself to a lame, short-tempered, and nearly middle-aged Frenchman!'

Claudia took hold of his hand and laid it against her cheek, but all she said was, '*Stupido!*'

He released himself after a moment, knowing that something had changed; it wouldn't be possible to pretend any more that he believed in the adolescent fixation theory; this intense, enchanting, maddening girl *wasn't* an infatuated schoolgirl – she was Llewellyn's daughter even more than she was Maria's; and the moment had come and gone when he could leave with his promise intact of not hurting her. He was involved now, with her and the Matthias family, and even strangely glad to be concerned at last with someone other than himself.

After a little while Claudia made one of her father's expansive gestures, putting aside what they'd been talking about.

'I asked Mamma about last night's party . . . she wasn't helpful! It was all very pleasant, she said – even meeting Llewellyn's unknown daughter was pleasant! *You'll* have to tell me how the evening really went.'

Jacques frowned at the sudden demand, then shrugged aside the memory of whatever had made him frown. 'I'm sorry to say I can't do much better – pleasant is what it was; no mad rave-up, no knock-down, drag-out fight . . . just a civilised dinner party, with even Llewellyn behaving himself, and making a favourable impression on the chief guest!'

Claudia didn't smile as he expected. 'Mamma said Signora Acheson looked very striking, and Jessica beautiful . . . was that your opinion also?'

'Roughly,' he agreed after a moment's hesitation. 'Giancarlo certainly found your half-sister worth watching; it tried even *his savoir-faire* to pretend that he didn't mind escorting Elvira Acheson home instead of Jessica.'

'Llewellyn is very taken with her too,' Claudia confessed sadly. 'I don't know that I can spare her any of *his* affection. You said we shouldn't hate her, but I *do* . . . Lorenza's heard the gossip about her and Giancarlo along the *rio*. It was bad enough before, being ignored; but it's much worse now that she knows he *isn't* ignoring Jessica.'

'Then persuade her to go away, *cara*,' Jacques said almost impatiently. 'She can't spend the rest of her life moping for a man who doesn't want her, nor can Rasini fall in love with her just because the rest of you want him to. A man makes his own choice in this matter.'

Claudia allowed this statement to stand without challenging it, and still didn't smile. Instead, she got up, depositing a little kiss on his cheek as she did so. '*Arrivederci, tesoro* . . . I'm glad we've got the future settled.'

He watched her walk away through the rain that was beginning to fall steadily. The rest of the day would have to be spent indoors, but that wasn't what made him frown – he had plenty of developing work to catch up on. It was the conversation with Claudia that was troubling him. The future was settled, she'd said happily to a man who'd always regarded himself free to go in any direction he pleased. She was there, for the moment in the centre of his life – charming and almost indispensable; but on the margin of his mind there hovered a different woman altogether who, even though she made no claim, refused to be forgotten. That complication wasn't enough, it seemed; Fate had decided to give the situation a final ironic twist by combining girl and woman in a tense relationship of their own.

The day following Emilia's dinner party had been allocated to Jess's expedition to Padua with Elvira Acheson. She regretted it now; she could imagine a journey spent trying to discourage her employer from delving into the tangled affairs of the Matthias family. But she arrived at the Danieli to find Elvira reluctant to go at all. The thaw predicted by Giancarlo had arrived overnight, and the snow was being worn away by the showers of rain that more properly belonged to a Venetian winter. It was true that the city in these conditions scarcely seemed to materialise out of the all-encompassing element of water, but Jess was dismayed to find her travelling companion strongly inclined to cancel a journey which must begin with a sodden boat-ride before she could even board a train for terra firma.

'I'm afraid we *need* to go,' she insisted with what she hoped was a friendly smile. 'If we can't find what you want, things will have to be ordered, and if we put off going today it might still be raining tomorrow!'

'A certainty, I'd say,' Elvira pointed out coldly. 'Whatever Nathan likes to think, this is no reasonable place to live. I had to come in February to be sure of that.'

Jess glanced round the comfort of the sitting room, remembered the luxury of the home being prepared across the canal, and felt her own store of patience rapidly dwindling, 'It probably rains in New York, and it certainly does in London, at most seasons of the year.'

'I know *that*, but this is the only place where I have to wade through water to get into what passes for a taxi!'

'Part of the rich tapestry of Venetian life,' Jess suggested, trying to smile again. 'Like hauling up your mail on the line you've let down to the postman!'

'If you live in a top-floor garret,' her employer agreed still more coolly. 'I have no plans for that.'

Patience exhausted altogether, Jess's reply came with a snap. 'Nor do you have to queue up to fight your way on to the *vaporetto*, or trudge about in the rain every time you need a loaf of bread.'

The reproof was a mistake, and she couldn't blame Elvira for resenting it. There was no occupation more futile than trying to make a rich woman remember what life was like for ordinary people. Nathan's wife could as easily be expected nowadays to put herself in the place of an average Venetian housewife as Battistina could imagine *not* spending her days in the devoted service of other people. The homily merely stung Elvira into stalking downstairs and allowing herself to be handed into the waiting boat, but she stared out of its streaming windows in offended silence until they were settled in the train, and from then on buried herself in the pages of *Harper's Bazaar*.

The day improved a little when they got to Padua. It had stopped raining, there was shopping to be done, and – obedient to Nathan's teaching – Elvira had enquired of the Danieli's concierge where lunch should be eaten. Ensconced at a table in the Ristorante San Clemente, her ill-humour began to fade; there was some serious investigation ahead, but first she felt entitled to regain the upper hand.

'I suppose *you* think we should have gone to some miserable *tavola calda* and eaten polenta,' she said, pleasantly aware of having just ordered quails and out-of-season asparagus instead.

Jess shook her head. 'Anything but polenta . . . it's a dish I can find no virtue in!' She looked across the table at her companion and made the apology that she knew was required. 'You're the boss, and you can eat where you like. I had no right to lecture you about life in Venice . . . I'm sorry.'

Elvira's nod agreed with that, but she relented sufficiently to make a confession of her own.

'Still, you're right about it being a peculiar place. Nathan must know that . . . he's been times enough before; but things that would fret him anywhere else don't seem to here. I can't figure out why that is, unless a very reasonable man needs something in his life that *isn't* reasonable.'

She put the problem aside with a faint sigh, sipped the white wine recommended by an attentive waiter, and meditated her best approach to the subject chiefly on her mind. Tired of waiting for it, Jess asked a leading question of her own.

'Did you enjoy yourself last night?'

'Now and then,' Elvira admitted. 'Paolo Rasini is a charming, courteous man, but I can't say his idea of a lively conversation is the same as mine. He expected me to know which I preferred – Byzantine, Venetian-Gothic, or something he called High-Baroque! I smiled sweetly at him, and admitted that I wasn't sure which was which. He left me with Jacques Duclos after that, I'm glad to say – you can always trust a Frenchman to find something interesting to talk about.'

Determined not to be drawn into discussing Jacques, Jess went back to Elvira's attempt at conversation with the Count. 'Your husband's committee, along with many others, has been carrying on a crusade here – rescuing wonderful buildings that would otherwise be in ruins by now. Are you really not interested in what they're doing? You don't have to be an expert to get a little involved.'

'I *am* involved,' Elvira insisted with a return to sharpness. 'I shall give very good parties for Nathan, I shall be nice to all the people he hopes will dip into their pockets, and I shan't complain that there's water everywhere I look.'

She was right in her own way, Jess reflected, and the only remaining puzzle was why Nathan Acheson had chosen to help preserve a place that his wife almost seemed to fear. But Elvira took advantage of the pause to make a sudden incision of her own.

'*You* took the party by surprise last night, I must say, in more ways than one! Everyone noticed the way you arrived with the Countess's grandson, but on top of that you had a father you hadn't owned up to.' Disapproval tinged her voice more openly as she went on. 'We were brought up more strictly where I come from – no drugs, and no sex outside the sacrament of marriage. I suppose that sounds old-fashioned to you.'

All-middle-American rectitude was in her face, tempting Jess to shock her still more by laying claim to a life of abandoned immorality in London, but she fought with herself and managed to answer differently.

'Gerald Smythson married my mother. I think of *him* as my father, and his ideas are quite as old-fashioned as yours.'

Balked in this direction, Elvira launched herself in another.

'I told Paolo Rasini about having to see the lawyer, by the way . . . wickedly spiteful articles *not* being quite the welcome Nathan deserved. The Count had to agree, but I could see he'd rather not have done – aristocrats preferring to stick together on principle, I suppose.'

'I doubt if Count Paolo would think Mario Ghisalberti entitled to cheat just because his ancestors once helped to govern Venice.'

Elvira smiled triumphantly. 'The Rasinis can do no wrong according to you, but I *have* been here before. It took me a while to make the connection, but when Maria Matthias referred to her husband as Llewellyn I remembered the Americans who used to come back to the Danieli last year when we were there. They'd been on a tour, had tea with a countess, and brought back a souvenir to prove it . . . a genuine one, because they'd even seen the artist at work. Of course they had – that was the object of the visit!'

'So where's the deception?' Jess asked as calmly as she could. 'Your Americans saw inside a lovely, historic house, met a great lady, and bought a painting that they can be proud of.'

'There's no deception, but as a scheme it's *very* neat!'

Suspecting that her father would almost certainly agree, Jess took refuge in a dignified silence that Elvira rightly interpreted as defeat. From then on she refused to be hurried over lunch, changed her mind three times about a table for the dining room, and took an immovable dislike to every Chinese carpet offered for the marble floor of her vast bedroom. Altogether, Jess reckoned, it was turning out to be one of the most disagreeable days she could remember, made worse by the knowledge that much of her pleasure in working on the *palazzo* had somehow seeped away.

On the train ride back to Venice, Elvira leafed through a new selection of magazines, but finally broke the silence that Jess had allowed to fall between them.

'I suppose I was expected to agree to a carpet I didn't like in case the salesman's children might be starving.'

The expedition was finishing as it had begun, with their opening disagreement obviously still rankling. Jess tried to remember that the petulant-sounding woman opposite her might be tired of being so often without her husband, that she didn't much care for the alien city he'd sent her to, and was anything but sure she wanted a *palazzo* there at all.

'The carpet man looked very prosperous,' Jess conceded with a tired smile. 'And I'll also admit that I'm thankful we *don't* have to fight our way on to a crowded *vaporetto* at the railway station!'

It was all the *amende honorable* she could manage, but it seemed not to be enough; Elvira's expression clearly said that a little more acknowledgement of being in the wrong wouldn't come amiss. Unable to supply it, Jess opted for silence instead while her companion mulled over impressions from the evening before, and selected from them what might ruffle the composure of the woman who sat staring out of the train window.

'Poor Maria Matthias must have felt embarrassed last night . . . having *you* there,' she suggested delicately. 'But she seemed very glad to talk to me about her own daughters – both of them beautiful and talented, I gather. One of them is working with the utmost devotion for Jacques Duclos. *He* confirmed that too – insisted she'd become quite indispensable.'

'So I've heard,' Jess agreed, determined that she would sound indifferent if it was the last thing she did. She told herself that she didn't hate Nathan Acheson's wife; it was just that they were turning out to be not very compatible. But, thank God, the interminable day was almost over – already they were clattering across the causeway and in another minute or two would be back in Venice. She need only shepherd her client towards a water-taxi and bid her goodnight. With one last effort she could surely manage that. But Elvira had a final shot in her locker, and she fired it as she stepped out of the taxi in front of the hotel. 'You seemed rather taken with the Countess's grandson, but I doubt if there's anything to be looked for there; Nathan always says I can pick out the no-hopers, Jessica.' Then with a smile she swept into the Danieli and Jess was free at last to redirect the taxi man to her own hotel.

Chapter 13

Walking to the *palazzo* next morning, Jess made a deliberate effort to see the small, water-cradled city around her objectively – was it as beautiful, as doomed, or merely as irrelevant as one partisan group or another claimed? It was probably all those things at once, she feared, and was immediately reminded of Jacques' first instruction that she must see Venice steadily and see it whole, for therein lay the truth.

As usual at the *palazzo*, she went in by the garden entrance and, also as usual, stopped for a moment to visualise the courtyard as it would look in its spring and summer beauty. No bare stone walls then – they'd be clothed in jasmine and honeysuckle and climbing roses. On summer evenings lemon trees in tubs would shed their pungent fragrance on the air, and a small bronze Pan in the middle of the pool would pipe an accompaniment all his own to the sound of falling water. But the Achesons would be gone by then, to avoid the crowds that Nathan didn't like; and, restored to glory though it was, the great house would still be without life. No longer one of Giancarlo's fellow-waverers, Jess felt convinced at last that Marco was right. Only the continued presence of its own people could keep this or any other city properly alive.

Still thinking about it, she climbed the outer staircase, walked inside the house, and immediately sensed its different atmosphere. The men started early, and were normally hard at work when she arrived – but not this morning; instead, idle for once, and gripped by some tension she didn't understand, they simply huddled together in the corridor. Before she could ask why, the foreman Luigi Arredo came towards her and said that she must follow him into Elvira's beautiful, empty drawing room. At the far end, where a row of tall windows overlooked the canal, Luigi's hand pointed downwards and she could see what he directed her to – their cluster of mooring-poles, recently repainted in stripes of blue and white, with gleaming re-gilded finials, were now daubed with scarlet paint. It still dripped down like blood into the water – ugly in itself, but menacing as well for the sense of vindictiveness that it seemed to convey. Avvocato Bossi had been wrong, she thought numbly; nothing was finished after all, and the problem *hadn't* gone away.

Luigi looked at her white face, wondered whether to offer

105

pre-Carnival high spirits as an excuse, and decided against it. Why make bad worse by lying about it to an intelligent woman?

'It's not only here,' he muttered. 'Three or four other *palazzi* have been given the same treatment.' He felt ashamed to admit it – such crudeness wasn't the Venetian way; but on the other hand, who could really blame young men for growing impatient? In Italy, at least, there often seemed no alternative to violence if injustice and corruption were to be brought to light.

Jess swallowed the nausea in her throat and tried to speak calmly. 'We must report it to the Questura. They may want to come before we can clear up the mess. Will you telephone, please, but start the men working again inside first. They can't stand in the corridor all day, looking miserable.'

She would have to speak to Elvira herself, but she needed first to think what she would say. There was no certainty that Marco was involved, but the timing of the vandalism seemed so deliberate that she couldn't believe it wasn't a response to the message she'd asked Llewellyn to deliver; in that case, Marco was almost sure to be implicated in some way.

Luigi returned from his telephoning to say that the Prefect's men had already examined quite enough red paint; the scrubbing-down of the *pali* could start immediately. Jess picked up the telephone and dialled the number of the Danieli, having decided only to report the damage and say that it was being dealt with; but Elvira's uneven voice warned her that she need scarcely say anything at all.

'You could have saved yourself the trouble of making up your mind whether or not to ring – I've already heard from Bossi. For an Italian, with local sympathies, he's been quite energetic.'

Jess got a firm grip on her temper and spoke as calmly as she could. 'It seemed necessary to tell the Questura first. Their only advice was to clean up the mess, and that's what the men are doing now.'

'Bossi did a little better – he got the police to admit that they know who's involved.'

Feeling sick again, Jess anticipated what was coming next. Fate had, she reflected, a damnably ironic sense of timing. Marco and his friends chose the very moment when she'd decided they were right to behave with altogether stupid recklessness. But she'd been silent for too long, and Elvira's voice came rasping along the line.

'You're not saying anything; understandably so, I suppose, when Marco Matthias is a leading member of the lunatic brigade we're up against. Perhaps you even reckon that your half-brother and his friends are justified in what they do.'

Jess took a deep breath but saw no option other than to nail her colours to the mast. 'Assuming that they *are* to blame for the nastiness outside, of course their methods are very wrong; but could you try to

106

understand what they're protesting about? It's not just what happens to one small piece of Venice; they're deeply angry with the people who have too much power over their lives – venal officials, clever lawyers, and dishonest politicians.'

'That's their problem, not mine and Nathan's,' Elvira pointed out implacably. 'All I'm sure of is that the sooner we hand Count Ghisalberti back his *palazzo*, the better. It's the only mistake I've ever known Nathan make, to think we might want a home here.'

Jess waited for her to add that her own mistake had been in her choice of a designer, but if this *was* a temptation, she resisted it and slammed the telephone down instead. Even so, it left their relations seriously strained – to the point, Jess feared, where for the first time in her professional life dismissal by a client seemed not impossible. But a worse thought was the family storm that might be raging at the *pensione* if Marco *had* been involved in the damage outside.

Feeling tired and sad, she forced herself to put that anxiety aside and concentrate on the job that, for the moment at least, was still Smythson's. Her open diary, blandly assuming that the day was normal, reminded her of an appointment to be kept, but it now seemed inappropriate enough to pitch her into hysterical laughter: could there be anything sillier than rushing across the Lagoon, to buy lace for a bedroom that Elvira most definitely didn't want? Still, it offered temporary escape from the four walls she seemed to have been locked up in for weeks, and in any case Gerald would insist that appointments weren't made to be lightly ignored. With some instructions given to Luigi, she left the building almost at a run, and collided sharply with a man on the pathway outside. She was steadied and held, and found herself staring at Jacques.

'We heard about the damage to the poles,' he said briefly. 'Llewellyn wanted to come but I said I was coming this way and would call instead.' He looked at her strained face and spoke more gently. 'Are you all right? You came out of the gate as if the hounds of hell were after you.'

She pulled herself free of his hands – impersonal hands, they felt, with no inclination to prolong the moment of contact. Well, she had no inclination for it herself, didn't want the help of this reluctant Frenchman.

'I was in a hurry, that's all – I've just time to catch the *vaporetto* for Burano if I run most of the way to the Fondamenta Nuova.'

Jacques waved a hand at the boat now idling alongside them. 'There's no need to run; we'll take you.'

The offer was made and assumed to have been accepted, because without waiting for her to answer he turned and walked towards the boat. She could have equally burst into tears, or shouted after him that she wouldn't set foot in his boat, but his boatman leapt on to the path and held out a friendly hand. There was nothing to do but try to smile and allow herself to be helped on board.

'Llewellyn was anxious about you,' Jacques said when she was standing beside him, 'but Lucia assured him that you'd be all right. The *inglesi*, she said, were famous for being stubborn in the face of adversity. She should know – she's scarcely old enough to remember the last war but her eldest brother was in the Resistenza, and killed as the Germans were retreating northwards.' He made the little gesture with his hands that she found she remembered – the subject, though not forgotten, was shelved for the time being. 'I suppose Elvira Acheson was upset by this morning's piece of stupid hooliganism,' he suggested next.

'More angry than upset – she thinks the Achesons deserve better of Venice, and to that extent I agree with her. The saddest thing about it is that from being unsure, she's now convinced of not wanting to live here. So I'm going to Burano to buy lace for the house she doesn't want that other people *did* want very passionately. And if you're about to tell me that it's part of life's usual barmy perversity, please don't!'

Jacques offered her at last the rare, sweet grin that rearranged the creases in his face, wiping away all trace of ill-humour or derision. 'It's when life doesn't run true to form that you need to worry . . . then indeed is "chaos come again"!'

Jess's own face suddenly relaxed. 'A man with a quotation for all occasions, and they aren't even in his own language. What can you manage in French, I wonder?'

'Oh, I keep that for making love in,' he suggested calmly. 'That's when a man needs his mother-tongue.'

Silenced, Jess concentrated on the route they were taking. She watched for dear life the traffic on the busy Rio San Lorenzo, and told herself that it amused Jacques Duclos to lay aside coolness occasionally to trap her in a moment of shared amusement. It was only in her imagination that it hovered on the edge of being something not so harmless. She was prepared now, and not likely to be misled by it again. Then, almost at once she was startled by their next manoeuvre. Instead of making for the *vaporetto* station, the boatman was heading out into open water.

'It's the Fondamenta I need,' she pointed out quickly.

'Burano, you said. We *were* going to Murano, but Daniele won't mind going somewhere else first instead.'

She knew when it was pointless to argue. He'd made up his mind that even a phlegmatic *inglese* might sometimes be glad of a helping hand. His own work could wait for an hour while the poor, silly creature was set on her way.

'Burano it is then . . . thank you,' she said quietly, and saw him nod before he turned to talk to Daniele.

She was glad to be left alone for the rest of the brief journey. The morning had been unsettling in a number of different ways, but she was calm again by the time Daniele nosed his way skilfully through the throng of fishing boats towards the quay. On terra firma again, she was given his instructions for finding the lace school – described as carefully as if some bursting metropolis awaited her, instead of a small, hugger-mugger island whose houses were painted in vibrant ochre, or maroon, or Prussian blue – no pale, pretty pastels for the Burinelli, it seemed.

She smiled at the thought, now able to speak cheerfully to Jacques as she said goodbye.

'Thank you again for bringing me; I hope I haven't wasted too much of *your* morning's work. I can get back easily enough on the *vaporetto*.'

He merely waved her on her way, but when she reached the end of the quay she suddenly turned to look back. He was still there, apparently now intent on capturing on film the scene in front of him – fishermen scrubbing down decks after a night at sea, and their talkative, black-shawled womenfolk haggling over the price of the morning's bream and red mullet. They didn't seem to mind him watching them, even stepped up the animation of the moment just because he was there, smiling at them. It was something else to store away in her memory . . . better, too, to think about that than feel unbearably lonely as she walked away.

It was time to remember also why she was there, not to linger wondering whether she might always be going to feel lonely in future, because while she went one way Jacques Duclos would almost certainly go another.

Chapter 14

The Scuola dei Merletti wasn't difficult to find, but Jess spent longer there than she meant to, engrossed in an ancient tradition of lace-making that had been rescued when it was almost at the moment of extinction. With her purchase made of the most exquisite point-lace of all, and with the school ladies' advice freely given as to what she should see, where eat lunch, and why ever leave Burano for Venice, she was finally allowed to say goodbye. There was just time, if she hurried to the quay, to catch the *vaporetto* on its way back from Torcello.

Instead, outside the school she collided again with the man who'd brought her there.

'This is silly,' she said as crossly as lack of breath allowed. 'I thought I made it clear that I could safely be left here alone.'

She was given much more than her ill-humour deserved – a smile that for once had no edge of derision to it. A successful morning on his own account seemed to have left him content to be there. 'The message was perfectly clear, but you can't come to Burano and not eat fish – the good people here don't like it.'

She could see that it was the moment to insist on going straight back to Venice; she even seriously tried to listen to the stern voice of duty.

'I'm sure the fish is delicious but I ought to be back at the *palazzo*, not loitering here – Marco's friends might amuse themselves next by trying to burn it down.'

'In which case I doubt if *you* could stop them. Forget dull care, Jessica, and look around you instead. The sun is out, the mist has disappeared, and the world is suddenly rather beautiful!'

It was true, she now realised; the world *was* as he described it, and perhaps his discovery had been made with the same shock of pleasure she was feeling herself, because his face was suddenly alight with a kind of wild, sweet gaiety.

'All right – lunch, but only if it doesn't take too long,' she managed to insist in a last-ditch clutch at caution that Jacques sensibly ignored. With her hand tucked inside his arm – perhaps in case she changed her mind – she was led towards the restaurant Daniele had recommended.

Da Romano's wasn't elegant but it was well known, he'd explained, for serving fish that smelled and tasted of the sea. While waiting for the *risotto di mare* to be cooked, they drank cool white wine that came from the mainland to the north, and nibbled shrimps taken, the *padrona* said, from the water that morning.

'This is a nice place,' Jess murmured almost to herself when their hostess had walked away. 'This island, I mean. The people who live here seem content with themselves and with their neighbours. It isn't a very common virtue nowadays.'

'They're proud of being Buranelli,' Jacques agreed. 'Being one of them himself, Daniele has enlightened me. They're ready to accept the tourists who swarm here in summer, but not ready to be changed by them. The men who aren't fishermen might have to go across to Murano to work in the glass factories, but the *motonave* brings them home at night, because this is where they belong. Life has been harsh in the past, and their homes are still precarious, perched on a sandbank in the Lagoon, but that sense of danger probably binds them together.'

'The precariousness is exactly what Elvira Acheson fears about Venice,' Jess admitted. 'The ancient sea walls are still there out beyond the *lidi*, but she needs a more immediate barrier between her and all that water always nudging at the city's doorsteps! I can't help feeling sorry for her in that respect, even though we don't see eye to eye in other ways.'

'Why . . . do *you* feel threatened here?' Jacques enquired, refilling their glasses from the carafe on the table.

She shook her head before she answered in words. 'No, but I'm accustomed to living nearer to the sea than Elvira is. For the first few days that I was here, though, I felt more lonely than ever before in my life. I've had time to realise since then that it hadn't much to do with Venice – it was the state of mind I'd arrived in.'

'How is the state of mind now?' he asked.

'Much improved, thank you! I'm even able to take Llewellyn in my stride, and that's more than I expected. When my mother died just before Christmas my formidable grandmother, who lives in New York, wanted me to make a fresh start there. She rather despised me for turning her offer down, but I think Llewellyn's wife would say that the Fates meant me to come here instead!'

She smiled at the idea, then turned smile and attention instead to the small waiter who had came to serve them. Her ways were very pleasant, Jacques noted again with a sudden shock of delight, and her beauty of so unassertive a kind that he'd missed it to begin with. More fool he; but she needed knowing, did Jessica Smythson. Hers was the attraction of slow release, not the instant smash and grab at a man's attention that women nowadays relied on. Chance had brought them both to Venice; he could so easily have missed her.

'Is the New York offer still open if you change your mind?' he asked suddenly.

'I expect so, but I shan't take it. My grandmother's friends are certain to be people like herself – well connected, rich, and powerful; another of my Venetian discoveries has been that I'd rather work at less exalted levels!'

'Elvira is proving a handful, I suppose that means, and Marco's antics must have made things more difficult for you. He wasn't directly involved in this morning's episode, by the way. In fact he tried to persuade the other members of the *gruppo* that such tactics would end up losing them friends. But he won't tell the *polizia* that, and as far as they're concerned he and his friends are all tarred with the same brush.'

'I ought to disapprove of Marco – he certainly disapproves of me. He's a blinkered, even bigoted young man who makes no allowances for other people's mistakes or prejudices. But I couldn't help liking him. He's got Llewellyn's fire and his mother's sweetness – a rather dangerous combination – and it sounds as if his sisters resemble him.'

'Maria blames their characters on Llewellyn's Welsh ancestors – she thinks her own antecedents were more reasonable!'

Jess smiled, but then looked thoughtful again. 'I now have to remember that I had Welsh ancestors too! One way and another this visit to Venice is giving me worse emotional hurdles to climb over than I've met before. Life in London with my dear, gentle Gerald didn't prepare me for Llewellyn and his brood.'

She inspected her companion across the table, sensing that at least one hurdle had disappeared. Earlier hostility could scarcely be remembered now, and the warmth and happy magic of the present moment seemed indestructible; nothing could spoil their happiness in being together, and they were *both* sure of that.

'What about your own character . . . who is to blame or thank for that?' she asked.

'My mother, mostly. I was born selfish, but Fanny admits that it's not my fault – she's very disinclined herself to see anyone else's point of view! She has no maternal instinct at all, having always wanted what she finally got – a highly successful stage career. My father directed films rather brilliantly, but what he did was too innovative, too thoughtful, for most cinema-goers. He died thinking himself a failure, but he was a nice man, and he adored Fanny. She's still charming and intelligent and the best of company, as Llewellyn found years ago, but a conventional homemaker she is *not*! Perhaps that's why I grew up believing that a settled life was something only dull people had.'

'And to prove it, I suppose,' Jess said, 'you became a news cameraman, roving the globe.'

113

'That's right – no ties, and no responsibilities except to my job and the people who shared it with me. It worked well enough until I went to Africa last year and our little group got ambushed – for taking photographs that the ruling military junta didn't like. My friends were killed, my chances of being fit enough to work again afterwards seemed slight, and the girl I'd been living with in Paris walked out on me.'

'*Not* helpful or kind,' Jess managed to say quietly.

'Not surprising, either, given the circumstances. Her younger brother had been one of the men with me in Africa and she couldn't help thinking I might have taken better care of him. I've had the same dreadful thought myself often enough since then.'

Jess contemplated the wreckage that had been made of his life and no longer wondered about the state of mind in which she'd first encountered him. But Jacques was following a train of thought of his own.

'We both seem to have missed out on conventional family life: perhaps that's made *you* disinclined for it too.'

Jess shook her head. 'I didn't go short of a family, even if it wasn't exactly conventional. The man my mother married after Llewellyn left was also her cousin; they'd been brought up together in the house we still live in. Gerald's parents are dead now, but his sister is there – it was she who first took Llewellyn to the Dutch House where he met my mother, and it was the same aunt who wrote to him about me when she knew I was coming to Venice. Aunt Imogen is as certain as my grandmother of how to organise other people's lives, but less often right, I'm afraid.'

Jacques grinned at the slight tartness but had still another question. 'Do you regret that Llewellyn knows?'

'No – I'm rather glad he does now, although I'm afraid that Maria and their children can't help wishing I wasn't here.' Jess hesitated a moment and then risked a question that he might resent. 'Why no devoted minder helping you today, by the way?'

He gave a little shrug. 'Even Claudia is occasionally obliged to put in an appearance at college.' Then, as if compelled to honesty, he went on, 'I miss her when she's not with me. Apart from knowing Venice almost stone by stone, there's no doubt that she was born to be a journalist. She talks to anyone we meet, high or low, and within minutes they've become her friends for life. It's an invaluable gift for the career she's got in mind.' He stopped, as if wanting to proceed carefully. 'You used the word "devoted" just now; it's what she is at the moment. But I'm *not* the love of her life. One of these days she'll wake up and see me for what I am, and then she'll smile at me very kindly and be off, over the horizon, looking for her next adventure.'

He believed it, Jess thought, even though Maria's expression at the

114

Countess's dinner party had surely revealed a different understanding of her daughter. Unsure what to say next, it was a relief to see the *padrona* arriving at last with their bowls of steaming risotto. When she'd gone again, the recollection of Jacques' photography on the quay offered a safer subject, and she asked him how his Venetian portrait was progressing.

'I'm basking in undeserved glory at the moment,' he admitted. 'My editor doesn't know that it's almost impossible to take a dull photograph here, so what I've been sending him – enormously helped by the captions Claudia's proving to be very good at – has been praised rather extravagantly! In fact, Henri thinks he's got my *next* assignment planned – pairing this perverse winter view of Venice with an equally perverse summer one of New York. It's quite an interesting idea, as a matter of fact, and I suspect my friend of having other places in mind as well – Sydney, perhaps, or Hong Kong.'

Jess agreed quietly that it *was* interesting, and refused to admit to herself that a little magic had suddenly disappeared from the day. The sun had disappeared as well, and outside the restaurant Burano would have become in reality what it probably always was – a small, unenchanted island smelling of fish and salt. She could even remember what she'd run away from that morning, and must now go back to. The day had been briefly gilded with joy, but magic never lasted – nor, probably, was it meant to.

'You're looking mournful,' Jacques said suddenly. 'Why, Jessica? Don't you like the idea of adventure? Can you really claim not to want to go and see what's round the next corner?'

She tried *not* to look mournful, decided that if she died in the attempt she'd at least attempt to sound amused. 'I'm thirty-eight, my dear sir, not eighteen, and the idea of settling down has quite an enticing glow about it! Perhaps I wasn't born to be a rover.'

He brushed the idea aside. 'I don't believe it . . . Llewellyn's daughter not adventurous?' Her hand was resting on the table and his suddenly covered it. 'Listen, Jess. My affair with Annette was almost over before Luc was killed. She wanted marriage and stability – not unreasonable in themselves, but scarcely what I was going to be able to provide. In any case, nothing is for ever. Pleasures can't be made to last just because we give each other futile promises that they will.'

Jess left her hand where it was to make *that* pleasure last a little longer, but she was proud of the teasing note in her voice. 'And you're also still disinclined for a settled life in case it might be dull!' She was learning to dissemble as well as any old Venetian.

'Dull or not, how are we to know what we're always going to want? How can two separate human beings, whatever their intention or their hope, ever promise each other not to change? How can they suddenly become blind to all life's other possibilities?'

She withdrew her hand; it was time now. 'Reasonably, not at all, I suppose,' she agreed, trying to smile. 'But I'm afraid I'm like Annette – wanting to give permanence a chance at least. And now I shall stand your argument on its head and claim that she and I are more adventurous than you – what could be braver than entrusting your happiness to another human being? I like the idea myself!'

Jacques was silent for a moment, then his next question was asked coolly. 'I suspect you have the other human being in mind. I don't see Giancarlo as one of the world's movers and shakers; at least *he* won't quarrel with your great ambition to settle down!'

She'd been right to sense a change; their lovely, easy companionship had suddenly fled, and they were back to confrontation again. But she smiled as if it didn't matter. 'Elvira made the same leap of imagination – just because we arrived at the Countess's party together.'

'I didn't imagine the way he looked at you. He's a safe choice, Jess, but I can't see him providing much joy or gaiety – he's already as set in his ways as his grandfather.'

The derision in his voice pricked her into sudden anger. 'What do you expect? His life has been stalked by tragedies that you know nothing about. For the moment I find him a charming, interesting, and kind companion. What else he might become has nothing to do with you. And now it's time I went back to Venice . . . I shouldn't have lingered here at all. I can catch the *vaporetto*.'

'You can go back as you came, with me,' he said sharply. He settled the bill, and a moment later they were outside. The afternoon had become overcast, and Burano looked as depressing as she'd feared. They walked in silence for little while, until Jacques found something to say.

'Is dudgeon high or deep? I can never remember.' She half turned to look at him and saw apology mixed with amusement in his face. 'Dear Jess, I'm sorry . . . forgive the sneer at Rasini, please. I'm not usually so quick to judge someone I don't know.'

'Dudgeon forgotten then,' she said with a faint smile. 'I think you'd like Giancarlo if you did get to know him.'

They were back at the quay, and the boat was still moored there, but Daniele had seen no need to hurry back from his own lunch. Jacques turned her round to face him, with hands gripped on her shoulders.

'I don't want to know Rasini; but I *do* want to know *you* . . . I want it enough even to be tempted into making the sort of promises I disapprove of! But I have some disentangling of my own to do first.' He studied her with an expression half smiling and half rueful. 'You're the last thing I bargained for here . . . a quiet, stubborn English creature who could all too easily lodge herself in my mind and heart . . .'

'Like a fishbone in your throat!' she suggested unsteadily.

116

'Remember that this is a wickedly deceptive place . . . nothing is what it seems.'

His smile faded, and he cupped her face in his hands. '"The isle is full of sweet airs that give delight, and hurt not",' he quoted softly. 'Dear Jess, would a parting kiss also give delight and hurt not?'

He didn't wait for an answer, and for as long as the kiss lasted there was nothing left in the whole world but themselves. Then Jacques raised his head, and saw Daniele, now waiting patiently by the boat.

'That seemed real enough to me,' he murmured unsteadily, 'but perhaps it's as well we've been interrupted, however much I should like to proceed! I'm in a bind at the moment, my dearest Jess, and I must get *that* sorted out, while you think about the future yourself.'

She was handed into the boat, scarcely aware of Daniele's interested gaze, vaguely trying to remember what she was supposed to think about. For the moment all she asked was to be left wrapped in the memory of a sweeter delight than any she had known. She was grateful to see Jacques station himself beside Daniele at the steering-wheel; there was nothing more to be said now . . . there might never be any more if his disentanglement couldn't be accomplished; but at least she had a small, gleaming pearl to add to her necklace of Venetian memories.

Back at the *palazzo* she was capable of registering that the mooring-poles were pristine again, but she could also remember clearly how the morning had begun, and the report she must make to Elvira. Jacques helped her on to the pathway, touched her cheek in a gentle farewell gesture, and then got back into the boat. He said nothing, and nor did she; instead of an island of sweet airs, the real world seemed to be all about them again.

She slowly climbed the stairs that she'd flung herself down hours ago it seemed, thanked Luigi for the men's hard work, and then picked up the telephone to call Elvira.

But even here there was a change. Elvira's morning rage might have belonged to a different woman – she was happy at last, and would still have sounded carefree as a lark, Jess realised, if the entire destruction of the *palazzo* had now to be reported. The explanation was simple when she reported gaily that Nathan Acheson had telephoned; he was this very minute on his way to Venice, and she was already plunging into the arrangement of a party that would lavishly welcome him home.

Jess put down the receiver at last, only aware herself of deathly tiredness as the culminating sensation of a day that had held too much emotion. With the last effort she need make, she would eventually bid the men her customary, calm goodnight and walk soberly back to the hotel where, this being Wednesday, she knew that in the dining room *fegato alla Veneziana* awaited her.

Chapter 15

Nathan Acheson arrived in Venice in the inconspicuous way that he preferred to travel the world. In rare moments of irritation Elvira refused to understand this low-key method of progress. Other important men enjoyed making a little stir, and even if *he* didn't, a stir was what she felt the rest of the world expected. Nathan always smiled when she said so, not inclined to explain that it amused him to be taken for an ordinary American, grey-haired, middle-aged, and harmless-looking.

But of one thing she was convinced all over again now – her husband became a different man in Venice. In New York or London he was the most private kind of magnate, doing good by stealth, ignoring the media, and going out of his way to avoid the society hostesses and hangers-on who lay in wait. Only here did he become approachable. She believed what she'd confided to Jess – that it was the sort of has-been place that shouldn't have appealed to him at all. Venice only went at its own maddening pace, and even then according to rules that no one else could follow. It didn't matter at all to her that its constant need of money absorbed quite a lot of the Acheson wealth – if not here, he'd give it away somewhere else; but the sight of St Mark's Square under a foot of water had convinced her that she'd been right all along – Venice was bearable when she had Nathan there; but only just, even then.

The morning after his arrival, while she was locked in happy party-planning with her hotel advisers, he strolled along the Riva to find his usual boatman. Warned in advance, Giorgio was waiting there, gondola sanded down and freshly painted for the coming season. Within the city it didn't occur to Nathan to use anything else but its own beautiful, archaic form of locomotion. He shared Giorgio's view – motorboats might be necessary out in the Lagoon; here they destroyed the natural tempo of the place, and did much damage to its crucial underpinnings.

His friend was pessimistic when asked about the future.

'Things are not good, *signore* . . . the young people still leave each year, and who can blame them? On the mainland they can find real jobs – not just be summertime waiters; they can buy modern houses, and best of all own a motorcar. What's life for today's young men without a *macchina*?'

119

'What about you?' Nathan asked.

Giorgio rested on his oar for a moment while he gave a little shrug.

'I'm too old to start again; otherwise I'd be tempted as well. It gets harder and harder to make a living here. We charge too much, we cheat, we grumble, the visitors say. What do *they* do? Crowd out the Piazzale Roma with their stinking cars and buses, spend as little as they can, and expect *us* to smile and sing them love songs!' He looked at his passenger with sudden anxiety. 'Not only foreigners, you understand . . . Italians are just as bad; some are worse!'

Nathan did understand; to a true-born Venetian other Italians *were* much the same as foreigners. Even their language sounded different, and what did they care about the Republic's past centuries of glory? Nowadays the power was in Rome, the culture in Florence, and the money in Milan; nowhere else mattered.

Nathan was tempted to ask the boatman what he thought of foreigners buying up Venetian property, but it scarcely seemed fair when the man couldn't afford the luxury of a truthful answer.

'Can you wait for me?' he asked instead. 'I don't know how long I shall be, or where I'll want to go next.'

Giorgio's face relaxed into a smile. '*Non importa, signore* – I shall be here.'

A moment or two later, sitting at her usual work table, Jess was startled by the knowledge that someone else was in the house. If she hadn't closed the garden door properly perhaps Llewellyn had guessed she was there; perhaps Jacques had decided that there'd been time enough for thinking since their visit to Burano. She'd slept badly since then, and concentrated on her work with difficulty. Still she hadn't been able to make up her mind about those heart-stopping moments on the quay, and what – if anything – they signified. In the context of the present day they need have signified nothing at all except a snatched enjoyment. But in the long, dark stretches of the night she seesawed vertiginously between one certainty and another, trying to remind herself that she was in the city of sorcery and illusion, but somehow convinced nevertheless that everything that was happening *was* going to matter for the rest of her life. In some curious way that neither reason nor common sense could justify, she and Jacques had recognised a shared delight, however briefly. But nothing else matched about their lives, and if *she* had drawn back a little, so most noticeably had he. She was left like a high-wire artiste, dangerously aloft and trying to keep her balance.

But it wasn't Jacques Duclos walking through the house. The man who stood in the doorway a moment later was a stranger; he cut nothing of her father's flamboyant figure, nor did he in the least resemble the Frenchman who occupied her mind. She might have taken him for a minor official of some kind if she hadn't already learned that even the humblest Italian bureaucrats were always dressed as if about to make a killing in the City. It seemed, therefore, safe to make a guess at this visitor's identity.

'Welcome to Venice, Mr Acheson,' she said, getting up to hold out her hand. 'I thought your wife expected you tomorrow, but I must have misunderstood.'

'I *was* expected then,' he agreed. 'Do you make a habit of working an Saturdays, may I ask?'

'On Sundays too if I'm very short of time! But I was able to give the workmen this weekend off – they've done so well that another few days should see all the redecoration finished.'

'Could you not have given *yourself* the weekend off in that case?'

Jess smiled at the question, wondering for a moment what he would say if she simply confessed to having grown attached to the great, empty building around her; in her imagination it seemed to be more ship than house, moored on the green waters of the canal, creaking and shifting a little and moving with the current. It would probably sound high-flown, and she doubted whether Nathan Acheson was a man who could spare time for whimsy.

'I was checking accounts,' she explained instead. 'Serious business that's better done in peace and quiet when no one else is here!'

'Very true,' he agreed gravely. 'Are you steeling yourself to tell me that your original estimate was too low?'

'No,' Jess said, looking surprised. 'Smythson's wouldn't have survived if we made that sort of mistake. I was told what you were prepared to spend – I've designed everything accordingly.'

'And you'd also like to point out, only you're too polite, that I've fallen into the trap men like me *do* fall into – we imagine that everyone else is so much less smart than we are!'

More surprised still, Jess registered the fact that Nathan Acheson was smiling. She'd fallen into a trap herself, judging him in advance, and deciding that he would be easy to dislike. It was an opinion she might now have to reconsider, but even so she felt no temptation to return a too-smart answer; he'd probably had years of practice in putting rash employees in their place.

'I expect you've come to see what we've been doing,' she suggested instead. 'I'll leave you to wander about on your own, until you're ready to inspect my sketches of how the rooms will look when they're finished.'

It left unspoken the possibility that Elvira's dislike of the Matthias family might now not require her to finish them at all, but she decided that it was a topic best left to him to air. He merely nodded and walked away, leaving her to contemplate what she would do if he came back dissatisfied. She could try informing him that she felt too tired to start again, or insist that her dear, elderly expert next door thought no mistakes had been made, but what notice would a self-made American millionaire take of the opinion of an impoverished Venetian aristocrat? Elvira had certainly made *her* view clear that Count Paolo was a pathetic dinosaur stranded on the shores of time.

She was still considering this when Nathan strolled past the kitchen door on his way to the bedrooms. The expression on his face was the unrevealing one she supposed he wore when thinking about the purchase of another oil-well or some new television station – no one was to be allowed to guess whether he was keen to buy or not. But she was discovering in herself the same dislike that Marco felt for what men like him represented. If Elvira was right, and her husband's philanthropy took the form of empty, extravagant gestures, she'd wish she'd had nothing to do with the *palazzo*.

Her sketches were spread out for his inspection when he finally returned, and he studied them without saying anything. Determined that she wouldn't be the one to reopen the conversation, she made some coffee instead and brought it to the table.

'It isn't going to look as I expected,' he announced, just as she was beginning to think he might not say anything at all.

'And not as you wanted?'

The blunt question suddenly made him smile openly. She thought he should do it more often, so great was the improvement over his usual impassive expression.

'I've seen the inside of a lot of palaces here,' he said, still not answering her. 'Most of them *looked* very grand and seemed extremely uncomfortable. A few had thrown tradition overboard and gone to the other extreme; they call it minimalist, I believe – it seems disastrous to me. I don't know how you'd describe what you've done here, but I couldn't ask for anything better.'

Jess let out the breath she'd been holding, recognising that what she'd been given by Nathan Acheson was his highest form of praise. 'Your next-door neighbour, Count Rasini, thinks it's all right too,' she admitted. 'I was holding him in reserve in case you needed convincing!'

This time Nathan even chuckled over his coffee, but there was nothing amiably vague about the glance he directed across the table.

'I was nervous,' he admitted astonishingly, 'even though your grandmother is a woman whose judgement I respect. *She* assured me that you would know exactly what to do here, but I couldn't help suspecting that it would be outside your previous experience.'

Jess tried not to look surprised by Elizabeth Harrington's faith in her; it wasn't her grandmother's way to be dogmatic about something she could only take on trust. But a more crucial worry was beginning to loom large. Elvira *must* have talked to him by now, and Jess couldn't be sure whether he postponed referring to the Matthias family to keep her in suspense, or reckoned them not important enough to mention at all. Finally it seemed the latter, when he shot a different, unexpected question at her.

'Do you get the impression that Elvira isn't happy here?'

He'd taken off his spectacles, the better to examine the sketches laid out in front of him, and for the first time Jess felt that she was being allowed real access to Nathan Acheson. She was also, she realised, being asked for the truth.

'I don't think she's enjoyed being here on her own, but that will change now.' It seemed not quite enough and Jess tried again. 'Venice in wintertime can't help looking a bit like a sacrificial goat, tied up and waiting to be devoured by the sea outside. That's been quite a problem for Elvira, but there's been another, more personal one to unsettle her as well. I expect she told you about it, but she might not have wanted to say that one of the young men involved in the campaign against you happens to be my half-brother, Marco Matthias.'

'I know as much of the story as she knows,' Nathan admitted. 'It's quite an unusual visit you've had here.'

The understatement was so heroic that for a desperate moment she was torn between the need to shout with laughter or weep. God knew what a man like Nathan Acheson would really make of Llewellyn; but her guess was that he'd share Elvira's outraged disapproval. It wasn't so long ago that she'd shared it herself. She got a grip on self-control again and tried to speak calmly.

'Perhaps you've already decided to take some kind of action against the newspaper or against Marco and his friends; Elvira certainly believes they deserve it. But will you just let me say one thing? Unlike Count Ghisalberti, at least they want nothing for themselves and mean well towards Venice. They want it to survive quite as much as you do, though probably in a different way. That seems to be the terrible difficulty here – even the people who love Venice most can't agree about what should happen to it.'

Nathan's expression gave her no hint of what he was thinking, but, aware of where her own sympathies now seemed to lie, she made one last effort on her half-brother's behalf. 'I expect you always deal through lawyers – someone in your position is bound to, of course; but if you talked to Marco yourself you'd understand how passionately he believes in a living Venice, not a museum-piece to a dead past.'

'People in my position, as you put it, have one unfair advantage in life,' he pointed out calmly. 'We're never bound to do anything. My dealing can be done in any way I like, here or anywhere else.'

Curiosity at last overcame Jess's reluctance to be given a much more annihilating snub.

'I've wanted to ask . . . *why* here, Mr Acheson? I know Venice needs help, but so do many other places.'

He took so long to answer that she supposed him making up his mind just to walk away; then she realised that he was simply looking back into his own past before deciding what to say.

'I came here first by accident nearly twenty years ago,' he finally began to explain. 'I was on my way back from the Middle East and the plane was grounded for a day. I was irritated by the delay, but to pass the time I hired a boat to bring me over to the city. I watched it materialise out of the Lagoon and thought I was dreaming – I dare say everyone does who sees it for the first time, because it isn't like anywhere else. I went home determined to bring my daughter back with me when she was old enough to be enchanted by it. Before I could do that she killed herself – a reckless teenager trying to convince a much older, sophisticated lover that she couldn't live without him. My ex-wife and my son blamed me – I ought to have "bought" the man for her; he was certainly for sale.'

Jess had known of an earlier Mrs Acheson – Pinky Todd had told her in London of the woman Nathan had divorced, for adultery and much else besides. Their son had apparently gone the ruinous way of many young men with huge expectations, but no mention had been made of a dead daughter.

'It took me a year or two,' Nathan went on quietly, 'but eventually I came back, and saw the extent to which Venice was falling apart – quite literally by then. I began to contribute, thinking of it as a private memorial to my daughter. It still is, but something else has happened as well. *This* has become the place where I refuse to fail, because my feeling is that if I do, the city itself will fail. Hubris talking? No, I don't think so.'

Uncertain of her voice, or of what she could safely say, Jess sat watching the man across the table while his own inward eye still lingered on the past. People not acquainted with his story would have thought him someone to envy, she supposed, but life took no care to exempt even the most powerful men from the punishments it decided to impose.

'I wish that Marco could know how you feel about Venice,' she said finally. 'It would make a great deal of difference.' She hesitated over whether to ask about Elvira, who seemed not to understand what kept her husband there, but Nathan answered the unspoken question anyway.

'I chose not to burden my wife with that particular piece of the past – she had enough to come to terms with.' Arrested by his next thought, he frowned at Jess. 'I don't know why I told *you* about my daughter – I never mention it as a rule.' Almost as if he blamed her, he stared at the quiet face of the woman sitting opposite him. Her whole aspect and her self-control seemed not to match the outlandish story Elvira had given him; but on the other hand, his redoubtable friend Elizabeth was her grandmother, and her father scarcely sounded a quietly ordinary man. Perhaps he should have expected Jessica Smythson to be a little unusual.

Jess supposed that he still worried about his wife, and wondered how to go about giving advice to someone probably not much in the habit of taking it.

'Elvira is angry at the moment; Venice hasn't provided the welcome she thinks you deserve. I can't help believing that she'd feel differently towards it, Mr Acheson, if she knew the reason that brings you here.'

'So do I now,' he agreed surprisingly. Then he permitted himself a faint smile. 'I know about her being good and mad! She even had some thought of excluding the Matthiases from the invitations to her party, but I hope I might have talked her out of that.'

He stood up as if to leave, but pointed at one of her sketches lying on the table.

'You've left an empty space above the fireplace, I see.'

Jess had the grace to blush. 'I suppose I thought that if it were *my* fireplace I'd . . . well, I'd commission a painting to hang there.'

'A . . . a Llewellyn, perhaps?'

She took the fence at a rush. 'He's getting bored with San Marco and the Rialto bridge. A Lagoon picture would go well in the room, and he does them very beautifully.'

Nathan made a noncommittal little sound, but she suspected him of having a struggle not to smile again.

'Don't toil over bills all day,' he said as he walked towards the door, then stopped again. 'Isn't it lonely for you here by yourself?'

'It doesn't *feel* lonely, and I may never get another chance to have a Venetian *palazzo* all to myself,' she explained solemnly.

He nodded, seeing nothing strange in that, smiled at her with unexpected warmth, and went away.

Jess remained there for most of the day, but found herself with not a great deal to show for it when she finally left. Invoices held no lure when her mind persisted instead on dwelling on a sequence of different images, one merging into another just as the reflections in the water outside constantly re-formed themselves.

She locked the door behind her at last and walked slowly back towards her hotel. It wasn't Carnival yet but already groups of revellers were making merry in the Campo San Vio. They looked young and carefree, content enough with what the evening brought in the way of immediate pleasure not to worry about the future. One of them gestured to her to join the throng, but she smilingly shook her head, trying not to feel all the more lonely. She wanted to have someone she knew holding her hand . . . didn't know for certain who it should be; but did know for sure that being self-sufficient had lost its charm – damn Venice for that unwanted piece of knowledge. The revellers moved on, and now the square was only full of shadows, and silence. She followed slowly, wishing that she'd been brave enough to go with them after all.

Chapter 16

After careful thought and consultation, Elvira finally omitted from her invitation list the name of the Patriarch of Venice. A Carnival ball might *not* be to His Eminence's liking, broad-minded though the Roman Catholic Church was known to be in matters that touched on worldly pleasures. Otherwise, she expected everyone who counted in Venetian society to attend, along with all the influential foreigners who resided there or figured on one or other international rescue committee like Nathan's. But there must also be room, she decided, for those local families who, even though not thoroughly patrician or utterly rich, could contribute *something* in the way of merit or beauty to a company she wanted to be dazzling.

In this last category the Matthias family had been considered, and rejected as being unsuitable, but when she told Nathan that she therefore meant to exclude Jessica Smythson as well, his expression told her that she would have to think again. Even so, she lodged the most spirited protest she could.

'Jessica is half-sister to a revolutionary firebrand, and her natural father is a free-living bohemian artist, Nathan. I *don't* think we should include *any* of the family among our guests.'

He looked suitably grave for a moment, then offered his wife the smile that other people saw so rarely.

'My dear, you're right, of course; but remember this *is* Venice, where firebrands and bohemians have never caused much of a stir! We shall have a beautiful house to thank Jessica for . . . she *must* be invited, don't you think? The Matthiases live along our rio – would it not seem churlish to ignore them?'

She agreed reluctantly, only comforted by the idea that Jessica Smythson might have preferred not to have to spend an evening confronted by such unreliable relatives. Even with no real grudge held against her for secrecy or unwelcome lectures about the deserving poor, Elvira was nevertheless inclined to eye her interior designer with a certain stiffness on the rare occasions when she called at the *palazzo* to inspect progress.

Finally, two separate invitations went to the Pensione Alberoni, one addressed to Jacques, and the other to Maria and Llewellyn. They arrived while the family were, unusually, eating breakfast together. Jacques opened his first, and smiled across the table at Maria.

'I'm invited to rub shoulders with the high and mighty at Elvira's Carnival extravaganza at the Danieli – I expect you and Llewellyn are, too.'

'We all are,' Maria said quietly after reading her card. 'The girls *and* Marco as well.' She glanced at Llewellyn but he was staring at the ceiling, and she could see him already beginning to contemplate what he would wear – powdered hair, of course, and perhaps a domino of scarlet silk.

Claudia clapped her hands, but Marco was the first to speak. 'Don't accept for me, Mamma. I've better things to do than get myself up in fancy dress to suit the whim of a rich, idle woman; in any case, it wouldn't be right.'

Llewellyn's bright gaze was lowered to fix itself on his son. 'Quite so,' he agreed affably. 'Never accept food from the hand you're trying very hard to bite. But I don't think that need stop the rest of us enjoying a delightful binge before the rigours of Lent close in.'

Maria wondered for a distracted moment what self-denial her husband had it in mind for once to undergo, but Marco stared at his elder sister. She was the only real supporter he had in the family. His mother did her best, even managed to seem sympathetic to his friends, but he knew very well what she believed: only heavenly intervention would make the world a less imperfect place. Lorenza understood what was required of her – she must refuse the invitation and range herself with those who wanted to rid Venice of people like the Achesons. She more than half agreed with them; but just for once the certainty was growing in her mind that she was going to disappoint Marco, because there was no doubt that Giancarlo would be included with his grandparents on the *signora's* invitation list. The gossip along the *rio* rubbed salt into the wound of his indifference to her, but the Achesons' ball offered one last hope of making a blind man see what he was missing. The vision wasn't complete yet, but already she could imagine herself in exquisite Carnival disguise – a shepherdess from some Arcadian springtime maybe – floating into the Danieli's ballroom like a beautiful, irridescent butterfly. Dazzled by the sight, Giancarlo would discover whom the mask concealed and understand at last the treasure he'd been ignoring for so long. Not even for her brother could she forgo the triumphant moment when she would smile at Giancarlo and then walk away.

Unable to look at Marco, she spoke to her mother. 'Signora Acheson is a stranger here. It would seem very unkind to refuse . . . don't you think so, Mamma?'

Jacques watched and listened with pity, understanding Lorenza's need and her mother's cruel dilemma. Maria would want her daughter to shine and be happy. But she'd watched Giancarlo usher a different

128

woman into his grandmother's *portego* with such charmed, proprietorial pride that she must pray Lorenza need never see them together.

While their mother hesitated over an answer, Claudia registered her expression and knew that persuasion might be required. Go they must, of course, to the most exciting ball they'd ever been invited to; but more was at stake than that. As certainly as Lorenza intended to dazzle Giancarlo, she herself meant to emerge for Jacques into irresistible adult beauty. She'd discounted Marco's impression of their half-sister – he was too kind and inexperienced a judge; but Daniele's worrying account of a visit to Burano had reached her quick ears. A kiss meant nothing . . . a nearly middle-aged Englishwoman desperate for a little attention had probably asked for it, and Jacques, too, was kind. But Claudia intended him to see Jessica alongside herself . . . it was all that would be needed, she felt sure.

'Lorenza's right, Mamma,' she said firmly. 'It *would* be unkind to refuse. But in any case, it isn't for Marco to say what we may enjoy.' She smiled ravishingly at Llewellyn, sure of loud support from a man who dearly loved a party. But for once Maria spoke first, sounding sad but certain.

'The Questura will have told Signora Acheson about Marco and his friends. For Jessica's sake we are being offered a courtesy that she expects us to refuse. Jacques must go, of course, if he wants to, but not the rest of us, I think.'

It was so rare for her to assert herself that Llewellyn shifted uncomfortably in his chair, and then temporarily abandoned the field of battle for his studio, muttering that he would think about the matter there. Sensing defeat, Lorenza threw a despairing glance at her mother before she quietly left the room; Jacques looked at Claudia's rebellious face and hastily announced that if she was coming out with him, she must come *now*.

The two left alone together stared miserably at each other. 'I'm sorry, Mamma,' Marco blurted out. 'I'm spoiling things for the rest of you. I wouldn't if it wasn't important . . . but it *is*. If we don't fight people like the Achesons, Venice won't belong to us any more.' He tried to smile at her, wanting to make her look less sad. 'There's no reason for *you* not to go . . . the girls want to, and after all, the *signora has* invited you.'

'Claudia expects the entire company, including Jacques, to hold their breath when she walks into the room, and she'll be bitterly disappointed when they don't. Lorenza wants Giancarlo to look only at her, and *he* will see no woman but Jessica.' She saw the expression on Marco's face and managed a wry smile. 'Not "important" like your problems? I'm afraid Lorenza and Claudia don't think so, and I agree with them – happiness isn't an unreasonable thing to want, my son.'

'I'm sorry, Mamma,' Marco said again, knowing because he knew most things about her that she could also have been speaking of herself. Llewellyn hadn't been the husband of any woman's dreams.

Maria shook her head. 'It's not you, *tesoro* . . . it's Jessica. I try not to hate her, because I'm sure she *isn't* hateful and she's a part of Llewellyn, as the rest of you are; but she can't help hurting my girls. It's a sort of punishment, I suppose, for what happened in London all those years ago.'

Marco got up from the table to envelop her in a loving hug, then carefully smoothed a strand of hair that he'd disarranged. 'Let them go to the party, Mamma ... let them see what they can do. You worry about them too much – anywhere but here they'd be living on their own by now.'

'I know,' Maria agreed. 'Llewellyn says I shouldn't worry about *you*, either, but I'm afraid it's something mothers do!' She waved him away, and rang for Lucia to clear the table. It wouldn't be long before her husband reappeared with some ingenious reason of his own for not missing Elvira's party, and she had to decide what she would say.

The morning brought Jess, as well as her own invitation to the Danieli ball, a surprise suggestion from Giancarlo that gave her greater pleasure – would she come that evening to a performance of Verdi's Requiem in the church of La Pietà? Indeed she would, and not only for the sake of listening to the music. Her working days kept her mind occupied, but the long, lonely evenings were a different matter, and she spent too much of them wondering whether her interrupted conversation with Jacques would be resumed.

In the darkest moments of the night it seemed that it was best not finished at all; what he'd said of himself was proof enough that they were incompatible. An ill-matched love affair had ruined her mother's life; she wasn't about to make the same mistake herself, even if a love affair was what Jacques had in mind. But that she doubted. A little magic had dusted the Burano air . . . nothing more durable than that.

She wasted time imagining a lunatically improbable future – a visit with him to New York, and meetings there with her grandmother. Elizabeth Harrington and Jacques would get on well together; no stupid hesitations for either of *them*, no second thoughts. Life offered options from which a rational creature selected the most desirable; that was how her grandmother would behave. Elizabeth would recommend her to turn a deaf ear to the tiredness in Gerald's voice when he telephoned. She would have no difficulty in fitting herself into the life of a self-sufficient man; *he'd* have to make adjustments, she would say. But Jess had no faith in the idea of Jacques Duclos making adjustments. It would be altogether better to stop thinking about him at all, and an evening spent with Giancarlo would mean that she could turn her attention to a more deserving man.

As they walked along the Riva degli Schiavoni that evening he explained what she vaguely knew – the church they were making for housed most of the city's concerts while the burnt-out Fenice Theatre was still being rebuilt. But its musical reputation went back two hundred and fifty years to the golden age when Vivaldi composed music for its famous orphanage choir. Even so, Giancarlo was careful to limit expectation now in case she was about to be disappointed.

'Don't judge us by London or Paris standards, Jessica – this is provincial Venice, remember!'

She smiled at him, shaking her head. 'I'm not to be caught like that, dear sir. This is indeed Venice, where the rain is wetter, women are more beautiful, palaces more numerous, and in short everything else is better than anywhere else on earth!'

He laughed out loud – perhaps for the first time, he thought, since the day Jeanne had died. His grandfather was right; the woman beside him had the priceless gift of enhancing life for other people. It wasn't a matter of beauty or sexual appeal or even intellect, though all these things came into it. There was just some grace about her that warmed anyone whose life touched hers. He ushered her into the Pietà's ornate vestibule, where half Venice already seemed to be crammed, and left her while he went to deposit their overcoats. Jess saw the party from the Pensione Alberoni in her first glance round – Llewellyn talking with a dark-haired girl and . . . Jacques Duclos. There was time to clutch at self-control, and pin a smile to her face. She couldn't help thinking for a brief, glad moment that Jacques looked pleased to see her; then her father took over . . . coming exuberantly towards her.

'Dear girl – what a marvellous surprise! Look . . . Lorenza's here as well; you two haven't met yet, though it's high time you did.'

He'd established for her which daughter stood there, but Jess could see in Lorenza's beautiful, unsmiling face no vestige of the pleasure she was being required to share.

'We didn't expect to see you *here*,' she said pointedly. 'My father always insists the English have no music in their souls.'

'It's probably a Welsh opinion,' Jess suggested, 'not necessarily to be trusted!' She hoped for a glimmer of amusement to melt the girl's aloofness, but saw none; permitted herself a small smile for Jacques, then spoke to Llewellyn instead. 'Claudia's soul *doesn't* crave music?'

He glanced at Jacques before answering. 'Too much time is spent not doing her college work – tonight an essay had to be written. But it's also true, I feel ashamed to say, that she's got no musical soul *or* ear – the "Marseillaise" and "God save the Queen" sound exactly the same to Claudia.' He frowned over such a failure, but put it aside to consider his eldest daughter. 'Now, my dear Jess, you can't sit alone – you and I will swop seats. Lorenza will much prefer it – she says I

131

embarrass her by singing louder than the choir!'

Before Jess could explain that no change was needed, Jacques' expression suddenly altered; Giancarlo was edging his way towards them, and it was certain that he wasn't doing that for the pleasure of joining the party from the Pensione Alberoni. 'You've no need to worry about Jessica,' the Frenchman said coolly to Llewellyn. 'She's not here on her own, and her noble escort is just arriving!' He held out an arm to Lorenza and smiled at her with warm affection. 'Shall we go in, *cara?* I loathe being pushed and shoved at the last minute.'

She gave a brief nod in the direction of the man who'd come to stand beside them, ignored Jess altogether, and then sweetly agreed with Jacques – they'd be more comfortable in the auditorium. Left behind by his companions, Llewellyn did his best to pretend that no coldness was hanging on the air.

'What about hot chocolate afterwards at Florian's?' he suggested. 'Shall we meet you there?'

Jess saw Giancarlo hesitate and answered for them both. 'Thank you, but I think I'll say no – I have to make a very early start tomorrow.' She smiled at her father to soften the refusal. 'Enjoy the music – I shall, despite Lorenza's doubts. She seems to want to forget that I can claim some Welsh blood myself!'

Before he could find an answer, the warning bell told them to take their places, and a few minutes later the first notes of the Requiem Aeternam floated out into the high, dim spaces of the church. Jess shared a smile of anticipation with the man beside her, and promised herself that she would simply concentrate on what she'd come to listen to. There'd be time enough later on to remember the hatred in Lorenza's dark eyes, and the desolating knowledge that in the game of taking sides that Llewellyn's family seemed to insist on, Jacques had suddenly decided to range himself with them.

Chapter 17

Breakfast at the *pensione* the following morning began normally enough. Marco had already eaten and left, and the rest of the household straggled down more or less together. But they seemed, Maria thought, quieter than usual; she even had to ask how the concert at La Pietà had gone.

'Not quite up to standard,' Llewellyn finally answered after a pause. 'The choir needed a bit more fire – they were supposed to be singing full-blooded Verdi, not a sixteenth-century Mass by Palestrina.'

'Papa enjoyed it even so,' Lorenza suddenly decided to point out. 'He was delighted to find his English daughter there.'

Maria just had time to register the rare formality – it was 'Papa' this morning – no friendly 'Llewellyn' – before he banged on the table.

'She has a name, *cara* . . . why not use it?'

As if he hadn't spoken, Lorenza smiled at her mother, and Jacques thought he could guess what was coming next. This quiet member of the family had decided to assert herself at last.

'Mamma, Marco was right about the Achesons' invitation, and so were you. I *shan't* be going, even if anyone else does.'

Jacques emerged from his own thoughts to register the self-control that a young woman could achieve by sheer will-power. If pride had allowed it, Lorenza would have broken down and wept, because whatever vestige of hope or wishful thinking she'd managed to cling to through the years of growing-up had finally had to be abandoned last night. The wastage of so much time past was bad enough, but she was confronting a future that looked even worse – stretching ahead, empty now even of dreams and visions.

He stared next at Claudia, and saw desperate puzzlement in her face at her sister's change of heart.

'Giancarlo escorted Jessica to the concert last night,' he explained quietly.

She stared for a moment at Lorenza, and finally understood the message Jacques had given her; there would be no going to the ball for either of them. With a nearly cheerful smile she went to wind her arms about her sister. 'You're right, *tesoro* – it's bound to be a stuffy affair. If Jacques doesn't want to go we'll have a Carnival party of our

133

own here instead – much more fun than some silly, snobbish ball at the Daniele.' She smiled at Llewellyn, daring him to start shouting a protest, but it hovered in the balance. Claudia had made her sacrifice, and Jacques knew that it was time to make *his*. He turned to Maria, sitting pale and tense at the other end of the table.

'*Cara*, I've got an even better idea. I must make a visit to Paris next week – why not let the girls come with me? It's not quite spring, but I don't suppose they'll mind. My mother has an enormous apartment, and she loves having guests to stay. They can amuse each other while I'm slaving away with Henri Clément.'

Maria watched the smile he offered Claudia's suddenly enchanted face, and sent a silent remonstrance to the Blessed Virgin Mary – life was never as simple as she needed it to be. Claudia emphatically *shouldn't* become any more spellbound by Jacques than she already was; but his offer had been made out of kindness and Lorenza desperately needed to escape from the claustrophobic, too-intimate watch of the neighbourhood. She watched her daughter's taut mouth relax a little at the mere thought of getting away from Venice, and knew what she must say.

'I'm sure Lorenza is entitled to ask for a holiday. It's more doubtful whether Claudia can convince her tutors that *she* needs a rest, but we haven't known her powers of persuasion fail yet!' She smiled at the faces watching her, and made an effort to sound cheerful. 'Now, my dears, you must arrange your own lives – I have a *pensione* to run, *non è vero?*'

A moment later, in the privacy of her little office behind the hall, she could stop smiling, try to stop thinking about her family, and concentrate instead on the enquiries and bookings for the coming season that now arrived by every mail. But concentration kept wandering, always coming back to the secret prayer she was ashamed of – that Jessica would leave Venice and not return. She was afraid of blurting it out in words one day, knowing that if she did Llewellyn would never forgive her.

Not working, but watching from the window beside her desk, she saw her husband stride out first, shabby old cape flowing about him as he marched through the bare garden. Poor, dear man, he'd wanted to go to the *signora's* party, but even *he* had realised that it would be impossible to go alone. She frowned next at the sight of Claudia dressed in jacket, mini-skirt, and scarlet leggings – not anyone's idea of the serious student in search of learning, but Maria knew what her support for Lorenza at the breakfast table had cost her. At last the front door banged behind Jacques and Lorenza as well, and there was no excuse not to turn her attention to the heap of correspondence in front of her.

Midway through the morning, she looked up from the letter she

134

was reading as the door opened. Lucia was bringing her morning coffee, but also indicating with a backward nod the presence of a visitor in the hall.

'*Il signor* Acheson,' she said, in a passable imitation of the name she'd been given.

'Then bring another cup, please, *cara*,' Maria managed to say above the sudden pounding of her heart. With the calmness of despair she watched the stranger, hat in hand, advance into the room and offer her a little bow. She couldn't decide whether it was wickedly unfair to be left to deal with this man alone, or whether Providence had thoughtfully determined not to have Llewellyn present to make matters worse. Count Paolo always insisted that Nathan Acheson was a good friend to Venice, but it only seemed to emphasise his right to quarrel with them. Maria supposed that this was what he'd come for.

'My husband is not here, *signore*,' she began. 'If you would prefer to call again . . .?'

Nathan waved the idea aside, but stared at the littered desk in front of her. 'If I've called at a bad time I'll go away,' he suggested pleasantly. 'Otherwise please allow me to stay and talk to *you*.'

Maria waited for the housekeeper to come and depart again, poured coffee for them both, and tried to speak as if her visitor was making a purely social call.

'A new season begins soon and a *pensione* needs people to come and stay in it, just as Venice needs people too. But we hope for . . .' she hesitated over a word and produced one that Nathan might have been tempted to smile at if she hadn't looked so anxious, '. . . *nice* visitors, who will understand our problems and treat a place that is old and frail with the proper respect.'

Nathan smiled at her over his gold-rimmed spectacles. 'In other words, no more pop festivals to leave a sea of filth in the Piazza . . . and not too many unmannerly day-trippers arriving every morning like a plague of locusts!'

Her worried face relaxed a little. 'Exactly!' If the entire visit was going to be conducted in this harmonious spirit she thought she might manage it after all, but with his next sentence they were suddenly on dangerous ground.

'My wife is waiting to hear from you, I believe, about her party.'

Maria nerved herself to look at him, seemed to see only polite interest in his face, and then discovered that his eyes, though shrewd, were not unkind. But she wasn't skilled at what Llewellyn called the lie permissible; it would have to be the truth, however deeply she got entangled in it.

'We couldn't agree about whether to accept or not,' she said baldly. 'Not Marco, of course, though we were grateful for your wife's

135

courtesy; but the rest of us. I have written to the *signora* now, asking her to excuse our absence.' Nathan didn't answer, and she was obliged to go on. 'I'm sure you've been told about my son, Signor Acheson. His behaviour must seem very bad to you, and although he would readily explain it, I cannot.'

Warming to this troubled, honest woman, Nathan took off his spectacles to observe her more closely. She looked an unlikely mother of a hell-raising son, but he'd had experience himself of the grief a wayward child could bring on its parents. He drank some coffee, put down his cup, and then unhurriedly continued the conversation. 'I make a habit of visiting the Rialto markets when I'm here. Early this morning I saw a young man who it now occurs to me looked very much like you – could he have been your son perhaps?'

Maria nodded with faint pride. 'I expect it was Marco. My brother trusts him to run a large fruit and vegetable business there. No one works harder . . . or with more devotion.'

'But other things concern him as well, I gather,' Nathan pointed out coolly. 'He takes a great interest in Venetian politics, for instance . . . perhaps has ambitions that have nothing to do with the price of asparagus and artichokes?'

She thought she heard belittlement in the visitor's tone of voice, and, nervousness forgotten, galloped into battle for her son. 'He sees things that are wrong, and wants to change them. He loves Venice, and hates the people who might destroy it. I find nothing wrong with that myself.'

'Nor I, *signora*,' he agreed gently, 'and I already know – from talking to Jessica Smythson – how Marco feels about Venice!' He took a card from his pocket and laid it on the desk. 'I like to go out walking but I'm back at the Danieli between eight and ten each morning. Perhaps your son would be kind enough to telephone me? I should like to meet him.'

She nodded, suspecting that Marco would want to refuse; but she would implore him to do this one thing for her if he did nothing else ever again. Nathan had retrieved his spectacles and was now staring at a picture hanging on the wall.

'I'm to commission a painting,' he murmured. 'I shouldn't despise the Rialto bridge myself, but Miss Smythson insists that your husband is getting bored with that. Will you ask *him* to talk to me as well?'

Maria stared at him in astonishment. 'Did . . . did Jessica suggest a Llewellyn painting?'

Nathan's elusive smile reappeared as he stood up to go. 'Certainly not – she *told* me that it was what the room needed! Thank you for the coffee, *signora*. I can see myself out.'

She sat there after he'd gone, partly relieved, but deeply perplexed as well. Marco was problem enough, but suddenly he was outweighed now by the thought of her husband. Jessica's recommendation would, in one way, give him enormous pleasure; in another, she feared, it would leave him haunted by the possibility of failure. Emilia's little 'views' were what he painted now . . . he hadn't even attempted anything else for years; but he would have to now, or be seen to refuse an important commission. It seemed that Jessica couldn't help upsetting them all; Maria groped for the English word in her mind – catalyst, that was it . . . someone who changed other people without having to change herself. It seemed on the face of it very unfair.

Jess could see the finished *palazzo* in her mind's eye now. On the *piano nobile*, where the Achesons would live, nearly all was ready except for the finishing touches being put to the kitchen and bathrooms by Luigi and his men. The rooms were mostly empty still, but the furniture and hangings that would make them complete were already beginning to arrive. On the floor above, an apartment was also being got ready for the servants Elvira would need, to look after them, and to watch over the house in their absence. The remaining rooms, Jess supposed, would remain empty, surplus to the life of a couple who would always be surrounded by much more than they required.

She had returned from a hurried mainland shopping trip, and was working in the kitchen as usual when she heard voices in the corridor. A late-afternoon visit from Elvira was unusual, but she'd certainly heard the click of feminine heels on the stone floor. Then Luigi spoke from the doorway, '*Ecco la signorina,*' and disappeared. Jess looked up to see a girl left standing there, and knew in some hidden corner of her mind that she'd been expecting this visit; the surprising thing was that it hadn't happened before.

Not as beautiful as her elder sister, Claudia still had more than enough of beauty's most essential ingredients – a mane of dark, curling hair, huge eyes, and the clear skin of youth and perfect health. But she had something else that Lorenza lacked – it was the inheritance of their father's extrovert verve that brought *this* face so vividly to life.

'Claudia Matthias, I think,' Jess said with a faint smile, 'and I don't suppose I need introduce myself either!'

Claudia was irritated to have lost the advantage of surprise, but relieved as well. Marco had been wrong – the woman in front of her looked quite ordinary after all. She didn't resemble Llewellyn, and that was comforting too.

'I'm doing research for a college project,' she announced, more or less truthfully. 'It's a report on housing here . . . or, rather, the lack of it for *Venetian* people, who can't afford what rich foreigners can pay.'

'You should consult your brother; he's the expert,' Jess suggested pleasantly. 'I only work for the sort of non-Venetians that he objects to. Perhaps you object to them too?'

'We *all* do,' Claudia insisted, co-opting her parents into Marco's protest movement. 'It doesn't matter to *you* what's happening here – I expect you think we should be grateful to rich Americans like the ones who employ you.'

'I already know from Marco that you aren't, but couldn't you both try to remember Mr Acheson's generosity towards Venice? It isn't his fault that he was born an American!' She was sure now that neither housing research nor friendly interest had brought Claudia there, but a clash had somehow to be avoided, because it seemed unthinkable to trade insults with a girl half her own age. Claudia waved aside her suggestion with an expansive gesture copied from Llewellyn.

'People like the Achesons give money they don't miss for reasons of their own – usually to buy their way into what remains of our high society. Unless aristrocrats cheat as Mario Ghisalberti does in order to stay rich, they're always poor and their homes are falling to pieces.'

Jess resented the implication that the Rasinis were among those who could be bought, but she was momentarily checked by the knowledge that she couldn't deny what Claudia had just said. She wasn't at liberty to reveal Nathan's true interest in Venice, and for all this girl knew, patrician friends and neighbours *might* seem to be one of his aspirations when he clearly possessed everything else.

Made happier by the feeling of having scored, Claudia sharpened her attack. 'I expect you're glad to know people like Count Paolo yourself, not being used to them as we are. Giancarlo will be *il Conte* one day.'

'So he will, but not for a long time yet, I hope. I'd like his grandfather to live for ever.'

This half-sister was maddeningly hard to pin down, frustratingly difficult to quarrel with for someone who was accustomed to the immediate flash of tinder against spark. Her English blood made the difference, Claudia supposed – they were known to be *flemmatico*; but it was a difference that she was finding it unexpectedly hard to deal with.

'I knew you were much older than us,' she now pointed out, abandoning finesse, 'but I'd imagined a *little* resemblance, even allowing for your English mother.'

No less than the rest of Llewellyn's family, Jess realised, this member of it was anxious not to let their inconvenient relative imagine that she was welcome in Venice. Given her own reluctance to meet *them*, such relentless discouragement had its comic side, but to her surprise there was grief in it now as well; she would have liked them to accept her.

'We'll agree on not young,' she answered wryly, 'and nothing like the Matthiases. If that's what you came to be sure of, you can safely go back to your work, and I can return to mine.'

'It's *not* what I came for.' The denial was sharp and swift, rejecting the raft of humour that Jess had mistakenly struggled to cling to. Claudia's preference was always to relish the dramatic possibilities of life; the other player in this scene was performing it differently and throwing her off her stride. None of the advantages were on Jessica's side – she hadn't even been born with the sacramental blessing of Church and God Almighty on her true parents; it was all wrong that she could still sound serene, and faintly amused.

'I've come to say what Llewellyn *won't* say because he feels guilty about you,' Claudia blurted out. 'This house was promised to Marco's *gruppo*; they know you're here, and they know his connection with you because he was foolish enough to tell them about it. They think they understand why he wouldn't join in painting the mooring-poles, and next they'll be saying he's been bought by these rich Americans you work for.'

'Could they be as stupid as that?' Jess asked reasonably. 'I should have thought it was perfectly obvious that he's unbuyable – by *anyone*.'

Balked of an objection there, Claudia had to change tack. 'Llewellyn's paintings help to keep the *palazzo* next door watertight. It seemed fair if Lorenza was going to live there one day, and that was certainly what the whole neighbourhood thought would happen. She waited for Giancarlo to recover from the death of the French girl, and pretended not to take any notice of Battistina's silly gossip about you and him. But seeing you together last night changed that. She refuses to go to the Acheson's ball now, and she *wanted* to, more than anything.'

Jess wished it needn't matter, but it did. The angry pain she'd seen in Lorenza's eyes was for the dream of much more than an evening out that was finally being given up.

'Giancarlo has been kind – probably to please his grandparents,' she pointed out gently, wondering how true that was. He'd been a charmingly attentive escort at the concert, which would be his behaviour to any woman he was with; but there had been more warmth in it than that. He'd taken her hand on the way home, to guide her up a flight of steps over a canal; but they'd walked the rest of the way like that . . . and if he'd found that a comfort, so had she.

Claudia's impatient shrug dismissed the Count and Countess as a red herring, before she changed course again. 'Llewellyn's rather enchanted with himself for having fathered another daughter, but Mamma now has to know that he had a different life in London – another woman that he loved. That isn't very pleasant for *her*.'

It was probably true, Jess reflected, but Maria's sad watchfulness at the Countess's dinner party hadn't been on her own account. Contentment for *her* was bound up in the well-being of her family, and she could perhaps see it threatened now, in one way or another, by the very woman Llewellyn would have liked to foist on them. Jess put the memory of Maria aside and braced herself for what was certain to be the most painful bone of contention of all. It came at last but not in the way she expected. If it hadn't seemed so inconceivable, she might have imagined that for a moment her young half-sister sounded sorry for her.

'I suppose the poor things can't help it, but Llewellyn always *says* that Anglo-Saxons go a bit mad in Venice.'

'I've been trying not to,' Jess suggested cautiously, hoping that that was true as well.

'It's not something *you* can judge,' she was informed with a fresh hint of sharpness. 'After all, Giancarlo isn't the only one you've been throwing yourself at – there's poor Jacques as well.'

They'd reached it now, Jess realised – the nub of the matter; the compulsion behind Claudia's visit.

'Has Jacques complained?' she asked in a carefully neutral voice.

'Of course not – he wouldn't. It was Daniele who told me about your visit to Burano.' She fidgeted with some pencils on the table in front of her, eyes looking down at them, and lashes making a dark fan against the creamy softness of her skin. Jess saw clearly how young she was, and how vulnerable. It would be easy to hate Jacques if he didn't understand this himself, and simply took whatever was offered. Casting about for what might be truthful without causing hurt, Jess lost her chance; Claudia was speaking again herself.

'It was an upsetting day for you – Jacques would have wanted to be kind . . . it's one of the things I love about him.' She smiled suddenly for the pleasure of saying that, and Jess could see her for the girl she was – Maria's kindness and Llewellyn's vivid intelligence combined in a mixture that a man would have to be blind not to find irresistible.

'He has to go to Paris,' Claudia went on, 'to discuss the book with his publisher friend . . . well, it's *our* book, he says, because I've written captions that Monsieur Clément likes. I'm going with him, of course, and we're also going to take Lorenza, to give her a change from Venice.'

'You've been very helpful, I'm told,' Jess observed after a small pause, in a voice that didn't tremble.

'Jacques *needed* help, especially when he first came; but it's just that we've found we can work perfectly together.'

'He won't always be here,' Jess took the risk of pointing out. 'He said something about New York . . . other places as well.' But even as she made the suggestion she knew with desolate certainty what was coming next. The mixture of delight and triumph in the flushed face opposite her made it clear.

'I shall be going with him to New York; I shall stay with him always. He pretends that he'll be able to manage without me, but only because he feels obliged to. I'm supposed to want a younger man, who doesn't have damaged legs, and women he knew before he came to Venice. As if any of that matters.'

Jess listened to the echo of that bright, proud confidence in the quiet room . . . compared it with her own expressed longing to settle down; how unintrepid she must have sounded . . . how suburban, she could imagine Elizabeth Harrington saying with a grimace of distaste. Claudia rushed on, made insistent by her listener's silence.

'You're English – well, half anyway – and probably rather set in your ways, and unable to understand that I don't want anything for myself – only to help Jacques. We aren't quite lovers yet, of course, because he's afraid Mamma would think he was behaving badly. But away from Venice we can be everything to each other and I shall make sure he never needs another woman.'

Numbly, Jess acknowledged to herself that this ardent, passionate girl was capable of doing exactly what she said. In response, what could Jessica Smythson safely claim? That being English didn't exclude her from the desires of normal women? That, instead of mere kindness, the most enchanted ease and intimacy had briefly gilded her Burano visit with Jacques? But perhaps that was only how it had seemed to her; perhaps every woman he met was required to fall a little in love with him. She couldn't be certain of any of *these* things, but she was heartbreakingly sure of something else; his airy claim that Claudia's attachment to him was an adolescent's passing whim was either wildly wrong or deliberately deceitful. Like the rest of Llewellyn's children, this one did nothing by halves; she would live and die loving Jacques Duclos unless he ever chose to make her hate him instead.

At last, aware that it was her turn to say something, Jess forced her brain to frame a crucial question. 'Has Jacques asked you to go with him to New York?'

'Not in so many words,' Claudia confessed almost shyly. 'He pretends that he ought to make me promise to stay here. We rather joke about it but I know he guesses – it's why he looks so happy whenever he mentions New York.'

Jess didn't answer for a moment; instead she busied herself with writing something on a scrap of paper which she slid across the table.

'My grandmother's name and address – call on her when you eventually get to Manhattan, and give her my love. She was a brilliant journalist herself, and she's still in a position to give you a great deal of help – you *and* Jacques.'

Claudia folded the paper carefully and stowed it in her pocket, not sure why she didn't feel happier with the way the interview had gone. She'd said what she meant to say . . . now and then perhaps a little more than she'd quite been justified in saying; still, as Llewellyn always said, when the stakes were very high, one had to play for death or glory.

'You'll be glad to get back to London,' she suggested almost kindly now. 'I expect it's where *you* belong, although Jacques says it strikes a Frenchman as being a very unsympathetic city. He reckons the Entente Cordiale never amounted to much either!'

'I'm sure he's right,' Jess agreed briefly, unable to listen to any more of his views about the English. 'Now, hadn't you better go and get on with your housing report? It's time we said goodbye.'

Claudia nodded, trying not to feel dismissed. She would have preferred to be the one to end the conversation, but Llewellyn's other daughter had already turned her attention back to the sketch in her hand, and there was nothing left to do but walk away.

Alone at last, Jess went doggedly on with her work, but when the long day was over she made the detour that was becoming habitual on her way back to the hotel. From the high, central span of the Accademia bridge, she could see the great, final curve of the Grand Canal. It was the view that every visitor to Venice knew and every artist painted. Even on a damp and dismal evening in late February it should have looked beautiful. But she seemed to be staring at a theatre backdrop, not a living city. Too many of the palaces lining each bank were shuttered or dark. Lights were needed to throw their brightness on the moving water, but warmth, and music, and laughter had fled too long ago, leaving only emptiness behind.

She was trapped for a moment in the sensation she'd experienced at Donna Emilia's dinner table. Whatever Giancarlo might say about the safety of the city, the play *was* nearly over. The thousand-year performance had been glorious – she could imagine it in her mind's eye – but the ending was in sight. The great argosies, laden with silks and spices from the East, had long since moored along the Zattere for the last time; the Doge's golden *bucintoro* would never again set out on Ascension Day for its wedding assignation with the sea.

Someone brushed against her, dispelling the bright vision of the past. There was no brilliant colour after all, no cheering crowds, no clamour of church bells. She was alone and lonely in the cold dusk, in a beautiful but dying city. It seemed an appropriate place in which to have had her own brief, inconsequential dream. Now she need only go back to her room and write a neat *finis* to it – a letter to Jacques that would effectively tie up the loose ends left by their Burano conversation. So much agonising there'd been about it, but it had been unnecessary after all. A harsh, half-hysterical laugh was shaken out of her, disturbing another passer-by; and because she was being stared at, she hurriedly turned away.

Chapter 18

Morning was dawning earlier now, with a hint of softness in the air. It seemed to promise that, if not yet quite a fact, the return of spring was at least becoming more likely day by day.

Outside the hotel after breakfast, Jess suddenly changed her mind. The intricate draping of yards of muslin at Elvira's bedroom windows could wait for an hour; first she needed a walk along the Zattere. There'd been a stupid moment of faintness yesterday, born of tiredness and strain. She'd almost overbalanced, measuring windows on a ladder, and only saved herself at the expense of a sprained wrist that was now strapped up. She told herself that it was fresh air she was short of.

She passed small groups of Sunday worshippers – women, mostly – making for Mass at Sant' Agnese or San Spirito. They called out a greeting, having grown used to seeing the tall *Inglese* walking about the neighbourhood; she wasn't one of them, *naturalmente*, but they liked the look of her nevertheless.

Jess stood on the wide pathway for a while, watching the mother-of-pearl colours of the water deepen as the sun rose. It seemed very strange that soon she wouldn't be there to marvel at the perfect composition made by San Giorgio Maggiore, set between sea and sky. She was on the horns of her usual dilemma, unable to decide what she wanted most – to stay for ever or run away.

'*Buon giorno,*' said a quiet voice behind her.

She swung round to see Count Paolo raising his ancient hat. 'I have a sick friend to visit,' he explained, 'but may I escort you somewhere first?'

'Thank you, but I'm only on my way to the *palazzo* for a morning's work.'

'On a Sunday? Can the *signora* be as unreasonable as this?'

She smiled at his shocked expression and shook her head. 'Don't blame Mrs Acheson. It's I who am in a hurry to finish, but I also rather enjoy having that lovely old building to myself . . . all its ghosts feel friendly to me!'

The Count nodded, not finding this strange, but another anxiety remained. 'You were looking sad when I arrived – Venice is not to blame for *that*, I hope. And, my dear, I see that you have damaged yourself.'

She spread out one thin hand, encompassing the view all round them. 'I was saying goodbye . . . not to the famous buildings that everybody knows, but to the hidden alleyways and shabby, perfect squares. Each one is complete – parish church in one corner, old stone well-head in the middle, hump-backed bridge, and green canal wandering by . . . Venice in miniature!'

'You're afraid these things won't still be here when you come back? My dear, Giancarlo and his colleagues will see to it – they devote their lives to keeping the Serenissima safe for us.'

'I know,' Jess agreed, unable to disturb him by pointing out that some of the city's problems might defeat even them. She hesitated a moment, then offered her friend a different truth. 'My worst doubt is about whether to come back at all. It's often a mistake to repeat certain experiences, and I feel Venice might be one of them for me. I read somewhere that one should never form attachments because they "jar with Fate"!' She saw sadness in *his* face, and thought he remembered his own lost attachments. 'It's pure selfishness,' she added hurriedly, 'not wanting the little gap I might leave here to have disappeared even before my plane touches down at Heathrow. It's mistaken pride in fact – expecting Venice to notice that I've gone at all!'

Paolo shook his head. 'I know from Emilia that the gap will never disappear for your father, nor will it for us. Because of you, Giancarlo has learned to appreciate Llewellyn, and I, instead of disapproving of the little enterprise he runs with Emilia, now see *his* generosity and my wife's sound Venetian instincts! That is much to have achieved, but you've given us great pleasure as well. We shall all miss you, Jessica.'

The affection in his voice touched her to the point of tears, but there was something else as well – some hope relinquished that had seemed promising for a while. *Damn* busy, well-meaning Battistina and all the neighbour ladies who listened to her. Jess longed to insist that the hope had never been real – Giancarlo had emerged from his shell simply *because* Jessica Smythson wasn't any threat to the austere life he'd chosen for himself. Well, thank God it was so; otherwise he'd be someone else whose peace of mind Claudia could tell her she'd wantonly destroyed.

She took herself in hand enough to turn and face her friend. In the bright morning light he looked old and frail, and his eyes were full of some knowledge that she didn't have. If she left it too long to come back again, he wouldn't be here. There was aching sadness in the thought, but she drove it away to smile at him.

'I'll call to say goodbye to Countess Emilia.'

He lifted his hat again, gave his little bow, and walked away. There was nothing to keep her standing there – she need only command her feet to move; but she was suddenly assailed by all the memories she wouldn't be able to leave behind when her homeward plane soared away from the Lagoon. She'd managed – rather brilliantly, she thought – to shut away the recollection of Claudia's visit. Now it was flooding over her in a wave of angry pain, and jealousy that finally had to be admitted to. The girl had what she lacked herself – youth, beauty, and a hunger for adventure. Above all, she had the single-mindedness of vision that young love inspired. No one else's needs, no ties, no duties would hold *her* back from going with Jacques wherever he went. Jess thought of them together in Paris or New York – thought deliberately to blot out the vision in her mind of his smile and his kiss on the quayside at Burano. She hadn't imagined the joy of it – shared at the time, her heart still insisted, while he forgot for a moment the web of kindness and family affection in which he'd become ensnared. He hadn't set out to capture Claudia's passionate heart, but it had happened, and to fight over him with a sister half her age was unthinkable. Her letter would have reached him by now, making light of a few moments he probably regretted. She could imagine him breathing a sigh of relief – the silly English creature hadn't taken him seriously after all, thank God; one complication the less!

Jess pushed the intolerable thought aside and swung blindly round to start walking again. She cannoned into an unnoticed bollard beside her and felt pain surge up her leg from ankle to knee. She clung for a moment to the lump of stone that had hurt her, torn between the need to laugh or burst into tears. What might she do next – tumble headlong into a canal? A passer-by stopped, looking concerned, but she managed to mutter, '*Fa niente, grazie.*'

She was almost unaware of a boat slowing down, reversing, and idling until its young driver leapt out on to the planking, holding a mooring rope. He inspected her white face, and trembling hands still clutched round the bollard.

'You've hurt yourself. Where shall I take you – to the hospital?'

'Not necessary, Marco, thank you. I banged my leg and will probably have a colourful bruise to show for it, but I'm perfectly all right now . . . ready to walk back to the *palazzo*.' She smiled to prove it, unaware that it seemed to make her air of distress all the more noticeable.

'I have two other islands to visit,' he said abruptly. 'It's a good morning to be out in the Lagoon . . . if you'd like to come with me.'

He made the offer as if he expected it to be refused, and Jess thought that it was certainly what she intended. But she heard herself say, instead, 'Yes, I *would* like to.'

She was helped into the boat, wondering what madness had possessed her to share the morning with one of the people she most wanted to avoid. Nor was Marco's expression encouraging as he offered her a reefer jacket to supplement the thin tweed she was wearing. It wasn't, she thought, going to be a talkative journey; he was probably silent from habit, living in a household that included Llewellyn and Claudia. But he surprised her by suddenly launching into words that had a belligerent edge to them.

'I'm supposed to be grateful to you . . . for talking about me to Nathan Acheson.'

'But you'd rather *not* be, of course,' Jess suggested sharply. It was all the day needed – another reminder of how little she was wanted there.

His thick brows drew together into a straight black line. 'You shouldn't have bothered. I'm not a child to be let off some punishment I'm thought to deserve.'

'No . . . you're an uncommonly stubborn thorn in the flesh of anyone who might want to help you.'

He blinked at the unexpectedness of the attack. Anticipating tactful agreement, he had the feeling that he'd poked a sleeping tigress by mistake; but pride refused to let him yield any ground.

'Such help is another word for interference, in our view, especially from foreigners. All we ask is to be left alone, to deal with our problems in our own way.'

'And while you argue, and *fail* to deal with them,' Jess pointed out, 'Venice will crumble into a dying lagoon and lose the last of its young people to the mainland. Co-operation may not be what springs naturally to the minds of a nation of last-ditch individualists, but couldn't you at least give it a try?'

He stared at her for a moment, painfully aware now as he had been at their first meeting that differences of age, environment, and even some opposing inherited genes made her not as he and his sisters were. The result was to leave him at a disadvantage he resented.

'I expect you find us laughable,' he said at last. 'We're good at making ice-cream, and designing clothes and beautiful, fast cars, but hopeless at something serious, like governing ourselves. Well, I think I *know* what Venice needs.'

'Then talk to Nathan Acheson, please. He's a highly successful businessman, and however much you may resent it, he has the power to help you get things done.'

But there was no change in Marco's expression of mulish obstinacy and, defeated by it, she refused to repeat her plea; this likeable but pig-headed youngster must go to perdition in his own way. Instead she asked where they were heading. Marco pointed to the island they were approaching.

'There you are – San Lazzaro; as the name says, it was our leper colony once upon a time, but it's been home to generations of Armenian monks for a couple of hundred years. They're rather jolly as monks go, and disposed to like the English because they remember Lord Byron very kindly.'

'Which is more than can be said of most of his Italian watering-places,' Jess admitted.

Marco was almost surprised into a grin, but he remembered just in time that his intention had only been to help Llewellyn's English daughter, not to enjoy her company.

'The Armenians have always been great printers and binders,' he explained stiffly. 'I've come to collect a book for my uncle.'

Jess allowed him to land alone, sensing that he would prefer it, and content in any case to rest her bruised shin-bone. He was soon back, pointing the boat this time towards a very different landfall – the bell-haunted seclusion of San Francesco del Deserto. It seemed an unlikely place to appeal to Llewellyn's son, but she doubted if Marco ever resembled his flamboyant father.

Here, he had something to deliver, he explained – a painting of the monks' patron saint that Llewellyn had had cleaned and reframed for them. It seemed so beautiful and peaceful a place that Jess was sorry to leave, but when they'd said goodbye to the gentle Franciscans and were moving homewards again she asked the question that exercised her mind. 'Brother wind . . . sister water – it's an admirable way of life, but not one that I could manage; what about you?'

She saw Marco's shoulders lift in the gesture she was becoming familiar with. 'I've got different work to do. But in twenty years' time when I can't stand the madhouse of our politics any longer I might find myself begging the brothers back there to let me in!' His brief smile appeared, but his eyes looked sad; the silver-coloured lagoon, its secret islands and sandbanks and changing channels, were all known and deeply loved. He belonged here, and the grief of going away was something he was already having to struggle to accept.

'Is *that* your future – politics?' Jess asked.

Marco frowned over the question, but it had been asked gently, and with interest; not as if she were laughing at an ambition that seemed ridiculous.

'I'll be twenty-five in three months' time – old enough to offer myself as a socialist candidate. But I haven't spoken of it at home yet, or told my uncle. Zio Pietro will disapprove – he has no time for politicians.

'Llewllyn will expect everyone to vote for you, and so will your mother, although privately I'm afraid she'll be praying that you *don't* end up in the den of vipers that Rome is known to be!'

'Perhaps,' Marco agreed with a faint smile, 'but she'll decide in the end that since the Blessed Virgin Mary's influence can't help being very strong in the Eternal City, I shall be watched over well enough!'

Jess imagined it to be the end of the conversation; now they would head back for Venice and, once landed, Marco could hurry away from his unwanted passenger. Instead, she saw him steer towards one of the clumps of wooden posts marking the channel they were in. He made the boat fast and then, with an unexpectedly charming grin, produced a wicker basket.

'It's one of my mother's few rules in life, and actually a very sensible one: never trust yourself to this unpredictable stretch of water without food and warm clothing!'

He unwrapped ham and bread and olives, and apologised for the fact that a thermos of coffee wouldn't be any substitute for a glass of good red wine. Jess agreed but accepted the food gratefully; her appetite had been sharpened by the sea air, and earlier desolation was somehow tempered by she didn't know quite what – perhaps the brief call at the Franciscans' peaceful sanctuary, perhaps some change in her companion; his hostility had also been abandoned, and now she sensed in him not only the need to talk, but also some hidden warmth towards herself.

'We aren't going to the Achesons' ball,' he said abruptly. 'Llewellyn wanted to, of course, and so did my sisters until they suddenly changed their minds; but it will be a stupid extravagant affair, just intended to impress people.'

'You're very severe,' Jess pointed out. 'Rule number one for a budding politician – remember that most of your voters will continue to want to enjoy their cakes and ale even if *thou* art virtuous!'

'Shakespeare, I suppose. He died a long time ago.'

'Very true . . . we needn't give him a moment's thought.' The Bard disposed of, Jess returned to watching a sea bird perch on the neighbouring clump of *bricole*, while it assessed its chance of getting the remains of the picnic.

'Is it an English habit . . . to smile without smiling?' Marco suddenly asked. '*You* do it, I've noticed, but Llewellyn doesn't. In fact, he's bad-tempered altogether at the moment – not smiling at all. Mr Acheson has asked him to paint a picture, but it isn't going well, Mamma says. She wishes the commission hadn't happened.'

Jess threw the last of her bread to the waiting bird, then turned to face Marco, determined that if this was to be their last conversation he should finally understand her. 'Claudia came to see me yesterday. She didn't mention the painting, but she told me that I've upset your mother for a different reason. I've also made difficulties for you with your friends, and hurt Lorenza deeply into the bargain. I didn't mean to do any of these things – I came here intending never to see any of you at all, and that is what *should* have happened.' The list of sins omitted any reference to Claudia herself and Jacques; not even to Marco could she mention them.

He took a long time to answer what she'd said. 'You don't have to pay too much attention to my little sister. Mamma understands

Llewellyn . . . after all, she chose him instead of the rich undertaker my grandmother had picked out as a son-in-law! We're all very glad she did, as a matter of fact.'

'*Anyone* but an undertaker,' Jess agreed, smiling in spite of herself. But she grew serious again. 'Lorenza is certainly unhappy, though . . . I saw her at La Pietà, and was made to feel to blame.'

'You shouldn't have been – she was like that long before you came . . . it's time she forgot about Giancarlo. Mamma realises that, and so does Jacques – it's why he's taking her and Claudia to Paris. She needs to get away from all the people here she thinks feel sorry for her.' Marco carefully poured out coffee and handed Jess a mug. 'We didn't know what to make of Jacques when he first arrived. Mamma was very anxious, because it soon became clear that Claudia was going to fall in love with him. But it's all right now – he'll take care of her, and let her think that *she's* taking care of him!'

'It sounds a very neat arrangement,' Jess managed to agree.

Aware of the sudden sadness in her face, Marco added a diffident little apology for his sister. 'I expect Claudia sounded bossy when she came to see you . . . she always does think that she knows best. But you needn't take notice of at least half of what she says – we never do.'

She drank her coffee so as not to have to answer, and finally, to her relief, Marco set them moving again. They travelled without talking until he'd steered them back into the Rio della Fornace beside the *palazzo*, but on terra firma again she kept hold for a moment of the hand he held out.

'Thank you for that outing . . . I enjoyed it . . . needed it, in fact! Now I'm going to ask you to do something else for me. Go and see Nathan Acheson, please, *not* looking as if you refuse to believe a word he says, but ready to listen. It's my impression that he wants to help you, and he certainly can – so *let* him, won't you?'

Marco's eyes inspected her face – she looked less pale and strained now; he was glad he'd taken her out with him. They'd been wrong about her all along, though he hadn't ever meant to think that when Llewellyn first owned up to having an English daughter. He would have liked to say so, but the words on his tongue somehow didn't sound like the ones in his mind.

'When will you be going home?'

Her faint, wry smile acknowledged how anxious they still were to get rid of her. 'Very soon – you won't have to put up with me much longer. *Ciao*, Marco!'

She'd let herself in through the gate and walked away while he was still working out where he'd gone wrong. He returned unhappily to his boat and puttered slowly home, thinking that his mother was right as usual – she always said that it was very easy to hurt other people, even without meaning to. He'd wanted to help Jessica, suspected that it would be easy to learn to love her almost as he loved Lorenza and Claudia. But he'd hurt her instead.

Chapter 19

Battistina always longed for Monday to come round again. The weekend loosened her finger on the pulse of local events, and an early tour of the neighbourhood was required to catch up on anything that had escaped her.

So it was this morning, but she was fortunate – her call at the *fornaio's* was well timed, coinciding with Bianca Bruni's. Now, along with *il caro Conte's* favourite bread, there was news to take home as well. Added pleasure – she might even be able to share it with someone sooner; a slight detour across the bridge and she could intercept the family's English friend, spotted on the far side of the *rio*.

'*Buon giorno, signorina* . . . I hear the servants for the Palazzo Ghisalberti have been chosen. Well, Bianca Bruni deserves some good fortune – any woman does who marries a Neapolitan! But I hope the Signora Acheson understands what that means?'

Unable to speak for Elvira and not sure what it meant herself, Jess decided not to ask. Letting Battistina for once have to guess what other people knew, or didn't know. She murmured instead that she was late for an appointment and hurried away before they could move on to what was probably coming next – some hopeful query about her own next outing with Giancarlo.

But inside the *palazzo* five minutes later, Luigi confirmed that this time Battistina's information was at least correct. The *signora* had telephoned to say that the new housekeeper was coming to be shown the empty apartment on the top floor.

'We've had a visitor already this morning,' Luigi went on. 'He was disappointed not to see you, but Signor Llewellyn said you'd understand. He needed to see where the picture he's supposed to be painting is going to hang. I showed him the *signora's portego*, and suddenly he began to smile as if he liked the look of it . . . well, it *is* very beautiful.'

Jess listened to the longest and most complimentary speech she'd heard Luigi make, but she was remembering what Marco had said about their father. Coming to inspect the room wasn't an odd thing for him to have done; and it was only worrying if it meant that he still couldn't bring himself to start painting. But if he'd gone away looking cheerful, there was that much comfort to cling to.

An hour later, in the middle of supervising the hanging of a beautiful Venetian mirror in Elvira's bedroom, she was interrupted by one of the workmen, ushering in the nervous woman he'd found hesitating outside.

'I can come again,' Bianca Bruni suggested, having introduced herself almost inaudibly, 'if the moment is bad . . .'

'The moment for looking at your new home can't possibly be bad,' Jess said with a friendly smile. 'Let's go upstairs; after that I'll show you round down here.'

She led the way to the floor above, expecting the apartment's bright, light-filled rooms to please the silent woman by her side, but Bianca didn't even smile. Only the gleaming bathroom that they reached last broke through her defences and then a prayer muttered in Italian was torn out of her. 'Mother of God, *please* let us stay.'

She saw from Jess's face that the prayer had been heard and understood, and a faint tinge of colour brought her gaunt face to life. 'Often we *haven't* been able to stay,' she felt obliged to admit quietly.

Their failures could have been nothing to do with her, Jess wanted to say. Bianca Bruni had the look of a woman who would work until she dropped, and covet nothing she didn't own . . . except perhaps the unattainable gift of security. Unaware that her hand still stroked the basin's shining taps, the visitor suddenly felt compelled to explain things to this stranger whose smile was kind.

'The *signora* will hear what people say about my husband; perhaps *you* could tell her first . . . explain a little, please. Giuseppe is a good worker, but he was a child in Naples after the war. They were *taught* to steal . . . just to stay alive, you understand. Now it's a habit with him; not stealing exactly . . . just not letting go to waste the things that other people are fools enough to leave lying about.'

Keeping Venice tidy, Jess thought, with a flicker of amusement she wished she could share; but the grief in Bianca's face didn't allow for humour, and it was doubtful whether Elvira would appreciate the nice distinction Guiseppe's wife made about his habits if things started disappearing from the *palazzo*.

'The *signora* doesn't understand enough Italian to listen to what people say,' Jess explained gently. 'She will only know what happens *here*. If you can get your husband to remember that, I'm sure you'll be able to stay. Now come downstairs and have some coffee with us.'

Bianca obediently followed her, even though the friendly suggestion seemed very strange. Being led to the kitchen reassured her, but she said very little until it was time to leave. Then she pointed to the crates of china and glass, obviously waiting to be unpacked, that occupied most of the floor space.

'*Signorina*, we are to be told by the *signora* when to move in . . . perhaps in one week, she said. But already there is work here that we

152

can do. We would rather work than be paid for doing nothing.'

Life might have made her anxious, but pride was still intact, Jess noticed with pleasure. 'Come tomorrow,' she suggested. 'I shall have explained to Signora Acheson by then that some help would be very welcome.'

Bianca's tight mouth managed a rare, shy smile before she went away to explain to Guiseppe the miracle that the Blessed Virgin had sent them.

Jess debated what, if anything, to say to Elvira about her light-fingered Neapolitan, and hadn't made up her mind by the time the lady herself walked into the *palazzo*. With her great party only a few days away, the call was unexpected, and Jess tried to guess from her expression what had caused it. Describing the housekeeper's visit, she made no mention at first of Guiseppe – simply ventured the opinion that the flat upstairs had looked to Bianca like the Kingdom of Heaven itself.

'So would it to you,' Elvira pointed out, 'if you'd seen what they live in at the moment.' She glanced around the room they were in – her own new bedroom – where Jess had been coaxing cascades of snowy muslin at the windows into beautiful folds and drapings. Then she fixed shrewd blue eyes on her interior designer.

'You look tired . . . no wonder, with all your family fuss on top of the work you've done here. We shall have the loveliest home in Venice, but I'm afraid I haven't admitted that until now, for one reason or another.'

'Because you're still not sure of liking the place,' Jess pointed out with a faint smile. 'Why *should* you feel grateful?'

'I'm sure now, at least, of having to get used to it. I didn't understand what it meant to Nathan, but now I know the reason he's here. I'll not say what it is, but it changes things.' With a kind of dogged honesty, she made herself go on. 'I could see straightaway that he'd love what you've made of the *palazzo*, and that made things worse. I was afraid he'd *want* to stay when I didn't. But he understands that I only feel safe here with him.'

Jess was distracted for a moment by the realisation of what she'd been trusted with – Nathan had expected her *not* to tell Elvira that she knew about his daughter. But it was probably how men like Nathan succeeded – knowing when and where to put their trust.

'I'm glad you'll have the Brunis here when you're away,' she said diffidently. 'I gathered from Bianca that their life has been hard, partly because Venetians and Neapolitans don't always mix very happily. Guiseppe has been a . . . a worry to her, even though she's rather proud of him.'

It was Elvira's turn to smile. 'Tactful Jess! I've known immigrant Italians like him in New York. I shall keep an eye on him and, as he's already promised me, his life will be ours from now on!' She hesitated for a moment and then went on almost shyly. 'I'm going to start looking after myself as well – begin by taking Italian lessons, and a course in Venetian history. I even aim to wipe the eye of Count Paolo with my expertise before I've done!'

'Good for you,' said Jess, and meant it. Amid the emotional turmoil of these weeks in Venice, her failure to get on with her employer had seemed almost trivial, but it had been a disappointment nevertheless. It was a pleasure to be in harmony with her again.

'I must go,' Elvira announced. 'Our costumes for the party are being delivered this morning. I rather favoured the idea of Caesar and Cleopatra, but I couldn't get Nathan to take it seriously. We shall just be beautiful eighteenth-century Venetians instead. What about you?'

'Nothing so grand. A client once taught me how to construct an Indian sari, but I never imagined it would come in useful!'

Elvira's nod approved, and then she smiled and went away, having decided not to ruffle new-found peace by admitting that none of the Matthias family would be gracing the Daniele on Saturday night.

With no ambition to go herself, and very nearly ready to return to London, Jess had seriously considered not staying for the party. She'd mentioned it to Gerald on the telephone, only to have him insist that of course she must stay, and take time to enjoy what she hadn't been able to see of Venice as well. But that evening, instead of her step-father's voice along the wire making his usual call, she heard Pinky Todd – trying to sound calm, but not succeeding very well.

'Jess love, it's me tonight instead of Gerald . . . a little bit of bad news, I'm afraid, but nothing to get in a stew about.'

'Tell me . . . *tell* me, please, quickly.'

'Well, he was taken into hospital last night – a heart attack, Imogen thought. It *wasn't*, Jess, and he's soon going to be allowed home. He'll have to be a bit more careful in future, but angina isn't the end of the world. That's why Imogen didn't ring earlier – not until we were sure.'

Jess eased her grip on the telephone clutched in her hand, and told herself that Pinky was right; there was no need to feel that the foundations on which her life rested had suddenly been kicked away.

'The boss says you're *not* to rush home, Jess.' Pinky's voice filled the silence, sounding firmer now. 'We can manage easily until you've finished there.'

'I almost have. Two more days will do it, but only if you *promise* me he's all right; otherwise I'll fly home tomorrow and come back when I can.'

Pinky insisted – cross her heart and hope to die – that the promise *could* be given, and Jess accepted it. Then, with the conversation at an end, she sat down to force her disordered mind to concentrate on what had yet to be accomplished. There was, thank God, almost nothing still to be delivered, and very little left to do. She could leave Venice, and not have to come back. The memories she must take home with her would fade in time . . . the images and reflections of this water-girdled, hallucinatory place would dwindle and die before long.

Maria set out to climb the stairs to the studio, hesitated, finally changed her mind again. Whatever the reception she might get, Llewellyn couldn't be left there any longer, alone and defeated. For several days past he'd come down to meals wrapped in a silence so morose that even Claudia had been intimidated, and then disappeared again. Maria knew why – the Acheson picture wasn't working.

She pushed open the studio door and, as she feared, saw him standing at the window. But he swung round, and his exhausted face sent her running across the room to put her arms round him.

'*Tesoro* . . . it doesn't matter . . . forget the painting.' Breathless and agitated, she would have gone on but he interrupted her.

'It *does* matter, Maria,' he said unsteadily.

'No, no . . . we'll tell Mr Acheson you changed your mind. I'll telephone now, this morning . . .' Llewellyn's hand was laid gently across her mouth, and then she saw that he was smiling.

'No need to make excuses for me – I've *done* it, *amore* . . . the bloody painting's finished, and this time it's all right.' He swept her into a painful hug and then released her again. 'Come and look.'

Staring a moment later at what was still propped up on the easel, she sent up a little prayer of thankfulness. Yes – even she could see that it was all right; in fact, it was very beautiful.

'I kept on starting again, and each time I tore the bloody thing up failure crept a little closer,' Llewellyn muttered beside her. 'Then, like that chap on the road to Damascus – Saul, wasn't it? – I saw light, and knew what I had to do. I went to the *palazzo* to find out where the damn thing was meant to hang. Jess wasn't there, but the colours she'd chosen for the room *were*, and I came away with the picture in my mind. I shan't even ask Nathan Acheson if he likes it. He knows about oil-wells and such . . . I know about *this*.'

'Jessica will like it,' Maria said suddenly. 'That *I* know, my dear.' She saw Llewellyn smile and felt obliged to be entirely truthful. 'I came close to hating her for this, although I was very ashamed.'

Llewellyn inspected her face for a moment, aware for once even in the midst of his own excitement of a core of sadness that his wife would not admit to. He knew the reason for it, too.

'You're afraid that loving Jessica – as I already do – means that I must have loved her mother a great deal and missed *her* ever since.

155

Sweetheart, apart from the fact that she was a dancer who was beautiful, I can't remember Gillian Carstairs at all.' He cupped Maria's face in his hands to make her look at him and see that he spoke the truth. 'I *can* remember Fanny, but she was a young man's fancy too – all fireworks and summer lightning! You know what I was by the time I crawled into your mother's *pensione* – a failure, rather more dead than alive! But with love and generosity you put me together again ... God knows why; I certainly didn't deserve such good fortune.' He kissed her trembling mouth gently, and then smiled at her. 'Dear heart ... it's all right now, isn't it? Everything's as it should have been at last.'

She nodded, unable to speak, while he mopped away her tears.

'We've been miserable for days, but tonight we'll celebrate, *amore*,' he promised jubilantly. 'But first I must go and bully my old friend, Cesare, into framing my picture for me quickly.' He kissed her again before he let her go, struck by something he hadn't bothered to notice before. Smiling and happy, his dear Maria was very nearly beautiful. It was very careless of him to have missed that until now.

By the late afternoon of her last day, even the missing painting had arrived – brought by Daniele, not by Llewellyn himself. Looking at it installed in its place above the huge hearth, Jess found it hard to believe that the artist had had any doubt or difficulty about it. In the serenest washes of colour – blue, pink, cream and pistachio green – he'd summoned up the essence of a small marine village reflected in the Lagoon in the heat and stillness of a summer afternoon. She watched the contented faces of the men clustered round it, and heard Bianca suddenly murmur beside her, '*Pellestrina – non è vero? Ero nata lassù, io.*'

Pellestrina it undoubtedly was, they all agreed, and Jess understood what their satisfaction meant – they now reckoned that the beautiful room was finally complete. She said goodbye to them with regret, having gradually worked her way through their Venetian wariness and reserve to real warmth and friendship. Bianca was also finally prevailed upon to go home, and she was left alone in the great house for the last time, to finish writing her report.

She was making a final tour of the rooms when a knock sounded on the door above the outer staircase. Llewellyn, perhaps, or even Count Paolo? She no longer wondered if it could possibly be Jacques ... didn't know whether he was already in Paris by now. But it was Nathan Acheson who stood waiting there.

'I hoped I'd catch you still here, but I was afraid of startling you if I just let myself in.'

'I was almost on the point of leaving,' Jess explained. 'I couldn't resist a last look round, but at least it means I can give you my final report, instead of delivering it to the Danieli.'

Nathan's expression was gravely kind. 'Elvira told me your news about Gerald Smythson when I got back from a visit to the mainland. We are so very sorry, Jessica.'

'Thank you, but he's been allowed home – I rang again at lunchtime – so I'm able to sound calm and optimistic. Everything that I can do here has been done, and there was even an unexpected bonus this afternoon . . . may I show you?'

She led him to the *portego*, but waited until he'd had a chance to look at the painting before she went to join him.

'Bianca recognised it – she was born on Pellestrina.'

After a long pause Nathan replied, 'I'm tempted to say that your father shouldn't be working here, in a provincial backwater. On the other hand, here without doubt is what he can paint so magically. I knew the picture was ready, by the way – there was a note waiting for me at the Danieli. He will accept no payment for it – it's to be a gift, he says.'

Jess's smile transfigured her tired face. 'Llewellyn's way of relieving them of the obligation they feel towards you because of your kindness to Marco – how typical of him!' She was suddenly afraid that the man beside her would misunderstand and make the mistake of refusing the gift, but as if he read her mind, Nathan shook his head.

'It's a rare pleasure for me – I'm usually expected to be the one who gives!'

But afterwards, walking down the staircase with him, she thought that there was probably another reason for the gift – Llewellyn had been making a libation to the gods for having rescued him from failure.

She persuaded Nathan that he could safely leave her where their route diverged, and said goodbye to him with the feeling that she was parting from a friend. Now she could either walk back to the hotel, pack, and go to bed; or she could listen to a small, insistent voice in her mind telling her that there was something else left to do. When her feet obeyed it by trudging past the bridge she should have crossed, she knew the choice had been made; her packing would have to wait a little longer.

Chapter 20

The last lamp along the pathway showed her the name she was looking for – the Pensione Alberoni; but the house was more imposing than she'd imagined, standing behind yet another unexpected Venetian garden. The door was opened by a stranger – a domestic of some kind, judging by the starched apron she wore – and Jess flogged her brain for Italian words to explain her visit. She'd scarcely embarked on them when another door opened inside, and Llewellyn himself walked into the hall.

'Jessica . . . my dear girl, come *in*.' He hurried towards her, hands held out in welcome. 'I'll tell Maria you're here – she's in the kitchen trying out some new Italian dish or other.'

'No . . . don't interrupt her, please. I only came to . . . to say goodbye to *you*. I'm leaving for London in the morning.' She stood in the lit porch, unaware of the extreme whiteness of her face and her exhausted air. 'I still have to go back to the hotel to pack.'

'Something's wrong. Don't stand there, girl – I insist on a glass of wine at least while you tell me what it is.'

She was led inside the hall, to a small, comfortable room that had the look of a study. Llewellyn pushed her gently into a chair, and heard the little sigh of relief she couldn't help giving.

'I had a telephone call from London two nights ago,' she explained, trying to sound calm. 'Gerald had had what seemed to be a heart attack. It wasn't that, although he must learn to live with angina from now on. I've spent the last two days rather frantically clearing up so that I can go home tomorrow. If I'd worked a bit harder all along I could have finished sooner . . . stopped him doing too much without me.' Her voice broke a little, and Llewellyn gave her hand a little pat.

'Wait, my dear – I'll be back in a moment,' he said, and disappeared.

She did as she was told, suddenly grateful to have someone else tell her what she must do – because tiredness and anxiety and regret were combining in a wave that threatened to overwhelm her.

'The others are out,' he explained, as he bustled back into the room. 'Claudia dragged them off to some Carnival *spettacolo*. Now, drink a little wine, my dear, and stop worrying. Gerald's a comparatively young man, and I'd guess his life has been entirely

159

blameless – free of every kind of wicked excess! There's no reason at all why he shouldn't recover.'

Jess nodded, sipping as instructed, but trying to focus her mind on what he'd just said. 'Marco mentioned something about Paris . . . I thought they would have gone by now.'

'They leave on Saturday – Jacques' idea to distract them from not going to Elvira's party. It's the sort of thing he *would* think of, because he seems to have become part of the family. Even Lorenza's getting excited about going, and God knows it's time she did.'

Jess drank her wine, half anxious to leave, half wanting to stay. 'The painting is beautiful – Nathan Acheson thinks so too, and he's also very touched to have been given it.'

Llewellyn's grin flashed. 'I like taking very important people by surprise!' Then he grew serious again. 'Have Marco's bloody silly goings-on made things difficult for you with the Achesons?'

'It's not all *his* fault,' Jess confessed. 'I haven't helped by finding myself suddenly out of sympathy with the goings-on of the super-rich! Though I'm bound to say that Nathan Acheson isn't a man to give millionaires a bad name; quite the reverse, in fact.'

Llewellyn poured more wine into her glass. 'I gathered that – he came here one morning, and Maria was terrified, but by the time he left she'd fallen in love with him. She thinks that he even wants to help Marco. If so, I suspect we have you to thank. Powerful Americans aren't noted for their kindness towards impertinent young men who get in their way. I know you've got to go now, but you will come back, Jess, won't you?' he asked suddenly. 'Dammit, girl, I *insist* on it.' His voice was richly emotional, but she no longer thought him theatrical or absurd. He was as he'd been made, and she even recognised in him things that she hadn't understood were in herself.

But unable to point out that his other children might never want her any more than they did now, she gave a faint nod and put down her glass. 'Say goodbye to Maria for me. If I don't go and get packed I shall fall asleep on my feet!'

He stared at her for a moment, thinking how dearly familiar she'd become with so few meetings. With no resemblance that he could see, she seemed in some strange way the most, instead of the least, known of his children. She wouldn't recognise *him* in the same way, of course, but he must accept that as the punishment he deserved.

'I'll take you to the airport tomorrow.'

She was touched by his kindness but shook her head. 'Thank you but there's no need. The hotel will order a taxi.'

Ready to leave, she turned on impulse to kiss him goodbye, but as she did so, the front door opened and a small knot of people suddenly surged in. They halted at the sight of her, conversation suddenly suspended, and neither she nor they found anything to say; only

Llewellyn struggled against the sudden tension in the air.

'Jessica, my dear, who don't you know among this crowd?'

She had to force herself to look at them – Claudia flushed and Lorenza beside her very pale. Behind them, Marco was trying to look unconcerned, while Jacques' eyes watched her with what seemed like cruel indifference; only Giancarlo Rasini remained calm, bowing with his usual indestructible *savoir-faire*. Before she could explain that she now knew them all, Claudia rushed headlong into speech, to prevent what she'd been going to say.

'The fireworks were a wash-out, so we came home, and brought Giancarlo along as well. You didn't say you were going to be entertaining a visitor, Papa.' She sounded aggrieved, but seeing the frown gathering on Llewellyn's face, Jess forestalled the explosion that seemed imminent.

'I *wasn't* expected, and I'm just on my way out.' She couldn't help but look at Jacques, but the kindness she needed wasn't there, and she spoke to the others. 'I came thinking *you* wouldn't be here; I came to say goodbye to your father. I've been called back to London because my dear Gerald is ill. I hope your . . . your Paris trip turns out well.'

She thought none of them was going to answer at all, but finally, in a voice that sounded ironed flat of all emotion, Jacques managed it.

'I expect you're not sorry to be going – home being where your heart is.' He offered the others a glancing smile. 'Jessica explained it to me once – hers is *not* the spirit that built the British Empire. She doesn't crave adventure abroad!'

In the little silence that followed, only Claudia responded to his lead. 'It's what the English can't help feeling – everything about their system at home is better than anyone else's!' She was aware of tension in the air, dangerous as a live electric wire; Jacques' face seemed now to be carved out of stone, but his eyes were fixed on Jessica, and the angry sadness in them frightened her into blundering on. 'You English won't ever make good Europeans.'

'Probably not,' Jessica managed to agree. 'I expect our hearts aren't in it.' Desperate for help, she smiled at Giancarlo. 'I'm so glad to see *you*. I'd hoped to call and say goodbye to your grandparents, but I ran out of time. Now, I've still got packing to do, so I'll wish you all goodnight and leave.'

She made for the door which someone – Marco, she thought – held open for her, and stepped thankfully into the friendly darkness.

For those left standing in a trance of stillness in the hall, it was Giancarlo who finally released them. For once he was smiling almost warmly at his host.

'Claudia was kind enough to insist on my coming in, but I only called to apologise to Maria for *not* staying. I have work waiting to be done at home. *Buona sera, e mille grazie!'*

Nothing in voice or manner suggested how aware he was of the storm about to break. Social grace wouldn't fail *him* in any catastrophe, Jacques decided with blind rage; there was something to be said for a long line of ancestors skilled in the art of surviving in the face of every kind of danger. But it was Llewellyn, of all those present, who saw in Giancarlo's decision to leave the only service he could render them, and who for once matched its restrained courtesy with a dignity of his own.

'Perhaps you're wise, my dear boy. Maria isn't entirely sure how the *bigoli* in salsa is going to turn out! My compliments to Donna Emilia and your grandfather.'

Giancarlo was free to leave, and his going seemed to restore Lorenza to life. With the door scarcely closed behind him, she was the first to speak, in a voice more high-pitched than usual.

'He's going to run after *her* – I could see it in his face.'

'Of course, *cara* . . . he's silly about her, but . . .' It was as far as Claudia got before a roar from Llewellyn interrupted them.

'Be *quiet*, both of you . . . all of you. After getting bad news from London, Jessica was tired and upset. Did any of you offer her even the kindness of a greeting? No, you did not. I have to feel ashamed of my own children.'

Used to her father's good opinion, Lorenza now looked ready to weep. Sinking their recent differences, Marco put an arm about her shoulders for comfort but didn't speak. Claudia faced her father, eyes huge and dark in the pallor of her face.

'We can't *feel* kind towards her . . . J-Jessica, I m-mean. Why pretend? We *want* her to go home.'

'Christ Almighty, child – can't you understand? This *is* her home, as much as it is yours. She's one of mine, the same as you are, but instead of loving her I've given her nothing – not even the name she ought to have had.'

There was no mistaking the anguish in his face. Claudia never minded her father's sudden flurries of ill humour – almost enjoyed her battles with him. But this was different; what seemed to threaten them now was an upheaval they couldn't survive. She knew what someone caught in an earthquake must feel, with all known certainties and landmarks gone. Her proud boast had been that Llewellyn didn't need Jessica; she couldn't believe that now. His face had said that he would always need her as one of his children. But, most terrible of all, she was no longer sure about Jacques Duclos; his eyes were still fixed on the door Jessica had left by and, as surely as she knew anything, she knew that his mind was full of her. White-faced and trembling, she stared at him, asking mutely but desperately to be reassured. After only a tiny pause he went, at least, to stand beside her before he spoke to Llewellyn.

'My impression has been all along that Jessica didn't *want* anything you could offer her; she's a woman determined to go her own way.' Then he turned to smile at Claudia, and a spinning world righted itself again; with Jacques smiling at her, there was nothing she couldn't survive.

The unbearable scene was suddenly interrupted; Maria was opening the door from the kitchen regions. Claudia saw her hesitate, confused by some weight of emotion in the air. It made a pause, so full of dramatic possibilities that the moment couldn't be lost, and she seized it thankfully.

'Mamma . . . Papa . . . all of you . . . listen! It's time to tell you that when Jacques goes to New York I'm going with him.'

Aware of riding a wave of danger that both exhilarated and terrified her, she almost shouted at them. 'He'll *need* me; of course I'm going.'

The man beside her said nothing at all. The ring of faces watching him made him feel like a performing bear; his turn to dance had come. He was trapped as surely as any tied animal, but the trap was of his own making. He must accept it or die of self-disgust. Claudia was making him a gift no man could refuse. The woman he wanted in her place had just walked out, but he'd lost her well before that. The letter she'd written him still burned in his memory, laughing at the idea that they'd found something worth holding on to. He was unaware of the long, breath-held silence all around him until Claudia's ragged voice spoke again, now begging for reassurance.

'Jacques, you *do* want me . . . don't you?'

'Yes . . . I want you,' he agreed quietly, and knew that in a way it was even true.

Maria let out a small sigh, not knowing which she'd feared more – his acceptance or rejection of Claudia's offer of herself. Time would tell how the story was to end, but it wasn't the simple, happy one she'd beseeched the Virgin Mary to give her daughter. There'd been anguish in Jessica's face as well, but she couldn't allow herself to be riven by that as well. Instead she must somehow make a grab at normality.

'Supper,' she managed to stammer, '. . . I came to say that supper was ready.'

'Then let us go and eat it,' Llewellyn said with desperate gaiety. 'God knows our revels *here* are ended!'

Outside the *pensione's* garden gate, Jess found that escape looked less desirable. The darkness seemed intense, the canal was unpleasantly near, and she was becoming aware of hurrying footsteps behind her. Not for a second did she allow herself to hope that they belonged to Jacques; it seemed altogether more likely that the crowning unpleasantness of her last evening in Venice would simply be the rare experience of being mugged. Then a moment later she heard a voice she recognised.

'Jessica . . . wait, please.'

As she turned round, a lamp on the bridge beside her threw down illumination enough to show her Giancarlo's face. The mixture of highlight and shadow made it almost theatrically beautiful in an austere, masculine way, but, as usual, he looked drained of life as well.

She said what first came into her head. 'You work too hard . . . I hope Venice is properly grateful.'

'It's still here – that's our reward.'

One subject disposed of, she flogged her brain for another. 'I didn't quite see you as a man who'd turn out on a cold, damp evening to enjoy fireworks, even at Carnival time.'

'I didn't – I was on my way home when I met the Matthiases. I walked with them and Claudia pressed me to stay for supper.'

Jess wondered whether to enquire why he'd changed his mind, decided against it, but could think of nothing else to stand there in the night and discuss.

'When did you eat last?' he suddenly asked.

'I can't remember . . . yes, I can – a roll at lunchtime.'

'I thought so.' His hand took hold of hers, and pulled her firmly along beside him. Short of an outright tussle, there was no chance of going in a different direction, but she made an effort to protest when it became obvious that they were walking towards the Palazzo Rasini.

'Please . . . I'm much too scruffy to sit down to dinner with Donna Emilia, and I'm in rather a rush besides.'

As if he hadn't heard, she was led up the stone staircase, but not to the entrance she had used before.

'My own quarters,' he explained briefly. 'Rather less impressive than my grandmother's. You can be as scruffy here as you please, and leave as soon as you've eaten.'

She could see his point – the room she was shown into was on a smaller scale than the ones downstairs, and up here the shabbiness wasn't disguised by faded grandeur. But the furnishings offered comfort of a kind – armchairs covered in worn velvet, overflowing bookshelves, and an old Persian rug whose colours still glowed gently on the uneven floor.

'Not up to the elegant standards *you* require,' he said with a smile, 'but it feels like home to me. Battistina cleans, and she also insists on leaving more food ready than I can possibly eat. It will take five minutes to reheat.'

Thankful that she wasn't required to be useful, Jess examined the bookshelves instead – where books on German philosophy rubbed shoulders with the poems of Robert Frost, and Simenon's Maigret stories in French kept company with the English derring-do of Richard Hannay. That last discovery made her smile – she could imagine Buchan's old-time gentleman-adventurer appealing to Giancarlo.

In less than the five minutes he'd promised, her host reappeared. 'If you will forgive the informality of eating in the kitchen, it's warmer there.'

'You're entertaining someone who *likes* kitchens,' Jess insisted. She had reached the stage of tiredness where argument was beyond her – if he'd said that they were going to have supper on the roof, she would have followed him there unquestioningly.

But Battistina's casserole of chicken and herbs, and the wine Giancarlo poured, restored her enough for normal conversation. Unable to talk of her own affairs, especially of the scene he'd witnessed at the *pensione*, she asked about the *palazzo* instead.

'It's one of the oldest, and also one of the smallest, thank God!' he explained. 'But protecting it from weather, salt air, and seawater is going to be beyond us before long, even with the help of your father. I don't mind for myself, as long as my grandparents are able to live out their lives here. After that, if it's not to crumble into dust, I suppose I shall offer it to the Municipality, or some international committee like the one Nathan Acheson concerns himself in.'

His face expressed only the slightly rueful concern of a man asked to part with some small object of virtue. Jess was nearly sure the impression given was a heroic lie, but she knew better than to drive him into a corner where he must say so.

'Are you acquainted with Mr Acheson yet?' she asked instead. 'My guess is that Count Paolo will have no difficulty in liking him.'

'My grandfather would like anyone who came prepared to rescue Venice from decay.'

'There is *that*, of course,' Jess conceded with a smile, 'but what Nathan rescues will be rescued with love as well as money, and Count Paolo will judge *that* to be a greater merit.'

'*D'accordo!*' He was silent for a moment before shifting the conversation on to more personal ground. 'Apart from the sad reason that takes you back to London, *will* you be glad to go home?'

She didn't answer at once – remembering with painful vividness the scene that his question harked back to. He would have needed to be insensitive and blind to miss the agonising discomfort of those moments in the *pensione* hall, but she was equally aware of something differently disturbing in the air now. In the isolation of the room, in the strange quietness of the traffic-free city around them, she felt suddenly exposed and afraid. The anxiety wasn't for herself – Giancarlo Rasini was probably the last man on earth capable of forcing himself on a reluctant woman, and even his downbent head now removed the pressure of an inspection that might seem unfair. But she felt, nevertheless, that his whole heart and mind listened for the answer she would give. She reminded herself of the girl he'd lost, and of his insistence that he'd put away hope of happiness in future; but Count Paolo had spoken of a change in his grandson. It would seem more than she could bear if to this kind, gentle man as well as to the others her visit had brought nothing but unhappiness.

'I'm very anxious about my stepfather,' she answered carefully at last. 'He's been my guide, counsellor, and best friend ever since I was a child; I don't know how I'd manage without him now. But apart from that, Elvira's job here has been demanding. So to answer your question at last, yes, I do look forward to getting home.'

He sat with hands folded round his wine glass – beautiful hands they were for a man; she remembered noticing that about him before at the Countess's dinner table. Then he asked another question.

'Llewellyn's other children haven't made you welcome here. Why not?'

Jess achieved an almost Venetian shrug. 'Each of them seems to have a different reason, but the blame is mostly mine, I think. I arrived with a lifetime's prejudice against my father. I managed to get over that, but I'm not used to being part of a close-knit family. I came to Venice quite determined not to know them, so it was only fair to find them equally set against knowing me!'

She tried to sound composed, no longer harrowed by the memory of the scene in the *pensione*, with Jacques' anger compounding her own pain. She wished that she needn't take away with her so clear a picture of *this* man watching over the dear, frail couple downstairs amid the crumbling beauty of a house that must be made to last out their lifetime. She would rather not have been able to picture him in this quiet room, with Battista's casseroles to keep him fed and only his books for company. She wanted to offer him friendship . . . love . . . herself – anything that would fill the room with life, and deny her aching fear that both of them might otherwise end up lonely.

The silence in the room was so heavy with suspense that she wondered whether the conviction that had taken hold of her had been made explicit in words. *Had* she said what was in her mind . . . made him so aware of the desolation the evening had left her with that he must feel compelled to save her from it?

She was on the verge of rushing into some mad, inconsequential speech when Giancarlo rescued her by suddenly taking over the conversation himself.

'Your wrist is bound up – my grandfather said you'd had an accident.'

'It was carelessness – I'm quite used to ladders, and don't make a habit of falling off them!'

166

She managed a smile that faded when his eyes met hers. His face was tragic, and she thought she knew what he would say next.

'That first day I came here and you asked me to share your lunch, I saw the truth of what my grandfather had said about you. Jessica Smythson was a woman we could all learn to like very much . . . Paolo even put it more strongly than that, and I'm sorry to say that he was right.'

'Why sorry?' she asked faintly, when Giancarlo paused for a moment.

'My grandfather said we could learn to love you,' he went on, as if she hadn't spoken, 'and he was right.' A faint, sweet smile touched his mouth for a moment. 'We shall get over it, and talk calmly about our dear Shylock's daughter, when she's safely back in London life, away from the danger that comes of being loved by the Rasinis!'

Jess understood him now . . . knew with a quietly breaking heart that no offer she could make, no promise that his love *wouldn't* harm her, no anger at his refusal to at least *try* for happiness, would make the slightest difference. He was the man that he'd become, and she must leave him lonely in that quiet, peaceful room because it was the choice he'd made. All she could do was pretend she didn't mind . . . *that* he would require of her.

'It's beautiful beyond words here,' she said at last; 'but I think I must have the genes of my English grandfather in my blood. *He* was a countryman, and I find I'm getting tired of cities – if I stayed here I might soon be like Falstaff, "babbling o' green fields!"'

He nodded by way of answering, struggling with the knowledge that at any moment now she would get up and leave. Once she was no longer there, he told himself, he could manage perfectly well – it was while he must still watch her smile, and breathe the faint perfume she wore, that self-sufficiency seemed not only arrogant but absurd. Habit would reassert itself again, of course, and what now felt like despair would be nothing but the tiredness left by a long winter of anxiety out in the Lagoon.

Jess saw the tiredness easily enough. 'Please don't come out with me again,' she said gently. 'There's no need; I can find my own way back.'

A flicker of amusement brought back warmth to his face. 'I'm afraid there's every need. Battistina won't have missed our arrival, and I should say it's more than my life is worth to let you walk out again unescorted!'

There seemed no answer to that and she allowed herself to be shepherded down the staircase. Her own exhaustion now felt like a dead weight she might have to bear until the end of time; but by concentrating on every step she took it would be possible to reach the hotel without collapsing on the steps of one bridge or another and begging to be left there. At last the entrance was in sight, and only one more effort was needed.

'Thank Battistina for the lovely supper, please, and don't completely wear yourself out in the Serenissima's ungrateful service!'

The hand she held out was taken but not immediately released. Her drawn, pale face, harshly lit by the lamp beside the door, was devoid of make-up – an arrangement of features not remarkable enough to add up to beauty or imprint itself unforgettably on his memory. But somehow that was what had happened, and he hovered on the very edge of blurting out what filled his mind – that she couldn't go away because, no matter what the risk, he so badly needed her to stay.

She pulled her hand away at last, while he still struggled to remember that he'd survived without a different girl after a Paris taxi had annihilated her. Jess touched his cheek briefly with her lips and he felt her tears on his face. Then she walked into the hotel and after a moment he turned and went away.

Chapter 21

The morning dawned windless and muffled in a thick sea mist. Out on the water, Jess could feel its moisture beading her eyelashes, even taste salt on her mouth. She wasn't sorry for the obscuring silver veil flung over what she was leaving, but there was anxiety as well, that caused her to consult the boatman about the possibility of a flight delay.

He waved the fog aside with an Italian's charming readiness to tell his listener whatever she wanted to hear. *'No, no, signorina . . . un po' di nebbia non importa.'*

But a little mist did matter at the airport. All outward flights were held up for the time being, although the tannoyed announcements managed to sound as optimistic as the boatman had been. At any moment, a cheerful voice seemed to suggest, the necessary little breeze from Heaven would arrive, and the *passagieri* could be airborne again. Failing the breeze, Jess had time to telephone Imogen and hear that Gerald was safely ensconced at the Dutch House; all was peaceful there.

Still waiting to be called through to the departure lounge, she was sitting over a cup of coffee to pass the time when someone arrived beside her at the counter. The automatic *'buon giorno'* she was about to offer was halted in her throat as her neighbour spoke himself, rather breathlessly.

'I was afraid I'd miss you. I went to the hotel first, but you'd already left.'

His face was set in a frown, and she realised that she hadn't yet seen him smile wholeheartedly. Marco Matthias was altogether a very earnest young man to be Llewellyn's son.

'I told your father that I didn't need seeing off.' Then her voice changed. 'There's nothing *wrong* . . . is there?'

'Nothing wrong in the way you mean, but we're all trying to pretend that last night didn't happen,' he admitted ruefully. 'Llewellyn flew into a rage after you'd gone – bad enough in itself, but it seemed much worse when he finished up just . . . very sad. We're also in disgrace with Mamma, who fears that we were unkind. Jacques is the only one who seems cheerful – I expect it's because he's looking forward to seeing Paris again.'

Marco stared at the pale face of the woman beside him – so different from the rest of them in almost every way. If *she* suffered pain they wouldn't be allowed to know . . . she'd smile instead. It was hard to believe that she was Llewellyn's daughter – they'd had *that* much excuse for not understanding her; but however noisily they denied it, she was part of their family, now and always.

Jess watched the departures screen above them and saw that it was beginning to show signs of life. 'We might be called through soon now.' She smiled at Marco, even though his own expression was still overcast. 'Thank you for troubling to see me off. Come and visit me in London one day – I'd like you to,' she suggested.

'One day I will,' he agreed, 'but I'll see Nathan Acheson first, and I promise to be *very* polite to him!'

The earnestness of it made her grin more broadly, and he smiled back, suddenly released from the misery of the previous evening. He wanted to laugh out loud, hug her, shout that she belonged to them; but already the screen was insisting that it was time for her to leave. He leaned forward to kiss her, watched her walk away until a crowd of other passengers cut off his view. Then there was nothing left to do but locate his boat outside, and steer home across the Lagoon.

In terms of general greyness, and cold, damp air, there wasn't much to choose, Jess reckoned, between London and the city she'd just left. But in other ways what she was returning to had become frighteningly unfamiliar. She sat trying not to cringe in the taxi taking her home from Heathrow as parallel lines of traffic threatened to converge, carelessly annihilating her between them. It wasn't feasible that in the mere six weeks she'd been away the capital had grown larger, noisier, more fume-laden; she'd simply become accustomed to being without cars . . . to a city built to a less inhuman scale altogether.

At least her home was recognisable – the curved white gables that gave the house its name still faced the entrance to Holland Park. But she'd forgotten the boldly painted front door, and its deep Prussian blue was suddenly an agonising reminder of somewhere else. Instead of standing in a busy London street counting out money for the taxi fare, she was back on a little island in the middle of a lagoon, listening to Jacques' grave voice explaining that she couldn't leave it without eating fish.

About to point out that he'd rather not wait all day, the cabbie was struck by the pallor of her face and almost forgot himself enough to offer to hump her luggage as far as the front door. But Jess shook away the vision of Burano and, because he was still staring doubtfully at her, managed to say that air travel was a disorientating business – whisking people's bodies from place to place but omitting to take their minds along as well. He didn't smile and, not one of Nature's

170

philosophers, merely reckoned that the aeroplane was here to stay. Then he pocketed his fare, and drove away, and she was back where she belonged. The old sea-witch city and all it had contained were memories now, to be revisited in her mind only when they'd become less sharp and painful.

Her aunt had the front door open while she was still unearthing a key. Imogen looked tearful and short of sleep, but she produced a wavering smile at the sight of Jess standing there.

'Darling – it's so *good* to see you. It seems *ages* since you went, and Gerald's missed you. I promised to wake him the very moment you arrived. He drifts off to sleep a lot, but the doctor says that's good for him.'

'Then don't wake him, Immy dear,' Jess said quickly. 'Let him rest; I'll see him later on.'

'A cup of tea first? It's the only thing one longs for abroad and it's never available. Or if it is, it isn't drinkable. I made Gerald move into my guest room down here, by the way, but in the kitchen we'll be as quiet as mice and not disturb him.'

While the tea was being made she nevertheless talked without stopping, covering the days from the evening of Gerald's collapse until the morning of his return home. But at last she got round to her niece. 'Now, darling . . . tell me about Venice. I can still scarcely believe that you saw your father; but I absolutely *knew* that I must write, however set you were against meeting him. It was all *meant*,' she finished up triumphantly.

She sounded ineffably sure that whatever she thought was right, but Jess dealt firmly with the spurt of irritation her aunt always aroused in her, and answered in the pleasantest voice she could manage.

'I'm glad you wrote. Llewellyn asked me to give you his love. He said you'd been a good friend.'

Imogen's plain face flushed with sudden colour. 'He was irresistible as a young man; I dare say you can understand that, even now. I suppose I fell in love with him, but as soon as he caught sight of Gillian . . .' She still hadn't forgotten the pain of watching that, Jess thought, but some sweetness in her that they hadn't sufficiently appreciated had kept her from embitterment. Perhaps there'd also been time enough to reflect that *she* would have been more certainly abandoned than beautiful Gillian had been.

'I'll tell you about Venice later, Immy,' Jess suggested gently. 'Now I'm just going to look in on Gerald, and then I must ring the studio and talk to Pinky.'

Her stepfather was in an armchair by the window overlooking the garden when she went in. He was awake, but not reading the book lying open in his lap. In elegant silk dressing gown and matching cravat he looked, she told him, like a character in a Noël Coward play instead of someone who'd worried them half to death.

'Dear Jess,' he said contentedly, 'I could only hear the sound of Imogen's voice, but I knew you were back . . . the house doesn't feel empty any more.'

'You *look* all right. Does the doctor say you are?'

'There's nothing to worry about. I was given a little warning, that's all – most considerate of whoever keeps an eye on our affairs!'

'Are you going to stay down here?' The question was wrung out of her by her aunt's choice of décor that he was now surrounded by – wind chimes, camel rugs, and butter-yellow walls.

'According to Immy's feng shui teacher, this colour is especially life-enhancing,' Gerald explained solemnly. 'She thought it would be good for me! I can survive it for a day or two, until I feel more like climbing stairs.'

'Be grateful it wasn't Chinese red – she's fond of that as well.'

They smiled at each other, content in their deep, mutual affection. They shared an eye for the frequent daftness of life as well, and it was something she realised that she'd missed in Venice. She stooped to kiss him and then stood up.

'I'll tell you about Venice later on – merely insist for the moment that Elvira's *palazzo* looks a dream; you'll need to be a little stronger for the whole saga of my Italian goings-on! I need to unpack and telephone Pinky while *you, caro signore*, rest some more.'

'You sounded just like your grandmother then,' he complained.

She grinned and went away, knowing that her real intention was to avoid talking about Venice until she was sure she could. It wouldn't take long to see it as a brief episode belonging to the past – if not quite forgotten, certainly no longer relevant to her real life. But for the moment the pain about her heart was real enough. Regret for something scarcely realised but irretrievably lost buried her, every now and then, in a suffocating wave, but she was learning to wait for it to break and recede, promising herself that the onslaughts would slowly become less frequent until she ceased one day to notice them at all.

At the studio the following morning Pinky beamed a welcome and then wept a tear or two of relief. 'I'm a silly old fool, Jess,' she muttered, mopping at her face, 'but I was terribly afraid we were getting into a mess. It was Gerald's way of making the time go quicker till you got home, but he took on too many things. Some of them were commissions he'd have refused before – said they were too boring. Poor Jane is stuck with one of them now – a show flat in Belgrave Square . . . you know the sort of thing – all money and no taste!'

But, bored or not, Gerald had still worked in his usual meticulous way. Notes, sketches, and scale drawings were all there, ready to be worked on; and, skimming through them, Jess said that with the burning of some midnight oil they'd be able to manage well enough.

'You look – if I'm allowed to say so – as if quite a lot of midnight oil has been burned already,' Pinky said candidly. 'I suppose Mrs Acheson was rich, ignorant, and a pain in the neck!'

Jess smiled but shook her head. 'Not a pain at all, although we *did* have our differences that had nothing to do with the job. The commission was nerve-racking, but a dear and kindly Venetian expert in the *palazzo* next door shored me up with generous amounts of praise. In the end both the Achesons were content, I think, with their new home.'

Pinky had known Jess since she was a small girl, fascinated by the rainbow-coloured bolts of silk and velvet that filled the studio workroom. The two of them had been friends for thirty years, but friendship didn't, in Miss Todd's stringent view of things, excuse what she called nosiness. She would have given a great deal to know the rest of the Venetian story, but until Jess offered to talk about it, they'd better just get on with bringing the studio back to order again.

At home, though, the moment came when the subject of Venice couldn't be avoided any longer. Gerald was back in his own apartment now, and murmuring of starting to work again, at least to the extent the doctor would allow. He began by making an apology one evening when dinner was over, and they were in his own peaceful sitting room – with not a bit of ethnic exuberance in sight, and Imogen safely practising her Andean pan-pipes downstairs.

'I'm sorry, Jess – I landed you with commissions I shouldn't have accepted . . . all the more foolish of me when I knew I wasn't feeling in very good nick.'

She poured coffee and put it in front of him. 'A couple of them have been good experience for Jane – she's been working like a Trojan, by the way, and as a pupil of yours she's doing you proud.'

'So all is well at the studio, as Pinky confirms. But I don't think all is well with you, my dear Jess.'

It was irritating, even very unfair, when she thought she'd buckled on each day the smiling composure their clients expected and held back until the dark night watches the aching sadness that always lay in wait.

'A lot happened in Venice,' she muttered at last, as a way of beginning the story.

'I realise that. If it isn't painful, I'd like to hear about your father. I can just remember him coming here with Imogen – a mercurial, talkative young man, with the sort of face that any artist worth his salt would long to paint – not handsome, but compelling.'

'It's rather how he still is,' Jess admitted with a smile, 'except that he isn't any longer young. He had the good fortune to find a kind and gentle wife who's made him almost respectable, though perhaps not quite as respectable as their children would like!'

'But *you* were agreeably surprised, I think.'

She nodded, turning memories over in her mind like a child deciding which bright shell to pick up next. 'Yes, I liked him, even not intending to. I don't think of him as my father; just someone I can't help feeling linked to. He *is* a fine artist, by the way. Imogen was quite right to keep him from starving in London!'

'And the children?' Gerald persisted gently when she halted again.

'Lorenza is like her mother, though more beautiful; painfully growing out of a fixation on a man who isn't fixated on her. Marco is a successful young businessman, but his heart is set on preserving Venice for the Venetians. He has a perilously sweet nature for the political career that seems to be required of him before long. Lastly, there's Claudia – Llewellyn's favourite, I think, because she's got his relish for life, and his gift for charming other people. She intends to be a journalist, and I shall recommend her to my grandmother; Elizabeth would love her.'

'Quite a family,' Gerald commented. 'I hope they understood what they were getting in you?'

'For one reason or another, I'm afraid they didn't. They didn't take to me at all!' She smiled at his expression. 'It doesn't matter – I'm not going back, although Llewellyn, at least, invited me to.' Anxious to move away from talking about the people at the *pensione*, she embarked chattily instead on the divisions separating the city's modernists and preservationists, and confessed that because of them her own relations with Elvira Acheson had almost broken down. 'I even became rather stupidly anti-wealth,' she admitted finally. 'Nathan Acheson cured me of that, although I suspect that he isn't typical of most very rich men.'

Gerald listened with interest, but led her firmly back to personalities again. 'Imogen heard from Llewellyn. He wrote to thank her, of course, but I think his main need was to brag about you. You might not have hit it off with *his* family, but it seems that you certainly did with other people.'

Gerald inspected Jess's withdrawn expression and suddenly plucked up the courage to tackle what needed to be said. 'After your grandmother's last visit we talked about making a fresh start. It's what led to your going to Venice in a way. My dear, if it *was* that – a new beginning – you mustn't imagine that you aren't free to go on with it; you most certainly are. I won't have you imagining you're indispensable here. Think again, please, if you turned down something there that is needed for happiness. I should like to be able to boast of you living in a Venetian *palazzo*!'

She shook her head, grateful for the fact that she could now guess what Llewellyn's letter to Imogen had said.

'You heard about Giancarlo, I expect. He's the grandson of the Matthiases' dear friends, the Rasinis. Apart from the awkward fact that he's the man Lorenza set her heart on, he's made up his mind to embrace a life of self-denial. Happiness has brought tragedy in the past; now he won't look for it again.'

She spoke with such regret that Gerald supposed he'd identified the grief about her that troubled him. 'If there's really no hope there, you could still think about Elizabeth's New York offer,' he suggested quietly. 'She'd love to have you.'

'*No* . . . not New York!' She feared she'd shouted the words at him, and his startled expression confirmed it. She'd spilled her coffee too, and had to mop it up with hands that shook a little. 'I've no wish to go there,' she managed at last to say quietly. 'But I *shall* write to my grandmother about Llewellyn's daughter, Claudia. She's been helping someone called Jacques Duclos work on a photographic portrait of Venice. His next assignment is to be in New York, and . . . and naturally Claudia wants to go there too. I think Elizabeth would like them both, and enjoy helping them.'

Gerald nodded, but returned to the subject of herself with the persistence, she thought, of a terrier at a rabbit-hole.

'So, you're happy to settle down again in London, Jess?'

She couldn't help wincing at the expression he'd used, and knew that to some extent, at least, she'd given herself away. Unable to lie to him, she achieved a smile instead.

'I forgot to mention that Jacques Duclos is a sophisticated, war-scarred Frenchman with whom Claudia has fallen wonderfully in love. Until I remembered my mother's disastrous infatuation for Llewellyn, I was even tempted to fall in love with him myself! But I'm far from being eighteen, and in any case there's Claudia . . . half my age, half my sister, and much more ready than I am to follow Jacques to the ends of the earth. So, to answer your question, my new fresh start is here.'

There was, her expression warned him, no more to be said, and with what he recognised as a mixture of sadness and shamed relief, Gerald allowed the subject of her going away to drop. He must somehow forget that glimpse of desolation in her face.

175

Chapter 22

What Jess insisted to herself was the real world – without Venetian mist and magic to blur, and dazzle, and confuse – took hold again. Spring was returning, and even in London the season was beautiful. With Gerald working at a slower pace than before, she left the running of the studio to Pinky, while she guided Jane Harrison and trained their new assistant. Even so, she made herself plunge into a social swim that she'd been happy to reject before. New friends, even a half-hearted attempt at a love affair, seemed necessary now to prove that she wasn't damaged, desolate, or pathetically distraught; Jessica Smythson was herself again, though ready to admit that what had happened to her in Venice might never be entirely forgotten. It was what life *was*, after all – the slow accumulation of important memories.

Of the people she'd met there, it was Llewellyn who seemed most determined not to be hidden away to some banished corner of her mind. His letters now arrived regularly – conversations on paper described them better, she thought, because he wrote as he spoke, and she had the impression that she was actually listening to him.

Elvira's ball had taken place without him; consequently, however splendid, it was bound to have lacked a certain something. But his dear Jess would be astonished to know that her grandmother, in Venice for the ball, had called at the *pensione* afterwards. Elizabeth Harrington – in New York, of course, all those years ago when he'd met Gillian – had wanted to meet them, she said. The meeting had gone off surprisingly well, all things considered, and Maria was now happier about Claudia going to New York – Elizabeth had promised to look after her.

Llewellyn's next letter also had unexpected news: Lorenza, left behind in Paris when Claudia and Jacques returned to Venice, was going to stay there for a while. Fanny Duclos had said she needed a companion while she endured an enforced rest from the stage. But Maria put it down to Fanny's kindness – she intended to take her beautiful, sad guest in hand. Jess read the letters, answered them carefully, and tore up any replies that sounded less than serenely content with life. Gerald was well, she was busy, God was in his Heaven and all was right with the world.

Then came another surprise. She got back to the studio late one

177

afternoon, after two days spent working out of London, to find Pinky curtseying to the telephone she'd just put down.

'Sorry, Jess, your presence is requested at the Hyde Park Hotel – Grandma's back in town! She always sounds so damned autocratic that I never have the nerve to say it might not be convenient.'

'No more do I,' Jess admitted. 'Cowards, both of us.'

She wondered, on the way to the hotel, what had brought Elizabeth back to London, and then felt a prickle of superstition along her nerves – it had been that previous pre-Christmas visit that had been responsible for sending her to the lagoon city. This time, she insisted to herself, Elizabeth could have nothing to suggest that would turn her life upside down again. Even so, her grandmother's opening remark, after the first sharp inspection, was unexpected enough.

'I've been attending some of Nathan Acheson's committee celebrations . . . in my role of generously subscribing member.'

'In . . . in Venice, of course,' Jess suggested faintly.

'Where else? That *is* what the committee's busy saving! I saw what you'd done for Elvira's *palazzo* . . . I have to congratulate you; you're even better than I thought.'

The rare praise was worth having, but Jess had other questions to ask. She wanted first of all to hear her grandmother's version of the meeting with Llewellyn; it was something she was sorry to have missed – worthy opponents they must have been, measuring up to one another before they locked horns in battle.

'I met the Matthias family there,' Elizabeth announced. 'I should have made a point of doing so anyway, after getting your letter, but of course Nathan and Elvira introduced them as well. The Frenchman you mentioned had gone back to Paris, unfortunately – from what they said, he sounds interesting. Never mind – I shall catch up with him in New York.'

Jess clung to the thought of the Matthiases. 'Are you going to tell me how you got on with my father?'

Elizabeth frowned at the question. 'How do you expect? We both behaved like civilised human beings – no blood flowed. I could even see what captivated Gillian all those years ago. He must have been a magnetic young man – he makes his presence felt even now; in any case, Walter taught me to prefer men who know what they think.'

Jess spared a moment to consider the thought that had come into her head. Comparing Jacques with Giancarlo Rasini, there wasn't any doubt which of *them* her grandmother would prefer. She and Jacques were two of a kind . . . no adjustments needed for doubt, no allowances for viewpoints not their own. Elizabeth would despise Giancarlo, but for once she would be wrong. Jess had found herself often thinking about him, understanding better now the unselfish strength of purpose that made him different from other men.

'If Walter taught you to prefer intelligent men, it explains why you like Nathan Acheson,' she finally suggested.

Elizabeth nodded, but refused to be lured away by the red herring. 'My dear Jess, a little while ago I suggested that you should give New York a try. You turned the idea down, mostly out of loyalty to Gerald, I suspect. The quality is rare nowadays and I don't undervalue it, but it shouldn't rule your life. If you think his illness ties you down even more, you're *wrong*, and he would be the first to say so.'

'He's said it already,' Jess announced with a certain amount of pleasure. 'But the estimate of what I owe him has to be mine, not his or anyone else's.'

Elizabeth's faint smile held no rancour, and for once a kind of grudging approval. 'You don't grow any less stubborn with age. I used to blame my dear William for that, but I can equally well see Llewellyn cutting off his nose to spite his face; so how could you *not* be pig-headed! It's probably why your father's finished up in Venice, painting souvenir views. I hope *you* won't settle for whatever seems the easiest option.'

Jess struggled to remember that the elegant, unsparing woman sitting opposite her had been conditioned by success; she couldn't help feeling that she was bound to be right, nor that the rest of the world must suffer the near-certainty of being mostly wrong.

'What Llewellyn had the good sense to settle for in the end was contentment,' she nevertheless corrected her grandmother sharply. 'It doesn't stop him putting aside Donna Emilia's "views" occasionally to paint pictures that even you might feel privileged to own.'

Elizabeth considered this while she flicked at a piece of fluff that spoiled the perfection of her dark suit. 'All right, that puts me in my place; but I'm not really concerned with your father . . . only with you. In my experience life doesn't make a habit of repeating its best offers – you have to catch them on the wing or miss them altogether.'

The point of the remark pierced more sharply than she knew, but after a moment Jess answered with determined cheerfulness. 'Claudia Matthias would agree with you. She wants to tread *your* path to high achievement, and Venice doesn't offer nearly enough scope . . . that's why I wrote to you about her.'

'I realise that. She was professional enough to tell me that I'd got a fact wrong – me! – but she also offered me a kiss in case the contradiction had been painful! I doubt if she even needs any help, but events have made her some sort of relative by marriage, and in any case I shall keep an eye on her for her mother's sake. She can use one of the empty rooms in my apartment, unless she's going to sleep with Jacques Duclos as well as work for him.'

Jess's expressionless face offered Elizabeth nothing except the certainty that something she should have known about was being deliberately withheld. It was irritating to a woman whose life had been dedicated to the principle of ferreting out whatever information other people mistakenly tried not to disclose.

'We were talking about *your* future, not Claudia's,' she persisted nevertheless.

'My future doesn't need talking about – it's fine as it is.' Jess smiled to soften the refusal, but she was clinging desperately now to the only certainty she had left. However unadventurous a mess her life turned out to be, by Elizabeth's or Jacques' standards of success, it would at least be of her *own* choosing. 'How long can you stay?' she asked, to switch the conversation away from herself.

'I'm booked on a flight tomorrow morning. I've enjoyed the visit, but I've probably seen some of my European friends for the last time. I'm getting too old to keep crossing the Atlantic.'

She almost managed to sound wistful – a state that Jess was well aware she normally despised. There wasn't the least need to feel guilty or anxious about her. She had an abundance of friends eager to be useful, and money enough to buy any service that friendship didn't supply. But for once there did seem to be a shadow of sadness behind her usual, astringent, parting shot.

'Gerald can't help behaving like an old maid, but I shan't forgive him if he makes *you* dull too.'

Torn as usual between resentment and a certain unslayable admiration for a woman she couldn't help feeling proud of, Jess promised to do her best to keep dullness at bay. She kissed her grandmother's cheek, and the smile they finally exchanged seemed a shared salute – full of respect and affection on both sides, and tempered as usual by considerable regret.

The New York summer had arrived – earlier than usual, and much more uncomfortably hot . . . or so the people Jacques talked to claimed, with a sort of resentful pride. Suffocated by the layers of engine fumes and heat that lay trapped in the deep canyons of the city, they had to learn to live without fresh air; but for the time being Manhattan was unbearable by day, and not much cooler at night. Jacques could only agree with their summing-up, adjusting his light filters yet again to absorb the glare of sun on glass and steel.

It wasn't all bad – he appreciated the fizz and crackle of New Yorker humour, admired the driving, restless vitality of the place, and found in its extraordinary architecture images of stunning beauty to set beside the ever-present undercurrent of brutality and violence. But he waited for the day when he could be sure of having done justice to it all and then go home; the word seemed faintly shocking in his mind – he hadn't ever thought in terms of 'home' before.

Claudia watched him when she knew his attention was engaged

elsewhere. She'd expected by now to be so thoroughly familiar with him, so intimately connected, that she would never have to guess what was in his mind or heart. It hadn't happened, and she asked herself every day why not – probably because fifteen years separated them, and try as she would she'd been unable to make them not matter. He'd lived that much longer, knew things about life that she didn't know.

But what she did know beyond any doubt was her failure to make him happy. He wasn't enchanted by New York, as she was, and that had come as a surprise; but the much more terrible truth to face was that he wasn't enchanted by her. Totally though she'd offered herself, and passionately though she'd sometimes been taken, she was becoming a little more certain day by day that her lover and friend was retreating away from her. There was the sheer grief of that to deal with, but puzzlement and pain as well – she'd left Venice for New York confident that failure was impossible.

One evening, over a final cup of coffee in the restaurant below Elizabeth Harrington's palatial apartment block, she *asked* to spend the night with him; they normally slept together at his suggestion, and only at his hotel, not in the room upstairs that Elizabeth had said was hers.

Jacques sat with hands gripped round his coffee cup . . . deep in thought, it seemed, about the suggestion she'd just made. It had been a mistake, she realised; he was an old-fashioned man in certain unexpected ways, and one of them was his preference to lead, not follow, when it came to making love.

'It doesn't matter,' she said before he could answer. 'You're tired . . . it's been a long day.'

'For you as well, *tesoro*.' He smiled at her, aware at last that his abstraction had made her anxious. 'Not that *you* look tired; this city seems to suit you as well as it does Elizabeth.'

It was certainly true . . . with dark hair fashionably cropped and clothes worn with the right air of casual chic, she was a Manhattan girl now, with a little added Venetian allure. He knew that she was noticed, especially by other men. They even looked measuringly at *him*, wondering how easy it would be to dislodge him from her life.

'What news on the Rialto?' he suddenly asked, knowing that she still insisted on being kept informed of what went on at home.

Her enchanting smile reappeared. 'Good news, and you'll never guess what it is. Marco's going to work for Nathan Acheson of all people. Mamma isn't sure of the details yet, and in any case he's got to teach someone else to look after Zio Pietro's fruit and vegetables; but the new job will be to do with buying up and renovating old houses. I expect Marco showed Mr Acheson my college housing report. *That* will have convinced him that something needed to be done.'

She believed it, Jacques thought, being certain that if anything important happened she must have had a hand in it. The miracle was that, even being as pleased with herself as she was, she remained none the less lovable; some touch of Maria's sweetness always saved her.

'You aren't the only one with news,' he pointed out next. 'I had a rare letter from Fanny this morning. Lorenza has fallen in love with two small children, but that's by no means all. It seems that she's learning to like the children's father as well!'

'I've heard about them already,' Claudia admitted unenthusiastically, 'and I agree with Mamma. We certainly don't want Lorenza eating her heart out for ever over Giancarlo; but a middle-aged stage designer working in Paris, and two stepchildren abandoned by their mother, is not what we'd have *chosen* for her.'

She watched him, knowing that the news of Lorenza had been offered to distract her from the subject of where they were to spend the night. It was time to be brave – Llewellyn had always taught her that she must walk towards, not away from, a fear.

'Talking of choices, much as she loves you, Mamma probably wouldn't have chosen you for me,' she said, as lightly as she could. 'But I expect she realises now how wrong she'd have been.'

There was time, too much time, to wait for what he would say; she couldn't guess from his face, even though she'd have sworn that every line etched into it by grief and laughter was familiar to her now.

'*You* haven't chosen me for ever, *tesoro*,' he said at last, with a faint, rueful smile. 'I'm only the first rung on the ladder you're going to climb with Elizabeth's help.'

She smiled the answer away; no need yet to take it seriously. 'Don't be silly, Jacques. You know as well as I do that we belong together. You haven't enjoyed being here as much as me . . . I'm not sure why, because I thought you'd love New York; but it doesn't matter. We'll soon be ready to go back to Paris, to dazzle Henri with our work. Then we'll insist on a holiday before we tackle Hong Kong or Sydney. That's what you need – a little break.'

Her voice sounded confident, but he could see the shadow of fear in her huge dark eyes. She was beautiful and dear, and he was sick to his heart for what must come next. But it had to be said now . . . was already long overdue.

'*Tesoro*, I shall go back to Paris alone. I want you to stay here, with Elizabeth.'

'You mean just while you see Henri Clément?' She didn't believe that it was what he meant, but she could pretend until she saw him shake his head. He stretched his hands out across the table and held hers in a grip that hurt.

'Listen to me, please, little one. You've given me more help than I

182

can ever repay, and more generous love than I deserve, but it's time for us to part company now. I should have insisted on it long ago . . . now I must.'

She heard a note in his voice that frightened her, so sad was it but so firm. If she wasn't sufficiently strong and certain, she might lose him now. Unbidden, the thought came into her mind of Llewellyn's English daughter. That one would stay calm in such a crisis, and *she* must stay calm too, not shout and storm and weep as she might once have done.

'Elizabeth's been talking to you,' she said quietly, 'telling you about the wonderful job she can get for me here. I don't want it, *amore* . . . I want to stay with you.'

Jacques felt memory stir and send a shaft of pain through his heart. How carelessly he'd promised Maria months ago that he wouldn't hurt her daughter. He knew they were being observed by people at other tables, who sensed some crucial tension in the air; he wanted to shout at them to get on with their own muddled lives. But the discomforts and regret being heaped on him now were only what he deserved. He released Claudia's hands and spoke almost roughly.

'*Think*, my dear – I'm nearly twice your age . . . a slightly shop-soiled wanderer, *not* the brave young Lochinvar of your imagination. You have everything still to do and see whereas I've discovered in myself an extraordinary and different ambition – I'm even getting tired of travelling.'

Intuitively her mind made the very leap that he prayed it would avoid. Instead of being in a crowded New York coffee shop, she was back in the hall of her mother's *pensione*, watching him stare at Jessica Smythson. Hysterical laughter destroyed the self-control she'd promised herself, and tears began to trickle down her face.

'It's my dear half-sister, isn't it?' she asked wildly. 'You're still hankering after her because she seemed more interested in Giancarlo. If you think *she'll* be of any use to you . . .'

Jacques stemmed the rush of words by laying his fingers over her mouth. 'Hush, my dear, please. Leave Jessica out of this discussion – she made it very clear that her life is in London. What has happened to *us* is nothing to do with her. I arrived in Venice hating myself and the rest of the world. I found with you and your family more kindness and warmth than I'd known before – the truth is that you all brought me back to life again. But gratitude blinded me to the mistake I was making. You wanted me to fall in love with *you* – instead I learned to love you as I love the whole Matthias family.'

Claudia looked at him with tear-drenched eyes, but she was quiet again, self-control regained with an effort he recognised. 'I think you *did* fall in love with Jessica – I don't know why; I saw it that night at the *pensione* even though I refused to believe it. *Something* about her

183

is still haunting you, even when we're in bed together. You told me once that I mustn't hate her, but I shall . . . always.' She saw his fingers open in a gesture that said more than he would ever put into words – his grief for her, and for himself recognition of what had been found too late and irretrievably lost. Even her anger seemed pointless now in the face of such an admission.

'I *shall* stay here . . . Elizabeth wants me to,' she said at last, 'and I love New York.'

He nodded, unable to deny what she'd said about Jessica, or reply to it. 'The book will be ours, jointly,' he murmured instead. 'Photographs – Jacques Duclos; text – Claudia Matthias. Yours will turn out to have been the greater contribution.'

She accepted it as her due. Then she stood up, stared at him for a long moment, and swept towards the door. He supposed she knew that she was being watched by everyone there. She was living the most tragic moment of her life so far, and consciously or not an audience was being used to sustain her through it. He thought Llewellyn would have said she was behaving just as he expected of his daughter.

Jacques followed her out after a moment or two, and walked the considerable distance to his own hotel. The night life of the city all around him went unnoticed and unheard – the only things he was aware of concerned himself – he'd lost Claudia for a fantasy born of the serenissima's damnable tricks. It left him empty again, just as he'd arrived in Venice. Claudia's warmth and beauty *should* have been enough, God knew, for *any* man, but the certainty had grown with every day and night they spent together that she wasn't the woman his need had fastened on. Jessica Smythson was that woman. He'd known it for the truth the night she was saying goodbye to Llewellyn at the *pensione*. He'd known it in his heart every time he forced himself to make love to Claudia. That pretence had finally had to end, but there was no one to put in Claudia's place. Jessica's letter had made that brutally clear. Fate at its most ironic had seen to it that *he'd* been the one to fall victim to an illusion, not her.

Chapter 23

An assignment in the north made the long summer bearable. It wasn't every interior designer who got the chance to convert a baronial keep in the wilds of Inverness-shire into a new home for a desert princeling. But Jess found her Arab client courteous, knowledgeable, and unexpectedly endearing as well. The ever-falling early-autumn rain was something she could have done without, but seeing a sophisticated, worldly man watch it with the entranced pleasure of a child at a toy-shop window transformed her own view of what the heavens poured forth.

When her work was finished, his invitation for her to stay on was flatteringly pressing. He was offering her, she knew, much more than a lavish holiday. She appreciated the delicacy with which it was done, and for a mad moment even hesitated over whether to accept the offer or not. Being loved by such a man would be an experience that would never come her way again, and her unsatisfied heart and body craved love. But a remnant of wisdom said it wouldn't do – what she craved was another man altogether. It was the face of Jacques Duclos that haunted her restless dreams at night.

But she went back to London reluctantly – the Highland scenery had been hard to leave behind. Travelling south, she thought of something she'd once said to Giancarlo Rasini – a long time ago, it seemed now. Cities *were* dehumanising; she would find herself some small, green country place still geared to the rhythm of the seasons, where stars were visible on clear nights, and the air tasted of rain. Pinky Todd would smile incredulously at the idea, as any dyed-in-the-wool Londoner might, and even Gerald would thank her for the offer of out-of-town weekends and probably refuse. It didn't matter – she'd enjoy her bolt-hole all alone if need be, just as soon as she was able to find it.

With the thought still in her mind, she paid off her taxi from Euston and turned in at the gate of the Dutch House. The elegant glass canopy that had once led to the front door hadn't survived the last war, but Gerald had never had it replaced, preferring the house without it. She thought for a moment that it was he who stood there waiting for her, but it was a man less tall and thin, and he was wearing formal evening dress, with the half-hidden gleam of ribbons and decorations.

Looking incongruously grand, being Nathan Acheson, he seemed entirely at ease at the same time.

'I rang Smythson's, Jessica. Your very pleasant colleague said that you were expected back here this evening, and gave me your address; but perhaps this is an inconvenient moment to call – you're tired from travelling.'

She smiled as she shook his hand, aware of being deeply pleased to see him. 'I've been sitting for hours in a comfortable train – it's a more restful way of spending the day than usual!'

'I have half an hour to spare before I must present myself at a Mansion House dinner. I hoped you wouldn't mind if I called on you.'

'I don't mind at all, but you'll have to forgive a climb – I live on the top floor,' Jess told him.

She led the way upstairs and into her sitting room, feeling puzzled now as well as pleased that he should be there. A spare half-hour could have been passed more easily watching television in his hotel suite, and Holland Park was scarcely anyone's idea of a convenient stopping-place on the way to the City.

Offered a drink, Nathan chose mineral water, explaining gravely that when financiers and bankers met to discuss the poverty of the Third World they first dined and wined themselves rather lavishly. Jess poured sherry for herself and then turned round to find him studying the room with care.

'Restful . . . and I envy you *that*,' he said, pointing to a small knee-hole desk gleaming like silk with age and much polishing.

'A junk-shop find years ago. Gerald was very put out that I spotted it first!' She smiled at him over her glass. 'Is Elvira with you in London?'

'No, this is just an overnight visit. I left her with friends in Paris.'

'My grandmother called here on her way home at the beginning of the summer – she enjoyed herself in Venice.' Jess hesitated a moment and then risked her next question. 'Is Elvira happier there now?'

Nathan's normally impassive face showed a trace of regret before it was banished again. 'She would move to the Gobi Desert if I asked her to, and she's making more of an effort with Venice than I deserve. She agrees that it's important for us to be there, but I doubt if she'll ever share my feeling for the place.'

'And the Brunis – are they still with you?' Jess ventured next.

'Most certainly – Bianca is an excellent, though anxious, housekeeper. Elvira hopes eventually to teach her to smile!' Jess's expectant face asked the question she didn't dare put into words, and Nathan answered it. 'Guiseppe is invaluable too. Some terracotta urns were required for the courtyard – ancient, weathered ones, Elvira naturally specified – and he was obliging enough even to provide *them.*'

186

'He's a Neapolitan, I expect you know,' Jess said, apparently apropos of nothing already mentioned.

'I didn't realise it sufficiently to begin with; I do now. It turned out that the pots, though beautiful, weren't his to provide.'

'So . . . what happened?'

Nathan took another sip of water. 'I bought the *palazzo* they came from.'

'Of course,' Jess managed after a moment's pause. 'How . . . how sensible!' She wouldn't smile, she promised herself, for fear of offending him – would somehow stifle the giggle she could feel rising in her throat. But she struggled in vain – the giggle became a laugh that seemed to echo round the room, and the blankness in his face only made things worse She gulped and mopped her tears, saw his own mouth twitch, and realised that he was now in the same helpless condition as herself.

At last, more or less restored again, they looked at one another with great contentment. 'It wasn't really funny,' Jess tried to explain, 'just absurd!'

'I know – *that's* what made it funny.' Nathan replaced the spectacles he'd had to remove and inspected her through them. 'You look better now – you were tired when you arrived, and I'm sure Elvira would say you're much too thin.'

It wasn't the sort of comment he normally made, and he heard himself say it with astonishment. But it wasn't the first time he'd behaved out of character with Jessica Smythson, and he could see that it might easily become a habit.

'It's been the sort of summer here that I don't like – hot and sticky,' she explained, 'and we've been very busy; but I can take a breather now.' She was of the opinion herself that the laughter of a moment ago had been mistakenly relaxing; reticence could easily have been mislaid, and if she wasn't very careful she'd be pouring out to this most unexpectedly sympathetic of listeners all the loneliness of the past few months and the constant strain of trying to look cheerful. She took another fortifying swig of sherry, and wondered whether to remind him that his spare half-hour must be nearly up.

But, unhurriedly, he was glancing round the room again, as if collecting images that pleased him.

'In a more perfect world I could stay here and enjoy the simple supper I hope you'd offer me,' he said regretfully. 'As it is, I must go and drink warm champagne, eat caterers' food, and listen to bright young men telling me how the world's problems can be solved.'

'You don't sound as if you're going to agree with them,' Jess ventured.

'Well, I might, if I could see how to do what they suggest without ruining the rest of us.'

He stood up to leave, and Jess walked with him down the stairs and out into the October dusk.

'I'm afraid you're going to be late if you can't find a taxi immediately,' she said, but he pointed to a car drawn up at the kerb just ahead of them.

'That little flag on the bonnet seems to make policemen part the traffic for us very considerately.'

'Like the Israelites and the Red Sea!' Her transfiguring smile appeared as she looked at him. 'I'm afraid you're even more of a very important person than I realised.'

Nathan waved the idea aside, but had one more surprise in store. 'I should like to call on you and Gerald Smythson in Sloane Street tomorrow. Shall we say nine thirty?'

She agreed, waved him on his way, and went indoors to spend the evening in fruitless speculation. She waited for Gerald to return from dining with one of his grander clients, and then went downstairs to warn him of the following morning's appointment.

'My guess is that Nathan wants something done in New York,' she suggested. 'If you feel well enough to make the journey, I think you'd enjoy working for him. Otherwise, may we please turn the offer down . . . even at the risk of offending someone I like very much indeed?'

She smiled to show that she was rational and calm, just stubbornly bent on staying in London. 'I suspect my grandmother of lobbying again – it's time to insist that we can find our own commissions!'

It sounded a lame excuse to her own ears, but it was the best she could do. Admit the true reason she would not – that the Achesons and her grandmother were too intimate friends; that Claudia, she knew from Llewellyn's letters, was still living in Elizabeth's apartment, with Jacques no doubt also close at hand. She could manage very well as long as she never had to see them together.

'I won't . . . *can't* . . . go,' she had to add unsteadily, trying to smile instead of bursting into tears, 'not even to save Smythson's reputation.'

Gerald patted her clenched hands, and looked at her with immense affection. 'Sweetheart, then don't; leave *me* to worry about Smythson's reputation!'

Nathan arrived punctually the following morning, looking none the worse for whatever strategic battles had been fought at the Mansion House the evening before. Jess introduced him all round, and then retreated to her own work table. If he wanted to enlist Smythson's help he must talk to Gerald, whom she felt sure he would like; she need take no part in the discussion. But Nathan had his own way of conducting business, which was simply to lasso the member of the herd he had his eye on.

'I'm delighted for your own sake that you're looking so well now,

Mr Smythson, but also for mine – because I hope to persuade Jessica to do some more work for me. I realise that she wouldn't want to leave London if your health were still an anxiety.'

Gerald appreciated the courteous phrasing – not many powerful men, in his experience, put themselves to the trouble of being so thoughtful. It behoved him to make an equal effort, even if it was only to phrase a refusal very politely.

'How kind of you to ask for Jess again. My health *isn't* a problem now, provided I behave sensibly, but your difficulty, I'm afraid, is more likely to be with her. She's very tired of being away from home, having been constantly on the move this year. Even her grandmother has failed to entice her to New York, so you'll have to forgive her for saying no to you as well.'

He was aware of having said too much or not enough, but at least Nathan Acheson could understand that he was being refused and take his leave. Instead, the quiet American was shaking his head. '*Not* New York in my case,' he corrected calmly. 'It's Venice that I hope to entice her back to.'

Caught at the disadvantage of not knowing whether it made the proposition seem better or worse, Gerald bravely admitted it. 'A return to Venice didn't occur to either of us. I think you'll have to put the proposition to Jessica yourself.'

He left the room and they returned together, with only the one word muttered in her ear. Nathan smiled at her but still spoke to Gerald. 'How much do you know of what happened during Jessica's previous visit?'

'Most of it, I think. I heard about her half-brother's rather too radical friends, and the articles in the *Gazzettino*, and of course the ongoing battle between the die-hard preservationists and the Viva Venezia brigade!'

'I was one of the preservationists, of course – still am,' Nathan admitted. 'But the interior designer Elvira hired, though perhaps not very radical herself, *was* inclined to take us to task for not listening to our opponents' point of view.'

'She sounds to have been impertinent,' Jess mumbled. 'You should have ignored her.'

'I might, but unfortunately she happened to be right.' He smiled faintly at the surprise on her face, but went on with his story. 'I know the marvellous work that has been done by the British Venice in Peril fund; our American committees have contributed their share, and so have dozens of others, and I'm still convinced that this work had to be undertaken. But when Marco came to see me – rather unwillingly, I suspect – I made him guide me about the city . . . made him confront me with the problems he assumed I knew nothing about. I didn't know nearly enough, it turned out – some of the poverty and decrepitude still visible there scarcely seemed to belong to what we think of as prosperous northern Italy at the end of the twentieth century.'

'For Marco it's a crusade,' Jess insisted. 'That means that he's blind to his opponents' legitimate interests. He's even willing to ignore their rights if they clash with what *he* sees as justice, but it's for other people that he wants it – never for himself.'

'Which makes him a hopeless proposition as a politician,' Nathan pointed out. 'He couldn't learn to be dishonest enough. It's partly why I offered him a different job.'

'Doing what?' she asked rather breathlessly.

'Running a housing trust, financed by me initially, but eventually self-supporting. The trust will buy up derelict *palazzi* and tenement houses, and convert them into apartments that aren't a disgrace for human beings to have to live in. The architect – you know him, Guido Moro – will judge which buildings are suitable. Marco's job will be to supervise the work, select the tenants, and administer the trust.'

'A large task for a young man,' Gerald pointed out.

'I know,' but Nathan sounded pleased. 'Large enough, I hope, to satisfy even *his* appetite for social reform!' He saw the anxiety in Jess's face and suddenly smiled at her. 'Don't worry – I'm not burdening him with more than he can manage. He's intelligent, well versed in the practicalities of running a business, and devoted to what the trust is going to do. He may need a little help to begin with, but he will do very well.'

'Do I now see where Jessica comes in?' Gerald asked quietly.

'As the trust's design consultant, I hope. The structural matters will be for Moro to handle, but the apartments themselves – to be rented out unfurnished – will need to be planned and decorated. Then Marco must discover who needs rehousing most urgently. I should like our tenants to be mixed – young and old together, not separated as they so often are nowadays. I imagine a visit from Jessica every three months or so would be required to begin with – perhaps less frequently later on.'

She was still silent, and it was Gerald who felt obliged to say something. 'The job sounds wonderfully worth doing, but good working relations would be essential. Jess would have to decide whether they're achievable in this particular case – she might easily fear they aren't, given the personalities involved.'

A flicker of amusement brought her strained face to life. 'I *would* have doubted it last winter, but both Marco and Signor Moro must now be so happy with the trust's philosophy that I don't see why harmony shouldn't reign!'

She still hesitated, nevertheless, unable to explain to Nathan, at least, why she was so reluctant to go back to Venice. There was no fresh emotional upheaval to fear, and she'd spent a wearying summer burying every memory that could possibly disturb. But other people had been involved – the family at the *pensione*, and especially Giancarlo. She wanted now, more than anything else, not to damage whatever peace of mind *he'd* struggled to find.

'Does Marco know you're offering the job to me?' she finally asked.

'Of course, and he hopes you'll take it.'

There was enormous pleasure in knowing that, apart from Llewellyn himself, someone else in the family would be glad if she went back. She was aware, too, of the huge compliment lurking in Nathan's offer, and of the difficulty of refusing it when she'd been so volubly on the side of those who believed Venice needed exactly what he now proposed. With care, she could avoid meeting Giancarlo, and the two who would want her back least – Lorenza and Claudia – weren't there themselves; perhaps it *would* be possible to go after all.

At last she made up her mind. 'I'd like to take the job if it really can be managed in brief visits. When will the first building be ready to work on?'

'It's being worked on now,' Nathan confirmed cheerfully, 'and it's the *palazzo* from which Guiseppe liberated his pots! Marco is setting up his office in the empty rooms at the Palazzo Ghisalberti. He and Moro ought to be ready for you by the middle of November, I think. Marco will be in touch with you about that, and my people in New York will confirm all the business details between us. Elvira and I are going there soon, but we shall be back in Venice before Christmas.' Then he turned to look at Jess, and she wondered how she could ever have thought him cold and unfeeling.

'I was afraid you were going to turn us down. Marco's faith in me would have been shaken before we'd scarcely started!'

Then with a little bow to each of them, he was gone, leaving them staring at one another.

'You're smiling about something,' Gerald said. 'The pleasure of going back to Venice?'

'No, I'm not even sure that it *will* be all pleasure. I was thinking of Giuseppe Bruni. He has a theory that nothing should go to waste, and I foresaw some problems there; but I should have guessed that Nathan would turn out to be a man after his own heart!'

She went back to Venice on a grey November day that happened to mark the first anniversary of her mother's death. It seemed to have been the longest year she'd ever known, and the most crucial . . . the one she would have to use as a yardstick for measuring all subsequent joy and sadness. But throughout the flight back to the Lagoon she told herself with the earnestness of a child repeating a vital lesson that this was a different time, a different visit; *nothing* that had happened before would happen again. There was no unknown father to meet or to avoid, and no residue of bitterness to hold against him for Gillian's wasted life and death; she wouldn't even be thrown off balance by Venice itself this time – she was prepared for it now. She made up her mind, reluctantly, to avoid all the Rasinis – it wouldn't be difficult, because the *palazzo* to be worked on was nowhere near their own. The only other place to avoid was Burano; if she didn't go there, she could manage not to think of Jacques at all.

The change from her previous visit was emphasised at once by the sight of Marco waiting for her in the arrivals hall. Despite what Nathan had said, she still wasn't entirely sure of her half-brother's welcome until she saw him smile; then suddenly it seemed right to have come.

'I was afraid you'd remember that we hadn't allowed you to enjoy Venice very much,' he admitted. 'Llewellyn is like a cat with two tails, partly because he was proved right! He *said* you wouldn't turn Mr Acheson's offer down.'

'What else has been happening?' Jess asked as they steered away from the traffic leaving the airport. 'When I last heard from him, Claudia was still in New York, and Lorenza in Paris.'

'Lorenza's back, though not for long. She's getting married – to the man she met in Paris, Filippo Adani . . . in fact, you'll be here for the wedding next week!' Marco gave his familiar little shrug, expressing anxiety for something he could do nothing about. 'Mamma thinks it's all much too sudden, but Lorenza's more than old enough to know what she wants, and she insists that it's Filippo and his two children. In the New Year at least they'll be moving nearer to us – he's going to be La Scala's chief designer.'

'Well, that must be a comfort to your mother – Milan's a good deal closer than Paris,' Jess pointed out.

'Scarcely – to a good Venetian, "abroad" is anything west of Padua! Claudia's coming home for the wedding next week but afterwards she'll go back to New York.'

'With . . .' Jess cleared the huskiness from her throat and tried again. 'With Jacques, of course.'

'No, he's in Paris now, working with his publisher, I believe.' Marco frowned, apparently at a boat foolhardy enough to cross the channel ahead of them. 'Claudia wrote to say that although their work was finished, she was staying on. Thanks to your grandmother, she's having too good a time to leave, and she's just landed a job with one of the top women's magazines. She *sounds* delighted with life but it isn't what I expected, all the same – I thought she'd go wherever Jacques went, for ever and a day. Women are more than I can fathom out at times.'

He turned to look at Jessica, and risked what he hadn't meant to say. 'We thought *you* were going to take on Giancarlo – Battistina told the neighbourhood so.'

192

'She's not often wrong, but for once she was,' Jessica mumbled unsteadily, while her agitated mind and heart tried to deal with what he'd said about Claudia and Jacques. She would have staked her life on the girl's devotion . . . so it must have been Jacques who'd decided that even *her* bright, adventurous spirit wouldn't be enough. Perhaps he didn't intend any hurt, but the terrible pity of it was that women went on failing to see how little they could change or hold him.

Marco registered the pain in her face, and cast about for something harmless to say. 'Madame Duclos is coming down for the wedding – well, she was bound to when it was through *her* that Lorenza met Filippo. Mamma's getting nervous . . . afraid she won't be able to hold her own with Parisian chic – I don't know why, when she seems to me to be everything that's beautiful.'

Jess managed to summon up a smile. 'It might help if you and Llewellyn told her so more often. There's nothing like a compliment or two to bolster a lady's self-esteem in the face of stiff competition!'

Marco's answering grin, combining amusement and affection, was a pleasure in itself, but he did better still. 'Dear Jess . . . I'm so *glad* you decided to come; I was afraid you wouldn't.'

'And I'm glad you're glad, but now you can tell me about our first assignment.'

'Well, it's up in the north of the city – in the Cannareggio, and therefore furthest from the wealth that the tourists bring in. The neighbourhood is badly run down, and the trust's first *palazzo* was derelict when we bought it. But Guido Moro is well on with the building repairs already. He's got Luigi Arrendo with him, by the way, and the same workmen you had at the Palazzo Ghisalberti.'

'Then we can't fail to transform a ruin into something beautiful.'

'That's what I think too,' Marco agreed contentedly.

With some resistance from her half-brother – and more, she suspected, from Llewellyn – she'd insisted on saving time by staying in a nearby hotel, instead of in the *pensione*. But her true reason for avoiding it couldn't be admitted to. Her image of it, and the confrontation in the hall before she'd left Venice that first time, were etched into her memory. If she ever walked through the door again she would instantly relive her half-sisters' animosity, and see Jacques' angry face disclaiming all knowledge of a woman who'd stepped back from the danger he represented. No, she wasn't going back to Maria's *pensione* if she could avoid it. Nor, she was now deciding to herself, would she go to Lorenza's wedding, even if Llewellyn tried to invite her. By working hard and long hours, she could be finished and back in London by the time the day arrived.

Chapter 24

The *palazzo* that Guido Moro was rescuing for Nathan followed the traditional layout of such buildings. Without damaging its outward façade, he said, three reasonably sized apartments could be contrived on each of the three floors – nine families therefore comfortably housed; twenty or thirty people able to live decently where they belonged, instead of joining the exodus to the mainland. From the outside the building would be undisturbed; within, it would brilliantly solve the technical problems destroying so much of the city. Methane gas, instead of oil, for heating would cause no air pollution, and its own small sewage treatment plant would result in only purified waste going into the canal. Nothing less than this, Guido said sternly, was now acceptable.

Jess was greeted by Luigi and his men with smiling warmth, but this she'd been fairly confident of receiving; they'd parted as friends. Nathan's architect was a different matter. In her previous collaboration with him, Guido Moro had been a morose, unfriendly partner; now, she scarcely recognised him for the same man. When he even invited her to dine with him at a local *trattoria* one evening, she took the risk of saying so.

'I was angry with myself then, not *you*,' he explained almost shyly. 'I felt I'd been bought by Nathan Acheson's money, talked into doing something I disapproved of.'

'But the other you that cherishes old buildings and can't bear to see them destroyed at least knew that the Palazzo Ghisalberti *was* being preserved.'

His heavy, bearded face broke into a smile. '*Esattemente* . . . I was torn in two – nothing is straightforward here!'

It raised a painful echo in her mind of other conversations, but before she could put them aside, Guido Moro spoke again.

'You had problems of your own to begin with, I believe. Marco thought it best to explain to me about your connection. I should never have guessed it, but now and then I see a little likeness between the two of you. I know his sisters too, of course, but you don't resemble *them* at all.'

Jess agreed that this was so, and led the conversation back to the next building the trust might hope to tackle. But at the end of the evening she reverted once more to the subject they'd begun with.

'You spoke of being bought by Nathan Acheson. We all are, to the extent that he pays us for what we do, but I'm sure his own view is quite different. I think that what we're involved in now is a private memorial to someone he loved, as well as his public gift to Venice. He sees *us* as helping to build it for him.'

'It makes a difference,' Guido agreed gravely. 'But in any case, I know there's no shame at all in what we're doing now.'

Having won her battle with Llewellyn about not staying at the *pensione*, Jess felt obliged to yield to another pressing invitation. The Feast of the Madonna della Salute would fall, as usual, on 21 November. She *must* – he insisted – take part and share supper with them afterwards.

'It isn't something you can be here and *miss*, Jess,' he roared down the telephone. 'Think of it – three hundred and fifty years after the event we still solemnly thank God and each other yet again that the plague is over! We build a bridge of boats across the Canal Grande, and get our only chance of the year to see the Basilica as Longhena intended it to be seen, with the great doors facing the water thrown wide open. Of *course* you've got to come.'

She agreed that she must, and accepted the rest of his invitation because she could see no way of avoiding it. It meant, at least, that she would be able to apologise in person to Maria for not staying on for the wedding; no invitation need even be given, because she would be on her way back to London.

The festival *was*, as Llewellyn had said, something not to have missed. The Venetians weren't more noticeably enthusiastic churchgoers than other people, but they still seemed to prefer their religious occasions to go reverently. The packed bridge of boats and crowded church celebrated an intervention from on high that, for the people gathered there, might only have happened yesterday. Afterwards, walking beside Llewellyn on the way home, Jess explained the problem she was still wrestling with.

'Marco once said to me that Venice couldn't manage both past and present – there simply wasn't enough space. But I realised tonight that its life isn't divisible; past, present, future too, are all part of the extraordinary entity that is Venice. Jacques Duclos said something similar when I asked him why he photographed it in its winter desolation. It's the whole thing we have to cherish – old, new, preserved, restored, glorious, or ugly as sin!'

'Marco's beginning to understand that too,' Llewellyn said slowly. 'It wouldn't have happened not so long ago, but the other day I overheard him explaining to a stroppy delivery man that if he couldn't drive his boat at a speed that wouldn't endanger the underpinnings of precious, *ancient* buildings, he could give up doing any business with the trust at all!'

'Marvellous . . . *dear* Marco! No wonder Nathan knew who to pick for the job.'

Llewellyn smiled at her from under the brim of his old hat. 'Maria thinks you won't stay for the wedding – change your mind, girl, please.'

But they were back at the *pensione*, and although she shook her head, there was no need to answer. Jess knew that Maria wouldn't try persuasion herself, and the reason was clear. Lorenza didn't want her, and on this occasion it was only what Lorenza wanted that mattered. The self-possessed girl was untalkative until almost the end of the evening, said only a polite thank you for the small, lovely piece of Murano glass that Jess had selected as a present, and then issued a surprise invitation to see some other gifts already collected in her bedroom.

'I hope you'll be very happy with Filippo,' Jess said when they were alone. It seemed a trifle sparse, but she'd decided that with this unfriendly sister she must err on the side of too little rather than too much.

'I shall make sure that we *are* happy,' Lorenza answered with some firmness. 'It's a matter of making up one's mind to it, and deciding what one wants. *You* don't seem able to – poor Giancarlo must be tired of waiting.'

Wearily, Jess parried once again a suggestion she was growing tired of. 'Giancarlo isn't being kept waiting by me and he makes his own decisions about happiness.'

'You didn't want him in the end, you mean. Did you change your mind about Jacques Duclos as well? Battistina would have it that you were smiling at Giancarlo, but Mamma saw you watching Jacques at the Countess's dinner party. I suppose you know he's back in Paris? Claudia pretends not to mind, because she won't have us pity her, but she can't hide the truth from me. Jacques is bringing his mother down for the wedding, and of course I want Fanny to be here. But he won't stay and I can't pretend that I want him to now.'

'And nor do you want me. Well, without either of us you should be able to have a happy day.'

Lorenza's unsmiling face agreed that this was so, and Jess thought that Maria was right to be anxious about her daughter. But just as they were about to return downstairs, Lorenza suddenly gave in; the need to make this alien Englishwoman understand had become too insistent.

'People think I don't love Filippo because he isn't beautiful and grave and grand, like Giancarlo Rasini. He's an ordinary, nice, clever man who can scarcely believe even now that I only want to make him

197

and his children happy; but it's what I *shall* do. Is there anything wrong in that, Jessica?'

Her voice and flashing eyes flung down a challenge that, after a moment's pause, Jess accepted.

'There's *nothing* wrong in it,' she answered quietly, 'and I doubt if he's ordinary at all. I think you're very lucky.'

It was raining again . . . just as Jacques remembered it had been nearly a year ago when he'd stumbled into the *pensione* for the first time. They weren't going there now; he'd explained to Fanny that they must make the other wedding guests an excuse. Maria would have her hands full, looking after Filippo's relatives and friends. He would treat his mother to a brief stay at the Gritti Palace instead. Fanny had accepted the offer, rather preferring it to a *pensione*, however comfortable. They were on their way to the hotel now in a water-taxi, but she was looking about her unenthusiastically.

'It needs sunlight,' Jacques insisted quietly beside her. 'Rain washes away the magic, and you see only the decrepitude.' She grimaced, then smiled disarmingly, and he registered again with a small twinge of fear how vivid and attractive she still was – fair hair artistically touched with highlights, face perfectly made up, clothes just as perfectly judged. He'd found himself worrying about that on the journey down: Llewellyn couldn't help being the impressionable man he was, and Fanny – dearly though he loved her – was herself. She could no more resist exerting herself to please and captivate than a bird could fold its wings and not fly. Much suffering had been caused in the past year, but Jacques passionately wanted not to be involved in any more. He would have spared Maria this ordeal if he could . . . now found himself framing a small, unaccustomed prayer that his mother would understand how different she was from the sophisticated, worldly women known in Paris.

'I'll take you to see the sights before I leave,' he promised. 'Well, as many as we can cram in.'

Fanny shook her head. 'Your father dragged me round San Marco and the Doge's Palace years ago; once was probably enough, I think – murals that went on for ever round the walls, and fat gods and goddesses sprawled across miles of painted ceiling!'

She expected to see him smile, but she didn't know what he was suddenly remembering – a rainy morning at the Ca'Rezzonico, watching Jessica Smythson examine just such a fleshy ceiling.

Fanny glanced away from his withdrawn expression, but risked a comment that she tried to make sound light. 'I'm sorry you're going to rush back to Paris before Claudia arrives, but I suppose I see why.'

'You *know* why,' he insisted. 'I only came at all because I owed an explanation to Maria and Llewellyn. I don't expect them to be pleased to see me; why should they be? I've used and abandoned their daughter.'

Fanny didn't argue, nor say to him as she might have done to someone else that he'd treated Claudia as Llewellyn had treated *her* in Paris all those years ago. Men and women behaved as they must, in her considerable experience; the only essential thing was to accept the fact with fortitude and grace. She'd managed to teach Lorenza that, and the wedding they were gathering for was the happy result.

Inside the Gothic splendour of the Gritti Palace she smiled encouragingly at her tired-faced son. 'Darling, you didn't sleep on the train last night, and nor did I, but I shall be ready this evening for dinner at the *pensione*, looking my dazzling best – I'm not going to have Llewellyn thinking I've grown into a poor old hag!'

'No chance,' he said with the faintest of grins. 'But it will serve you right if Maria takes the wind out of your sails. Don't hurt her, please, Mamma.'

Fanny heard the little note of anxiety in his voice and shook her head. 'Of course not, dearest . . . how could I when she was so kind to you?'

He accepted it as the reassurance he needed, but even so he escorted her across the canal that evening with calmness under very imperfect control. One way and another the dinner party was more likely to be a test of everyone's endurance than a pleasure. But even so, when Llewellyn came out on to the path to greet them, he acknowledged to himself the possibility that Fanny's charm and Llewellyn's irrepressible verve might salvage the evening for them. And so it proved.

Dressed to kill in his best velvet smoking jacket, Llewellyn kissed the guest's hand and cheek, then smiled at her.

'Fanny, my dear . . . welcome to Venice. Lorenza said there was nothing to fear, but I couldn't help it . . . time has passed, alas . . . you *might* have grown just a little tired and frail! Silly of me, I now see. You're the very spirit of youth and beauty!'

His silver hair came as a shock, and there were unquestionably lines etched into his brown face that hard-lived years had put there; but Fanny could smile with the radiance of relief – the unthinkable *hadn't* happened; Llewellyn hadn't grown old and ordinary. She wouldn't forget her promise to Jacques, but it didn't mean that they couldn't now enjoy this reunion.

They were swept indoors on a wave of bonhomie that Jacques felt extended to himself as well, but his heart missed a beat at the sight of Maria waiting for them. She was dressed in black as usual, greying hair drawn back from her face and fastened in a complicated coil. Watching her greet his mother, Jacques thought them as different as two women could be. Fanny must recognise that too, please God, and adjust her Parisian behaviour a little.

'It's time we met,' Maria was saying quietly. 'I don't know how to thank you enough for the help you gave Lorenza. She set out for Paris in despair, and came back happy.'

Fanny looked at the quiet-faced, plump woman in front of her – Llewellyn's chosen life-partner. She wasn't insensitive enough not to see why; here were all the strength and gentleness even he would have needed.

'*You* were kind to Jacques . . . he told me you *all* were,' Fanny said almost gravely. 'Despite what's happened since, we seem to have become a family.'

Maria's expression wavered into a smile. She looked past Fanny to where Jacques stood behind his mother, and then held out her hands. He took them and pulled her into a hug that expressed all the love and regret he couldn't put into words. Then he released her and gently smoothed her ruffled hair.

'I'm sorry . . . so very sorry,' he murmured only to her. 'But Elizabeth Harrington *will* take care of her – she promised me.'

'I know . . . she wrote to me as well . . . such kindness. We have Jessica to thank for that.' Maria smiled mistily at him, and then it was Marco's turn to be introduced to Fanny. The worst was over, and Jacques felt his jangled nerves relax; the visit was going to be all right after all.

It was Marco, a few minutes later, who told him that Jessica was back in Venice. There was more talk, something about them working on a *palazzo* together, but he missed most of it. He could only think that she might have walked in on them that evening while he was unprepared. Perhaps it was a pity that she hadn't; he might have found that he could manage a meeting very well – call himself cured.

'She'll be here for the wedding?' he eventually managed to ask, but saw Marco shake his head.

'No – we couldn't persuade her . . . at least, I couldn't; I'm afraid Lorenza didn't try very hard.' He made a brave attempt to grin at Jacques. 'You've had time to discover that my sisters are a law unto themselves!'

'*All* your sisters,' Jacques agreed unsmilingly. 'Beget only sons, I should, when the time comes . . . I believe they're much less trouble.'

Marco's hand touched his shoulder for a moment, shaming his earlier fear that he might be made to feel unwelcome. Maria's goodness was in them all, but perhaps especially in this quiet young man.

Chapter 25

Jess spent long hours working with her colleagues or alone, driven by an overwhelming sense of urgency to complete what she must do, and leave. She refused Llewellyn's invitations, and scuttled about the city whenever she had to go out, feeling the need of some Carnival disguise. It might have been comic in its absurdity if there hadn't been aspects about it that *weren't* comic. She salvaged her conscience in one direction, at least, by writing to Emilia Rasini. Her time on this trip was too short for visiting . . . they were, please, to forgive her for not calling, and must take care of themselves most carefully until she came back.

Her most pressing need was to hide from Jacques, whom she knew from Marco was now in Venice with Fanny Duclos. A faint and unadmitted hope that he might come looking for her had withered and died by the morning of Lorenza's wedding day, when at last she was free to leave. With the morning flight to London fully booked, she had hours to fill, and no safe hiding-place except the hotel. She could take refuge instead in some corner of the great, dimly gleaming Aladdin's Cave in the Piazza, but she'd never much liked San Marco, except for its gallery of glorious horses. Then suddenly a solution to her problem seemed simple after all – she would go to the Torcello Madonna. Peace of mind had been recovered there once before, and she would be likely to have the Lady to herself in midwinter.

In fact, the cathedral was sprinkled with visitors – Japanese, mostly, busy with their cameras as usual. Watching them, Jacques wondered if they saw anything of what they photographed, or understood at all the mosaic images that covered the wall in front of them. The pictured story of the Last Judgement, realised with Byzantine richness and precision must once have been compelling to the Lagoon inhabitants unable to read; but what could these people from a totally different culture make of it now?

He moved on towards the eastern end of the church, just in time to see someone get up from her seat and walk towards the exit. She was a slender woman in a grey tweed suit, looking out of place among the small, casually dressed tourists. With the long-legged stride he remembered, she'd almost covered the distance to the door before he'd recovered from a few seconds when his heart seemed to have stopped beating.

He caught up with her on the green outside, and although she faltered for a moment he thought she managed the first dislocating start of recognition better than he'd done himself.

'I saw you leave,' he muttered. 'You rather tower over a flock of dainty Orientals.'

There was no other greeting, and he sounded angry; she was too tall, she thought distractedly, as well as everything else. But blood was flowing round her body again, and she could even find something to say.

'I heard you were in Venice. I'm going home this afternoon. Having stayed in here too long, I see that I'm going to miss the next boat back, but Llewellyn introduced me once to a nice little café lady – I shall go and see if she remembers me.'

Uninvited, Jacques walked beside her; she didn't know why when he still looked so frowningly aloof. A moment later, because she *was* remembered, they were shown into the room where she and Llewellyn had once drunk coffee on a cold January morning – it seemed an endless time ago. There was something neatly symmetrical about this visit, she reflected – here she'd met her father for the first time; here she would finally say goodbye to Jacques Duclos. After the gap of months since he'd left Venice he'd become a stranger again. It was a relief to know that – she couldn't have endured a meaningless leap into ease and intimacy again. If he looked tired and drawn, it was no concern of hers; if he was regretting the break with Claudia, that was entirely his own affair. In a quarter of an hour at the most she could get up and say a careless goodbye, and leave him there to whatever train of thought kept him withdrawn and silent.

Jacques roused himself to thank the *padrona* for the coffee she brought, and listened patiently while she explained that the visitors' season was almost over – now, *Dio mio*, there'd be the loneliness and the winter rain and storms in the Lagoon to survive until next spring. She *liked* the foreigners herself, though some Torcello people didn't. She padded away at last, and he was free to look at Jess – reddish-fair hair tousled by the breeze, cheekbones a little more prominent than before, as if she'd lost weight. Quite an ordinary face when all was said and done. He was angry with himself all over again for having held it so ineffaceably in his memory, but it seemed reasonable to be still more angry with *her*, for causing him so much pain.

'You decided not to attend Lorenza's wedding?' he asked in a voice that suggested more of the bloody-mindedness she'd once or twice confessed to; she was still not going to be a part of her father's family, by her own deliberate choice.

'I'm not going for the same reason as you,' she pointed out. 'Lorenza didn't want me.'

It sounded so unarguable that he was forced to change tack. 'I saw quite a lot of your grandmother in New York – she was very helpful and kind. I gathered from her that Gerald Smythson made a good recovery.'

The mention of New York seemed dangerous, and she was careful to concentrate on Gerald. 'Yes . . . he just has to pace himself more slowly, that's all.' It seemed to bring them to another conversational dead-end, but it was the best she could do – to initiate a subject seemed beyond her.

'Marco told me about the Acheson Trust. *Pace* Lorenza, at least *he* seems to enjoy working with you.'

A smile lifted the strain from Jess's face for a moment. 'Yes, but most of all he enjoys his new job; it fits him like a glove. He's so contented with what he's doing that even the spitefulness of some of his so-called friends doesn't worry him – they think he's gone over to the other side, but he knows that what the trust is doing is right.'

She sipped coffee, waiting to be cross-examined again, but Jacques took her by surprise. 'Now it's your turn to ask a question.'

She thought carefully and produced one. 'What comes after the New York book? I seem to remember you mentioning Hong Kong or Sydney.'

'It's not decided yet. What about you? Rumour hinted that you might end up here with Rasini; is that still on the cards?'

'I'm afraid rumour lied,' Jess said calmly. 'I merely came to do a job for Nathan Acheson. If not to attend the wedding, what brought you back?'

He hadn't remembered that her eyes were quite so clearly grey or that her glance was so direct. She'd probably be unable to lie or prevaricate even if her life depended on it. 'My mother hates travelling alone so I decided to bring her. But I should have come anyway – to make my peace with Maria and Llewellyn. I expect Marco's told you that Claudia will go back to New York after the wedding. I wanted to reassure them that she'll be safely under your grandmother's wing. Elizabeth Harrington is a very clear-sighted, formidable lady – it says a lot for Claudia that they've taken to each other so well.'

Jess thought he sounded intolerably casual – thank God, with not much harm done, he could now move on again.

'Nice for them, and a great relief for you,' she suggested. 'How convenient to be able to pass the responsibility on . . . how useful for the man who steers clear of commitments that look in danger of going on too long!'

His eyes were bright with anger at the gibe but he answered quietly. 'I'm the man who makes no promises he can't keep . . . I told you that once before. Have you forgotten the occasion?'

The reminder was deliberate, spurring her to more sharpness. 'No, I haven't forgotten, but what a good thing we discovered how little we could ever suit each other. I'm afraid it's been more painful for Claudia to come to the same understanding with you.'

Instead of shouting at her as she expected, Jacques' voice was suddenly heavy with regret.

'I made *my* mistake here, right at the beginning, when I was feeling too damned sorry for myself to worry about anyone else. Claudia was determined to be helpful, and I'm ashamed to say that I took comfort from the warmth she offered – I wasn't even above being a little flattered; she made me feel alive again. By the time I woke up to the danger, it was too late – she'd come to see me as the damaged hero she must always love.

'I should have refused to have her in New York – would have done but for *your* brutal slap in the face. After that, it didn't seem to matter; where else would I find so delightful a helpmate? I still believed that she'd eventually straighten herself out. There were times when I thought it was happening – God knows, I was often bad-tempered and unreasonable enough to put a saint off. At other times I almost thought my own determination not to hurt her would be enough to see us through. But she knew the effort I was making, and in the end it was she who forced me to admit that I had to go back to Paris alone. She was angry, of course – she's Llewellyn's daughter – but also deeply hurt. I tried to love her, *did* . . . do love her in fact, but not in the way she needed.' An unamused smile touched his mouth briefly. 'I was right all along – I shall make a point of travelling alone in future!'

She would have liked to hate him, but it wouldn't be possible; she knew that for certain now. Nor would she be able to forget him, even if she never saw him again. It seemed a dreadful waste that none of them, Jacques, Giancarlo, Lorenza, Claudia, or herself, had been able to catch true happiness on the wing and make it stay.

'I must go,' she said at last, standing up to leave. 'If I don't catch the next *vaporetto* back to Venice I shall have to rush to make my flight.' She stared at him, thinking that since it was the last time she would ever see him she could be truthful. 'I came over here in order to avoid bumping into you – an act of cowardice that got its due reward! Maria would say I should have expected Fate to have the last word.'

She waited for some edged remark and a smile that would make her bleed a little more inside, but instead he spoke gravely. 'I came to say goodbye to this extraordinary place – I shan't ever want to see it again.' He stared at her, as if contemplating what else there was to mention. 'I remember what you told me. No step into the unknown for Jessica Smythson. At the age of – what was it, thirty-eight? – adventure was banned; security was to be the rule. Well, here's a final challenge before you scuttle back to safety.'

Before she could foresee what would come next, she was pulled against him and his mouth found hers in a hard, hurtful kiss that had no possibility of tenderness in it. Released at last, she wiped it away, but her fingers trembled and she had to hide them in the pockets of her jacket. A sort of smile changed the harsh planes of his face.

'Why not give adventure a chance, Jess . . . forget the safe life and come back to Paris with me for a night or two,' he suggested unevenly. 'Still no promises, of course, and the pleasure I rashly anticipate might be yet another of my mistakes . . . but at least we could find that much out for certain!' He tilted her face up so that she had to look at him. 'But you won't join me on the night train, will you? "Kissing the joy as it flies" isn't your idea of a safe, sensible life!' His bright, mocking eyes seemed to laugh unkindly at her, and she was reminded with a stab of pain of their first meeting at the Ca'Rezzonico. They were back to where they'd started, but with far too much emotion lived through in between.

'No, I shan't join you,' she said slowly. 'But perhaps only because you didn't ask me for the right reasons. Goodbye, Jacques – enjoy your self-sufficient travels in future.'

She managed a faint smile and then headed blindly for the door, telling herself that she must concentrate on running if she was not to miss the boat.

Jacques stayed where he was trying to blank out of his mind one more failure with Jessica Smythson. He'd invited her to Paris in the reckless, stupid way she was certain to have refused, and he knew why – he was afraid! The self-sufficient traveller of the past had lost his way, needed for happiness a woman who didn't seem to need him. She would have refused however he'd asked . . . he told himself that over and over again while the long minutes dragged away. Then suddenly he stood up, but in a mad dash to the door remembered that the *padrona* had still to be paid. She wasted still more precious time, and although he ran as fast as he repaired legs would carry him, he reached the jetty in time to see the boat pulling out into midstream. Jess was finally out of reach, and in an hour or two she'd be on her way back to London.

She'd packed her suitcases, paid her bill, even pretended to swallow a few mouthfuls of lunch. Now there was nothing left to do but sit in the hall; in another half-hour she could leave for the airport. Her mind had been forbidden to think of the morning's meeting; instead, she tried to imagine the wedding party at the Pensione Alberoni, and wished too late that she'd walked into one of the city's many churches

205

to offer up a little prayer for Lorenza's happiness.

It seemed for a moment when a girl came walking through the doorway that she'd been conjured up by a disordered, overwrought imagination. How could it be Claudia standing there when she had to be somewhere else, involved in the celebrations? But it *was* Claudia, with a coat thrown over her long silk dress, and a wreath of flowers still entwined in her dark hair.

'Marco said when you'd be leaving, but I was suddenly afraid of not having left enough time,' she announced breathlessly.

White-faced and, for some reason she didn't properly understand, very close to tears, Jess stared at her. The day was proving altogether too much, and she wasn't nearly prepared enough for yet another bruising confrontation.

'I have to leave soon,' she tried to say calmly. 'And shouldn't *you* be at the wedding feast?'

An impatient gesture borrowed from Llewellyn waved the idea away. 'I'll go back when I've said what I came to say. I'm full of wine and wedding euphoria at the moment; otherwise I should probably have stayed away.' She considered Jess for a moment with huge, over-bright eyes . . . they were not made that way by wine, Jess thought; Claudia was being driven by some compelling emotion that now found release in a rush of words.

'Has Marco told you that I'm only here for the wedding? After that I shall fly back to New York . . . to the sort of job I've always dreamed of. Jacques didn't like Manhattan, and now the poor dear man thinks I'm leaving him behind . . . climbing my ladder without him. I suppose I am in a way.'

Not sure what she was expected to say, and very afraid of saying the wrong thing, Jess made the best effort she could. 'I gather you've been getting on very well with my grandmother, and she isn't an easy lady to please.'

Claudia nodded. 'She thought I could do much better than tag along behind someone else . . . even a man she likes as much as Jacques.' But the need to mention his name again was too much, and suddenly her voice rushed on, ragged and hoarse with emotion.

'He and I *were* lovers in New York – I warned you of that, didn't I? Apart from helping him, and I *knew* I could do that, I thought I could make him completely satisfied and happy. He *was* for a little while, but gradually I had to accept that something was wrong . . . I wasn't quite the woman he needed, however much I loved him.'

The confession was torn out of her, but she didn't weep. She been changed by the months in New York – not just in appearance, but in self-control and adulthood, Jess realised.

Wanting to give comfort, she offered all she could. 'The woman who could keep Jacques happy doesn't exist, I think.'

'He seems to think *you* could,' Claudia said more quietly now. 'I don't understand why, and I expect he's wrong; but I know it's the idea he has. It's all quite hopeless, of course, when *you* only want to settle down and hide away from adventure.'

'Hopeless indeed,' Jess agreed faintly, 'but thank you at least for telling me.'

'Thank Marco,' Claudia contradicted her. 'He said I had to come and see you. I still might not have done, but I remembered your face that night in the *pensione*, when you were going back to London, and decided that Marco was right. But you won't do anything about it – you're not brave, as Llewellyn taught me to be.'

Now there was real comfort to give. 'Perhaps you're right about me, but you're wrong about Jacques. I happened to bump into him this morning, and he made things very plain – we women complicate things; apart from enjoying their incidental pleasures, he prefers not to be encumbered with silly creatures who expect things to last.'

Claudia inspected her face again, with a kind of sad frustration. 'So nobody gets what they really wanted; they just have to make do. When Mamma used to say that it was how life was, I never believed her; I suppose I might have to now.'

Jess dredged up a smile through the depths of her own infinite regret. 'Marco's done better than that. I defy you to show me a more contented man!'

'That's true,' Claudia slowly agreed, 'and perhaps I'll be proved wrong about Lorenza. She looked so beautiful today that it's hard to believe she isn't happy.' The thought was put aside as Claudia turned her attention back to Jess. Her glance seemed determined to discover once and for all what it was about this Englishwoman that had appealed enough to Jacques Duclos to be the ruin of her own happiness. The very difficulty of pinning it down, she finally decided, *was* the thing itself – some attraction so elusive as to catch and hold the interest of a complicated man. She let out a long, concluding sigh, and then gave her familiar shrug. 'I must go back – they'll be wondering what's happened to me. We might never see each other again and I rather hope not, as a matter of fact. But I'll say thank you now for recommending me to Elizabeth Harrington. We've become the best of friends; she'll help me, and I shall look after her.'

'I know,' said Jess, 'and at least that's something better than just making do.'

Claudia gave a final little nod, hesitated for a moment longer, and then walked away.

Left alone, Jess looked at the hall clock, compared it with her own watch, and decided that she must leave within the next five minutes if she was to be sure of checking in at the right time. She got as far as the door, stopped, and walked back to her chair again. A quarter of an hour later she was still there, her only conscious thought now being that the London flight must leave without her. Beneath its repetition, her mind remembered something else with the agonizing frequency of a tongue touching an aching tooth – the terrible idea with which Claudia had dismissed her: she wasn't brave enough to be Llewellyn's daughter.

At last she got up stiffly, walked to the reception desk, and smiled at the girl who had been watching her for some time.

'If you have a railway timetable here, could you tell me when the night train leaves for Paris? I've decided to take a different route home.'

She was given the information, and a curious glance. Was the *signorina inglese* feeling all right? She looked a little pale, and the *viaggio in treno* would be tedious, would it not, compared with a short flight to London? Jess agreed with this sensible point of view, and stifled a sob of hysterical laughter that would make her friend behind the desk still more anxious. There were better words to apply to the journey she was going to make – ill-judged, perhaps . . . pathetic even, probably downright insane.

She rang the Dutch House and told Imogen that they weren't to expect her that evening; then she went early to the railway station and booked a vacant sleeper. Still with an hour to spare, she sat in the restaurant, pretending to eat pasta and cheese, and trying to make sense of the only book she had with her – a biography of Richard Wagner by someone who seemed to have loathed the man he'd oddly chosen to write about. The train arrived, and she climbed aboard, as furtively as any escaping jewel-thief, suddenly terrified of having Jacques find her there. The idea was so intolerable that she sat on her berth shaking with the relief of having avoided him. Two subsequent thoughts were slightly more rational – if she was going to continue to avoid him, the whole journey would be entirely pointless; and if she couldn't trace him in the Paris telephone directory, she would have no idea where he lived.

The night journey seemed far too swift; she needed it to last longer, suspended as she was between sleep and wakefulness, listening to the rhythm of the wheels, and the disembodied voices in the darkness calling out the names of places she would never see. She thought about the people who lived in them, and was vaguely comforted by the idea that they couldn't all be living purposeful, tidy, single-minded lives; *somebody* out there must be in the same excruciating muddle as she was herself.

They trundled in the dawn through the suburbs of Paris and, dressed much too early, she had to watch the whole dreary length of them unfold. No one here, it seemed, any more than the planners of London, had solved the problem of making the sprawling approaches to a capital city bearable. But not even suburbs could go on for ever:

they were running into the Gare de Lyon, and at any moment now she would have to leave the refuge her *wagon-lit* had become and crawl out of it into the uncertain world outside.

Chapter 26

Out on the platform she shivered in the cold morning air; it felt altogether sharper here, and she was aware of being in a country that was foreign in a different way from the one she'd just left. Her mind was slow to make sense of the signs, and her ears missed in the voices about her the soft dialect of the Venetians.

But Jacques she couldn't miss; he was standing not a dozen paces away, having just emerged from the next sleeping-coach. He looked very tired, as if he hadn't slept either, but just for a moment she thought she saw joy blaze in his face. Then his features were under control again and she supposed she'd been mistaken.

He came towards her and, as usual, his opening remark went straight to the point; would she ever be in a position to remind him that every language had its own pleasant phrases designed to ease the awkwardness of meetings? It didn't seem likely.

'You were *flying* back to London . . . that's what you said.'

'I changed my mind . . . suddenly remembered that I liked trains more than aeroplanes.' Even with no encouragement at all, she thought she could chatter on for ever about the pleasures of the night express . . . perhaps she was becoming unhinged. Jacques' expression, seeming to suggest that it was so, shocked her into giving him the simple truth. 'I changed my mind about your . . . your offer at Torcello.'

For a moment his face still offered no help, and she was obliged to stumble on. 'I seem to have made another mistake – it doesn't matter . . . I'll go straight on to London.'

At last the blankness in his expression melted into warmth. He framed her face in his hands and lightly kissed her mouth. 'No mistake has been made, sweetheart. Give me your suitcase and let us go home. You may like trains, but I can't stand railway-stations.'

She wasn't sure of her welcome, even now . . . felt embarrassed to be there as they walked out of the station to where a vacant taxi waited for a fare.

'I live in the sixteenth *arrondissement*,' Jacques said calmly when they were inside. 'Nice district, almost on the edge of the Bois de Boulogne, but I'm afraid my apartment will look rather down-at-heel to you. I'm not there enough to worry about it.'

She considered a sprightly comment that it was music to an interior decorator's ears, and decided against it. The insane desire to laugh that was taking hold of her must be resisted if it was the last thing she did, because she doubted that the man beside her was in a mood to enjoy the idiocy of this last and most mistaken meeting. On the whole it seemed safer to say nothing at all, but even this had its dangers. In the stuffy dimness of the taxi, she couldn't move far enough away from him to avoid the warmth of his shoulder against her own. She could easily have stretched out a hand to touch his and, shaken by her own longing to do so, she tried to remember that he was a cruelly self-sufficient man, able to do without the reassurance that other people occasionally found essential.

They reached the street he lived in – pleasant, as he'd said, even with the plane trees along the pavement leafless as they now were. The tall, narrow houses were graced by long windows, elegantly shuttered, but his own apartment was on the top two floors – *sous les toits*, he muttered. The front of the sitting room she was led into overlooked the street and the tops of the bare trees; a french window at the back would open on warmer days on to a tiny garden seemingly poised in mid-aid, but built on the roof of the kitchen below.

'I don't know why you were so disparaging,' Jess said – the first words she seemed to have spoken for a long time. 'It's charming here.'

But she doubted if he even heard what she said; his eyes were fixed on her face, almost as if he feared she might disappear the moment he ceased to stare at her. She couldn't read his expression – some happiness was there, but so, strangely, was some deep regret.

'You look exhausted, my dear,' he said very gently. 'I'd like more than anything in the world to take you to bed and make love to you – that *was* the offer, was it not? But I have to suggest instead that what you need is sleep. Go and shower away the night in the train while I make the bed freshly for you.'

She couldn't argue . . . was beyond knowing anything for certain, even whether he really wanted her there or not. But the idea of sleep was suddenly irresistible, and so was the need to do whatever this man, in his lovely, unexpected kindness, suggested. She was led to the bathroom with her suitcase, and left, but lying in his bed afterwards, she couldn't be sure whether to laugh or weep; one more scene with Jacques Duclos hadn't turned out as expected, and she had no idea what might come next.

She awoke to the dimness of the curtained windows to find herself not alone – Jacques was stretched out beside her. He turned towards her, smiling a little as he brushed a strand of hair back from her face. Then he gently kissed her and, as inevitably as the moon moves the sea, their arms enfolded each other. Regret was dead, and now failure was impossible. They were together and must love each other at last. Spent afterwards, but utterly content, Jess slept again and woke this

212

time to the brightness of midday, with Jacques putting coffee on the table beside her. He smiled down at her, thinking how beautiful she was, and trying not to wonder what he would do without her when she went away.

'Why are you smiling?' she wanted to know.

'I'm comparing you with the bedraggled, prickly creature I met at the Ca'Rezzonico a long time ago – the same Jess, but *not* the same at all!'

He resisted the temptation to kiss her again and tried to sound calm. 'I'm ravenously hungry, my heart, and so should you be, but we have no food here. If you'll be good enough to get dressed, I'll take you *out* to lunch instead.'

But when she went into the sitting room a quarter of an hour later, he was pouring white wine into beautiful old glasses; it seemed that food could wait.

'You said no to coming here yesterday morning,' he began quietly. 'Tell me why you changed your mind.'

She walked over to the window, to watch the Sunday quietness of the street while she decided how to answer. Then she turned to face him.

'It sounds silly now, after the joy of the past few hours, but at Torcello your offer sounded like some sort of punishment. Expecting no pleasure, we were simply going to discover how little there would be to enjoy.'

He nodded, accepting the truth of what she said, but repeated his question. 'So, believing that, why *did* you come?'

Jess took a sip of wine, then plunged into a confession she could see no way of avoiding. But the path ahead was perilous; somehow she must remain smiling, able to convince him that for her the world wouldn't grow dark when it was time to leave.

'Claudia came to see me, still in her wedding finery, just as I was about to set out yesterday afternoon. She seemed to think that being Llewellyn's daughter entitled – no, required! – me to put my money on the number marked "risk" just once in my life.'

'There *wasn't* any risk, though perhaps you weren't to know that. What do you propose to do next?'

She managed to smile this time. 'Eat the lunch you were kind enough to offer me, and then fly home, back to London.' His mouth twisted in an expression she thought she recognised, and she hurried on. 'London's not *your* scene, I know. You find it an unsympathetic city, and won't have any truck with the Entente Cordiale we were taught to believe in. Well, no more will I – Edward VII made it all up, I think.'

She was talking too much, chattering aimlessly, because Jacques was frowning at her – *not* frowning; watching with a hard, intent gaze she couldn't understand.

'When did the interesting subject of my preferences crop up – yesterday afternoon, with Claudia?'

'No, we only talked about New York,' she answered, wondering why it should matter enough for him to sound suddenly harsh. He came towards her and gripped her shoulders tightly.

'I remember every conversation we've ever had – there haven't been all that many of them. *Never* have you heard my views about London or the Entente Cordiale. If Claudia didn't mention them yesterday afternoon, when *did* she? As far as I know, the two of you only met that dreadful evening at the *pensione* the first time you came to Venice.'

Jess offered a part-truth now. 'She'd been to see me at the Palazzo Ghisalberti one day . . . just . . . just out of curiosity. Marco and Lorenza had both met me – she couldn't bear to be left out!'

'She always liked to know everything that went on,' he said quietly now, almost as if talking to himself. 'I suppose she heard that we'd gone to Burano together.'

'Daniele told her – rather graphically, I fear, being a romantic Italian! An English boatman wouldn't have even noticed.'

'And it was after she'd been to see you that you sat down and wrote your bright, brief, brutal letter . . . "*adieu, cher monsieur* – silly of us to have imagined we'd found something of value. No adventure required, thank you." It had nothing to do with having to go back to London; your stepfather hadn't been taken ill then.'

It wasn't even a question, but Jess felt obliged to answer. 'Claudia told me she was going with you to Paris, but already she'd made up her mind about New York as well. I *knew* that most of what she said was true – she *was* indispensable to you; and the rest seemed very likely, too – she was beautiful and bright and generous, and most certainly heart and soul in love with you. She was also convinced that you loved *her*, and I'd seen for myself that even *that* was likely to be true. I had very little to set against all that, and worst of all, she was my half-sister . . . a girl I couldn't bear to try to hurt or compete with. But I knew something else as well – you and I weren't looking for the same things . . . at least we'd had time to discover that.'

'It wasn't all we'd discovered even then,' Jacques insisted fiercely. 'Deny it if you like, but you'll be lying.'

She gave a little nod. 'I spent a long, lonely summer trying to deny it, and refusing to think of you and Claudia together in New York. Then Marco told me when I arrived back in Venice that you weren't still together. He didn't need to tell me how deeply Claudia would have been hurt, and I thought I might even manage to hate you for the damage you'd done. Unlike Giancarlo, refusing to make a grab at happiness for fear of hurting people, *you* would go on roaming carelessly about the world. You even confirmed it for me at Torcello

214

yesterday – no camp-followers required; you'd travel faster alone.'

She seemed to have been talking too long; even to her own ears her voice sounded hoarse and unfamiliar.

'You still haven't told me what changed things . . . trying to hate me, you came here. *Why?*'

No mad insistence that she loved trains would do now; it was the unvarnished truth she must give him.

'Claudia bravely decided to clear the air between us and . . . and absolve me, I think, of letting kinship stand in my way. She seemed to think that I was to blame for her failure with you but, being the unadventurous coward that I was, she was certain I wouldn't do anything about it. And the truth is that if she hadn't despised me quite so much, I *would* have gone back to London as planned, instead of making this . . . this little detour here. Claudia was angry as well as hurt – she's accustomed to pushing life into whatever shape she wants. It hadn't occurred to her that life might sometimes refuse to co-operate, or that people might occasionally behave in ways she didn't expect them to.'

Jacques nodded, but watching his face she couldn't believe that he damaged people as thoughtlessly as she'd claimed.

'What I said to you at Torcello was true, Jess,' he stated with a simplicity she had to accept. 'The blame was mine; my affair with Claudia was a mistake I shouldn't have made. At the moment she believes she'll never get over it, but she will; and in a year or two, being the girl she is, she'll be glad to make sure that I know she can scarcely remember the name of Jacques Duclos. I shall be happy when it happens.'

'What *does* come next for you . . . Hong Kong . . . Sydney?' she finally forced herself to ask.

His sombre expression faded into a kind of wry amusement. 'Neither of those. Much to Henri Clément's disgust, I made an unexpected discovery during those interminable months in New York. I kept thinking I wanted to come home! God help me, I even began to like the idea of settling down. I blame it on Maria and the *pensione*,' he added solemnly, by way of explanation. 'They gave me a taste for family life!'

She tried hard to sound amused, and sceptical. 'What does a brilliant cameraman do when he grows tired of roaming?' He'd have no ready answer to that, she thought, but she was wrong.

'Well, first of all he compiles his last photographic book. Henri is rather excited about the idea now – a portrait of Paris, before much of what we cherish about it is finally buried under car parks and ring roads. After that I shall become less of a sleeping partner in a company I inherited – my father set it up to make television documentaries. It will mean living in Paris, so perhaps I'll commission you to make this place more comfortable!'

She was able to smile at the idea, could see how that this heartbreakingly brief visit might be ended after all on a note of friendly normality.

'My assistant in London would jump at the chance. I'm rather tied up myself, commuting to Venice for Nathan Acheson. His new housing trust is typical, I suspect, of *all* his ideas – brilliant, simple, and workable. I feel honoured to be involved in it, and very content to be working with Marco.'

'Is that why you're happy to go back?' Jacques asked. 'You were very wary of Venice before.'

'There were too many anxieties. Now, I can imagine a time when the *pensione* might begin to feel almost as much like home as the Dutch House in London. Maria doesn't have to struggle with herself any more to make me welcome – in fact she seems to credit me with helping to keep Marco's head out of the lions' den in Rome! Lorenza is no longer being destroyed by unhappiness, and Llewellyn is himself again, painting wonderful pictures.' Jess risked a question of her own that she was anxious to know the answer to. 'How did Maria get on with your mother, by the way? Marco feared that she was anxious.'

Jacques' face was suddenly alight with remembered amusement, reminding her of moments when it had been easy to laugh with him. 'The two dear ladies got on so brilliantly that Llewellyn was left rather out in the cold. He made the best of it, I'm bound to say, and consoled himself by reckoning that his taste had always been exemplary!'

Then he asked a more serious question. 'How does Giancarlo figure in your happy new Venetian scenario?'

She took care to answer honestly. 'As a friend, I hope, eventually. I avoided the Rasinis this time, but I can't go on doing that without hurting them. I just wanted Giancarlo to get used to the idea of my comings and goings before we met again.'

'So you turned him down. I thought I was the one who hurt other people's feelings.'

'I think he turned me down . . . the people he'd loved most in the past had been taken away from him and he feared it would happen again. He feared for *me*, I think. If he'd been selfish enough to ask me to stay, I might have done . . . just so as . . . as not to have waste all round, as it then seemed.'

A faint, wry smile touched Jacques' mouth. 'Unlike me . . . selfish and arrogant customer that I am! I've learned quite a lot, my love, but not enough yet. That's why I made such a mess of things at Torcello. I wanted you so much, but I was knocked off balance and terrified that you'd turn me down again.'

His hands framed her face now, forcing her to look at him.

'Claudia was right in New York. Every man we met over there

envied me, but all I could think of was that I was there with the wrong woman. I knew exactly who I *did* want . . . but for always, Jess, not just for a night or two, because I know now that I shall love you for as long as I live. Dear heart, will you consider staying? If I promise *never* to be unreasonable, if I don't make the *slightest* fuss each time you go off to London or Venice . . . if I take the greatest care of you, *will* you stay and be my love?'

'You don't believe in promises,' she reminded him unsteadily, but she was beginning to smile, because what had happened at Burano was happening here, and his shabby room was being dusted with same golden magic of happiness.

He leaned forward to kiss her mouth, then smiled himself. 'Blame Venice, where I suffered Shakespeare's sea-change into something rich and strange . . . "Benedick, the married man", to mix his plays, who *insists* on settling down, and even wants to make not only promises but vows! So which of the fathers in your life should I apply to for your hand?'

'Can you be serious?' she asked almost wonderingly. 'No promises or vows are needed, my dearest.'

'I'm afraid they are – for *my* peace of mind, if not for yours. Now, answer my question, please.'

She tried to consider it rationally, and seriously.

'Llewellyn, I think. He'd be so enchanted to be asked, whereas my dear Gerald won't mind at all – although I hope you'll come back with me to London to meet him.'

The radiance in her face was suddenly dimmed, and he thought he could guess the reason.

'Your puritan conscience is waking up, my love . . . because we've finally managed to grab the pot of gold at the end of the rainbow. I know there are others who haven't, but they must look for different chances. I've seen too much human misery not to know that we can't feel responsible for it all – that way madness lies.'

'Giancarlo won't even look for chances,' she said with sadness, 'but at least he'll have his most precious reward if Venice is kept safe. Don't you feel, Jacques, that it *must* survive with men like him and Nathan and Marco insisting on it?'

'With my new-found pleasure in making promises, I assure you that it will,' he insisted seriously. 'And if you're still thinking about Claudia, I promise you that *she* will survive as well . . . she's Llewellyn's daughter.'

Jess's face broke into a reluctant smile. 'Yes, but he should have taught her it's a mistake to despise the English too openly.'

'I know – it makes them bloody-minded. You warned me of that at the beginning of our acquaintance! Claudia probably has more mistakes to make yet, but we shall go on loving her, and the whole

Matthias tribe.' Amusement crept into his voice again. 'I blame that on Venice too . . . to think I was a sensible, selfish, and wonderfully uncaring man until I crossed Marco's precious Lagoon! Now . . .' But she stifled the rest by laying her fingers over his mouth, and then hand in hand, still laughing, they walked out into the sunlight together.